LET THE
GAMES
BEGIN

Also by Niccolò Ammaniti

Steal You Away
I'm Not Scared
The Crossroads
Me and You

LET THE GAMES BEGIN

NICCOLÒ AMMANITI

Translated from the Italian by Kylee Doust

CANONGATE
Edinburgh · London

Published in Great Britain in 2013 by Canongate Books Ltd,
14 High Street, Edinburgh EH1 1TE

www.canongate.tv

1

First published in Italian in 2009 as *Che la festa cominci* by Giulio Einaudi
editore, Torino

British Library Cataloguing-in-Publication Data
A catalogue record for this book is available on
request from the British Library

ISBN 978 1 84767 941 3

Typeset in Sabon by Palimpsest Book Production Ltd,
Falkirk, Stirlingshire

Printed and bound in Great Britain by
CPI Group (UK) Ltd, Croydon CR0 4YY

This book is printed on FSC certified paper

MIX
Paper from
responsible sources
FSC
www.fsc.org   FSC® C020471

To Anatole,
who pulled me out of the box

PART ONE

Genesis

1

At a table in Jerry's Pizzeria 2 in Oriolo Romano the Wilde Beasts of Abaddon were holding a meeting.

Their leader, Saverio Moneta, aka Mantos, was worried.

The situation was critical. If he didn't succeed in taking back command of his sect, this might very well be the last get-together of the Beasts.

They had been haemorrhaging for a while. The first one to leave had been little Paolo Scialdone, aka The Reaper. Without a word, he had dumped them and become part of the Children of the Apocalypse, a Satan-worshipping group from Pavia. A few weeks later Antonello Agnese, aka Molten, had bought a secondhand Harley-Davidson and joined the Hell's Angels from Subiaco. And to top it off Pietro Fauci, aka Nosferatu, Mantos' right-hand man and founder of the Beasts, had got married and opened a plumbing and heating supplies store on the Abetone.

They were down to four members.

It was time to give them a serious talking to, tell them to get their shit together and pull in some new recruits.

'Mantos, what are you having?' asked Silvietta, the group's Vestal. A scrawny redhead with bug-eyes sticking out beneath thin eyebrows that sat too high on her forehead. She wore a silver ring in one nostril and another in the middle of her lip.

Saverio took a quick look at the menu. 'I don't know . . . A *marinara pizza*? No, better not, it gives me heartburn . . . Pappardelle, yeah.'

'They do 'em greasy here, but they're delicious!' said Roberto Morsillo, aka Murder, approvingly. A chubby guy almost six foot six, with long dyed-black hair and glasses covered in oily fingerprints. He wore a stretched Slayer t-shirt. Originally from

Sutri, he was studying Law at Rome University and worked at the Brico DIY centre in Vetralla.

Saverio studied his disciples. Even though they were all over thirty, they still dressed like a mob of head-banging losers. He couldn't remember how many times he'd told them: 'You've got to look normal, get rid of these body-piercings, and the tattoos, and the bloody metal spikes . . .' But it didn't make any difference.

Beggars can't be choosers, he thought to himself, downhearted.

Mantos could see his image reflected in the Birra Moretti mirror hanging behind the pizzeria's counter. Skinny, five foot six, with metal-framed glasses, he wore his dark hair parted on the left. He was wearing a short-sleeved, light blue shirt buttoned right up to the throat, dark blue cords and a pair of slip-on moccasins.

A normal-looking guy. Just like all the great champions of Evil: Ted Bundy, Andrei Chikatilo and Jeffrey Dahmer, the Milwaukee Cannibal. The sort of people you would see on the street and you wouldn't even give the time of day. And yet they were the Demon's Chosen Ones.

What would Charlie Manson have done if he'd had such hopeless disciples?

'Master, we have to talk to you . . . We've been sort of thinking . . . about the sect . . .'

Mantos was caught off-guard by Edoardo Sambreddero, aka Zombie, the fourth member, a haggard-looking guy who suffered from congenital oesophagitis: couldn't swallow garlic, chocolate or fizzy drinks. He worked for his father assembling electrical systems in Manziana.

'Technically,' he said, 'we, as a sect, don't exist.'

Saverio had guessed what he was up to, but pretended not to understand.

4

'What do you mean?'

'How long's it been since we took the bloody oath?'

Saverio shrugged his shoulders. 'It's been a few years.'

'They never talk about us online. But they talk plenty about the Children of the Apocalypse,' whispered Silvietta so softly that nobody heard her.

Zombie pointed a grissino at his chief. 'In all this time, what have we ever accomplished?'

'All those things that you promised . . . How many of them have we done?' Murder chimed in. 'You said we'd make loads of human sacrifices, but we haven't seen hide nor hair of them. And what about the initiation ritual with the virgins? And the Satanic orgies?'

'Well, for one thing, we did make a human sacrifice, we did indeed,' Saverio pointed out, annoyed. 'It might not have worked, but we made it. And the orgy, too.'

In November of the year before, on the train to Rome, Murder had met Silvia Butti, an off-campus student at the Faculty of Psychology at Tor Vergata University. They had a lot in common: their love for the Lazio football team, for horror films, for Slayer and Iron Maiden, basically for your good old 1980's-heavy metal. They had started chatting on MSN and hanging out on Via del Corso on Saturday afternoons.

Saverio had been the one who came up with the idea of sacrificing Silvia Butti to Satan in the forest of Sutri.

There was just one problem. The victim needed to be a virgin.

Murder had sworn to it. 'She and I have done everything, but when I tried to fuck her, she just wouldn't cave in.'

Zombie had burst out laughing. 'Did it ever occur to you that maybe she just doesn't want to fuck a fatso like you?'

'She's taken a chastity vow, you idiot. She's definitely a virgin,

5

no doubt about it. And anyway . . . I mean, if it turned out she wasn't one, what would happen?'

Saverio, the group's master and theoretician, looked worried.

'Well, it's pretty serious. The sacrifice would be worthless. Or even worse, it could turn against us. The powers of Hell wouldn't be satisfied, and they could attack and destroy us.'

After hours of arguing and online investigating, the Beasts had come to the conclusion that the purity of the victim was not a substantial problem. So they had set to work on a plan.

Murder had invited Silvia Butti out for pizza in Oriolo Romano. There, by the light of a candle, he had offered her *supplì* rice balls, salted cod fillets and a huge glass of beer in which he had dissolved three tablets of Rohipnol. By the end of the dinner the young woman could barely stand and was mumbling incomprehensibly. Murder had gotten her into the car and, using the excuse that they should go to see the sunrise over the lake of Bracciano, he'd carried her into the forest of Sutri. There the Wilde Beasts of Abaddon had used tuff bricks to build a sacrificial shrine. The girl, half-unconscious, was undressed and laid down on the altar. Saverio invoked the Evil One, chopped the head off a chicken and sprayed the blood over the naked body of the psychology student, and then they'd all done her. At that point they had dug a hole and buried her alive. The ritual had been performed and the sect had undertaken its journey down into Evil's tenebrous lands.

The problem had arisen three days later. The Beasts had just come out of the Flamingo cinema, where they had seen *The Texas Chainsaw Massacre: The Beginning*, and ran straight into Silvia. The girl, sitting on a bench in the gardens, was eating a *piadina*. She couldn't remember much about that evening, but she had the feeling she'd had fun. She told them how, when she'd come to her senses underneath the dirt, she dug her way to the surface.

6

Saverio had then signed her up as the sect's official high priestess. A few weeks later she and Murder were an item.

'Yeah, that's right, you did have an orgy,' Silvietta giggled nervously. 'You've told me about it a hundred times.'

'Yeah, but you weren't a virgin. And so, technically, the ceremony didn't work,' Zombie commented.

'How on earth could you think that I was a virgin? My first time . . .'

Saverio interrupted her. 'It was still a Satanic ritual . . .'

Zombie cut in. 'All right, forget the sacrifice. What else have we done?'

'We've cut a few sheep's throats, if I remember rightly. Haven't we?'

'Then what?'

Mantos unwittingly raised his voice. '"Then what?! Then what?!" Then there's the grafitti on the viaducts in Anguillara Sabazia!'

'Sure. Did you know that Paolino and those guys from Pavia disembowelled a nun?'

The only thing that the leader of the Wilde Beasts of Abaddon had managed to do was neck a glass of water.

'Mantos? Did you hear me?' Murder put his hand to his mouth, like a loudhailer. 'They disembowelled a fifty-eight-year-old nun.'

Saverio shrugged his shoulders. 'That's bollocks. Paolo's just trying to make us jealous, he regrets leaving us.' But he had the feeling that it wasn't bollocks.

'You watch the news on TV, right?' Murder insisted, unmerciful. 'You remember that nun from Caianello that they found decapitated near Pavia?'

'Yeah, so?'

'The Children of the Apocalypse did it. They picked her up at a bus stop and then Kurtz decapitated her with a double-headed axe.'

Saverio couldn't stand Kurtz, the leader of the Children of the Apocalypse from Pavia. He always had to be top of the class. Always the one coming up with extravagant stuff. *Good on you, Kurtz! Congratulations! You're the best!*

Saverio wiped his hand across his face.

'Well, guys . . . Don't forget how much of a hard time I've been having lately, what with the birth of the twins . . . the bloody bank loan for the new house . . .'

'That reminds me, how are the little darlings?' asked Silvietta.

'They're like drainpipes. They eat and shit. At night they don't let us get any sleep. They've got the measles, too. On top of it all, Serena's father had hip-replacement surgery, so the whole furniture shop is my responsibility. You tell me when I'm supposed to get something organised for the sect . . .'

'Hey, have you got any special offers at the shop?' Zombie asked. 'I want to buy a three-seater sofa-bed. The cat's ruined mine.'

The leader of the Beasts wasn't listening. He was thinking about Kurtz Minetti. As tall as a dick on a tin can. Full-time pastry chef. He had already set fire to a Kirby Vacuum Cleaner salesman and now he had decapitated a nun.

'Anyway, you're all ungrateful.' He pointed to them one by one. 'I've worked my arse off for this sect. If it hadn't been for me introducing you to the Worship of Hades, you'd all still be sitting around reading Harry Potter.'

'We know, Saverio, but try to understand us, too. We do believe in the group, but we can't keep going like this.' Murder bit angrily into a *grissino*. 'Let's just give it up and stay friends.'

8

The leader of the Beasts slammed his hands down on the table in exasperation.

'Or how about this? Give me a week. You can't say no to an extra week.'

'What are you going to do?' asked Silvietta, nibbling on her lip ring.

'I've been laying the groundwork for a mind-blowing piece of action. It's a really dangerous mission . . .' He paused. 'But don't think you can just cop out. We all know that talk is cheap. But when it's time to act . . .' He put on a whiney voice. '"*I can't, I'm sorry . . . I've got problems at home, my mother's not well . . . I have to work.*"' And he looked hard at Zombie, who lowered his head over his plate. 'No. We all put our arses on the line in the same way.'

'Can't you give us a hint?' Murder asked shyly.

'No! All I can say is that it's something that will send us right to number one on the list of Italy's Satanic sects.'

Silvietta grabbed a hold of his wrist. 'Mantos, come on. Please. Just a little hint. I'm so curious . . .'

Saverio shook himself free. 'No! I said no! You'll have to wait. If in a week's time I haven't brought you a serious plan, then thanks very much, we shake hands and disband the sect. All right?'

He stood up. His black eyes had turned red, reflecting the flames from the pizza oven.

'Now, disciples, honour me!'

The members lowered their heads. The leader raised his eyes to the ceiling and stretched out his arms.

'Who is your Charismatic Father?'

'You!' the Beasts said in unison.

'Who wrote the Tables of Evil?'

'You!'

'Who taught you the Liturgy of Darkness?'

'You!'

'Who ordered the *pappardelle* in hare sauce?' asked the waiter with steaming plates perched on his arm.

'Me!' Saverio stretched out his hand.

'Don't touch, they're hot.'

The leader of the Wilde Beasts of Abaddon sat down and, without saying another word, began eating.

2

About fifty kilometres away from Jerry's Pizzeria 2, in Rome, a little three-gear Vespa struggled up the slope of Monte Mario. Sitting astride the saddle was the well-known writer Fabrizio Ciba. The scooter stopped at a traffic light and when it changed to green turned into Via della Camilluccia. Two kilometres further on, it braked in front of a cast-iron gate on the side of which hung a brass plaque that read 'Villa Malaparte'.

Ciba put the Vespa into first gear and was about to face the long climb up to the residence when a primate squeezed into a grey flannel suit stepped in front of him.

'Excuse me! Excuse me! Where are you going? Have you got an invitation?'

The writer took off his bowl-shaped helmet and began searching the pockets of his creased jacket.

'No . . . No, I don't think I have . . . I must have forgotten it.'

The man stood with his legs wide apart. 'Well, you can't go in then.'

'I've been invited to . . .'

The bouncer pulled out a sheet of paper and slipped on a

10

pair of small glasses with red frames. 'What did you say your name was?'

'I didn't. Ciba. Fabrizio Ciba . . .'

The guy began running his index finger down the list of guests while shaking his head.

He doesn't recognise me. Fabrizio wasn't annoyed, though. It was obvious that the primate didn't 'do' literature but, for Christ's sake, didn't he watch television? Ciba presented a show called *Crime & Punishment* every Wednesday evening on RAI Tre for this very purpose.

'I'm sorry. Your name is not on the list.'

The writer was there to present the novel *A Life in the World* by the winner of the Nobel Prize for Literature, Sarwar Sawhney, published by Martinelli, his own publishing house. At the age of seventy-three, and with two books as thick as a law dictionary behind him, Sawhney had at last received the coveted prize from the Swedish Academy. Ciba was to do the honours alongside Gino Tremagli, Professor of English–American Literature at the Sapienza University of Rome. That old gasbag had been asked to participate just to give an official tone to the event. It was, however, up to Fabrizio to unravel the ancient secrets hidden within the folds of Sawhney's huge novel and offer them to a Roman audience notoriously thirsty for culture.

Ciba was getting fed up. He lost the polite tone.

'Listen to me. If you can forget about that guest list for a minute and take a look at the invitation – that white, rectangular-shaped piece of card which I unfortunately don't have with me – you will find my name on it, seeing as I am presenting this evening's event. If you want me to, I'll leave. But when they ask me why I didn't come, I'll tell them that . . . What's your name again?'

11

Luckily an attendant, with a blonde pageboy haircut and wearing a blue suit, appeared. As soon as she recognised her favourite author, with his rebellious fringe and big green eyes sitting astride the old-style Vespa, she almost fell over.

'Let him through! Let him through!' she screeched in a thin, high-pitched voice. 'Don't you know who this is? It's Fabrizio Ciba!' Then, her legs stiff with excitement, she walked up to the writer. 'I sincerely apologise. Oh God, this is so terribly embarrassing! I'm so sorry. I'd just gone off for a second and you arrived out of nowhere . . . I'm sorry, I'm so sorry . . . I . . .'

Fabrizio lavished the girl with a smug smile.

The attendant looked at her watch and rubbed her hand across her forehead. 'It's very late. Everybody will be expecting you. Please, go, go.' She shoved the bouncer out of the way, and as Fabrizio passed by her she shouted: 'Afterwards, would you mind signing a copy of your book for me?'

Ciba left the Vespa in the parking area and walked towards the villa, his footsteps as light as those of a middle-distance runner.

A photographer, camouflaged behind the laurel bushes, popped out onto the tree-lined avenue and ran towards him.

'Fabrizio! Fabrizio, do you remember me?' He began following the writer. 'We had dinner together in Milano in that *Osteria . . . La compagnia dei naviganti?* I invited you to come to my *dammuso* on Pantelleria and you said that you might come . . .'

The writer raised an eyebrow and gave the scruffy hippie, covered in cameras, the once over.

'Of course I remember . . .' He didn't have the faintest idea who the man was. 'Sorry, but I'm late. Maybe some other time. They're expecting me . . .'

The photographer didn't relent. 'Listen, Fabrizio, while I was brushing my teeth I had a brilliant idea: I want to take some photos of you in an illegal dumping ground . . .'

Standing in the doorway of Villa Malaparte the editor Leopoldo Malagò and the head of public relations for Martinelli, Maria Letizia Calligari, were gesturing to him to hurry.

The photographer was struggling to keep up, with fifteen kilos of equipment hanging around his neck, but he wouldn't be deterred.

'It's something out of the ordinary . . . striking . . . The garbage, the rats, the seagulls . . . Do you get it? The magazine, *Venerdì di Repubblica* . . .'

'Maybe some other time. Excuse me.'

And he threw himself in between Malagò and Calligari. The photographer, exhausted, bent over holding his side.

'Can I call you in the next couple of days?'

The writer didn't even bother to answer.

'Fabrizio, you never change . . . The Indian got here an hour ago. And that pain in the arse, Tremagli, wanted to start without you.'

Malagò was pushing him towards the conference hall while Calligari tucked his shirt into his trousers and mumbled, 'Look what you're wearing! You look like a tramp. The room is full. Even the Lord Mayor is here. Do your fly up.'

Fabrizio Ciba was forty-one years old, but everyone thought of him as the young writer. That adjective, frequently repeated by the newspapers and other media, had a psychosomatic effect on his body. Fabrizio didn't look any older than thirty-five. He was slim and toned without going to the gym. He got drunk every evening, but his stomach was still as flat as a table.

Leopoldo Malagò, nicknamed Leo, was thirty-five but looked ten years older, and that was being generous. He'd lost his hair at a tender age, and a thin layer of fluff stuck to his skull. His backbone had twisted into the shape of the Philippe Starck chair he spent ten hours a day sitting in. His cheeks sagged like a merciful curtain over his triple chin, and he'd astutely grown a beard, albeit not one bushy enough to cover the mountainous region. His stomach was as bloated as if someone had inflated it with an air-compressor. Martinelli obviously spared no expense when it came to feeding its editors. Thanks to a special credit card, they were free to gorge themselves in the best and most expensive restaurants, inviting writers, paper-smearers, poets and journalists to feasts disguised as work. The outcome of this policy was that the editors at Martinelli were a mob of obese *bons vivants* with constellations of cholesterol molecules floating freely through their veins. In other words, Leo – despite his tortoiseshell glasses and his beard that made him look like a New York Sephardim and his soft, marsh-green-coloured suits – had to rely on his power, on his unscrupulousness and his obtuse insistence for his romantic conquests.

The same did not apply to the women who worked for Martinelli. They began working in the publishing house as frumpy secretaries, and in the aggressive years they improved consistently thanks to enormous investments in themselves. By the time they reached fifty, especially if they had a high-profile position, they became algid, ageless beauties. Maria Letizia Calligari was an emblematic example. Nobody knew how old she was. Some said she was a young-looking sixty-year-old, some an old-looking thirty-eight-year-old. She never carried any identification with her. The gossipmongers whispered that she didn't drive simply to avoid having to carry her driving licence in her purse. Before the Schengen treaty came into force, she would go to the Frankfurt Book Fair by herself so that she didn't have to show her passport in front of any colleagues. But she had slipped up once. At a dinner party at the Turin Book Fair she accidentally mentioned that she had met Cesare Pavese – dead since 1950.

14

'Please, Fabrizio, don't rush poor Tremagli as soon as you walk in the door,' Maria Letizia urged.

'Go on, show us your stuff. Kick his arse.' Malagò pushed Fabrizio towards the conference hall.

Whenever Ciba walked into a venue, he used a secret ritual to get himself pumped. He thought about Muhammad Ali, the great boxer, about how he shouted and moved towards the ring encouraging himself: 'I'm gonna kill him! I won't even give him the chance to look at me before he'll be down for the count.' He did two little jumps on the spot. He cracked his neck. He tousled his hair. And, as charged as a battery, he walked into the grand affrescoed room.

3

The leader of the Wilde Beasts of Abaddon was at the wheel of his Ford Mondeo amidst traffic moving towards Capranica. The stretch of road was lined with shopping centres that stayed open late, and there were always delays. Usually, waiting in a traffic jam didn't worry Saverio. It was the only moment of the day when he could think about his own business in peace and quiet. But now he was running very late. Serena expected him for dinner. And he had to stop by the chemist's, too, and pick up some paracetamol for the twins.

He was thinking about the meeting. It would have been hard for it to go any worse than it did, and as per usual he had got himself into trouble all on his own. What made him think he should say that if he didn't bring in a plan within a week the sect could disband? He didn't have even a scrap of an idea, and it's common knowledge that laying down the guidelines for a Satanic mission takes time. He had recently tried to come up with some kind of plan, but nothing had occurred to him. Even the super-bargain month he'd organised at the furniture shop had been a washout, and he was still stuck there from morning till night, with the old man all over him as soon as he tried to take one step.

He had, though, stumbled on a bit of an idea a while ago: vandalise the Oriolo Romano Cemetery. On paper, it was a lovely plan. If carried out properly, it could work out really nicely. But when he'd taken it under closer consideration, he'd decided to abandon it. To begin with, opposite the cemetery there were always lots of cars coming and going, so it had to be done late into the night. The surrounding wall was also more than three metres high and scattered with pieces of broken bottles. Groups of teenagers hung out in front of the entrance gates and occasionally were even joined by the Porchetta sandwich van. Inside the graveyard lived the caretaker, an ex-soldier who was off his rocker. Absolute silence would be needed, but when uncovering graves, pulling up coffins, removing bones and piling them in heaps, a bit of commotion couldn't be avoided . . . although Saverio had even thought of crucifying the ex-soldier head-downwards over the mausoleum of the Mastrodomenicos, his wife's family.

Too complicated.

His mobile began ringing. On the display he read 'SERENA'.

Saverio Moneta had told her the usual story: a Dungeons & Dragons tournament. For two years now, to keep his Satanic activities under wraps, he had told her that he was a champion boardgame-player. But this wouldn't hold up much longer. Serena was suspicious. She kept asking him lots of questions, wanted to know who he played with, if he'd won . . . Once he had organised a fake match with the Beasts to reassure her. But when his wife had seen Zombie, Murder and Silvietta, rather than feeling reassured she had become even more suspicious.

He took a breath and answered his phone.

'Honey, I know, I'm running late, but I'm on my way. Traffic's hell. There must be an accident up ahead.'

Serena answered with her usual gentleness.

'Oi! Have you gone completely out of your mind?'

Saverio slumped in the front seat of the Mondeo. 'Why? What did I do?'

'There's a guy here from DHL with a huge package. He's asking for three hundred and fifty euro. He says it's for you. So, do I pay him?'

Oh God, it's the Durendal.

He'd bought the faithful reproduction of the sword of Roland, Charlemagne's paladin, on eBay. As legend would have it, it first belonged to Hector of Troy. But that dimwit Mariano, his building's caretaker, was supposed to intercept it. Serena wasn't meant to know a thing about the sword.

'Yeah, yeah, pay him. As soon as I get home, I'll pay you back,' said Saverio, feigning calm.

'Are you mental? Three hundred and fifty euro?! What the hell did you buy?' Then Serena turned to the DHL delivery man. 'Would you mind telling me what's in this box?'

While a spurt of peptic acids nibbled at his stomach wall, the grand master of the Wilde Beasts of Abaddon wondered why the fuck he had chosen such a mortifying life. He was a Satanist. A man who was attracted to the unknown, the dark side of things. But at that very moment there was no trace of anything dark and unknown except for the reason why he'd ended up in the arms of that harpy.

'Excuse me, what's in the box?' Serena asked the DHL man.

He could hear the delivery man's voice off in the distance. 'Ma'am, it's late. It's written on the delivery slip.'

Meanwhile Saverio banged the nape of his neck against the head rest and mumbled: 'What a mess . . . what a mess . . .'

'It says that it's from "The Art of War" from Caserta . . . A sword?'

Saverio raised his eyes to the sky and made an effort not to begin howling.

'What do you want a sword for?'

Mantos began shaking his head. A huge billboard on the side of the road caught his eye.

THE HOUSE OF SILVER. WEDDING LISTS.
UNIQUE AND EXCLUSIVE GIFTS IN PURE SILVER.

'It's a gift, Serena. It's a surprise. Don't you get it?' His voice had risen a couple of octaves.

'Who for? I reckon you've lost it.'

'Who for? Who could it be for? Have a guess?'

'What would I know . . .?'

'For your father!'

There was a moment of silence. 'My father? What would he do with this sword?'

'What else could he do? He can hang it over the fireplace, can't he?'

'Over the fireplace? In the mountains, you mean? In the chalet up on Rocca Raso?'

'Exactly.'

Serena's voice softened instantly. 'Oh . . . I didn't expect you to be so sweet and thoughtful. Pussycat, sometimes you really know how to surprise me.'

'I have to hang up now because I shouldn't talk on the mobile while I'm driving.'

'All right, pussycat. But come home quickly.'

Saverio hung up and threw the phone into the glove compartment.

4

In the conference hall of Villa Malaparte there were people everywhere. Many stood along the side corridors. Some university students were sitting cross-legged in front of the speakers' table. Others were perched on window sills. It was surprising that nobody was hanging from the Murano glass chandeliers.

As soon as the first photographer spotted the writer, the flashes started popping. Three hundred heads turned and there was a moment of silence. Then, slowly, a murmur rose. Ciba walked down the aisle while six hundred eyes watched him. He turned backwards for a second, lowered his head, touched his ear lobe and put on a fearful expression, trying to appear slightly awkward and embarrassed. The message his body language sent out was simple: *I am the greatest living writer on earth, and yet even I can run late because, despite everything, I am a normal person. Just like you all are.* He looked exactly the way he wanted. Young, troubled, with his head in the clouds. With his tweed jacket worn through at the elbow and his baggy trousers two sizes too big (he had them made in a kibbutz near the Dead Sea), with his waistcoat bought in a charity shop on Portobello Road, with his old Church shoes, which had been given to him the day he graduated from university, with his nose that was just a little too big for his face and that wild tuft of hair that fell over his green eyes. A star. An English actor who had been given the gift of writing like a god.

As he moved towards the table Fabrizio studied the

components of the crowd. He guessed that ten per cent were officials, fifteen were journalists and photographers, at least forty per cent were students (actually female students popping with hormones), and thirty-five per cent old bags on the verge of menopause. Then he added up the percentage of these wonderful people holding a copy of his book or the Indian's book to their chest. Easy done. His was a powder-blue colour with the title written in a bright blood red, while the Indian's was white with black writing. More than eighty per cent were powder blue! He managed to make his way through the last few bunches of people in the crowd. Some shook his hand, some gave him a brotherly slap on the back as if he had just returned from a stint on some celebrity reality TV show. Finally he reached the presenters' table. The Indian writer was seated in the middle. He looked like a turtle who had his shell slipped off and a white tunic and black-rimmed glasses put in its place. He had a peaceful face and two small, wide-set, watery eyes. A carpet of black hair combed back with hair oil helped him to not look like an Egyptian mummy. When he saw Fabrizio, the Indian bent his head forward slightly and welcomed him, pressing the palms of his hands one against the other. But Ciba's attention was immediately drawn to the female creature sitting next to Sawhney. About thirty years old. Mixed heritage. Half Indian and half Caucasian. She looked like a model, but those glasses perched on her petite nose gave her the air of a primary school teacher. A Chinese chopstick held her long hair together in a dishevelled manner. Loose locks, the colour of tar, fell around her delicate neck. A narrow yet voluptuous mouth, lazily open, stood out like a ripe plum above her pointed chin. She was wearing a white linen blouse, open just enough to show off her cleavage, which was neither too small nor too large.

A C cup, Fabrizio calculated.

Her bronze-coloured arms came to end in fine wrists covered in heavy copper bracelets. Her fingers were tipped with nails painted black. While Fabrizio took his seat, he peeked under the table to see if she was just as well-set down below. Elegant legs appeared from underneath a dark skirt. Her thin feet were wrapped in Greek-style sandals, and even her toenails were covered in the same black polish as her hands. Who was this goddess come down from Olympus?

Tremagli, seated on his left, looked up from his sheets of paper, a stern expression on his face. 'Well, Mr Ciba has decided to honour us with his presence . . .' He made a point of staring noticeably at his watch. 'I believe, if you agree of course, that we may begin.'

'I agree.'

For Fabrizio Ciba, the highly esteemed Professor Tremagli, without beating around the bush, was a huge pain in the arse. He had never attacked him with one of his poisonous reviews, but he had never praised him either. Quite simply, for Professor Tremagli, Ciba's work did not exist. Whenever he talked about the current, regrettable, state of Italian Literature, he began to go into raptures over a series of little writers only he knew, and for whom the sale of one thousand five hundred copies would trigger a family party. Never a mention, never a comment about Fabrizio. Finally, one day, on *Corriere della Sera*, when asked directly 'Professor, how can you explain the Ciba phenomenon?', he had answered: 'If we must talk of a phenomenon, it's a passing phenomenon, one of those storms greatly feared by meteorologists but which pass by without causing any damage.' And then he'd clarified: 'However, I haven't read his books thoroughly.'

Fabrizio had foamed at the mouth like a rabid dog and

thrown himself onto his computer to write a fiery reply to be published on the first page of *La Repubblica*. But when his ire had died down he had deleted the file.

The first rule for each true writer is: never, ever, not even on one's deathbed, not even under torture, reply to insults. Everyone expects you to fall into the trap and reply. No, you have to be as intangible as a noble gas and as distant as Alpha Centauri.

But he had felt like waiting for the old fogey on his front doorstep and ripping that fucking walking stick out of his hands and beating it down on his skull like it was an African drum. It would have been so enjoyable, and it would have strengthened his reputation as an accursed writer, one of those who answered literary insults with his fists, like real men, and not like fuckwit intellectuals using bitter comments in page three of the Culture section. Only thing was, that fogey was seventy years old and he would have ended four paws up in the middle of Via Somalia.

Tremagli, in a hypnotist's tone of voice, began a lesson on Indian Literature, starting with the first texts in Sanskrit dating back to 2000 BC found in the rock cave tombs of Jaipur. Fabrizio calculated that it would take him at least an hour before he made it to 2000 AD. The first ones to be anaesthetised would be the old biddies, then the officials, then everyone else, including Fabrizio and the Indian writer.

Ciba leant an elbow on the table and his forehead on his palm, in an attempt to do three manoeuvres at once:

1. Check out which officials were present at the event;
2. Work out who the goddess sitting next to him was;
3. Contemplate what he would say.

The first manoeuvre took a few seconds. The whole of the Martinelli senior staff was sitting in the second row: Federico Gianni, the managing director, Achille Pennacchini, the general manager, Giacomo Modica, the sales manager, and a rally of editors including Leo Malagò. Then the whole gynaeceum of the press office. If even Gianni had unnailed his arse from Genova, then that showed the Indian's book meant a lot to them. Who knows, maybe they hoped to sell a few copies.

In the first row he recognised the Councilman responsible for Culture, a television director, a couple of actors, a thread of journalists and some other faces he'd seen a thousand times but couldn't remember where or when.

There were little cardboard markers with the names of the participants on the table. The goddess's name was Alice Tyler. She was murmuring the translation of Tremagli's speech in the ear of Sarwar Sawhney. The old man, with his eyes closed, was nodding as regularly as a pendulum. Fabrizio opened the Indian's novel and realised that the translation was by Alice Tyler. So she wasn't just the translator for the evening. He began to seriously think that he had found his perfect woman. As beautiful as Naomi Campbell and as intelligent as Margherita Hack.

Fabrizio Ciba had been reflecting for some time on the idea of building a stable relationship with a woman. Perhaps this could help him to concentrate on his new novel, which had paused at chapter two for the past three years.

Alice Tyler . . . Alice Tyler . . . Where had he heard that name before?

He almost fell off his chair. It was the same Alice Tyler who had translated Roddy Elton, Irvin Parker, John Quinn and all the new breed of Scottish writers.

She must know them all! She must have had dinner with Parker and then afterwards he fucked her in a London squat,

23

amidst fag-ends stubbed out on the carpet, used needles and empty beer cans.

A frightful suspicion. *Has she read my books?* He needed to know now, straight away, immediately. It was a physiological need. *If she hasn't read my books and has never seen me on television, she might well think that I am just anybody, might mistake me for one of those mediocre writers who get by attending presentations and cultural events.* All of this was unbearable for his ego. Any balanced relationship, where he was not the star, caused unpleasant side effects: dry mouth, headspins, nausea, diarrhoea. If he were to seduce her, he'd have to rely solely on his charm, on his biting wit, on his unpredictable intelligence and not on his novels. And it was a good thing he didn't even take into consideration the hypothesis that Alice Tyler had read his works and hated them.

He came to the last point, the most prickly one: what would he talk about once the old gasbag finished his rambling speech? Over the past few weeks Ciba had tried to read the Indian's huge volume a handful of times, but after ten pages or so he had turned on the television and watched the athletics championships. He'd really made the effort, but it was such a deadly boring book that it had boiled his balls. He had called a friend of his . . . a fan of his, a writer from Catanzaro, one of those insipid, subservient beings who buzzed around him in an attempt, like cockroaches, to feed themselves on the crumbs of his friendship. This one, though, unlike the others, had a certain critical spirit, a certain, in some ways, bubbly creative ability. Someone whom he might, in an undefined future, get Martinelli to publish. But for now he assigned this friend from Catanzaro secondary tasks, such as writing articles for him for women's magazines, translating pieces from English into Italian, library research and, like now, reading the behemoth and composing a nice short critical summary that he could make his own in quarter of an hour.

Trying not to be too obvious, Ciba slid the three pages jotted down by his friend out of his jacket.

Fabrizio, in public, never read. He spoke freely, he let himself be inspired by the moment. He was famous for this talent, for the magical sense of spontaneity that he bestowed upon his listeners. His mind was a forge open twenty-four hours a day. There was no filter, there was no depot, and when he started in on one of his monologues he captivated everyone: from the fisherman from Mazara del Vallo to the ski instructor from Cortina d'Ampezzo.

But that evening a bitter surprise was awaiting him. He read the first three lines of the summary and blanched. It spoke of a saga revolving around a family of musicians. All of them forced, thanks to an unfathomable destiny, to play the sitar for generations and generations.

He grabbed the Indian's book. The title was *The Conspiracy of the Virgins*. So why was the summary about *A Life in the World*?

A terrible realisation. The friend from Catanzaro had made a mistake! That dickhead had cocked it up and done the wrong book.

He devoured the blurb in desperation. There was no mention at all of sitar players, but of a family of women on the Andaman Islands.

And at that very moment, Tremagli terminated his monologue.

5

He was crushed that the Durendal which had cost him three hundred and fifty euro would end up above his father-in-law's

25

fireplace. Saverio Moneta had bought the sword with the idea of slaying the caretaker of the Oriolo Cemetery, or in any case with the idea of using it as a sacrificial weapon for the blood rites of the sect.

The traffic moved forward at a walking pace. A row of palm trees, burned by the winter, were covered in coloured lights that twinkled on the bonnets of the Mercedes and Jaguars sitting in dealerships' forecourts.

There must have really been an accident.

Saverio turned on the radio and began searching for the traffic station. A part of his brain was working ceaselessly in search of another plan of action to propose to Murder and the others.

And what if, for example, we murdered Father Tonino, the priest from Capranica?

His mobile began ringing again. *Please . . . Serena . . . Not again?* But the screen displayed the words 'PRIVATE NUMBER'. It had to be the old bastard hiding his number in an attempt to fuck him over.

Egisto Mastrodomenico, Serena's father, was seventy-seven years old and yet he tapped away on the mobile phone and the computer keyboard like a sixteen-year-old boy. In his office on the top floor of the Furniture Store of the Thyrolean Master of the Axe, he had a whole battery of computers connected to video cameras, the likes of which would have made a Las Vegas casino-owner jealous. The productivity of the fifteen salesmen was monitored throughout the whole day, worse than being inside a reality TV show. And Saverio, who was the department manager of the Thyrolean furniture shop, had four cameras pointed on him alone.

No, I can't bear having to talk to him this evening. He turned the volume of the car radio up, trying to silence the phone.

Mantos hated his father-in-law with such intensity that he had got irritable bowel syndrome. Old Mastrodomenico used every opportunity to humiliate him, to make him feel like a poor wimp, a freeloader who held his job at the furniture store simply because he was married to the old man's daughter. He would insult him not just in front of his colleagues, but even in front of customers. Once, during a spring sale, he had called him a moron, shouting it into the overhead speaker system. Mantos's only consolation was knowing that sooner or later the bastard would snuff it. Then everything would change. Serena was an only child, which meant he would become the manager of the entire furniture shop. And yet a part of him had even started to wonder if the old man would ever die. He'd gone through it all. They'd removed his spleen. They'd ablated a sebaceous cyst from his ear and he nearly went deaf. He had an eye ravaged by cataracts. At the age of seventy-four years he had slammed his Mercedes at two hundred kilometres an hour against a tip-up truck waiting at the Agip petrol pump. He was in a coma for three weeks and he had come-to even more pissed off than before. Then they diagnosed him with intestinal cancer, but seeing as he was elderly the tumour was unable to spread. And if that didn't suffice, during the twins' christening he had slipped on the steps in front of the church and broken his pelvic bone. Now he lived in a wheelchair and it was up to Saverio to take him to work in the morning and take him back home in the evening.

The phone kept ringing and throbbing in the tray next to the gearstick.

'Fuck you!' he growled, but that bloody sense of guilt written in his chromosomes forced him to answer. 'Papa?'

'Mantos.'

It wasn't the old man's voice. And there was no way that he knew about his Satanic identity.

'Who's this?'

'Kurtz Minetti.'

Upon hearing the name of the high priest of the Children of the Apocalypse Saverio Moneta closed his eyes and reopened them. He squeezed the steering wheel with his left hand and with his right the mobile phone, but it slipped out of his hand like a wet bar of soap, ending up between his legs. He took his foot off the clutch to get to the phone and the engine began hiccuping and turned itself off.

Behind him horns were honking while Saverio shouted at Kurtz: 'Hang on . . . I'm driving. Hang on while I pull over.'

A motorcyclist on a big three-wheeled scooter knocked on the passenger window: 'You realise you're a fuckwit?'

Saverio picked up the phone, started the engine again and managed to pull over.

What did Kurtz Minetti want from him?

6

As soon as Tremagli concluded his speech, the audience began pulling themselves up in their seats where they had cuddled up, stretching their numb legs, patting each other on the back out of solidarity at having survived such a gruelling test. For a second Fabrizio Ciba hoped that it would end there, that the professor had used up all the time available for the event.

Tremagli looked at Sawhney, convinced that he would comment, but the Indian smiled and, once again, lowered his head in a sign of recognition. At that point the poisoned chalice was passed to Fabrizio. 'I believe it's your turn.'

'Thank you.' The young writer rubbed his neck. 'I will keep it short.' Then he turned towards the audience. 'You all look

28

a little worn out. And I know that, over there, a delicious buffet awaits.' He cursed himself the moment the words came out of his mouth. He had offended Tremagli in public, but he recognised in the eyes of the audience a spark of approval that confirmed what he had said.

He looked for a way in, any nonsense to get him off to a start. 'Ahhhh . . .' He cleared his throat. He tapped the microphone. He poured himself a glass of water and wet his lips. Nothing. His mind was a blank screen. An emptied chest. A cold starless universe. A jar of caviar without the caviar. Those people had come here from all across the city, facing the traffic, struggling to find a parking space, taking half a day off because of him. And he had fuck-all to say. He looked at his audience. The audience that were waiting with bated breath. The audience that were wondering what he was waiting for.

La guerre du feu.

A fleeting vision of a French film, seen who knows when, came down into his mind like a divine spirit and tickled his cortex, which released swarms of neurotransmitters that rained down on the receptors ready to welcome them and to awaken other cells of the central nervous system.

'Forgive me. I was distracted by a fascinating image.' He tossed back his hair, adjusted the height of the microphone. 'It's dawn. A dirty and distant dawn of eight hundred thousand years ago. It's cold, but it's not windy. A canyon. Low-lying vegetation. Stones. Sand. Three small hairy creatures, a hundred and fifty centimetres tall, covered in gazelle skins, are in the middle of a river. The current is tempestuous, it's a full-blown river. One of those water courses which, many years later, American families will travel down harnessed with inflatable life-jackets atop coloured rafts.' Fabrizio took a technical pause. 'The water is grey and it is shallow and freezing. It only comes up to their knees, but the current is bloody strong. And they have to cross the river and they move forward, placing each foot carefully. One of the three of them, the biggest, whose hair braided with mud makes him look like a Jamaican Rastafarian, holds a sort of basket tightly in his hands, one of those things made with small woven branches. At the centre of the basket a weak flame flickers, a miniscule flame prey to the winds, a flame that risks going out, poor little thing, which needs to be fuelled continuously with kindling and dried cactus pads, which the other two hold tightly in their hands. At night they take turns to keep it alight, curled up inside a damp cave. They sleep with just one eye closed, taking care that the fire doesn't go out. To gather wood, they have to brave the wild beasts. Enormous and frightening. Tigers with teeth like sabres, hairy mammoths, monstrous armadillos with spiky tails. Our little ancestors are not at the top of the food chain. They don't see it from the top downwards. They are in a good position in the hit parade, but above them are a couple of creatures with hardly a friendly little attitude. They have teeth as sharp as razors, poisons capable of nailing a rhinocerous in thirty seconds. It is a world full of thorns, spikes, stingers, of colourful and toxic plants, of miniscule reptiles which spray liquids like Cif bathroom cleaner . . .' Ciba touches his jaw and glances encouragingly towards the affrescod vaulted ceiling of the hall.

The audience were no longer there; they were in prehistory. Waiting for him to continue.

Fabrizio wondered why the fuck he had carried them back into prehistory and where he was hoping to end up. No matter, he had to continue.

'The three of them are in the middle of this river. The biggest one, the fire-carrier, is at the head of the line. His arms are as stiff as pieces of marble. He holds the weak bonfire in front of him. He can feel his muscles screaming in pain, but he moves forward, holding his breath. One thing he cannot do, fall over. If he falls over, they will no longer have the heat needed not to die of cold during those never-ending nights, the heat needed to roast the leathery warthog meat, the heat needed to keep the ferocious beasts away from the camping place.' He took a peek at the Indian. Was he listening? He appeared to be. Alice was translating for him and he was smiling, keeping his head slightly cocked, like blind people sometimes do. 'What's the problem, you are probably all wondering? What does it take to light a fire? Do you remember the history book in middle school? Those illustrations of the famous primitive man, with a beard and a thong, who rubs two rocks together next to a nice little bonfire like a diligent boy scout? Where are those bloody flint stones? Have you ever found one on a walk through the mountains? I haven't. You feel like lighting a cigarette while hiking, you're out of breath but a Marlboro is just what you need, you haven't got a lighter and so what can you do? Of course! Pick up two stones off the ground and – snap – a spark. No, my friends! That's not how it works. And these very ancestors, unlucky for them, live one hundred years before that genius, a nameless genius, a genius no one has ever thought of dedicating a monument to, a genius as important as Leonardo da Vinci and Einstein, who will discover that certain stones, rich in sulphur, when rubbed together make sparks. These three men, to make a fire, must wait for lightning to fall from the sky and burn a forest. An occurrence that does happen occasionally, but not that often. "Sorry, I need to roast this brontosaurus, I don't have any fire, darling. Go and look for a wildfire," says the Hominid mum, and off her son goes. She will see him three years later.'

The audience laugh. There are even a couple of brief spurts of applause.

31

'Now you understand why these three must keep the fire alive. The famous sacred fire . . .' Ciba took a deep breath and lavished a big smile upon the audience. 'Why I am telling you all of this, I have no idea . . .' Chuckling. 'On the contrary, I believe I do know why . . . And I think that you have all understood why, too. Sarwar Sawhney, this exceptional writer, is one of those beings who has taken on the difficult and terrible responsibility of keeping the fire alive and handing it over to us when the sky darkens and the cold settles in our souls. Culture is a fire that cannot be put out and re-lit with a match. It needs to be cared for, kept high, fuelled. And every writer – I consider myself to be one of them, too – has a duty to never, ever, forget about that fire.' Ciba got up from his chair. 'I would like everyone to stand. I am asking you, please. Stand up for just a moment. Here with us is a great writer who must be honoured for what he does.'

Everyone stood up amidst the din of chairs and broke into a wild applause for the old Indian man, who began bobbing his head, looking rather embarrassed. 'Bravo! Well done! Bravo! Thanks for being you!' someone, who had probably heard Sawhney's name for the first time tonight and certainly wouldn't buy his book, called out. Even Tremagli, reluctantly, was forced to stand and applaud that farce. A girl in the second row pulled out a lighter. Everyone else quickly followed suit. Flames lit up everywhere. Someone turned the big chandeliers off and the long room was lit by a hundred little flames. It was like being at a Baglioni concert.

'Why not?' Ciba pulled out his lighter, too. He saw the managing director, the general manager and the whole Martinelli group follow suit.

The writer was satisfied.

7

'Mantos, I have a proposal to make. Come to Pavia tomorrow for a business lunch. I've already got you booked on a flight for Milano.'

Saverio Moneta was on the side of the motorway to Capranica. He couldn't believe that the famous Kurtz Minetti, the high priest of the Children of the Apocalypse, the one that had decapitated a nun with a double-edged axe, was talking to him. He rubbed a hand across his burning forehead. 'Tomorrow?'

'Yes. I'll get one of my followers to come and pick you up from Linate.'

Kurtz's voice was reassuring and accent free.

'Um, what day is it tomorrow?'

'Saturday.'

'Saturday . . . Let me think.' It was impossible. The next day was the beginning of the 'Kid's Bedrooms Week', and if he asked the old man for another day off his father-in-law would pour kerosene over him and set him on fire in the shop car park.

He took his courage in both hands. 'No, tomorrow I can't make it. I'm sorry, but I really can't.' *I must be the first person who has dared to say no to an invitation from the greatest expert of Italian Satanism. He'll slam the phone down in my face.*

But Kurtz asked him: 'And when could you make it?'

'Well, actually, to be honest, I'm quite busy for the next couple of days . . .'

'Of course.' Kurtz seemed more surprised than annoyed.

Mantos took a risk: 'Couldn't we discuss it over the phone? You've caught me at a bad time.'

Kurtz breathed in deeply through his nose.

'I don't like discussing these things over the phone. It's not safe. I can only give you an idea. As you well know, the Children of the Apocalypse are the number one Satanic sect in Italy, and the third-biggest in Europe. Our website registers fifty thousand hits per day and we have a calendar rich with events. We organise orgies, raids, black masses and excursions to Satanic sites, like the pine forest of Castel Fusano and the Al Amsdin caves in Jordan. We also have a small theatre, where we show the greatest films of demoniacal cinema. We are also developing a half-yearly illustrated magazine called *Satanic Family*.' His voice had changed, it was becoming more animated. He must have given this speech a number of times. 'Our followers are spread out like leopard spots all across the peninsula. Our head office is still in Pavia, but at this point, given the situation, we have decided to expand and take a step forward. And here you come into play, Mantos.'

Saverio undid the button on his collar. 'Me? What do you mean, me?'

'Yes, you. I know that you have been having some organisational problems with your Wilde Beasts of Abaddon. It's a predicament familiar to a lot of small sects. The Reaper told me that you've had a number of deserters over the last season and there are only three of you left.'

'Well . . . To be honest, if you include me, there are actually four of us.'

'Furthermore, you still haven't done anything noteworthy except for, as I see on the forum, some graffiti worshipping the Devil on the viaducts of Anguillara Sabazia.

'Ah, you'd heard about that?' Saverio asked proudly.

'At this moment in time your sect is seriously ailing. And as you well know, with today's crisis there's not much hope you'll survive another year. Forgive me being frank, but you are an insignificant blip in the hard panorama of real Italian Satanism.'

Saverio undid his seat belt. 'We're trying hard. We're planning to recruit new adepts and carry out some plans of action that'll really put us on the map of today's Satanism. We're a small group, but we're really tight.'

In the meantime, Kurtz carried on all by himself. 'What I want to propose to you is that you disband the Wilde Beasts and join the cursed band of the Children of the Apocalypse. What I'm offering is for you to be in charge of Central Italy.'

'What do you mean?'

'You will be the managing director of the branch for Central Italy and Sardinia of the Children of the Apocalypse.'

'Me?' Saverio's heart swelled with pride. 'Why me?'

'The Reaper has told me good things about you. He told me that you've got charisma, willpower, and you are a fervent believer in Satan. And as you well know, to be the leader of a Satanic sect you need to love the forces of Evil more than your own self.'

'Really, did he say that?' Saverio couldn't believe it. He was convinced that Paolo hated him. 'All right. I'm in.'

'Wonderful. We'll organise an orgy in your honour at Terracina, where we've got a number of novices from the Agro Pontino . . .'

Mantos relaxed against the head rest. 'Murder, Zombie and Silvietta will be so happy to hear about this offer.'

'Hold it. The offer only applies to you. Your adepts will have to complete the application forms, which they can download from our website and send in to us. We will evaluate them case by case.'

'Of course.'

Kurtz's voice was flat again. 'As you well know, favouritism is the death of every business.'

'Right.'

'You'll have to come up to Pavia for a brief orientation, where we'll give you the basic notions of the liturgy we've adopted.'

Saverio looked out the window. The cars were still banked up. On the other side of the road, on some landfill covered in billboards, the local train to Rome whizzed past. It looked like a glowing snake. In front of an SMA supermarket people were crowding around with their trolleys. The moon, above the rooftops, looked like a ripe grapefruit and the Northern Star, the one that guided the sailors . . . That one there was the Northern Star, wasn't it?

I don't feel very well.

The pappardelle in hare sauce were to blame; they'd given him indigestion. He could feel an unpleasant pressure pushing up at the mouth of his oesophagus. He widened his jaw as if he was about to yawn, but instead produced a sort of gurgle, which he plugged with one hand.

Kurtz was still explaining: 'To begin with, you could share the responsibility with the Reaper . . .'

It's too hot in here . . . He couldn't keep track of the conversation. He pressed the button to open the window.

'You're a little behind in that area, but I'll give them to you, don't worry about it and then . . .'

A waft of air that tasted like chips and kebab from the kiosk in front of the shopping centre slid into the car. The rancid smell made him nauseous. He curved his back and held back a burp.

'We'll set up a series of Satanic masses around the Castelli Romani area, naturally under your direct control, and then you'll need . . .'

He tried to concentrate on Kurtz's monologue, but he felt as if he'd just swallowed a kilo of mouldy tripe. He undid the top button of his trousers and felt his stomach swell.

'Enotrebor, who's in charge of Southern Italy, has done some remarkable stuff in Basilicata and Molise . . .'

An Alka-Seltzer, a Coke . . .

'Mantos? Mantos, are you there?'

'What?'

'Can you hear me?'

'Yes . . . of course . . .'

'So, what do you say? Would next week work for you, if we meet and start drawing up a work plan?'

Saverio Moneta would have liked to say yes, that it was an honour, that he was happy to be in charge of Central Italy and Sardinia, and yet . . . And yet he didn't feel like it. He couldn't help but remember when his father had given him as a present a Malaguti 50. Saverio had wanted a scooter all through his high-school years and his father had promised him that if he got sixty out of sixty on his final exams, then he would give him one. In his last year Saverio studied his backside off and in the end he'd done it. Sixty out of sixty. And his father had come from work and shown him his old smelly Malaguti. 'Here you go. It's yours. I keep my promises.'

Saverio had expected to get a new scooter. 'But what do you mean? You're giving me yours?'

'No money for another one. This one not good enough for you? What's the matter with it?'

'Nothing . . . But how will you get to the factory?'

His father had shrugged his shoulders. 'Public transport. Nothing wrong with that.'

'But you'll have to wake up one hour earlier.'

'A promise is a promise.'

His mother didn't let him get away with it: 'How can you live with yourself, letting your father go without his scooter?'

In the following months Saverio had tried to use the Malaguti, but every time he hopped on it the image of his father walking out of their apartment building at five o'clock in the morning, bundled up in his overcoat, would appear before him. He started to get anxious, and in the end he had left it in the courtyard and someone stole it. So both he and his father had had to go without.

It had nothing to do with all of this and yet he felt he had done something worthwhile with the Beasts. And he owed part of it to that group of losers that followed him. He couldn't let them down.

Kurtz wanted to trick him. Just like his father had tricked him with the scooter. And the old man as well, when he said that he wanted to give him an important role within the company. Just like Serena had tricked him when she said she wanted to be his geisha, and that the twins, in the end, were just like one baby.

That's why he had become a Satanist. Because everyone tricked him.

What sort of a gift is a gift that every time you use it your father is forced to take the bus?

Saverio Moneta hated them all. Every single one of them. The whole of humanity who moved forward through trickery and exploitation of their peers. Sheltered by his hate, he had fed, he had regained his strength, he had shielded himself. Hate had given him the strength to endure. And in the end, Saverio had made it his religion. And Satan his god.

And Kurtz was just like all the others. *Who the fuck does he think he is, saying that the Wilde Beasts of Abaddon are an insignificant blip?*

38

'No,' he said.

'No what?'

'No. I'm not interested. Thank you, but I'll stay on as the leader of the Wilde Beasts of Abaddon.'

Kurtz was surprised. 'Are you sure you know what you're saying? Think about it. I won't make the same offer twice.'

'I don't care. The Wilde Beasts of Abaddon may very well be an insignificant blip, as you said. But even a tumour is only a single cell at the beginning, then it grows, it multiplies and it kills you. The Beasts will become a blip that everyone will have to contend with. Just wait and see.'

Kurtz burst into laughter. 'You're pathetic. You're over.'

Saverio put his seat belt on. 'Maybe. But as you well know, it's not certain. It's not certain at all. And anyway, I'd rather become a priest than work for you.'

He hung up.

The remains of the sunset had melted away and the shadows had descended across the land. The leader of the Wilde Beasts of Abaddon turned the indicator on and skidded off down the motorway.

8

The old Indian writer kept to himself, sitting in a corner with a glass of water in his hands.

He had arrived by plane from Los Angeles that morning, following two exhausting weeks of book presentations across the United States, and now he wanted to go back to the hotel and stretch out on his bed. He would try to sleep, but he wouldn't succeed in doing so, and in the end he would take a sleeping pill. Natural sleep had abandoned his body a while ago. He thought of his wife Margaret, in London. He would have liked to call her. Tell her that he missed her. That he would be home soon. He looked across to the other side of the room.

The writer who had spoken about the fire was surrounded by a throng of readers who wanted his name signed on their copy of his book. And for each person the young man had a word, a gesture, a smile.

He envied his youth, his relaxed desire to please.

He no longer cared about any of this. What did he care about? *About sleeping.* About getting in six hours of rest, with dreams. Even the trip around the world that he had been forced to do since winning the Nobel made no sense. He was a rag doll, thrown from one end of the globe to the other, to be exhibited to the public, taken in hand by people he didn't know, people he would forget about as soon as he moved on. He had written a book. A book that had taken ten years of his life to write. Didn't that alone suffice? Wasn't it enough?

During the presentation he had not managed to get past the introductions. Not like the Italian writer. He had read his novel on the plane. A small, fluid novel. He had read it out of scruple, because he didn't like to be presented by writers whose work he didn't know. And he had enjoyed it. He would like to tell the writer. It was not good manners to keep to himself.

As soon as the old man got up from his chair, three journalists who were waiting on the sidelines were suddenly all over him. Sawhney explained that he was tired. The next day he would be happy to answer their questions. But he said it so softly, so sweetly, that he was unable to free himself of these annoying flies. Luckily a lady arrived, from his publishing house, who shooed them away.

'What must we do now?' he asked the lady.

'There is a cocktail party. Then, in about an hour, we will go

40

and eat in a traditional restaurant, in Trastevere, which is famous for its Roman specialities. Do you like spaghetti carbonara?'

Sawhney placed his hand on her arm. 'I would like to talk with the writer . . .' Oh God, what was his name? His head wasn't working any more

The lady came to his aid. 'Ciba! Fabrizio Ciba. Certainly. Please stay here. I'll go and call him straight away.' And she threw herself, her high heels tapping, into the throng.

'You're not supposed to be asking me for my autograph . . . Ask Sawhney. He's the one who won the Nobel Prize, not me.' Fabrizio Ciba was trying to dam the sea of books engulfing him. His wrist was sore from the autographs he had signed. 'What's your name? Paternò Antonia? Pardon? Just a moment . . . Oh, you liked Erri, Penelope's father? He reminds you of your grandfather? Me, too.'

A chubby woman, clearly overheated, elbowed her way through the crowd and planted another copy of *The Lion's Den* in front of him.

'I came all the way from Frosinone just for you. I've never read your books. But they tell me they're real good. I bought it at the station. You are so nice . . . And so handsome. I always watch you on the television. My daughter is in love with you . . . And so am I . . . a bit.'

A polite smile was sculpted on his face. 'Well, maybe you should read them. You might not like them.'

'What do you mean? Are you serious?'

Another book. Another autograph.

'What's your name?'

'Aldo. Can you make it out to Massimiliano and Mariapia? They're my children, they're six and eight years old, they'll read it when they've gro . . .'

He despised them. They were a bunch of idiots. A herd of sheep. Their appreciation meant nothing to him. They would have gathered with the same enthusiasm for the family memoir of the director of the Channel 2 news, for the romantic revelations of the most uncouth showgirl in television. They only wanted to have their own conversation with the star, their own autograph, their own moment with the idol. If they could, they would have ripped off a piece of his suit, a lock of hair, a tooth, and they would have carried it home like a relic.

He couldn't bear another minute of having to be polite. Of having to smile like a moron. To try and be modest and gracious. He was usually able to conceal perfectly the physical revulsion he felt towards indiscriminate human contact. He was a master at faking it. When the moment came, he threw himself into the mud, convinced that he enjoyed it. He emerged from bathing in the crowds weary but purified.

However, that evening a ghastly suspicion was poisoning his victory. The suspicion that he didn't behave properly, with the discretion of a real writer. Of a serious writer like Sarwar Sawhney. During the presentation the old man had not uttered a word. He had sat there like a Tibetan monk, his ebony eyes offering wisdom and aloofness, while Fabrizio played court jester with all that crap about the fire and culture. And as per usual, the question upon which his entire career balanced sneaked into his mind. *How much of my success is thanks to my books and how much is thanks to TV?*

As always, he preferred not to answer himself, and instead drink a couple of whiskies. First, though, he had to shake off that swarm of flies. And when he saw poor Maria Letizia push her way towards him, he couldn't help but rejoice.

'Sawhney wants to talk to you . . . As soon as you finish, would you mind going to him?'

'Now! I'll come now!' he answered her. And as if he'd been summoned by the Holy Ghost himself, he stood up and said to those fans who still hadn't received their certificate of participation: 'Sawhney needs to talk to me. Please, let me go.'

At the drinks table he sank two glasses of whisky one after the other, and felt better. Now that the alcohol was in his body, he could face the Nobel Prize winner.

Leo Malagò came over to him with his tail wagging happily like a dog who's just been given a wild-boar pâté bruschetta.

'You legend! You knocked them all out with that little tale about the fire. I wonder how you come up with such ideas. Now Fabrizio, though, please don't get drunk. We have to go to dinner afterwards.' He folded his arm through Fabrizio's. 'I had a look at the book sales. Guess how many copies you sold this evening?'

'How many?' He couldn't help answering. It was an automatic reflex.

'Ninety-two! And you know how many Sawhney sold? Nine! You don't know how pissed off Angiò is.' Massimo Angiò was the foreign-fiction editor. 'I love seeing him so pissed off! And tomorrow you'll be splashed across the papers. By the way, how fucking hot is his translator?' Malagò's face relaxed. The look in his eyes suddenly softened. 'Imagine what it would be like to fuck her . . .'

Fabrizio, instead, had lost all interest in the woman. His mood was dropping like a thermometer in a cold snap. What did the Indian want from him?! To tell him off for the crap he had shot off? He plucked up his nerve.

'Excuse me a moment.'

He could see him in a corner. He was sitting opposite the window and was watching the tree branches scrape the yellow skyline of Rome. His black hair shone under the light of the chandeliers.

43

Fabrizio drew near carefully. 'I beg your pardon . . .'

The old Indian turned around, saw him and smiled, showing off a set of teeth too perfect to be real.

'Please, take a seat.'

Fabrizio felt like a child who'd been sent for by the head-master.

'How's it going?' Fabrizio asked in his high-school English, as he sat down opposite Sawhney.

'Well, thank you.' Then the Indian thought again. 'To tell you the truth, I'm a little tired. I can't sleep. I suffer from insomnia.'

'I don't, luckily.' Fabrizio realised that he had nothing to say to the man.

'I read your book. A little hastily, on the aeroplane, I do beg your pardon . . .'

Fabrizio coughed out a suffocated 'And?' He was about to hear the verdict of the winner of the Nobel Prize for Literature. One of the most important writers in the world. The man who had the best press reviews of anyone in the last ten years. A part of Fabrizio's brain wondered whether he really wanted to hear it.

I bet he hated it.

'I liked it. A lot.'

Fabrizio Ciba felt a shot of well-being float through his body. A sensation like what a drug addict feels when he injects himself with good-quality heroin. A sort of beneficial heat that made the back of his neck tingle, slid down across his jaw, shut his eyes, slipped between his gums and his teeth, went down his trachea, it spread out pleasantly boiling hot like Vicks VapoRub from his sternum to his spine, through his ribs, and skipped from one vertebra to another until it reached his pelvis. His sphincter tensed briefly and goosebumps shot up his arms. A warm shower without getting wet. Better than that. A massage without being touched. While this physiological reaction – which lasted a few seconds – took place, Fabrizio was blind and deaf, and when he snapped back to reality Sawhney was talking.

' . . . places, facts and people are unaware of the force that wipes them away. Don't you agree?'

'Yes, certainly.' He answered. He hadn't heard anything at all. 'Thank you. You've made me happy.'

'You definitely know how to keep the reader interested, how to move the best chords of your sensitivity. I would like to read something you've written that's a bit longer.'

'*The Lion's Den* is my longest work. I've recently . . .' – it was actually five years ago – ' . . . published another novel, *Nestor's Dream*, but that is also quite short.'

'How come you don't venture further? You most certainly have the expressiveness to do so. Don't be scared. Let yourself go without fear. If I may give you a piece of advice, don't hold yourself back, let yourself be taken by the story.'

Fabrizio had to stop himself from hugging that dear adorable old man. How true what he had said was. Fabrizio knew he was capable of writing THE GREAT NOVEL. What's more, THE GREAT ITALIAN NOVEL, like *I promessi sposi* to be exact, the book the critics said was missing in our contemporary literature. And after various attempts, he had begun work on a saga about a Sardinian family, from the seventeenth century until the present day. An ambitious project that was definitely much stronger than the *Gattopardo* or *I Viceré*.

Fabrizio was about to tell Sawhney all this, but a little humility held him back. He felt obliged to return the compliments. So he began inventing: 'I wanted to tell you that your novel had me literally inspired. It is an extraordinarily organic novel and the plot is so intense . . . How do you do it? What is your secret? It has a dramatic energy that left me shaken for weeks.

The reader is not only called on to weigh the consciousness and innocence of these powerful female characters, but, through their stories, how can I say it . . .? Yes, the reader is forced to transfer your point of view from the pages of the book to his own reality.'

'Thank you,' said the Indian. 'How nice to pay each other compliments.'

The two writers burst out laughing.

9

The leader of the Wilde Beasts of Abaddon was seated at the kitchen table hoeing into a plate of lasagne floating in a lake of reheated Béchamel sauce. It made him feel nauseous, but he had to pretend he hadn't eaten.

Serena, sitting with her feet up against the dishwasher, was painting her nails. As always, she hadn't waited for him for dinner. The television on the Formica worktop was showing *Who Wants to be a Millionaire?*, Saverio's favourite programme after *Mysteries* on RAI Tre. But the Wilde Beasts' leader's mind was far away. He kept thinking back to the phone call with Kurtz Minetti.

I am such a legend. He cleaned his mouth with the serviette. *What did I say again? No. I'm not interested.* Could he think of any Satanist on the circuit who would have had the guts to turn down an offer to become the manager of Central Italy for the Children of the Apocalypse? He felt like calling Murder to tell him about how he had told Kurtz to fuck off, but Serena might have overheard him, and then he also didn't want them to find out what that shithead Kurtz thought about the WBA. They'd be offended.

He was surprised at how powerfully and confidently he had pronounced that no. He couldn't help himself from pronouncing it again: 'No!'

'No what?' Serena asked, without lifting her gaze from the fingernails she was painting red.

'Nothing, nothing. I was just thinking . . .'

Saverio felt an urge to tell his wife all about it, but he held back. If she found out that he was the leader of a Satanic sect, the least she would do is file for divorce.

But that no might be the beginning of an existential turning-point. It was a no that would inevitably lead to an avalanche of no's that it was time to enounce. No to working on the weekends. No to having to babysit. No to him always having to take the rubbish out.

'There's left-over turkey from yesterday. Heat it up in the microwave.'

Serena was standing up and waving her hands.

'No,' he answered naturally.

Serena yawned. 'I'm going to bed. When you're finished, clear the table, take out the rubbish and turn off the lights.'

Saverio looked at her. She was wearing elastic denim shorts covered in rhinestones, patent white-leather cowboy boots and a black t-shirt with an enormous V for Valentino on it.

Not even the girls who hang out at the shopping centres put on that sort of get-up.

Serena Mastrodomenico was forty-three years old, and all those years of sunbathing had dehydrated her like a sundried tomato. She was very skinny, despite having given birth to twins less thank a year ago. From far away she looked great, with her toned physique, those balloon tits and that caffé latte-coloured complexion. But if you moved in closer and took a better look, you discovered that her derma was stretched and leathery like a rhinoceros's, and a tangle of thin wrinkles ran across her neck, the corners of her mouth and her cleavage. Her green eyes, sparkling and lively, sat upon cheekbones that were as shiny and round as two Annurcan apples.

She often wore open-toed shoes that showed off her tapered ankles and delicate feet. She preferred little summer dresses that left room for lacy bras and two synthetic hemispheres to stick out. She covered herself in more ethnic jewellery than a Berber princess at her coronation.

During their long years of marriage, Saverio had noticed that his wife was very popular with men, especially the younger ones. Every time he went down into the factory warehouse the couriers, a pack of letches, would pull him into their banter. They didn't even respect the boss's daughter.

'Your wife must be something to watch in bed. Forget about these young chicks, she's got experience. She'll open you like a sofa bed.' 'Go on, do a sex tape for us.' 'Save, how do you keep her satisfied? I reckon she needs a whole team of beasts . . .' 'She's the classic type of woman who acts all sophisticated, but in reality she's a total animal . . .' And other vulgarities it's best not to mention.

If those morons only knew the truth. Serena deplored sex. She said it was crude. She abhorred any type of nudity, and found body fluids and everything that was involved in physical relationships repellent (except for massages, and those only to be done by a woman).

But something in all of this didn't make sense to Saverio Moneta. If sex disgusted her so much, why did she dress like a playmate? And why, of all the vacant spots, did she always park the car right in front of the storeroom?

*   *   *

Saverio got up from the table and began putting things away. He didn't feel ready for bed, he was too excited. Luckily, the twins were asleep. The time was right to concentrate on the idea that would shake up the WBA and the rest of the world. He took out a note pad and a pen, and grabbed the remote control to turn off the television when he heard Gerry Scotti say: 'Unbelievable! Friendly Francesco from Sabaudia has made it, all hush-hush, to the question worth a million euro . . .'

The contestant was a fidgety little man with a sneer pulled across his mouth. It looked like he was sitting on a hedgehog. Gerry, instead, had the satisfied expression of a tabby cat who's just scoffed a tin of tuna. As if he was about to sprout claws and start scratching the couch. 'So, dear Francesco, are you ready?'

The little man swallowed and adjusted his collar. 'Pretty much . . .'

Gerry puffed out his chest and turned towards the audience, enjoying himself. 'Pretty much? Do you hear what he says?' Then, suddenly serious, he spoke to the people at home. 'Which of you wouldn't be nervous in his place? Put yourselves in his shoes. One million euro can change your life.' He began talking to Francesco. 'You said your dream was to pay off your house loan. And now what? If you won, in addition to your loan, what would you do?'

'Well, I'd buy my mum a car and then . . .' The contestant was suffocating. He gasped and managed to answer. 'I'd like to make a donation to the San Bartolomeo Institute of Gallarate.'

Gerry studied him down his nose. 'And what do they do, if I may ask?'

'They help the homeless.'

'Well done.' The presenter encouraged the audience to clap their hands and the audience responded with an uproarious applause. 'You're a philanthropist. Are you sure we won't see

49

you zooming around in a Ferrari? No, you can see that you're a good man.'

Saverio shook his head. If he won that sum of money, he would buy a medieval castle in the Marche region and turn it into the headquarters of the Beasts.

'Now, let's take a look at the question. Ready?' Gerry tightened the knot in his tie, cleared his throat and, while the question and the four answers appeared on the screen, he recited:

WHO WAS ABADDON?

A) AN ANGLICAN PREACHER OF THE 18TH
   CENTURY
B) A DEMON CITED IN THE APOCALYPSE
C) AN ASSYRIAN DIVINITY
D) A MAYAN RELIGIOUS FESTIVAL

Saverio Moneta almost fell off his chair.

10

After the revitilising injection to his ego, Fabrizio Ciba's mood was at stratospheric levels. He had written an important novel and he would write another one that was even more important. There was no need to question the reason for his success. Hence, when he saw Alice Tyler talking with the Martinelli sales manager, he decided that it was fine to intervene. He finished his whisky, messed up his hair and said to the Indian writer: 'Excuse me a moment, I need to say hello to someone.' And he went on the attack.

'Here I am, hello there, I'm Fabrizio Ciba.' He pushed in between the two, then said to Modica: 'And seeing as you are

bloodsuckers and you never pay me a cent for these presentations, I can do anything I want, so I'm taking the most charming
and talented translator in the world away from you and off
to drink a glass of Champagne.'

The sales manager was a chubby fellow, unhealthily pallid,
and the only thing that he managed to do was puff up like a
puffer fish.

'You don't mind, do you, Modica?' Fabrizio grabbed the
translator by the wrist and dragged her along with him towards
the refreshments. 'It's the only way to get rid of him, talk about
money. I wanted to congratulate you. You did a wonderful job
with Sawhney's book, I personally checked the translation word
for word . . .'

'Don't make fun of me,' she giggled, amused.

'It's true, I swear! I swear on the head of Pennacchini! I
checked every one of the eight hundred pages, and nothing.
Everything is perfect.' He put his hand on his heart. 'Just one
comment . . . Yes, on page six hundred and fifteen you translated "creel" as fishing basket and not as lobster pot . . .'
Fabrizio tried to look her in the eyes, but he couldn't take his
eyes off her tits. And that skimpy blouse didn't help. 'I'm sorry,
but shouldn't you translators be ugly and badly dressed?'

He was clearly sailing. He was back to being Ciba the
conquistador, the one for the most important occasions.

'So, when should we get married? I write the books and you
translate them, or the other way round, you write the books
and I translate them. No flies on us.' He poured her a glass of
Champagne. He poured himself another glass of whisky. 'Yes,
we really should do it . . .'

'What?'

'Get married, right?' He was forced to repeat himself. He had
the vague feeling that the girl wasn't exactly responding to his

advances. She wasn't your classic Italian bint, and maybe he needed to use a more subtle strategy. 'I've got an idea. Why don't we make a run for it? I've got my Vespa outside. Just imagine, everybody here dying of boredom, talking about literature, while you and I drive around Rome having fun. What do you think?'

He looked at her with the expression of a boy who has just asked his mother for a piece of cake.

'Are you always like this?' Alice slid her hand through her hair and opened her lips, showing brilliant white teeth.

Fabrizio purred. 'Like this how?'

'Well, this . . .' She paused for a moment in search of the right word, then sighed: 'Idiotic!'

Idiotic? What does she mean idiotic? 'It's the childlike part of the genius,' he proffered.

'No, we can't leave. Don't you remember? We've got the dinner. And Sawhney . . .'

'The dinner, I forgot. Right,' he lied. He'd overdone it, asking her to run off, and now he tried to dam the refusal.

She grabbed his wrist. 'Come with me.'

As he passed the table, Ciba snapped up a bottle of whisky.

Where was she taking him?

Then he saw the door leading to the garden.

11

It was obvious that Satan had used Gerry Scotti to communicate with him. How could it be that, of all the infinite number of questions that exist in the universe, the authors of the programme had chosen one about Abaddon? It was a sign. Of what, Saverio hadn't the faintest idea. But it was undoubtedly a sign from the Evil One.

The guy from Sabaudia had stuffed it up. He'd answered that Abaddon was an Anglican preacher from the eighteenth century, and had gone back home to his bank loan.

Serves you right. That'll teach you for not knowing who Abaddon the Destroyer is.

Saverio took a pack of Alka-Seltzer out of the drawer, dissolved a tablet in a glass and thought about the day. The last twelve hours had something prodigious about them. Everything had begun with his sudden decision to make the leap with the WB. Then turning down Kurtz Minetti. Now there was even the big question. He had to look for other signs of the presence of the Evil One in his life.

What day was it today? April 28th. What did the 28th of April correspond to in the Satanic calendar?

He went into the lounge room to get his laptop bag. The room was furnished with the ethnic Zanzibar collection. Square-shaped furniture made of black, oily wood inset with diamond-shaped pieces of zebra skin. They gave off a strange spicy odour that left you with a headache after a while. The Pioneer plasma TV was beneath an enormous mosaic Serena had created using shells from mussels and clams and coloured stones picked up on the Argentario. It was supposed to depict a mermaid sitting on the rocks, playing her long hair like it was the strings of a harp.

Saverio connected to the Internet and Googled for the words: 'Satanist Calendar'. He discovered that the 28th of April didn't mean anything. But the 30th of April was the Night of Walpurga, when there was the grand meeting of the witches on top of Mount Brocken.

He stood up, feeling confused. The way things had gone today, he was sure that April 28th was a Satanic day.

Even if, truth be told, only because the 28th wasn't far from the 30th, the Night of Walpurga.

He went over to the big box next to the front door. He cut the packing tape and opened it. Then, like an ancient paladin, he kneeled before the treasure, slipped his hands into the polystyrene shavings and extracted the Durendal. He lifted it using both his hands. The solid steel blade, the hilt in forged iron and handle covered in leather. He had hesitated at length over whether to buy a Japanese katana, but he'd made the right choice when he bought a weapon that belonged to his own cultural tradition. It was so beautiful it took his breath away.

He went out onto the small terrace, placed it before the moon's disc and, just like Orlando at Roncisvalle, he began to whirl it around. He would have loved to challenge Kurtz Minetti to a duel. In his office in Pavia.

Me with the Durendal and him with the double-headed axe.

He imagined himself dodging a blow, turning around and with a sharp swipe decapitating the head priest. Then he would simply say: 'Come to me! You will be Beasts.' And all the Children of the Apocalypse would kneel before his presence. That would be a great moment. Except for the fact that Kurtz Minetti, even though he was only as tall as a dick on a tin can, was a disciple of Sante Lucci, a Shaolin Master from Trieste.

Saverio pirouetted and destroyed the clothes horse. The very idea that that gem would end up above his father-in-law's fireplace in Rocca Raso made him feel sick.

The phone began ringing then quickly turned silent. Serena must have answered. Shortly after, he heard her shout: 'Saverio, it's for you. Your cousin. Tell him the next time he calls at this hour I'll shove his teeth down his throat.'

The leader of the WB went back into the lounge room and put the sword in its box, picked up the cordless and answered in a rushed tone: 'Antonio? What is it?'

'Hey there, cousin. How's it going?'

'Not bad. What's the matter?'

'Nothing. Actually, there is something. I need your help.'

That's all he needed. Didn't anyone think that even Saverio Moneta had troubles of his own, too? 'No, look . . . I'm up to my neck . . . I'm sorry.'

'Wait. You don't have to do anything. I know you're busy. But every now and then I've seen you hanging out with a group of kids . . .'

He's seen me with the WB. I have to be more careful.

'I'm up shit creek. Four Poles left me hanging at the last minute, so I'm looking for fill-ins. They need to carry cases of wine, set up tables in the garden, clear away. Stuff like that. Hard workers, but well-behaved ones. Even if they don't have much experience, all they need is the will to work and no misbehaving.'

Antonio Zauli was the head waiter of *Food for Fun*, a catering company in the capital city, which, thanks to the supervision of Zóltan Patrovic, the unpredictable Bulgarian chef and owner of the extremely famous restaurant *Le Regioni*, had become Rome's number one for organising banquets and buffets.

Saverio wasn't listening. *And if I decapitated Padre Tonino with a stroke of the Durendal? He's got Parkinson's so I'd just be doing him a favour, really. Tomorrow, after the paediatrician, I'll take the sword to the knife-sharpener . . . No, that would be copying Kurtz Minetti a bit.*

'Saverio? Can you hear me?'

'Yeah . . . Sorry . . . I can't help you out,' he faked.

'My arse, you can't. You weren't even listening to me. You don't get it. I am desperate. I put my backside on the line with this party. I've been working at it for six months, Save'. He lowered his voice. 'Swear you won't say anything to anyone.'

'What?'

55

'Just swear.'

Saverio looked around and realised just how ugly the ethnic lampshade was. 'I swear.'

Antonio whispered in a conspiratorial tone of voice: 'Anyone and everyone's gonna be at this party. Tell me a VIP. Anyone at all. Come on. The first name that springs to mind.'

Saverio thought about it for a second. 'The Pope.'

'Oh, come on. A VIP, I said. Singers, actors, football players . . .'

Saverio huffed. 'What do I know? What do you want from me? Who can I say? Paco Jimenez de la Frontera?'

'The centre-forward for Rome. Bingo!'

Now, if in the whole world there was a word Saverio Moneta hated, it was 'bingo'. He, as did all serious Satanists, detested popular culture, slang, Hallowe'en and the Americanisation of the Italian language. If it were up to him, everybody would still be speaking in Latin.

'Give me another one.'

Saverio couldn't take it. 'I don't know! And I don't care! I've got too much on my plate at the moment, I have.'

Antonio now put on an offended tone of voice. 'What's the matter? You're a weirdo, you know that? I'm giving you and your friends the chance to make some money, to participate in the most exclusive party of the last few years, to rub shoulders with famous people, and you . . . You tell me to fuck off?'

Saverio felt like ripping out his cousin's carotid artery and bathing in his blood, but he sat down on the couch and tried to reassure him.

'No, Anto, I'm sorry. Really, I'm not angry with you. It's just that I'm tired. You know, the twins, my father-in-law, it's been hard going . . .'

'Yeah, I hear ya. But if you think of anyone who could help

me out, give me a bell. I've got to find four kids by tomorrow morning. Think about it, OK? Tell them the pay's great and during the party there's even a concert with Larita and fireworks.'

The leader of the WB pricked up his antennae.

'What did you say? Larita? Larita the singer? Who did *Live in Saint Peter* and *Unplugged in Lourdes*? Who sings that song "King Karol"?'

Elsa Martelli, known artistically as Larita, had been the lead singer of the Lord of Flies for a couple of years, a death metal group from Chieti Scalo. Their songs had been the anthems of the Evil One and they had been much appreciated by the Italian Satanic community. Then suddenly Larita had left the group and converted to the Christian faith, been baptised by the Pope, and had undertaken a solo career as a pop singer. Her releases were a flavourless mix of new age, teenage love affairs and feel good sensations, and as such had obtained a huge amount of success in the world. But she was loathed by all Satanists.

'Yeah. I think it's her. Larita . . . The one that sings "Love Around You".' Antonio was no expert of pop music.

Saverio realised that the air had a nice smell, of earth and grass from the freshly mowed street islands. The moon had disappeared and it was completely dark. The windows vibrated and the ficus was restless, tossed about by a sudden breeze. It began to rain. Huge, heavy drops stained the bricks on the small terrace, and a lightning bolt, like a crack in the wall, tore open the shadow and for an instant the sky lit up like it was day with an explosion that shook the earth, set off burglar alarms and started dogs barking.

Saverio Moneta, seated on the couch, saw a fleet of large and twisted black clouds heading towards Oriolo Romano. One of them, the biggest of all, right in front of him, folded in half and stretched out, turning into a sort of face. Black eyes and mouth wide open. Straight after the shadows returned.

'Madonna of Carmine!' he sputtered instinctively. He ran to close the windows, where the rain was drenching the parquet floor. 'All right!' he panted into the receiver.

'All right, what?'

'I've found your three.' Then he beat himself on the chest. 'I'm the fourth.'

12

Fabrizio Ciba and Alice Tyler were sitting calmly on a marble bench opposite an oval-shaped fountain. On their right was a bamboo forest illuminated by a halogen floodlight. On their left, a hydrangea. Between them a distance of twenty centimetres. It was dark and cold. The lights from the villa behind them were reflected in the water, and on Alice's splendid legs.

Fabrizio Ciba took a sip of alcohol from the bottle and passed it to the girl, who lifted it to her mouth. He had to make his move quickly. It was so cold they risked paralysis. What to do? Jump her? *I don't know . . . You know how these Anglo-Saxon intellectuals can be.*

The dominator of the bestseller lists, the third-sexiest man in Italy according to the women's weekly *Yes* (behind a motorcycle racer and a sitcom actor with blond highlights), could not bear to think about being turned down. It would probably force him to undertake years of psychoanalysis.

The silence was becoming eerie. He took a shot: 'You've translated Irvin Parker's books, too, haven't you?' As he spoke he realised that it was the worst thing to say if he was aiming for a quick approach.

'Yes. Everything except his first one.'

'Ah . . . Have you met him?'

'Who?'

'Parker.'

'Yes.'

'What's he like?'

'Nice.'

'Really?'

'Very.'

No! This wasn't working. What's more, he felt she was distracted. The twenty centimetres between them felt like twenty metres. It was better to pull back in and leave it be. 'Listen, mayb . . .'

Alice looked at him. 'I have to tell you something.' Her eyes were shining. 'It's a bit embarrassing . . .' She took a deep breath, as if she was about to share a secret. 'When I finished reading *The Lion's Den*, I cried . . . I felt terrible, just thinking that I was supposed to go out that evening. I stayed at home, I was too shaken. And the next day I read it again and it was even more beautiful. I don't know what to say, it was a unique experience . . . It holds so many analogies with my own life.'

Ciba was overwhelmed with waves of pleasure, by endorphins trickling from his head downwards, swishing through his veins like petrol in a pipeline. Except that this time, unlike what happened with Sawhney, the pleasure channelled its way into the urethra, in the epididymides, into the femoral arteries and exploded inside his reproductive organ, which filled with blood, causing him a ferocious erection. Fabrizio grabbed her by the wrists and stuck his tongue in her mouth. And she, who was about to confess that she'd written him a long letter, suddenly found it between her tonsils. She muttered a collection of vowels, 'Ae u aei!', which meant 'Are you crazy?!' Instinctively she tried to free herself of the oesophagogastroduodenoscopy, but unable to do so she figured she was done for and put her hand in his hair, pressed her lips hard against his and began windmilling her small, thick tongue.

Fabrizio, feeling her giving in, wrapped his arms around her back and squeezed his chest up against hers, testing its firm consistency. She raised one of her marvellous legs. He pushed his erection against her. She then lifted her other marvellous leg. And he put his hand between her thighs.

Federico Gianni, the managing director of Martinelli, and his faithful steed Achille Pennacchini were leaning on the banister of the grand terrace that overlooked the garden and Rome.

Gianni was a dapper beanpole in his windswept Caraceni suits. When he was young he had played basketball in the A2 league, but at twenty-five years of age he had given up the sport to take on the management of a sports-shoe company. Then, who knows by way of which street and contacts, from starting in a small Milanese publishing house he came to land at Martinelli. He didn't know squat about literature. He treated books like shoes, and was proud of his way of thinking.

The exact opposite of Pennacchini, who Gianni had pulled out of the University of Urbino, where he taught comparative literature, and placed at the head of the publishing house. He was an academic, a literary man, and everything about him was proof of this: his round, tortoiseshell glasses that sat in front of blue eyes ruined by books, the worn checked jacket, the rough cotton shirt with the buttons on the collar, the woollen ties and striped cotton trousers. He spoke very little. Always in a soft voice. And he hesitated. It was never possible to understand what he was really thinking.

'Another one over.' Gianni stretched. 'I think it went well.'

'Very well,' Pennacchini echoed.

Rome appeared like an enormous dirty blanket encrusted with diamonds.

'This city is big,' Gianni mused, staring out at the panorama.

'Very big. It goes from Castelli across to Fiumicino. It is really immense.'

'How big would its diameter be?'

'Hmph, I don't know . . . At least about eighty kilometres . . .' Pennacchini guessed.

Gianni glanced at his watch. 'How long till we go to the restaurant?'

'About twenty minutes, maximum.'

'The buffet was disgusting. The two salmon sandwiches I ate were dry. I'm hungry.' He paused. 'And I need to piss, too.'

Following his boss's last statement Pennacchini bounced his head backwards and forwards like a pigeon.

'I may piss right here in the garden. Out in the open. There's nothing better than pissing in front of this panorama. Look down there, it looks like a storm.' Gianni leaned over the terrace and looked down into the darkness of the bushes. 'Can you check to make sure no one can see me? Actually, if anyone comes this way, stop them.'

'What should I say?' Pennacchini murmured, uncertain.

'To whom?'

'To whomever comes by this way.'

Gianni thought about it for a second. 'What do I know . . .? Entertain them, stop them.'

The managing director walked down the steps that led to the garden, unzipping his trousers. Pennacchini took position, like a Swiss Guard, at the top of the stairs.

13

Larita.

She was the chosen one. They would sacrifice the singer from Chieti Scalo to the Lord of Evil. During the party, Mantos would decapitate her with the Durendal.

'Beats a nun any day . . . I'll show you, Kurtz,' Saverio sniggered while he started jumping around the living room.

What would happen once everyone knew that the singer who had sold ten million copies across Europe and Latin America, and had sung in front of the Pope on Christmas Day, had been decapitated by the Wilde Beasts of Abaddon? The news would be printed on the front page of newspapers across the globe. It was would rank there with John Lennon and Janis Joplin . . .

Saverio hesitated. Was Janis Joplin actually assassinated?

Who cares. All he cared about at that moment was that, with such a deed, he'd be remembered for ever. Websites, forums and blogs would be dedicated to him. His face would be printed on thousands of young boys' t-shirts. And Satanist groups for generations and generations would be inspired by the figure of Mantos, and they would be charmed by his charismatic and psychotic personality, just like Charles Manson.

Saverio grabbed Serena's iPod from the credenza next to the front door. He was sure that his wife had something by the singer. And in fact she did. He pressed play. The artist began singing in her melodious voice, rich with octaves, about a love story between two teenagers.

Disgusting!

That disgusting woman had brought together the two things he hated most in the world: love and teenagers.

From the drinks cabinet he pulled out a bottle of Jägermeister and had a suck.

It was so bitter.

14

The marble bench was not exactly comfortable. Fabrizio Ciba and Alice Tyler were entwined around each other while puffs of the Western wind shook the bamboo forest. The writer had one hand against the cement wall and the other on the translator's tit. The translator had one of hers shoved in behind his back and the other inside the writer's pants. His belt was stopping, like a tourniquet, the flow of blood to her hand, and so the only thing she could do with her numb fingers was squeeze his dick. Fabrizio was panting in her ear while trying to free her tit from the imprisonment of her bra but, having no luck, he decided that he would explore her intimate areas.

They didn't notice the managing director, who, just ten metres away, was having a piss until they heard him sigh. 'Ahhh! I really needed that. What a feeling of freedom!'

The two of them froze like sole fish, and if they could have, like the *Solea solea*, they would have changed colour, camouflaging themselves with their surroundings. Fabrizio whispered: 'Shush, someone's here . . . Shush, please. Don't breathe.' They turned to stone, like two calchi from Pompeii. Both of them with their hands on the other's genitals.

Another voice. Far off. 'Ciba was good this evening.'

How many of them are there?

The voice nearest-by answered: 'You have to admit that our Ciba is the best at this sort of thing!'

'It's Gianni! The managing director!' Ciba explained, in a whisper.

'Oh my God, oh my God, oh my God,' she said. 'What if they see us?'

'Shush. Don't say anything.' Fabrizio raised his head. Gianni's silhouette stretched upwards from behind the hydrangea bush. Ciba lowered down again. 'He's having a piss. He can't see us. He'll go away now.'

But the managing director, who suffered from prostate trouble, kept shaking his thing in the hope of further downfalls.

'Not bad, that idea of the story of the fire! Total crap, but effective nevertheless. We should call on him more often for this sort of thing, he's magnetic.'

Fabrizio smiled, satisfied, and looked at Alice, who huffed, amused. What more could he want? He was snogging a sort of intellectual, mixed-race model, and at the same time he was being complimented with high praise from the king of his publishing house.

He touched Alice's clitoris. She shivered and sighed in his ear. 'Gently . . . gently . . . Otherwise I'll start screaaaaahhhh-ming . . .'

His dick had become a block of steel.

'Now, getting down to business . . . How far is Ciba into his new novel?'

'It's hard to understand . . . From what little I've read . . .' Pennacchini was speechless. It often happened that he would stop talking, as if someone had unplugged him.

'What, Pennacchini? What have you read?'

'I feel . . . Well, it's unfocused . . . More . . . How can I explain it . . .? Like a series of clumsy attempts rather than an actual story . . .'

Fabrizio, who was working at undoing his belt, came stock-still.

'It's crap, I get it. Like his last one, what was it . . .? *Nestor's*

Dream. I'm not at all satisfied . . . And it's only selling so-so. From someone who has sold a million and a half copies, I expected, frankly speaking, a lot more. With all that advertising we bought for him. Have you seen the quarterly returns? If it weren't for *The Lion's Den* . . .'

Alice, with a masterly sleight of hand, had finally freed his erection and began masturbating him.

'We need to discuss the contract for his next book. His agent is out of her mind. She demanded too high a sum. Before we sign, we have to think things through properly. We can't be strangled by someone who sells as much as Adele Raffo, at the end of the day, but she gets exactly half as much as him.'

Ciba thought he would faint. That son of a bitch was comparing him to an obese nun who wrote recipe books! And what was this story about renegotiating the contract? Pennacchini was nothing but a big fat fake . . . He had told Fabrizio that *Nestor's Dream* was a necessary book, the novel of his coming-of-age.

Alice, in the meantime, all fired up, wasn't listening and continued to massage him with a precise anti-clockwise movement of the wrist. However, to her great surprise, this wasn't getting the desired result in the least. His dick was literally shrivelling up in her hand. She looked at him, embarrassed. The writer was floored. 'What's happening? Is he coming here?'

'Please . . . Just a moment. Be quiet for just a moment.'

Alice heard a broken note in Fabrizio's voice. She dropped his flaccid appendage and started listening.

'Anyway, he's not going anywhere! Where could he go? No other publishing house is prepared to give him as much as we do. Not even half. Who does he think he is? Grisham? And what's more, I've heard that his show hasn't been confirmed for next year either. If they shut it down, Ciba will sink like a rock. We have to get him to lower his crest. In fact, next week, Achille, I want to meet with Modica and Malagò so we can work out how to proceed . . . He hasn't got another book in him. He's washed up.' A moment of silence. 'Ahhh!! I've finished. I'd been holding it in since the plane.' Then the sound of footsteps on the gravel.

Ciba was floating half off the ground, unable to react. Then he plummeted down, into the mud of planet earth, or better, onto the woman whose vagina he had his middle finger immersed in. A woman whom, what's more, he had only just met. And who worked in the same field as him. A stranger. A potential spy.

He picked himself up, red in the face and with the expression of a psychopath.

She covered her chest with her blouse and made an undefinable face.

Pity! She feels pity for me! Fabrizio realised. He pulled his finger out and cleaned it off on his jacket. What the devil was he doing? Had he gone crazy? He had thrown himself like a horny teenager onto a stranger while his publishing house was plotting against him.

I must respond to this outrage.

There was only one person in the world who could help him. His agent. Margherita Levin Gritti.

'Sorry, I've gotta go!' he said distractedly, while he stuffed his mollusc into his trousers and ran away.

She didn't move, not knowing what to think. Then she began buttoning up her blouse.

15

The leader of the Wilde Beasts of Abaddon had finally found the idea. He needed to meet with his adepts immediately and fill them in on the situation. It didn't matter that it was past ten o'clock. They were all at Silvietta's house watching a film.

With the lights off, he went into the broom cupboard. Well hidden behind the detergents and shoes, rammed into a plastic supermarket bag, were the uniforms of the Beasts. He had designed them himself, and then had them sewn by a Chinese tailor from Capranica. They were simple black cotton tunics (not like the showy ones of the Children of the Apocalypse, in gold and purple) with a pointed hood. As for shoes, after reconsidering many times, he had opted for black espadrilles.

Saverio went back into the living room and, trying not to make any noise, took the Durendal out of its box, and from the mantelpiece the car keys. He grabbed an umbrella and the bottle of Jägermeister, and was just about to lower the handle of the front door when the hall light came on, illuminating the Zanzibar collection.

Serena was standing in the doorway of the living room in her night gown.

'Where are you going?'

Saverio hunched forward, lowered his head and tried, unsuccessfully, to hide the sword behind his back. 'I'm going out for a moment . . .'

'Where?'

'I'm going to the shop to see a thing . . .'

Serena was confused. 'With the sword?'

'Yes . . .' He had to come up with some crap quickly. 'You see . . . There's this piece of furniture . . . It's a living-room piece that could hold it perfectly, and I wanted to check whether it fits. I'll go and come back straight away. It'll only take me a second. You go to sleep.'

'And what's in the bag?'

Saverio looked around him. 'Which bag?'

'The one you've got in your hand.'

'Oh, this one.' Saverio shrugged his shoulders. 'No, nothing. Just some clothes I have to give back to Edoardo. They're for a costume party.'

'Do you know how old you are, Saverio?'

'What sort of a question is that?'

'You tire me. Truly tire me.'

When Serena said that she was tired, sick and tired, with that worn out tone of voice, Saverio knew that within a few minutes they would start arguing. And an argument with Serena was never worth it. She was capable of obliterating you, of turning into something so terrible that you cannot even begin to describe it. The best strategy was to stop talking and smile vaguely. If she started shouting, the twins would wake up and whine, and then he would have to stay at home.

Let her talk. Superior.

'And you haven't just tired me. You know what Dad says? He says that of all the departments in the furniture shop, yours is the only one in the red.'

Saverio, despite what he'd just promised himself to do, couldn't take that.

'Too right! Thyrolean furniture sucks. Nobody wants to buy it! That's why your father gave it to me. You *know* that. This way he can . . .'

Serena interrupted him, strangely enough without raising her voice. She seemed so discouraged as to not even have the strength to scream.

'Oh! Thyrolean furniture sucks? Are you aware that for over twenty years my father sold solely and exclusively Thyrolean furniture? May I remind you that he was the one to bring it to the Lazio region? Do you know how many people have copied him since then? The wood-style furniture and what-not

68

only came thanks to that furniture you hate so much.' She crossed her arms. 'You have no respect . . . No respect for my father and not even for me. I am really so tired of covering for you, of hearing Dad insult my husband every day. It mortifies me.' She shook her head, embittered. 'Hang on . . . hang on . . . What did he call you last time? Oh, yes . . . a cockroach with no balls. Do you know where he'd have sent you by now, if you weren't with me?'

Saverio squeezed the handle of the Durendal like he wanted to snap it. He could have killed him, that old bastard. It would have been so easy. One clean slice of the sword between the third and the fourth cervical vertebrae.

'Can't say he's wrong.' Serena pointed at him. 'Look at you. You sneak out with a bag full of fancy dress, and a sword, and you go off to play with your mates . . . You are not thirteen years old. And I am not your mother.'

Saverio, his head lowered, began to dig the tip of the Durendal into the parquet flooring.

'We can't go on this way. I have lost all respect for you. I need a man. Do you ever ask yourself why I don't want to make love to you?' She turned around and went back into the bedroom. He heard her say: 'Off you go. Run along. You wouldn't want to keep your friends waiting . . . And take out the rubbish.'

Saverio stood on the threshold of the front doorstep for about a minute. Outside the storm didn't show any sign of calming down. If he went out now, his life would be a living hell for a week. He put the Durendal back in the box and returned the plastic bag with the tunics to the closet. He sucked on the bottle of bitter liqueur. He'd better sleep on the sofa-bed. Tomorrow morning Serena will have calmed down and they will be able to make up, or something along those lines.

He had to show her, though, that he wasn't a cockroach with

no balls. And to prove it there was only one way: get his department's quarterly budget under control and shut the old bastard up. There was still a month to go, and if he worked himself silly he could make it. He took another sip of alcohol and, with his head spinning, went into the bathroom to brush his teeth.

What was he thinking when he'd come up with the idea of killing Larita? To do so, he'd need to take a day off and, right now, under these expectations, it just wasn't do-able. And moreover, let's admit it, the problem wasn't simply his wife: the Wilde Beasts didn't believe in him either.

He spat toothpaste into the basin, dried his mouth and looked at himself in the mirror. His temples had turned almost completely white and the shadow of a beard on his chin was grey.

You're not thirteen years old. And I am not your mother.

Serena was spot on. Spot on the dot. If he didn't prove to her that she could trust him, she would never let him manage the furniture shop after her father was gone.

And I have two kids to look after. They can't grow up thinking their father is incompetent.

And it was only his fault if that's what everyone thought.

Enough! This whole story with the Satanic sect has to end. Tomorrow I'll call the Beasts together and I'll tell them the game is over.

He took off his shirt and vest. Even the few hairs on his chest were beginning to turn grey. He opened the shower tap, then shut it again. He opened his mouth wide in a silent scream. His cheeks were tracked with tears.

Why had he let himself go like this? What was the absurd reason that had made him lock himself in a cage with that harpy and throw away the keys of his existence? He had had so many ideas when he was young. Travel by train across Europe. Go to Transylvania to visit Count Vlad's castle. See the dolmen and the sculptures on Easter Island. Study Latin and Aramaic. He hadn't done any of these things. He had gotten married too young to a woman who loved holiday villages and sifting through factory outlets.

He went back to the basin and looked at himself in the mirror, as if he wanted to check that it was still really him. He picked up a towel and placed it over his head.

'Hang on . . . Hang on just a moment,' he said to himself.

He couldn't forget. This had been a special day and one fight with Serena shouldn't erase it. He could feel in every fibre in his body that this was the beginning of a new existence. All he needed was the courage to rebel. And it wasn't because of Gerry Scotti, and not even because of the big cloud with the face of Satan that had come to him like an omen. It wasn't even because of Kurtz calling to ask him to be his representative. It was because of that no. It had been so great. So gratifying. He couldn't ruin it like that. It had been the first time he had said NO. A real NO.

If you abandon the sect now, you must be conscious of the fact that from this point on your life will be a long series of YES. You must be conscious of the fact that you will go out slowly, amidst the general indifference, like a votive candle on an abandoned tombstone. If you lay down the Durendal now, and you go to sleep on the sofa-bed, there will be no more black masses, Satanic orgies, and graffiti on viaducts. Never again. And you will be unable to mourn them because you will be too depressed to mourn them. You decide now. Decide if you are your wife's slave or if you are Mantos, the grand master of the Wilde Beasts of Abaddon. Decide now who the fuck you are.

He took the towel off his head. He swigged down the last of the Jägermeister. He grabbed the clippers, turned them on, and he shaved his head.

71

16

Washed up.

Fabrizio Ciba was driving his Vespa down the winding road of Monte Mario. Foot to the floor, he curved right and left like he was Valentino Rossi. He was fit to be tied. Those cowboys from Martinelli had said that he was washed up and they wanted to slip him the pill. Him, the one who pulled them out of bankruptcy, who had sold more than all the other Italian writers together. Him, the one who had been translated into twenty-nine languages, including Swahili and Ladino.

'And you even cop twenty per cent of the sales of the translation rights!' he shouted as he swerved to overtake a Ford Ka.

If they thought they could treat him like the bulimic nun, they were making a big mistake.

'Who do you think you are? Everybody wants to publish me. You'll see when I publish my new novel, you worthless bastards.'

He began zig-zagging through the traffic of Viale delle Milizie. Then he threw himself down the tramway, screeching to a halt at a red light.

He had to go to another publisher. And then leave this fucking country. *Italy doesn't deserve me.* He could live in Edinburgh, amidst the great Scottish writers. He didn't know how to write in English, but that didn't matter. Somebody would translate his novels for him.

Alice . . .

He was struck by the vision of the two of them in a Scottish cottage. She, naked, would translate while he would prepare a dish of cacio and pepe rigatoni. He needed to call her tomorrow and ingratiate himself with her.

A raindrop as big as a coffee bean hit him in the middle of the forehead, followed by one on his shoulder, one on his knee, one . . .

'No!'

A downpour of rain exploded. People ran for shelter. Umbrellas were opened. Gusts of wind shook the banana trees on the sides of the road.

Fabrizio decided to keep on nevertheless. His agent's house wasn't too far away. He would have a warm shower and then they would organise their counter-attack.

He reached the Lungotevere Road. Millions of stationary cars were at a standstill in the underpass. Everyone honked their horns. The rain whipped the panels, the asphalt and everything else. Headlights created a blinding glare.

What the hell is happening?

Friday night + yobbos on the loose + rain = bumper to bumper traffic across town for the whole night.

Fabrizio hated Friday evenings. Hordes of barbarians came from the Prenestino, from Mentana, from Cinecittà, from i Castelli, poured themselves from the surrounding ring road into the historical town centre, Trastevere and the Piramide, in search of pizzerias, Irish pubs, Mexican restaurants and sandwich bars. All of them determined to have fun.

The writer cursed and threw himself along with the others onto the Lungotevere Road. He couldn't make any headway, though. The Vespa couldn't fit between one car and the next. He clambered onto the pavement, but even there it was hard to travel forwards. There were cars parked all over the place, thrown about like the Matchbox toys of a spoilt brat. He came, soaked through to his underwear, to a sort of bottleneck that funnelled into a lake. Cars drove through it, sending up waves like speedboats. He took a deep breath and threw himself in. He did the first twenty metres in a jubilee of splashes. The Vespa's wheels disappeared below a dark, freezing cold liquid. He began struggling. The water level was rising above the footboard. It was up to his ankles. The engine began to splutter, to stutter. Like an injured beast, the scooter shuddered forward, wheezing. Fabrizio begged: 'Come on, you fucker, come on, you fucker, come on, you piece of shit . . . You can do it!'

But the Vespa wheezed and died right at the deepest point.

Fabrizio Ciba got off, swearing to the Madonna. The water reached his calves. His feet squished in his old Church's. He started kicking the scooter. He couldn't believe that humanity, mechanics and nature had conspired in the span of forty minutes to take it out on him.

The cars, crammed with shaven-headed, tattooed monsters, drove by splashing him. They pointed at him, shaking their heads, laughed and drove off.

He took a look at himself. His jacket had turned into a horrendous dripping poncho. His trousers were wet and muddy.

His head lowered, shaking all over, he pushed the Vespa out of the lake. The rain dribbled down his neck, slid down his back between his buttocks. His feet had gone numb. He dumped the scooter and began walking.

Luckily, he wasn't far from his agent's house. He would sleep there. He'd get her to make him a cup of camomile tea with honey. He would take a couple of aspirin and get her to hug and reassure him. He would fall asleep against those warm breasts while she whispered sweetly that they were going to take Martinelli for a spin, big time.

He began to march, his mood improved, while blasts of wind pushed him from behind. The mournful shadow of Castel Sant'Angelo was shrouded in water. He crossed the bridge of

74

angels. The river in flood roared beneath his feet as it channelled between the pillars.

On the opposite side of the road a long snake of queued traffic stood unmoving and restless, honking horns and flashing headlights. Storm drains vomited grey torrents that ran impetuously along the pavements. All the roads, lanes and shortcuts that led to the historical centre were manned by groups of traffic police with hi-viz raincoats and traffic paddles, trying to stem the flow of cars. It looked like an exodus from a city under a bomb threat.

Fabrizio made his way between the cars and slipped into the first lane that appeared before him. He popped out in a little square where two guys had gotten out of their cars and were shoving each other over a free parking space. The two girlfriends, both blondes, both dressed like Versace models, were screaming from the car windows.

'Enrico! Can't you see he's a dickhead? It's useless.'

'Franco! It's not worth it, he's a piece of shit.'

Fabrizio walked by without even deigning to glance at them. He came at last to Via Coronari.

What a nightmare.

But it was over, he had made it.

17

'And so you don't want to make love to me?'

Serena opened one eye. To be able to fall asleep, she had taken twenty-five drops of sleeping medication. She raised her head slightly and saw the dark shadow of her husband at the bedroom door.

'What do you want?' she mumbled, feeling the bittersweet

taste of benzodiazepine on her numb tongue. 'Can't you see I'm sleeping? Are you looking for an argument?'

'You said that you don't want to make love to me.'

'Give it up. Leave me alone. I'm telling you . . .' she brushed him off, sinking her head back on the pillow. Despite her sleepiness, one part of Serena's brain noticed that Saverio's voice sounded different, very confident. And it wasn't like him to face her in such a direct way. *That idiot must be drunk.* She began scratching around in the drawer in the bedside table for her eye mask and ear plugs. She had spent the whole day in Rome looking for a potter's wheel and she was whacked. She did not feel like getting into an argument.

'Go on, say it again. Go on, if you've got the guts, say you don't want to make love to me.'

'I don't want to make love to you. Are you happy now?'

She found the eye mask.

'You prefer to be fucked by the guys from the dispatch office, don't you?'

Now he was overdoing it. He needed to be put in his place. She pulled herself up and growled: 'Have you gone crazy? How dare you? I'm gonna . . .' But she couldn't say any more because, despite having the light from the corridor in her eyes, it looked to her like Saverio was naked and . . . *No, I don't believe it . . . He's shaved his hair off.* A shiver ran up her spinal cord.

'Do you know what they say to me each time I go down into the warehouse? That you could be a porn star. And they're not that far off, after all, considering how you dress. You are such a slut! You are so slutty that you say that fucking is vulgar, but then you get a boob job.' And then he burst into howling laughter.

Serena was frozen stiff. She wasn't even breathing. Her heart was beating like crazy and the blood was humming in her veins. There was something not quite right with her husband.

And it wasn't because he'd suddenly become jealous or because he'd cut his hair. Yes, these were worrying symptoms. But the thing that terrorised her was his voice. It had changed. It didn't sound like him. It was deep and mean. And that mean laugh, like a psychopath's, like a man possessed.

Serena Mastrodomenico had always been aware that sooner or later her husband was going to snap. He was frustrated. Too downtrodden, too remissive, too nice with everyone. She liked him that way. He reminded her of those dray horses that pull the carriage and take beatings for their whole lives and then die, cut-down with fatigue. Deep inside, though, she knew that Saverio carried in him a hell that burned day and night. And she loved teasing him, to see how much he could stand, and whether every now and then he would let off a blast of anger. In ten years of marriage, it had never happened.

But it's happening now, for fuck's sake.

She remembered that film. It was the story of a model employee, with a perfect family, who gets stuck in traffic, lets go of the brakes and starts massacring people with a pump-action shotgun. Her husband was exactly the same as that guy.

Saverio moved slowly towards the bed.

'You don't know me, Serena. You have no idea what I am capable of. You believe you know everything, but you know nothing.'

Serena saw that her husband was holding the sword. She let out a little scream and pushed herself against the wall.

'Shut up! Shut up! You'll wake the babies! Ahhh . . . Exactly! Let's talk about babies. You think I don't know why you insisted we go in vitro? It's not because of our age. You thought I ate all that bollocks about our age. No! It's because I disgust you so much.' Saverio raised his arms, and the sword, showing off his nudity. 'Go on, tell me. Am I that disgusting?'

Serena Mastrodomenico was no expert on psychotic syndromes, despite having attended the two-year university course in Psychology. But popular wisdom suggested that you should always agree with a psycho. And in that moment it seemed to be the most appropriate behaviour.

'No . . . No . . . Of course you aren't disgusting,' she stuttered, surprised that she still had breath to speak with. 'Listen to me, Saverio. Lay down the sword. I'm sorry for what I said to you.' She swallowed. 'You know that I love you . . .'

He began to shake, overwhelmed by laughter. 'No . . . You're too much, please . . . Now you've gone too far. You love me! You love me? That's the first time I've heard you say it since I met you. Not even when I gave you the engagement ring, did you say it. You asked me if you could exchange it.' He turned his heard towards the window, as if someone was there. 'Do you get it? Do you get what it takes to be loved by your own wife? And they say that marriage is a tradition in crisis.'

She had to run for it. The window that opened onto the balcony was closed and the venetian blinds were down. And even if she managed to open it, they were on the third floor, and below was the tarmac of the car park. If she screamed for help, he would hit her with the sword. The only thing left to do was to beg for mercy and call on the good old Saverio, who had to be hidden somewhere inside the sick mind of this schizophrenic.

But that was unthinkable. In forty-three years, Serena had never asked anyone for mercy. Not even the Orsoline nuns who hit her on the knuckles with a ruler. Serena Mastrodomenico's personality had been forged according to the strict Lutheran ethics of the Thyrolean Masters of the Axe. Papa, who had spent his youth as an apprentice in a carpentry factory in Brunico, had told her that the most precious woods snapped but never bent.

And you, my darling star, are as hard and precious as ebony.

And you will never let anyone walk all over you. Not even your husband. Promise me. Yes, Daddy, I promise.

And so there was no way she would beg mercy of that useless bloodsucking piece of shit Saverio Moneta, son of a modest Osram factory worker and an uneducated housewife. She had cleaned him up, she had let him into her bed, she had got her saintly father to accept him, she had welcomed his worm-eaten sperm to make children with, and now that very man was threatening her with a sword.

Serena grabbed the alarm clock from the bedside table and threw it at him, grinding her teeth: 'Fuck you! Kill me! Come on, if you've got the guts. I'm not scared of you, you cockroach without balls!' And she gestured with her hands for him to come towards her.

18

The building where Margherita Levin Gritti lived was old and elegant, with a large entryway that hid a small door.

Fabrizio Ciba pushed the gold-coloured intercom button. A spotlight placed on top of a video camera shot a ray of light straight into his eyes. His teeth chattered as he waited half a minute before buzzing again. He looked at his watch. Ten past midnight.

From a stochastic point of view, it was highly improbable that she wasn't in. It just wasn't possible to line up this much bad luck in one thing after another. It would have been like throwing dice and getting seven ten times in a row.

He held down the button. 'Answer! Answer! Wake up!'

And, thank God, a voice answered: 'Who is it? Fabrizio, is that you?'

'Yes, it's me. Let me in,' he said towards the eye of the video camera.

'What are you doing here, at this time of night?' She sounded incredulous.

'Let me up. I'm soaked.'

The woman didn't speak, then: 'I can't . . . Not tonight. I'm sorry.'

'What do you mean?' Fabrizio couldn't believe his ears.

'I'm sorry . . .'

'Listen, something seriously terrible has happened. Martinelli want to give me the flick. Let me in,' he ordered. 'I'm not here to have sex.'

'I *am* having sex.'

'What, you're having sex? I don't believe it!'

'Why can't you believe it? What do you mean?' His agent's voice tensed.

'Nothing, nothing. Right, don't worry, let me in anyway. I'll fill you in quickly, dry off and call a taxi.'

'Use your mobile to call.'

'You know I don't use a mobile. Listen, you stop fucking for a moment and then you pick up again after. It's no big deal.'

'Fabrizio, you don't realise what you're saying.'

Ciba felt the anger expand inside his guts. 'You are the one who doesn't realise! Look at me, for fuck's sake!' He opened his arms wide. 'I'm soaked! I could get pneumonia. I feel sick! Open this bloody door, for fuck's sake!'

His agent's voice was firm. 'Call me tomorrow morning.'

'So you're not going to let me in?'

'No! I mean it, I'm not letting you in.'

Fabrizio Ciba exploded. 'Right, you know what that means? Fuck you! Fuck you and your pathetic woman-friend. I know it's the poetess, who else would it be? Whatever the fuck her

80

name is . . . Whatever, the two of you can both fuck right off, you big fat lesbians. You're fired.'

He walked off, kicking parked cars.

19

What a woman! What a lioness!

Saverio Moneta had always known that his wife had balls, but he didn't think she'd go so far. She was willing to risk her life to put up a fight. That's exactly why he'd decided to marry her. His father and his mother, and all of his relatives (even the ones from Benevento, who had only seen her once), had warned him that she wasn't right for him. She was spoiled, she would henpeck him, squash him, cut him down to the level of a Filipino servant. But he hadn't paid attention to anyone and married her.

He stretched out the sword and pointed it at her throat. 'And so you're not afraid?'

'No! You make me sick!' Serena spat at him.

Saverio smiled as he wiped his cheek. 'Huh, so I make you sick.' He slipped the tip of the Durendal in the buttonhole of the night dress, and with a flick of his wrist he clipped off the top button.

Serena was tense, her painted red claws ready to scratch him.

'Now I'm going to kill you.' Saverio clipped off the second button on her night dress. Her boobs, as big as two cantaloupes, with their small dark nipples scared into pointyness, appeared in all their synthetic splendour.

'What are you doing? You sicko! Don't you dare . . .' hissed Serena, her eyes two dark slits.

Saverio placed the blade beneath her throat and pushed her

up against the headboard. 'Quiet! Be quiet! I don't want to hear your voice.'

'You're worthless.'

He grabbed her by the hair and held her head down on the pillow. Then he flung the sword away and with his right hand squeezed her neck like one would a poisonous serpent, before throwing himself full force on top of her.

'So, now what are you going to do? What you gonna do? You can't move. You can't scream. You're scared, aren't you? Admit it, you're scared.'

Serena didn't give in. 'I'm not scared of anyone.'

Saverio realised he had a roaring erection and he wanted her like crazy. 'I'm going to show you . . .' He ripped her pants off and bit her on the buttock. 'I'm going to show you who's boss here.'

A suffocated scream came out of the pillow. 'If you try it, I swear on our children I'll kill you.'

'Kill me! Kill me, go on. I don't give a shit about my life anyway.'

He pushed her legs open and slid a hand between her thighs. He made room and penetrated her sharply. His dick sunk inside her right up to her boiling guts.

Like a cat gone crazy, she pulled her arm free and with a flash of her claws scratched four bloody stripes across his chest.

'You're raping me, you pig. I hate you . . . You don't know how much I hate you . . .'

Saverio, high on pain, was pumping away desperately. His head spun as the blood swirled in his ear drums.

Serena had managed to lift her face from the pillow and mumble, 'Stop it! You make me sick . . . You make me . . .' She was unable to go on because she began to arch her back, offering herself to Saverio.

Saverio realised that he had done it. The slut was enjoying it. Today was his day!

But now there was a problem. At that crazy speed, he wouldn't be able to hold out long. He could feel the orgasm climbing the tendons of his legs. It bit into his thigh muscles and, unperturbed by his own will, it was aiming straight for his arsehole and his balls. He thought of Sting. That son of a whore, Sting, who could apparently fuck for four hours straight without coming. How did he do it? He remembered that in an interview the English rock star explained that he learned the technique from a group of Tibetan monks . . . Something like that. Anyway, it was all a question of breathing.

Saverio, holding himself up with one hand on his wife's scapula and the other against the wall, began breathing in and out like a dodgy outboard motor, trying to slow the rhythm.

Beneath him, Serena was wriggling around like the tail cut off a lizard.

He grabbed her by the hair again and squeezed her tit. 'You love it. Say it!'

'No. No. I don't love it. It makes me sick.' And yet, she didn't look as if it made her sick. 'Arsehole. You're a disgusting arsehole.' She slapped the mattress and hit the clock radio, which awoke from its slumber and began singing 'She's Always A Woman' by Billy Joel.

Another unmistakable sign that Satan was on his side. Saverio told his disciples that he loved Sepultura and Metallica, but he secretly adored old Billy Joel. Nobody else wrote songs as romantic as his.

He squeezed his teeth and, with renewed vigour, began hammering her again. 'I'm going to snap you in two. I swear, I'm going to snap you. Cop this, you tart.' And he stuck a finger in her ass.

Serena's whole body stiffened. She stretched out her legs and arms, and lifted her head, looking at him with a pained expression. And then she gave in, sighing, and whispered: 'I'm coming . . . I'm coming, you fuck. Fuck you, arsehole.'

Saverio finally let himself go. He relaxed his thighs and came with his mouth open. Exhausted by the effort, sweating all over, he flopped onto Serena's neck and stuck his mouth in her hair. 'Now tell me you love me,' he sighed.

'Yes. I love you. Now let me sleep.'

20

Fabrizio Ciba had given up looking for a taxi on Corso Vittorio Emanuele. The long boulevard was packed with cars. The bass from woofers made the cars pulse. In a corner he saw a bar with lights on. He catapulted himself inside.

A suffocating heat. A head-spinning stink of sweat. People everywhere pushing each other in the narrow space. And they were dancing. On the bar. On the tables. An orchestra made up of wild Caribbeans was playing a crappy ear-piercing salsa.

A short guy with blond fringe and wearing a wrestling vest pulled up in front of him. He was wearing a sort of cowboy belt tied around his waist, loaded with shot glasses instead of bullets. He was holding a bottle in his hand. 'You look like crap. Have a tequila boom-boom. It'll do you good.'

Fabrizio necked it. The alcohol warmed his frozen innards. 'Again.'

The guy poured him another.

He necked this one two. 'Ahhhh! Better. Another!'

'Are you sure?'

Fabrizio nodded. He placed a soaking wet fifty-euro bank note on the bar. 'Pour and don't ask questions.'

The waiter shook his head, but obeyed.

Fabrizio made a disgusted face as he threw the shot into his stomach. Then he looked at the young man. 'Listen, my name's Fabrizio Ciba, and I have a . . .' He stopped. The short-arse's eyes showed only a glacial emptiness. He didn't have the vaguest idea who Fabrizio Ciba was. He was looking at him as if he was a hobo. 'Is there a phone I can use?'

'No. There should be a phone box in Piazza Venezia.'

Fine, the writer said to himself, he'd have to fall back on the usual method he used with idiots like this guy. 'Listen, I'll you give another hundred euro if you take me to Via Mecenate. It's not far from here, it's behind the Colosseum.'

The fringe-haired guy shrugged. 'I wish! But I've gotta work.'

'You can't do this to me! Fucking hell, I didn't ask you for the moon.'

The waiter poured a shot and slammed it down on the counter. 'Here, this one's on me, but then you piss off. That's a good boy.'

Fabrizio threw the tequila down in one go and wiped his mouth on his sleeve. 'If you're in trouble, no one helps you out, right?' He took two steps backwards and ended up on someone's feet.

A female voice complained. 'Ouch! This wanker smashed my big toe!'

He tried to look her in the eye, but the lights from the bar were pointed right in his face. He lifted his hand in apology, but a male voice barked at him: 'Listen . . . We've had enough of you. Look what you did to her!'

'So what? I don't get it . . . She's about as good-looking as a clam . . . Don't shellfish have a higher level of pain tolerance?' He closed his eyes and noticed that the music had stopped. 'I bet that none of these gentlemen . . .' He was unable to go on. He had to take a seat. He opened his eyes again and the room with all those fuzzy faces began spinning above him. 'What a terrible world yours is . . .' he slurred and tried to grab on to the short-arse, but instead collapsed on the floor amidst people's legs.

'Kick him out!' 'We've had enough!' 'It's always the same story round here.'

'All right . . .' He got up, with the help of someone.

And before he realised he was back outside, beneath the downpour. The cold and the rain were like the crack of a whip, and he felt a little more lucid. He'd cover the last one and a half kilometres home on foot in the rain.

He made it to Piazza Venezia with his eyes closed and his legs trembling, the cars honking at him. Via dei Fori Imperiali appeared before his eyes. It looked never ending. Off in the distance, like a mirage, the Colosseum glittered, shrouded in water. The rain struck hard on the sampietrini, which shone in the light of car headlights.

All he needed to do was walk with his head down.

I've gotta throw up, though.

He kept thinking back to that arsehole Gianni as he stabbed him in the back, that bitch his agent who hadn't let him in, and those pieces of shit in the bar.

Tomorrow . . . I'll get . . . a new agent . . . and I'll send a tough email . . . to Martinelli.

The Colosseum was getting closer. Lit up, it looked like an Italian Christmas cake.

Fabrizio was bushed, but he accelerated the pace using his last bit of energy.

I'll leave Martinelli.

He realised he was out of breath and that a frozen claw was ripping open his heart.

Oh God . . .

He lifted his gaze skywards and reached out his hand as if to hold himself steady with something. Then he tripped and the footpath bent in two and came up at him, hitting him on the cheekbone.

He registered that he was now lying on the ground and was falling unconscious. He vomited something acid and alcoholic, which diluted in a puddle.

Heart attack.

His head had transformed into a fiery ball. His ears housed a jet motor. The Colosseum, the road, the lights, the rain span around him, melting into shiny coils.

He tried to stand, but his legs couldn't hold his weight. He fell again. He began dragging himself towards the street on his arms, while cars drove past without even slowing. He lifted a hand and murmured:

'Help! Help! Please . . . Help me!'

Fabrizio Ciba, the international bestselling writer of *The Lion's Den*, the presenter of the culture programme *Crime and Punishment*, the third-sexiest man in Italy according to the weekly magazine *Yes*, understood that nobody was going to stop and help him, and that he would die in his own vomit opposite the Fori Imperiali. He could see the photo of his body melted on the ground. In the background, the Roman ruins.

It will be in all the newspapers. What will they write? Like Janis Joplin.

His arm flopped back down. He lay there wondering why, why did this have to happen to him?

I haven't done anything wrong.

Everything was turning hazy. All he could see were purple dots. He leaned his head on the ground and closed his eyes.

21

Mr and Mrs Moneta were lying on the bed. Outside, the storm was beginning to die down.

Saverio looked at his wife. She was sleeping facing the other way, a mask over her eyes.

Just after they had finished making love, Serena told him that she loved him. He shouldn't believe her. Serena was as treacherous as a scorpion. To get her to say it to him, he'd been forced to rape her.

But in the end she came.

A weakness of Serena's that would cost him dearly.

Tomorrow, when she thinks about what happened, she'll go crazy. She'll be even more selfish, overbearing and insensitive than ever. She might even tell her old man about it.

He was unable to hate her, in spite of everything. He'd had to stop himself from saying: 'Me, too. You don't know how much. More than anything else in the world.'

But now, with a clearer head, he felt differently. That word no kept buzzing around in his head. The gutless cockroach phase was over. The metamorphosis had ended, and now all he needed to do was take flight and disappear.

He'd made a promise to the Beasts, and he would keep it. He would sacrifice Larita to Satan and they would become the world's most famous sect. Saverio Moneta would prove to the world how sick they were in the head.

The police would catch them. That was certain. And the idea of spending the rest of his days in jail terrified him. There were really nasty people in there. Killers, mafia, real psychopaths. Of course, if he went to jail as Mantos, the Lord of Evil, the monster who had decapitated the singer Larita and bathed in her blood, they might all be afraid of him. And they would leave him alone.

Maybe . . . Maybe not . . . Maybe they're Larita fans. And they'll kill me like they did with that poor fellow Jeffrey Dahmer.

This whole jail thing was a real nuisance.

Unless . . .

He smiled in the dark. There was a way.

He got up from the bed. He opened the wardrobe. He took out a black tracksuit that he had bought with the idea of using it to go jogging, something he had ended up never doing. He slipped it on and pulled the hood over his head. He was walking out of the room when Serena mumbled: 'Where are you going?'

'Just go back to sleep.'

22

'Do you need a hand?'

What?

'Can you hear me? Can you hear me?'

What? Who?

Are you all right?

A voice. A woman.

Fabrizio Ciba squeezed opened his eyes. 'I'm not well . . . Help me . . . Please.' He grabbed the ankle of the black figure standing in front of him.

'Oh my God, but you . . . You're the writer . . . Of course, you are Fabrizio Ciba! What are you doing lying on the ground? I'm so excited to meet you.'

'Yes . . . Ciba . . . That's me . . . I'm Fabrizio Ciba! Please, help me, take me to . . .'

With the little clearheadedness he had left, Fabrizio realised that if he went to the hospital it would end up in the papers. And they would write that he was an alcoholic, or worse. 'No. Home. Take me home . . . Via Mecenate . . .'

'Of course, of course. I'll take you straight home. Did you know, you are my favourite writer? Much better than Saporelli. I've read all of your books. I loved *The Lion's Den*. Would it be indiscreet for me to ask you for your autograph? I don't have your book with me, though.'

Fabrizio smiled. He loved his readers.

'Now I'm going to get you into the car.'

He felt himself being lifted by the armpits. He saw a car with the doors open. The woman dragged him over and helped him into the back seat.

I'm still the best, I'm not all washed up . . ., he said as he fainted.

23

Zombie, Murder and Silvietta were enjoying a good chat about films.

They were spread out across a couch and they were passing around a homemade chillum made from a bottle of Rocchetta water. A grey-coloured mix of vodka and smoke sat on the bottom. The plastic sleeve of a Bic pen, which held a double-paper joint, stuck out of a hole. They'd just finished watching *Blackwater Valley Exorcism*. All three of them were enthusiastic about the film and had agreed that it was better than the much-acclaimed *The Exorcist*. For a start, everything was based on a true story and, according to their criteria, true stories are better than invented stories. Also, the first scene was unbelievable: Isabel, the daughter of a poor family of Texan farmers, ate a live rabbit. It was a fresh, uncontrived film, and you could see that the director and the actors had given it their all, despite the low budget.

Silvietta began rolling another joint. She was the group's official roller.

'What do you reckon, Zombie, is *Blackwater* better than *Omen*?'

Zombie yawned. 'Good question . . . I don't know.'

Silvietta yawned, too. 'I'm stuffed. This Moroccan is brutal.'

Murder lifted his back off the couch and stretched his arms. 'What about if we went to bed?'

The Vestal passed her tongue over the glue on the paper and, with a technical move, sealed the joint and lit it up. 'All right, let's smoke our goodnight joint.' Then she began tidying the heavy metal CDs, the tattoo magazines and the greasy bags from the fried courgette flowers and ascolane olives spread across the floor. When she overdid the grass, she got an attack of housewife syndrome. 'Zombie, why don't you sleep here?'

'Well . . . I don't know . . . Better not,' said Zombie as he searched for his army boots. 'Tomorrow morning I've gotta take my mum for some medical tests at Formello.'

It wasn't true, but the springs in the couch where they let him sleep were broken. And he hated always looking like he didn't have any women friends, which was true, by the way.

Also, those two swore that they hated couples in love, those lovey-dovey sorts and romantic crap like Valentine's Day, and yet as soon as they got the chance they would go off by themselves, as if he didn't exist.

What harm would it do them to sleep all three of them

together in the big bed? Not that he wanted to have group sex (even if, in fact, he wouldn't have minded), but hadn't they taken the Satanic oath of brotherhood? He just couldn't understand what Silvietta found so endearing in that hick, Murder. Zombie was a thousand times better. Agreed, he did have that problem with the gastric oesophagitis, but with the medicine he'd almost got it under control.

Zombie picked up a shoe off the floor. 'No . . . I'll go home. I prefer to.'

Murder carried his one hundred kilos of fat to the fridge in the corner kitchen. 'It's up to you.'

Silvietta threw the window open to clear the room of smoke. Outside, the rain had nearly stopped. She stayed there for a bit, staring out at the night, then she turned towards the other two.

'What sort of plan do you guys reckon Mantos wants to offer us?'

Murder pulled out an old jar of mayonnaise and inspected it. 'I reckon he doesn't have a clue. He's got no more ideas, he's flat. Didn't you see him at dinner? All antsy . . . I told you we should have gone along with Paolo and joined the Children of the Apocalypse. At this hour, right now . . . Think of the orgies, the sacrifices.'

Zombie tied bows in his laces. 'They're in Pavia. It's ages away. And I've gotta work.'

Murder stuck a finger in the yellow cream and lobbed it into his mouth. 'See how dead wrong you are. The Children of the Apocalypse organise their raids for the weekends. You go up there on Friday and on Sunday evening you come down on the train. Monday, you're back at work.'

Silvietta ran her hands through her hair. 'Yeah, I suppose . . . Even if, at the end of it all, between getting there and back, it costs a wad.'

Zombie scratched his jaw. 'I'll tell you something else. Saverio doesn't have the charisma of a Kurtz Minetti or, I dunno, a Charles Manson. Let's admit it, the Wilde Beasts of Abaddon are dead!'

'They were never even born,' Murder corrected him.

'No! That's not true.' Silvietta poured the washing-up liquid in the sink. 'It's just a phase. You know that Saverio's been having a lot of family problems. I really trust him, though, and I won't give up on him. If it hadn't been for him, I wouldn't have become part of the Beasts, and I would never have met you guys. And also we agreed we'd give him another chance.'

'Yeah . . . It's true. We owe it to him,' Zombie repeated, barely convinced.

At that moment the intercom buzzed.

Murder looked at the other two. 'Who the hell is that?'

Silvietta huffed. 'It must be the old lady from downstairs.'

'And what does she want?'

'She says that when we talk, she can hear everything. At the residents' meeting, the other time, she caused a stink. Just kept going on and on.'

Murder lowered his voice. 'So what should we do? Be mute?'

'No. But Murder, my darling, I've told you a thousand times to speak softly.'

'If there's someone who speaks loudly here, it's him.'

Zombie put his hand on his forehead. 'Of course. At the end of the day, it's always my fault.'

The buzzer rang again.

Silvietta moved towards the intercom. 'What do I do? Should I answer? What should I say to her?'

Murder shrugged his shoulders. 'Tell her not to be a pain in the arse.'

She took a breath and lifted the receiver. 'Yes?!' She was

93

silent for a moment, then pressed the button. 'All right. I'll let you up.'

Murder threw himself over the chillum, to hide it. 'Are you mental? You let her up?'

Silvietta opened the front door. 'It's Saverio.'

One minute later, the leader of the Wilde Beasts of Abaddon appeared. He was dressed all in black. Sunglasses. And had his hair shaved off.

Zombie moved closer to him. 'Saverio, what have you . . .?'

Mantos gestured to him to shut up, then, with a theatrical movement, he took off his sunglasses and looked them up and down, one by one.

'I know, you're thinking that the great Mantos is finished. That he's lost the spark, worrying about his family and work.'

Murder lowered his head guiltily.

Saverio stared at him, disappointed. 'Murder, you were the first person who I let read the Tables of Evil. You, you didn't even know what the Satanic courts were. You don't trust in your Master. This is a sect united by its faith in the Malign. Remember that it is extremely difficult to get into, and extremely easy to get out of.'

Murder murmured: 'Aw, come on, Saverio. I didn't mean to . . . I mean . . . you know . . .'

The leader of the Wilde Beasts of Abaddon looked out the window, then stared at them again.

'From now on, Saverio Moneta doesn't exist any more. He died on this stormy evening. From now on, only Mantos, the high leader, exists. What day is it today?'

'The twenty-eighth of April, I think,' said Silvietta.

'Mark this date. Today is the turning-point of an epoque. The Beasts will come out of the shadows and conquer the light.

This date will be added to the Satanic calendar and remembered with horror by the Christian calendar.' The leader of the Beasts raised his arms to the ceiling. 'I am the Charismatic Father. I am the wolf that carries death in the Good Shepherd's flock. I am the one that has had the idea!'

'I knew he was a legend,' Silvietta screamed excitedly at the other two. 'See? I told you.'

'Tell us, Mantos!' Murder stretched out his hand towards his rediscovered Charismatic Father.

The leader lowered his arms and pulled a CD out of the pocket of his tracksuit. He threw it on the coffee table in front of the sofa.

Zombie jumped backwards, as if it was a tarantula.

'Oh my God, what the hell are you doing with a CD of that bitch Larita?'

Mantos pointed at the disc. 'Did you know where she recorded this live performance? In Lourdes. Did you know that her song "King Karol", in honour of Pope Wojtyla, has been in the top ten for six months?'

Murder made a disgusted expression. 'Traitor . . . She converted to Christianity. She is an enemy of Satan.'

Silvietta sat down in her boyfriend's lap. 'Hey, don't be too harsh. I read an article in *People* where she explained why she abandoned the Lord of Flies. She was going out with Rotko, the lead singer of Remy Martin, and they both started down the tunnel of drug abuse. He's still a junkie, but she got free of it thanks to Don Toniolo. In rehab, she saw the light and converted to pop.'

Mantos shut her up. 'Larita will die at the hands of the Wilde Beasts of Abaddon. This is the mission.'

A heavy silence fell over the room.

A dog somewhere in the distance began to howl.

Zombie scratched his head. Silvietta bit her nails. Murder cleaned his glasses on his t-shirt, then let out a deep breath and said: 'That's huge! Really huge! I didn't expect anything like this.'

'How will we do it? Have you got a plan?' Zombie stuttered.

'Obviously. In Rome, tomorrow, there's going to be a party where all of the VIPs of Italy will be in attendance. Larita will sing during the party. We will be hired as porters. When the time is right, we will kidnap Larita and we will soak the earth in that bitch's blood.'

'But first we can bonk her, right?' Zombie asked, visibly excited.

'Of course, first we'll have a Satanic orgy. The next day, the Wilde Beasts of Abaddon will be on news programmes throughout the world. This is serious stuff we're talking about, not rumours of decapitated nuns. Each one of you will become a hero in the Satanic field, and an enemy throughout the rest of the world.'

Zombie caressed his throat. 'But they'll catch us for sure, Saverio. I don't wanna go to jail.'

Mantos shook his head. 'You won't go to jail.'

'How's that possible?'

'Don't worry.' The leader of the Beasts spun around slowly, then stopped and put his hands on his hips. 'They won't ever catch us. Because we will commit suicide.'

The Beasts studied each other silently.

Murder spoke first. 'Hey, hang on a second. Are you serious, Saverio? Isn't that taking it a bit too far?'

'First of all, don't ever call me Saverio again. Second of all, don't be afraid. Death will taste of sweet liqueur to us. We will find ourselves sitting beside Lucifer.' Mantos lifted his arms. 'Now kneel and honour your Charismatic Father.'

The three of them bowed down with their heads to the floor.

Mantos bent over, touched the crowns of his adepts' heads and, opening his eyes wide, began to laugh.

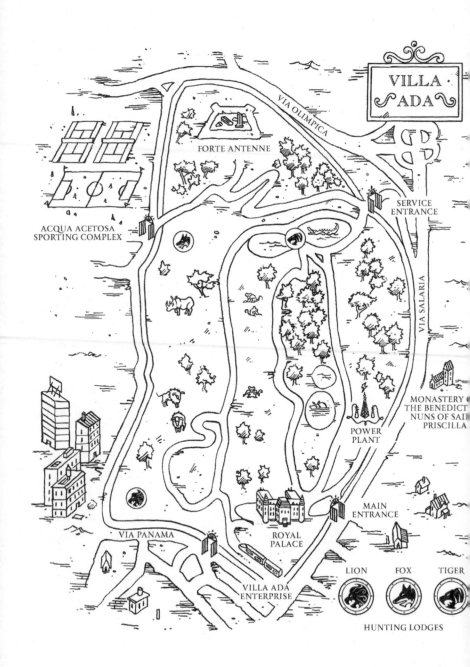

VILLA ADA

VIA OLIMPICA

FORTE ANTENNE

SERVICE ENTRANCE

ACQUA ACETOSA
SPORTING COMPLEX

VIA SALARIA

MONASTERY
THE BENEDICT
NUNS OF SAI
PRISCILLA

POWER
PLANT

MAIN
ENTRANCE

VIA PANAMA

ROYAL
PALACE

VILLA ADA
ENTERPRISE

LION   FOX   TIGER

HUNTING LODGES

When dining outside, the Romans often discuss which is the most beautiful park in the city. In the end, inevitably, first place is disputed by Villa Doria Pamphili, Villa Borghese and Villa Ada.

Villa Doria Pamphili, behind the suburb of Monteverde, is the largest and most scenic; Villa Borghese, right in the centre of the city, is the most famous (who hasn't been on the Piazzale del Pincio, which offers an unforgettable view over the centre of Rome and Piazza del Popolo?); of the three, Villa Ada is the oldest and the wildest.

In the modest opinion of the author of this story, Villa Ada beats the other two hands down. It's very big; about a hundred and seventy hectares of woods, lawns and thorn bushes squashed between Via Salaria, the Olimpica Viaduct and the Sports Centre of Acqua Acetosa. It still houses squirrels, moles, hedgehogs, wild rabbits, porcupines, weasels and a rich community of birds. It must be the sense of total abandonment and negligence, but as soon as you enter one of the woods there's a feeling of being in a forest. The city and its sounds disappear and you find yourself amidst one-hundred-year-old pine trees, laurel bushes, muddy tracks that wind around impenetrable blackberry bushes and fallen tree trunks, fields of poison ivy and large lawns covered in weeds. Amidst the branches you can catch a glimpse of old abandoned buildings covered in ivy, fountains taken to pieces by wild fig trees and bunkers destined, to who knows what purpose. If you aren't extremely familiar with the park it's best not to venture in there alone, or you risk getting lost for days. The subsoil of the Villa is covered with the Catacomb of Priscilla, where the early Christians buried their dead.

In the northern part, beyond the big artificial lake, is a tree-covered hill called Forte Antenne because at the end of the nineteenth century the Italian Army built fortifications upon it to defend Rome from French attack. When Rome hadn't yet come into existence, in that position lay the city of Antemnae. The name, according to the Roman historian Varrone, derives from ante amnem *(in front of the river)* because that is the point where the Aniene runs into the Tiber. From that position, the city dominated the river traffic that headed towards the ford at the Tiberian Island. In 735 AD Romolo conquered the city, its citizens were welcomed as Romans, and tenant farmers sent to occupy the land. From the third century AD onwards, the city fell into neglect and was abandoned. The highlands of Antemnae, during the centuries of Roman decay, housed the Alaric Goths who, coming from the north, prepared to attack Rome. Nothing more was said for centuries and centuries, until the seventeenth century. The area had become the farming estate of the Irish College. Then, in 1783, the land was bought by Prince Pallavicini, who built a country house on it. Ownership passed in the mid-eighteen hundreds to the Potentian Princes, and was sold in 1872 to the Royal Family, who turned it into their Roman residence. Victor Emanuel II, who was a great lover of the art of hunting, then acquired other lands that bordered with his, to turn it into his hunting lodge.

Upon his death he was succeeded by Umberto I, who moved his whole court to the Presidential Palace. The country house was bought for five hundred and thirty-one thousand lira by the Swiss Count Tellfner, the administrator of the Royal Family's assets, and he named it in honour of his wife, Ada, with whom it seems he was deeply in love.

In 1900 King Umberto I was killed by an anarchist. His successor, Victor Emanuel III, decided to move back to his grandfather's villa, and it was the official residence of the Royal

Family until 1946, the year in which the monarchy was ousted, and the king and his kin were forced into exile.

The villa now passed to the Italian Government, with the exception of the Royal Villa, which the Savoys generously granted to the Egyptian Government as a token of their gratitude for hospitality received during the exile of 1946. The building subsequently became the Egyptian Embassy.

From that moment onwards, Villa Ada became public property and was transformed into a city park. New roads were designed, specially equipped tracks for athletes were set up, artificial lakes were dug and many non-native trees were planted.

In 2004, in order to fatten the local government's coffers, the capital city's mayor decided to auction the entire area of Villa Ada for the astronomical sum of three hundred million euro.

The auction took place on Capitoline Hill on the 24th of December, amidst protests by infuriated Romans at what would go down in history as 'the big rip-off'. Bidders included celebrities of the calibre of Bono from U2, the Russian businessman Roman Abramovich, Sir Paul McCartney, Air France and a cartel of Swiss banks.

Unexpectedly, it was snapped up for the sum of four hundred and fifty million euro by Salvatore Chiatti, nicknamed Sasà, a businessman from Campagna (but otherwise of obscure origins) who had in the course of the nineties managed to amass an immense portfolio of real estate. He had at one point been in jail on charges of tax evasion and cattle-stealing, but thanks to the pardon he had been set free.

A few days later, in an interview with the daily newspaper Il Messaggero, the businessman explained the acquisition as follows: 'My mum always took me there when I was little. I *was driven by nostalgia.' A big lie, since Chiatti had spent his childhood in Mondragone, working in his father's garage. The journalist had gone on to ask: 'And what do you plan on doing with it?'*

'It will be my Roman residence.'

For a few years the Villa was closed. Locals formed a committee to return the park to the Romans. People said that Chiatti had actually bought it as an investment and was looking for foreign partners to transform it into a residential area, with golf courses, horse-riding clubs and go-kart racing.

In 2007 the renovations began. The boundary walls were raised by ten metres and rolls of barbed wire were placed on top. Every fifty metres along the walled perimeter were little towers hung with clusters of video cameras.

The Marquess Clothilde, the widow of General Farinelli, from her penthouse suite on Via Salaria was able to glimpse through the branches a slice of the park. The elderly woman had revealed to a journalist from the weekly magazine Panorama *that she could see workers coming and going non-stop. They were planting trees, clearing the land. And she had even seen two giraffes and a rhinoceros. The journalist, however, didn't give her credence because the Widow Farinelli was seventy-eight years old and had the beginnings of Alzheimer's.*

But the marquess had seen correctly.

Sasà Chiatti had built marshland, rivers and quicksand, and committed himself to repopulating the park. He had bought from the neglected zoos and abandoned circuses of the Eastern countries bears, seals, tigers, lions, giraffes, foxes, parrots, cranes, storks, macaques, Barbary macaques, hippopotamus and piranhas, and he had scattered them throughout the one hundred and seventy hectares of Villa Ada. All of the animals had been born and bred in captivity, hence docile and dependent on the food supplied by the guardians. They lived in a natural paradise where the primordial rules of prey–predator no longer existed. With the passing of the months, the diverse fauna had found a sort of balance. Each species had carved out its own ecological niche. The hippopotamus positioned themselves in the little lake next to the old kiosk of the cafeteria, and they didn't move from there ever again. The crocodiles and the piranha colonised the second artificial body of water, not far from the swings and the slides. Lions and tigers formed a colony on Mount Antenne. The Australian bats, huge beasts weighing six kilos each, took refuge in the catacomb. Beside the ex-Embassy, gnus, zebra, camels and herds of buffalo that Sasà had brought in straight from Mondragone grazed on a big grassy plain.

With the avian breeds, things were a little more complex. Stefano Coppé, lying on the ground next to his Burgman 250 scooter after having been rear-ended by an Opel Meriva on the exit between the Salaria and the Olimpica, saw a flock of vultures circling overhead and understood that the situation was serious. A pair of condors built their nest on the Rossetti family's balcony, in Via Taro, and tore Anselmo, the pet tabby cat, to pieces as he tried desperately to defend the small terrace. The athletes of the Acqua Acetosa centre witnessed kites and barn owls perching on the bars of the rugby goal posts. The fishmonger on Via Locchi was plundered of a sea bass weighing three kilos by a fish eagle. Parrots and toucans slammed into the windscreens of cars driving along the ring road.

Sasà Chiatti's idea was simple and magnificent at the same time: to organise a housewarming party so exclusive and sump-tuous that it would be remembered throughout the centuries to come as the biggest, globally important event to take place in the history of our republic. And he would go from being *famous as a suspicious real-estate magnate to being famous as a radiant millionaire and eccentric. Politicians, entrepreneurs, people from showbusiness and from the sports world would come to court to pay him homage, just like the Sun King at Versailles. But to achieve this, a party with music, dancing, buffet and cotillion would not be enough. It needed to be something so special and inimitable that everyone would be speechless.*

The idea came to him one night while he was watching Out of Africa, *starring Robert Redford and Meryl Streep.*

A safari! He would organise a surprise safari for the guests. His megalomania led him, however, to the decision that one was not enough. There had to be three of them. The classic English fox hunt, the African lion hunt with coloured beaters, and then the Indian tiger hunt, on elephants.

But in order for everything to work as planned, it was fundamental that nothing regarding the party preparation be leaked. All of the guards, workers and employees were forced to sign a confidentiality agreement.

He summoned the famous white hunter Corman Sullivan, whose claim to fame was having accompanied the writer Ernest Hemingway on the great hunt of 1934. Sullivan's age was undefined and ranged from eighty to one hundred years old. He suffered from chronic cirrhosis of the liver and had spent the last twenty years living in a rest home run by missionary nuns in Manzini Town in Swaziland, the small state bordering South Africa.

When he arrived at Fiumicino Airport, the hunter, in a weakened state because of a number of lung infections, had to spend three days in a hyperbaric oxygen chamber prepared for him at Civitavecchia. Then he was transported to Villa Ada in an ambulance. He spent two more days lying in bed spitting up blood and catarrh, waiting for the malignant tertian, which struck him cyclically, to drop. When he at last had the strength to walk, the old addict began working to organise the three hunts.

The fox hunt wasn't particularly complicated. Sasà Chiatti had restored the Savoy's stables and it held twenty-five pure-bred Lipizzans. And in the kennels he had a pack of beagles he'd bought from a pharmaceutical company that was going bankrupt. Even for the Indian-style hunt Sullivan didn't come across any complications. The real-estate magnate had bought four elephants affected with spotted dermatosis from a circus in Kracovia. The real problems arose with the lion hunt. They had to sign up about thirty beaters from within the communities from Burkina Faso and Senegal who roomed opposite the Termini station. They couldn't remember perfectly the art of hunting the big feline, but they guaranteed that they would do a good job, or at least survive the event. Seeing as he was at the station, Sasà also signed up some Filipinos to lead the elephants.

But his greatest stroke of entrepreneurial genius was to have his safaris sponsored by the designer Ralph Lauren, who chose khaki and hot pink as the dominant colours in the hunting uniforms.

Even the catering was planned in minute detail. Most parties lose points on the food, and at that stage you might as well bin everything else. Chiatti went all-out and called Zóltan Patrovic, the unpredictable Bulgarian chef-owner of the multi-award-winning restaurant Le Regioni. Each safari would have its own camp where the guests would take some refreshment with foods in the style of their hunt. The fox hunt camp consisted of big tartan rugs laid over a field of heather. There they would nibble on salmon, game and pudding, all

105

reinterpreted with the Zóltan Patrovic touch. For the tiger hunt, the guests would be received on three house boats moored on the artificial lake. Chiatti had them brought in from Lake Dal in Kashmir. The sherpas would serve basmati rice, curried chicken and other Hindustani delights. For the African safari, Corman Sullivan insisted that there be five field tents and barbecues where they could grill ostrich meat and lamb.

The party would begin at lunchtime and would end at dawn the following day. Rest tents, information booths and free drinks kiosks would be set up here and there throughout the park.

Here is the programme for the party that Salvatore Chiatti, together with Ingrid Bocutte, the great Viennese event organiser, and Corman Sullivan, invented after a briefing that lasted six days.

Programme

12.30 p.m.	Welcome Buffet
2.30 p.m.	Speech by Salvatore Chiatti to the Guests
3.00 p.m.	Organisation of the Hunting Groups. Wardrobe and Allocation of the Weapons
3.40 p.m.	Departure for the Safari
4.00 p.m. – 8.00 p.m.	Hunt
8.30 p.m.	Arrival at the Bivouac and Dinner
11.00 p.m.	Return to Villa Reale
12.00 a.m.	Midnight Matriciana
2.00 a.m.	Concert by Larita in Villa Ada
4.00 a.m.	Fireworks Display by Xi-Jiao Ming and the Magic Flying Chinese Orchestra
4.30 a.m	New and Revival Dances by DJ Sandro
6.00 a.m.	Croissants
7.00 a.m.	End

24

Fabrizio Ciba awoke convinced that he had been resurrected from a dead man's coffin. He raised his right eyelid and a blade of sunshine pierced his pupil. With his eyes closed he began passing his tongue, as swollen as that of a calf, across his dry lips. He moved his head slightly. The pain was so intense that it left him breathless; he was unable even to complain. It was like an alternative current was channelled through his shoulder blades, along the cervical vertebrae, crossing over his grey matter, flowing from his temples into his eyebrows and from there inside his eyeballs. He touched his hair. Even that hurt. He rolled onto his side to hide from the sunshine. His stomach seized and expanded, sending an acidic jelly up the writer's throat. He very nearly vomited. 'All right . . . all right . . . I'll keep still . . .' he begged desperately. He lay there, traversed by electrical currents up top and scratched by gastric acid down below.

What the hell did I do last night?

He couldn't even remember how he had got home. He remembered that he had been progressing along drunkenly on Fori Imperiali and it was raining. His legs had suddenly given out. After that, everything was black.

Am I at home?

It was a struggle, but he managed to look around and conclude that he was in his jocks, under a blanket, on the sofa of his flat in Via Mecenate.

An old alcoholic writer from Udine had shared his own recipe for a potion to be used in cases of terminal hangover . . . even if what Fabrizio was feeling was more akin to the after-effects of brain surgery than a hangover . . .

In a glass of water put three Alka-Seltzer, two Serenase, thirty-five drops of Algozone, eat a piece of bread and go back to sleep. You'll see . . .

You'll see what?

The writer from Udine didn't take into consideration the objective difficulty of concocting the pharmaceutical mix given the unstable condition Fabrizio was teetering in. And yet somehow Ciba managed to get up. He wobbled around the flat, grabbing onto everything. He went into the bathroom and with a huge effort prepared the potion. He drank it all in one gulp, burped and dragged himself back to the bedroom, where he closed the blinds, took the phone off the hook and slipped into bed. The touch of the fresh sheets, the smell of fabric softener on the pillow and the gentle weight of the duvet were the only pleasant sensations in the hell he had woken up to. He had the impression that the bed wrapped around him and protected him from all the baddies of the world, like the shell of a hermit crab.

He then died.

He came-to a few hours later. The sleep and the cocktail had worked. His temples still throbbed, and his limbs were as stiff as if he had scaled Monte Rosa, but he felt better.

He swayed around the flat, trying to take stock of everything. First of all he needed a cup of boiling hot coffee, a good old prosciutto and stracchino panini, and a shower.

Standing beneath the warm cascade, and with a full stomach, the bits and pieces of the evening fell into place. The outstanding facts were there:

1. Martinelli wanted to give him the bullet;
2. He had told his agent, his only ally, to go to hell;
3. He'd had a minor heart attack, stroke, or something like that.

The last point worried him the least. As he was chronically terrified of doctors and pain, Fabrizio Ciba minimised every health problem. It was the fault of those tequila boom-booms.

The other two points, however, tormented him enough. He had to put a plan together quickly. Gianni was right: no other publishing house would ever pay him as much as Martinelli.

He went out onto the terrace and leaned against the railing. Sky and sun were blended together into an opalescent thing that weighed like a fetid gas on the capital, and the racket caused by the traffic even that high up was deafening. Below, he could see the Colosseum, and around it the to'ing and fro'ing of tourists, coaches, centurions and sellers of souvenirs. He thought about their squalid lives, the evenings in pizzerias, the holidays. The car loan. The queue at the post office. Simple, common problems.

They're so lucky! They don't know what real suffering is. Why don't I work in a real-estate agency? Free of this creative anguish, of the responsibility of having to say intelligent things to humanity. And if I just stopped? If I gave it all up for ever?

The image of J.D. Salinger, the wonderful author of *Catcher in the Rye*, came to mind. *Jerome . . . you really are the best. Just like me, you barely wrote three books. Just like me, you wrote your masterpiece, then you disappeared and became a legend. I should do the same thing as you. With the royalties from* The Lion's Den, *in theory I could get away with it. I'll have to reduce my living expenses, though.*

Fabrizio Ciba spent, a piece of crap here, a bit of mucking around there, fifteen thousand euro a month. Even if his last novel, *Nestor's Dream*, was published more than two years ago and had sold fewer than two hundred thousand copies, it was thanks to *The Lion's Den* that he could afford that lifestyle. That little one-hundred-and-twenty-page novel was still at the top of the bestseller lists. It had been translated across half the world and Paramount had bought the film rights.

If Ciba was prudent, he could easily live until he was eighty without having to lift a finger from morning to evening. Sure, he'd have to give up the penthouse flat in Via Mecenate. And he'd have to sell his hideaway on the mountains of Majorca. And most importantly, to keep up that aura of mystery that surrounded Salinger, he shouldn't do any more interviews. No programmes, no guest appearances on TV, no parties, no fucking around. In short, he'd have to transform into a cloistered monk and annoy himself shitless in a solitary hermitude for the rest of his life.

Maybe it can be done in America. Nature, desert, open spaces . . . But where would I lock myself up in Italy? In a one-room apartment on the Boccea? And then I'd be all alone, in a hermitage, without any pussy . . . I'd commit suicide in a couple of weeks.

The word 'pussy' thankfully brought him back down to earth.

He had to get away. Spend a couple of days in Majorca. There, in solitude, he would have time to pick up his novel where he'd left it off since . . .

His brain made an undetectable click, as if a safety switch had cut off the circuit. The thought, just as easily as it had appeared, melted away and his attention returned to Majorca.

Sure, but all alone . . . Who could he take with him? It had to be a woman who would help to give a bit of a boost to his self-esteem. But especially one who wouldn't bore him silly with children, husbands and other mental hang-ups.

Alice Tyler . . . the translator.

No, too intellectual. And what's more, he'd made such an ass of himself that he wasn't sure she would agree to come.

110

Instead, he could pick and choose from the wealthy pot offered to him by the LUISS. At least seven female students from his creative writing course would have given up their civil rights to spend a weekend with him. There was this girl, too, Elisabetta Cabras, who was definitely a horny tart. She didn't know how to write for shit, but she had a natural talent for erotic scenes. You could tell that they were real-life experiences. Ciba imagined Cabras wandering naked around the swimming pool, with her big tits and a bloody mary in one hand, in front of the sun that drowned in the Balearic Sea.

He went back inside and sat down at the desk. The surface was messily covered with bundles of printed pages, books, bound papers, cans of beer and ashtrays overflowing with cigarette ends. He began looking for Cabras's essay, which he was sure would have included her mobile phone number. He knocked the mouse and the laptop screen lit up. There was the beginning of the second chapter of his new novel:

Vittoria Cubeddu had what is considered a clean Italian accent. On the contrary, the rest of the Cubeddu family spoke the slow, drawled dialect of Oristano. The house was also

He had spent three days writing those two sentences, obsessively continuing to change the adjectives, move the nouns, invert the verbs. Unwillingly he re-read it and then gagged on an acidic regurgitation. He slapped the computer closed.

'What the fuck is this stuff? This was supposed to be the new national novel! I am a tosser!'

And he paced around the flat, kicking the sofa and Moroccan pouffes. He sat down on the bed, gasping for breath. The pain in his temples began tormenting him again. He had to snap out of it. Deep inside him, buried beneath a sea of useless crap, there was still the spirit of the writer that he had once been. He had to get him to re-emerge. A blank slate, stop drinking, stop smoking and knuckle down and write, with the strength and passion he had at the beginning.

How was it possible? In four years he had abandoned five novels. The great Sardinian family saga seemed like the only novel that made any sense, and yet . . . It was useless, it was bullshit. Absolutely, he really needed to go and spend ten days or so in Majorca to clean up his mind.

While he began looking for Cabras's number again, the landline rang. He was sure that on the other end of the line there was definitely a pain in the arse. But he decided to answer anyway. It might be that bitch, his agent, ringing to apologise.

He put on an annoyed tone of voice.

'Hello? Who's speaking?'

'Ya poofter!'

Fabrizio closed his eyes and bent backwards, like a football player who stuffs up a penalty kick.

Paolo Bocchi. The quintessential pain in the arse. For reasons beyond his understanding, that creature kept buzzing around him like a mosquito thirsty for blood. Professor Paolo Bocchi always had access to any psychoactive substance that either nature or chemistry offered humankind.

A little bit of grass in Majorca, to be honest, wouldn't hurt at all.

'So, you old poofter, how are you?'

If there was anything which deeply annoyed him, it was the heavy high-school attitude that Paolo Bocchi had towards him. Just because they'd been in the same class together at San Leone Magno high school . . . That didn't give him the right to be so intimate with him.

'Come on, Paolo, I'm not in the mood today.' Fabrizio tried to keep calm.

'Tell me about it. Today I did two nose jobs and a lipo. I'm whacked.'

Professor Paolo Bocchi was head plastic surgeon at the San Roberto Bellarmino clinic. He had studied under the great Roland Chateau-Beaubois and was considered to be number one in the capital's plastic surgery field. He had restored the youthfulness to many old biddies. His only problem was that he sucked it up like an old woodfired oven.

'Hey! I did it! I read *The Lion's Den*. Can I give you my opinion? Fantastic!'

'Congratulations, it came out eight years ago.'

'How do you get into people's heads like that? You can really see them, the characters. I swear, better than a film. The nurses didn't believe I could read a whole book . . .'

'Well,' Fabrizio tried to cut him off, 'listen, I'm busy at the moment, I'm about to leave for Spain. In fact . . .'

A scream: 'What? What about Chiatti's party?'

Fabrizio smacked himself on the forehead. He had completely forgotten about Salvatore Chiatti's party. The invitation had come two months ago. A piece of square Perspex with gold letters written in bas-relief, strictly personal.

For a year everyone had talked only about that party. According to what everyone said, it was shaping up to be the most exclusive and over-the-top event of the last few decades. Missing that sort of affair seriously damaged one's VIP status. But Fabrizio just wasn't psychologically prepared to face mundane situations. To get through a social test like that, you have to be one hundred per cent, witty and chirpy as never before. And at the moment he was as witty and chirpy as a Ugandan refugee.

Salinger. Concentrate on Salinger.

Fabrizio shook his head. 'Naaaah, that megalomaniac mafioso builder? Never! It's so tasteless.'

'Are you out of your mind? You don't understand how much that crazy megalomaniac has spent. We're talking about millions, here! You can't miss something like this. Everybody'll be there. Music, arts, football players, politicians, models, everyone! The world's greatest circus. You could write a novel about it.'

'No listen, Paolo, I know these parties by heart. They bore you shitless. And it's exactly this sort of attention-seeking that I have to avoid. Think of Salinger . . .'

'Who?'

'Forget it. Anyway . . . I'll give you a call when I get back, right . . .?'

'Are you sure?' Paolo Bocchi was incredulous. 'I think you're fucking-up big-time. There'll be . . . how can I say it . . .' The great surgeon was a wizard with the scalpel, but a lexical disaster. 'You just don't get it . . . They'll be throwing pussy at you. Two days of drinking and screwing in the park. You're crazy.'

'I know, I know. Look, I've got problems with my publishing house. And I'm just not in the right mood.'

'Relax, I'll fix it for you.' Paolo Bocchi laughed deeply.

'Leave it. I've stopped using that stuff.'

'Whatever, do whatever the fuck you wanna do. But just so you're clear on this: Larita will be singing, too. It's the only thing that has leaked about the party. Do you get what that means?'

'Larita? The singer?'

'No, Larita the dry cleaner! Of course, the singer.'

'Who cares?'

'She's won I don't know how many Grammies and platinum discs.'

114

Fabrizio wanted to hang up. 'All right, Paolo, I'll think about it. Now just let me go.'

'Good boy, think about it. Nurse, hurry with that drain, it would be good to get out of here before Christmas . . .'

'Where the hell are you?' asked Ciba, speechless.

'In the operating room. Don't worry, I'm using earphones. See ya, mate.'

And the phone went dead.

Ciba went back into the living room to look for Cabras's essay. And he noticed a piece of paper stuck to the desk lamp.

Good Morning Fabrizio,

My name's Lisa, I'm the girl who brought you home last night.

Forgive me for saying so, but you were really in pieces. How much did you have to drink? I don't know what happened to you, but I'm happy to have been the one to save you. I was lucky enough to meet you in person and to discover that you're even hotter in real life than on TV. I could have taken advantage of you.

I undressed you and put you on the sofa, but I'm an old-fashioned girl and I don't do certain things.

And being here in your house, the house of my idol, of the best writer in the world is incredible.

It's too much. No one will believe me.

I'm never going to wash the arm that you autographed for me ever again.

I hope you'll do the same thing with your hip.

Fabrizio lifted his t-shirt. And he saw, in the region of his left buttock, the unreadable remains of a phone number. 'No! The shower!' He continued reading.

Always remember that you are the best, that everyone else is one hundred metres below you.

Now, that's enough compliments, you must be sick of people like me. Call me, if you feel like it.

Lisa

Fabrizio Ciba re-read the note three times, and with each reading he felt his body and his spirit perk up.

He said to himself, fully satisfied: 'You are the best. You are always the best, everyone else is one hundred metres below you. I could have taken advantage of you.' He pointed at the window and said: 'I love you, sweet Lisa.'

That's who Fabrizio Ciba is! Fuck you all!

He had the childish desire to scan the letter and send it to that bastard Gianni & co., but instead he turned the stereo on and slipped in a CD of an old live recording of Otis Redding. The woofer in the huge Tannoy speakers began to shake and the little blue VU meters of his old McIntosh amplifier began to sway as the singer from Georgia struck the first notes of 'Try A Little Tenderness'.

Fabrizio loved that song. He liked the fact that it began softly, relaxed, and then slowly grew until it changed into an unstoppable rhythm with the husky, kneaded voice of old Otis acting as a counterpoint.

The writer took a beer out of the fridge and began dancing naked in the living room. He jumped around like the great Muhammad Ali before a fight and yelled at the entire universe: 'Fuck you! Fuck you! I am Ciba! I am the coolest of them all!' Then he leaped up on the Gae Aulenti coffee table and, using the can as a microphone, began to sing. At the end of the piece he flopped down on the sofa, exhausted. He was breathing heavily, his stomach as swollen as the hull of a boat, but he was still strong. It took more than this to cut him down. He wouldn't run off to Majorca with his tail between his legs. It came naturally to him to think of the writer F. Scott Fitzgerald. He'd lived his life in sin, between wonderful parties and beautiful women.

He was back again. The old fighter.

Fabrizio Ciba began to hunt, amidst the papers and the mail that crowded his desk, for his invitation to the party.

25

The Wilde Beasts of Abaddon, on board their leader's Ford Mondeo, were stuck in traffic. The GPS navigator told them that they were a kilometre and a half from Villa Ada, but the road blocks on Via Salaria had created a traffic jam on the Olimpica and on Via dei Prati Fiscali.

Mantos, at the wheel, observed his adepts in the rear-view mirror. They had been very good. They had removed their piercings and washed up. Silvietta had even dyed her hair black. But ever since they had left Oriolo they had been quiet, long-faced, wearing worried expressions. He needed to rouse them; that was what a leader did.

'So, guys? Are you ready?'

'A little worried . . .' Murder's mouth was dry.

Silvietta nibbled at her lip. 'I've never been this nervous, not even for the General Psychology exam.'

Mantos put the indicator on, pulled over to one side of the Olimpica and looked at them: 'Do you trust me?'

Zombie's face had the same complexion as a boiled cauliflower. 'We do, Master.'

'Listen to me. The mission, as you know, is a suicide. There is still time for you to drop out. I'm not forcing anyone. But if you decide to stay, then we have to be a perfect team, as synchronised as a Swiss watch. We have to be ruthless and have faith in the Evil One who watches over our heads.'

At that point he turned on the radio and the chorus from Carmina Burana filled the car. 'O *Fortuna velut luna statu variabilis, semper crescis aut decrescis.*'

'Listen to me! We are the most evil of them. And I want Larita's head. Once inside the Villa, no one will foresee our attack. They'll all be having fun, drinking, they lower their defences and we will knock them down. Zombie, in the back there's a rolled up bathroom mat. Get it, but be very careful.'

The adept stretched into the boot and placed the roll into Saverio's hands. The leader of the Wilde Beasts of Abaddon laid the mat in his lap and slowly and solemnly he unfolded it.

A ray of sunshine shone through the window, making the iron sparkle.

'*Vita detestabilis nunc obdurat et tunc curat*'. The chorus continued its impetuous crescendo.

Mantos, struggling slightly, raised the weapon above the head rests.

'This is the Durendal, the precise reproduction of Orlando's sword used at Roncisvalle.'

'Nooooo!' the adepts said in unison. 'It's gorgeous!'

Saverio opened the car door. 'Let's get out of the car.'

Silvietta squeezed his shoulder to stop him. 'Wait, High Priest, they can see us.'

'It doesn't matter. We'll hide behind the car.'

The Beasts got out and crouched behind the Ford.

'Kneel down.' Saverio placed the blade of the Durendal on the heads of his adepts. 'Murder! Zombie! Silvietta! I, Mantos, your Charismatic Father, high priest of Evil and humble servant of Satan, name you Champions of Evil. May no one dare to break our oath, now and for eternity! We will go all the way with this mission. Unto the final sacrifice of our very own lives. Now let's kiss!'

The Beasts all hugged and kissed, feeling moved.

'What the hell are you doing? Have you lost your minds?'

They turned around.

Saverio's cousin, Antonio Zauli, at the wheel of his van, was looking at them, astonished.

'No . . . It's just that . . .' stuttered the leader of the Beasts.

'Come on . . . You're running late . . . You've gotta register. Jump in.'

He let them in through the West Gate, the service entrance. There were three entrances into the Villa. Two were closed and only to be used in case of emergency, while the third one, on the Via Salaria, was the main entry, to be used by the guests. Ten-metre-high impressive iron gates ran along tracks, controlled by hydraulic pumps.

The service entrance was patrolled by a private security service who checked the goods going in and coming out. Behind it lay the registration point, a two-storey structure made of glass and anodised steel. The staff, from the cooks to the beaters had to be registered before they could gain access inside.

The Wilde Beasts of Abaddon stood in line. There were about thirty people in front of them, mostly coloured.

'I feel like I'm at the airport,' Zombie, who had once gone to Köln to see an AC/DC concert, commented.

When it was their turn, a security guard made them complete a long questionnaire and sign a contract written in really small letters. Then he stamped an indentifying barcode on their wrists.

From there, crossing a low, dimly lit corridor, they came to a room with rows of metal lockers where they could leave their clothes and pick up their uniforms. Silvietta got dressed in the women's changing room. They had given her a black skirt, a white blouse and ankle boots with thick rubber soles. When she reappeared, the others began laughing and making fun of her. No one had ever seen her in a skirt. But they had to admit that she didn't look bad at all.

A notice board stated in many different languages that it was strictly forbidden to take any personal objects including mobile phones, cameras and video cameras inside the Villa.

'How will we get the sword through? And our tunics? We can't do the ritual without out tunics,' Murder whispered in Mantos's ear.

Mantos had hidden the tunics in his backpack, but held the bathroom mat rolled up around the Durendal under his arm.

He clearly hadn't considered this. So now what? The most important thing was to make them think that everything was under control.

'No worries. Take it easy.'

He took a deep breath and walked through the metal detector, praying the alarm wouldn't sound.

But that wasn't the case.

'Come over here,' one of the guards, weighed down by a bulletproof vest, gestured at him. 'What have you got there?'

Mantos unrolled the mat nonchalantly.

The guard shook his head. 'Weapons aren't allowed in.'

Mantos shrugged as if this was the hundredth time this sort of nuisance had happened to him. 'It's not a weapon. It's just a replica of a Durendal that belonged to Orlando and before him to Hector.'

The man took off his dark glasses, showing two little eyes

about as expressive as a bedside lamp. 'What do you mean?'

The leader of the Beasts looked towards his adepts, who, along with the security guard, were waiting for an answer. He smiled. 'I mean that it is exclusively of aesthetic value.' It sounded like an excellent answer to him. One of those definitive answers, for which there is no reply.

'What's it for?' the guy enquired.

'What's it for? Let me explain.' He took a big breath and jumped in. 'It's for cutting the roast meat. I'm assigned to the cutting of the red meats. And the clothes that I have in my backpack are needed for a magic show. I am Magician Mantos, and these are my three assistants.'

The security guard scratched the shaved nape of his neck. 'So, let me get this straight, you are a magician assigned to the cutting of the red meats?'

'Exactly.'

Some of the guy's few cast-iron certainties snapped. 'Just a moment.' He moved away to confab with someone who was probably his boss.

Then he returned and said: 'OK, you can go.'

The Beasts stiffly passed through the check-in area and came to a courtyard full of cases of wine, food and containers. On one side was a row of parked mini electric buggies like the ones used on golf courses. The square was surrounded by a metal fence and warning signs were hung along it: 'WARNING. ELECTRIFIED FENCE.'

As soon as they were alone, the Beasts were unable to hold back their joy.

'You legend, Mantos! You're the best!' Murder gave his master a couple of affectionate slaps on the back.

Silvietta huddled up to the high priest. 'Too cool, the story about the meat-cutting magician.'

'I wonder what those two said to each other. You threw them off,' Zombie sniggered.

'Enough! That's enough.' The leader tried to hold in check the praises of his adepts.

'Again?! So you're poofs, then?' Antonio yelled at them from behind the wheel of his buggy. 'Come on, hop in. Hurry up. I'll take you to the kitchen area. There's loads of stuff to do and the guests will be here soon.'

Mantos looked around. 'What's all this security for?'

Antonio pushed down on the accelerator: 'You'll find out in no time.'

They passed through the gates and drove along a small dirt path immersed in the forest. At first they didn't notice anything, and then Zombie thought he saw something jumping from branch to branch. Then they heard the shrill cries.

'Gibbons. Don't worry. They're harmless.'

'Nooooo . . . Unbelievable! Look!'

Zombie pointed at something past the forest. Where the trees thinned out began a huge field of green, green grass where gnus, gazelles and giraffes were grazing. Further on, in a slimy lake, they could see the muddy rumps of a pod of hippos. Flocks of vultures flew overhead.

Mantos was incredulous. 'It's like the zoo safari at Fiumicino.'

'That's nothing yet. Just wait and see,' Antonio smiled smugly.

On their right, hidden behind a row of holm oaks, they noticed a sort of miniature electrical plant. Huge transformers painted green to blend with the surrounding vegetation, created a dull humming sound. Colourful pipes stuck out of the structure and were rooted in the earth.

'This is the source that powers the whole park,' Antonio explained. 'Chiatti produces his own electrical power with gas. It's cheaper than buying it from Acea, given the amount of kilowatts he needs to supply the fences, light the park, and send electricity to the computer room.'

Ten or so zebras, with a couple of foals in tow, crossed the road in front of them. Silvietta was beside herself. 'Look at the little ones. They're so cute.'

They waited for them to go by and then continued their journey.

Saverio, in a disinterested tone of voice, asked his cousin: 'Has Larita arrived yet?'

Antonio raised his arms. 'I've heard that Chiatti reserved an apartment for her in the Royal Villa, but I don't know anything else.'

Shortly after, from between the tree tops an old three-storey building, crowned with a terrace and two turrets, appeared.

'This is the Royal Villa.'

The back courtyard of the house, hidden by tall boxwood hedges, was frenetic with the coming and going of men and machines, the tyres of vans, pick-up trucks and Land-Rovers kicking up dust. Teams of workers in green uniforms offloaded food, bottles, table cloths, glasses, cutlery and tables under the command of men dressed in black who hollered like they were in a military prison. Under a canopy, squatting in the dust, the coloured beaters, wearing thongs, were eating from tin cups something that looked to be tortellini in broth.

In a corner were some prefab buildings that gave off smoke and the smell of food.

'Those are the kitchens. Zóltan Patrovic will be here soon to check on how things are going. Please behave.' Antonio's expression turned serious. 'Don't be seen twiddling your thumbs.'

'Who is Zóltan Patrovic?' Silvietta gulped, feeling worried.

'You can tell you are all from Oriolo. He's a famous Bulgarian chef. He's very demanding, so do your jobs well.'

The four of them got out of the buggy.

Antonio pointed at a man dressed in black. 'Now go over to that guy there and ask him what you need to do. I'll see you later . . . And please, no fuck-ups.'

26

Fabrizio Ciba was waiting at the stoplight at the intersection between Via Salaria and Viale Regina Margherita astride his Vespa, which was puffing out black smoke. He had managed to find it and start it up again.

Two teenagers screeched alongside him, aboard a scooter, with their bum cheeks and their panties exposed from the top of their low-waisted jeans. They studied him for a moment, then they squealed excitedly and the girl sitting on the back asked him: 'Excuse me? Are you Ciba? The writer on TV?'

Fabrizio unleashed his ironical expression, showing off his whitened teeth.

'Yes, but don't tell anyone. I'm on a secret mission.'

The blonde girl asked him: 'Are you going to the party at Villa Ada?'

The writer shrugged his shoulders as if to say 'I have to go.'

The other young girl chewed gum and asked: 'You couldn't get us in, could you? Please . . . please . . . I beg you . . . Everyone's going to be there . . .'

'I wish, but I think it's impossible. I would have much more fun if you were there, too.'

The light turned green. The writer slipped into first gear and the Vespa sprang off. For a second Ciba saw himself reflected in the shop window of a boutique. For the occasion he had put on a pair of light brown linen trousers, a light oxford-blue shirt, a faded dark blue Cambridge tie that had belonged to his grandfather, and a grey-and-white striped three-button madras cotton J. Crew jacket. All strictly crushed.

The closer he moved towards Villa Ada, the more the traffic increased. Bands of police tried to detour the cars onto Via Chiana and Via Panama. A police helicopter buzzed above them. On the pavements the crowds crammed together behind barriers, held in check by riot police. Many of them were young protesters who were demonstrating against the privatisation of Villa Ada. Huge banners hung from balconies. There was a really long one that said: 'CHIATTI MAFIOSO! GIVE US BACK OUR PARK!' Another one said: 'LOCAL GOVERNMENT BUNCH OF THIEVES!' And another: 'GIVE VILLA ADA BACK TO THE ROMANS!'

Fabrizio decided to park the Vespa and reflect on an aspect he hadn't taken into consideration: his public image as an intellectual would suffer from his participation at Chiatti's party. He was a left-wing writer. He had made the opening speech at the national congress for the Partito Democratico, demanding an urgent commitment to Italy's dying cultural movement. He never turned down a presentation at the Leoncavallo or at the Brancaleone.

I still have time to go home, no one has seen me yet . . .

'Hey, poofter!'

Fabrizio turned around. Paolo Bocchi, at the wheel of his Porsche Cayenne, had pulled up beside him.

No way!

'Mr Writer, dump that old wreck and get in my car! Make a proper entrance.'

'Go on ahead, I've got to make a work call, I'll see you inside,' Fabrizio lied.

The surgeon pointed at a group of young men wearing

keffiyehs. 'What the fuck do those shitheads want?' And he drove off, honking his horn.

What to do? If he wanted to leave, he had to be quick about it. Photographers and television crews were circling hungrily in search of invited guests.

While he watched the kids from the halfway houses scream at the police 'You are arseholes, and arseholes you'll always be', Fabrizio was reminded of something that occasionally he inexplicably forgot: *I am a writer. I talk about life. In the same way that I denounced the felling of the thousand-year-old Finnish forests, I can badmouth a group of nouveau riche and mafiosi. A nice tough article in the Culture section of* Repubblica *and I'll sort the lot out. I am different.* He took a look at his crushed clothes. *You will never buy me! I'll show you all for what you are!* He climbed back on his Vespa, put it into first and faced the crowd.

The spectators in the crowd behind the barriers were beginning to change. Now there were more young girls and entire families with their mobile phones out, starting to take his photo and shouting at him to stop.

Finally he made it to the entrance, guarded by about twenty hostesses and a band of private security guards. A young blonde woman swathed in a tight grey suit came up to him.

'Good morning, pleased you could join us. We weren't sure whether you would come, you didn't RSVP.'

Fabrizio slipped off his Ray-Bans and looked at her. 'You're right, I'm terribly guilty. How can I gain your forgiveness?'

The girl smiled. 'You have nothing to be forgiven for . . . I just need your invitation.' Fabrizio took out the envelope. Inside it, along with the invitation, was a magnetic card. He handed it to the hostess, who swiped it over the reader.

'Everything is fine, Doctor Ciba. I recommend you park the

Vespa here on the left and walk the catwalk on foot. Enjoy yourself.'

'Thanks,' the writer answered and put the scooter into first.

He turned left past the red carpet which led up to the entrance, towards a clearing where BMWs, Mercedes, Hummers and Ferraris were parked. He put the Vespa on its stand, he took off his helmet and tidied his hair. While he was checking himself in the wing mirror, he heard a suffocated shout from behind the barriers: 'You fake!' He didn't even have the time to understand what was happening before something heavy hit his left shoulder. He thought for a moment that the Black Bloc had thrown a hail storm of sanpietrini stones at him. He went pale and backed away terrified, crouching down behind an SUV. Then, swallowing mouthfuls of air, he took a look at the offended shoulder. A Sicilian arancino, stuffed with rice and peas, had exploded all over his jacket and was slowly dripping onto his chest, leaving an oily dribble of mozzarella and boiling hot sauce. Fabrizio ripped the arancino from his shoulder as if it was an infected leech and slung it to the ground. Injured, mocked and humiliated, he turned towards the crowd. Three men with curly hair and beards were staring at him with hate in their eyes worse than if he'd been Mussolini (who happened to be arrested in Villa Ada). They were wearing jacket and tie, pointing at him and yelling in unison: 'Ciba, you bastard! Die, Ciba, die! You're a traitor.' The writer managed to dodge a maxi one-litre cup of Coke, which exploded on the bonnet of the SUV.

An armoured vehicle then spewed out a phalanx of riot police, who attacked the violent dissidents with truncheons. The three men tried to defend themselves with a barrier, but the guy who had thrown the arancino was hit on the eyebrow by a policeman and a stream of blood burst across his face, transforming it into a red mask. The other two ended up on the ground beneath a shower of truncheon blows.

A young policeman took the writer by his arm and dragged him backwards, screaming: 'Get away, get away from there!'

Fabrizio, feeling distressed and confused, followed him without taking his eyes off of the bloodied man who kept on shouting from his position on the ground: 'Bloody Ciba! You're just like all the oooooooothers! You traitorous hypocrite! You make me sick.'

While the riot police kept laying into him, flagship cars stopped by the red carpet and the invited guests walked their catwalk amidst the flashbulbs of fans and photographers. Fabrizio Ciba took refuge between the cars with his heart thumping in his chest. 'What the fuck . . .?' he gasped, drying the sweat on his brow. 'They're all crazy!'

'Are you OK?' the policeman asked him.

Ciba nodded.

'What are you waiting for? Go, go . . . It's dangerous here.'

Fabrizio felt like he would die. *No, no, I'm going back home.*

He couldn't leave. He could imagine the newspaper headlines: *The writer Fabrizio Ciba, challenged by CENTRI SOCIALI at Chiatti's party, flees.* Even though those three guys looked like anything but kids from CENTRI SOCIALI.

He was in the shit now and the only way out, at this stage, was to spend a couple of hours at the party and then go home and write a fiery article. He headed to the red carpet with his jacket stained with tomato and oil. He decided it was best to take it off and carry it nonchalantly over one shoulder.

At the front of the entrance to the Villa the situation was completely different. Big elegant cars kept on spitting out actors, football players, politicians and television showgirls amidst the clapping and the screams of the spectators who were squashed behind the barriers like chicken on a grill. He had never seen anything close to it, not even at the Festival of Venice. The VIPs waved and the women let people take photographs of their designer outfits. One girl managed to break through the barriers and threw herself at Fabio Sartoretti, the comic from *Bazar*. But the bodyguards nailed her to the ground and threw her back into the crowd, which sucked her straight in.

Ciba took his courage into both his hands and walked with his head down, hoping nobody would recognise him, towards the red carpet. But seeing his fans waving at him so warmly, he couldn't resist and began waving back.

At that moment a BMW with darkened windows braked in front of the catwalk. From the car emerged a pair of tanned legs that seemed never to end. Then the rest of Simona Somaini came out. Miss Italia 2003, who had then gone on to become a successful actress with the show *SMS From Beyond*, was wearing a bikini that showed her back, and a fair part of her bum, while it lightly covered her breasts but not her flat, tanned stomach. He recognised next to her the famous showbusiness agent Elena Paleologo Rossi Strozzi, who looked, compared to the diva, like a pygmy with tapeworm. Although Ciba was still shaken by the incident with the arancino, as soon as he saw that pure-bred filly he thought that his day wasn't going to be so bad after all. And most importantly, he thought about the fact that they'd never fucked, and how that needed to be rectified.

Fabrizio threw open his chest, tucked in his stomach, put on his ineffable cursed writer expression. He lit a cigarette, stuck it in the corner of his mouth and walked by her distractedly.

'Fabri! Fabri!'

Ciba counted to five, then turned around and looked at her

with a perplexed expression on his face, as if he was looking at a work by Mondrian.

'Hang on . . . Hang on . . .' Then he shook his head. 'No . . . Sorry . . .'

The actress wasn't really offended, more disorientated. In the last few years the only time someone hadn't recognised her was when she went to visit her Uncle Pasquale in the Blind Institute in Subiaco. Now, she simply thought that the writer was short-sighted.

'Fabrizio? It's Simona. Don't tell me you don't remember me?'

'Recanati, perhaps?' Fabrizio said the first name that came to mind. 'For that conference on Leopardi?'

'*Porta a porta* last month!' Somaini would have liked to pout, but the Botox wouldn't let her. 'The sad story of little Hans . . .'

Ciba slapped himself softly on the forehead. 'Shit, it's the Alzheimer's . . . How could I forget the Venus de Milo! I've even got your calendar in my bathroom.'

Somaini let out a bird call similar to the sound of the curlew in mating season: 'Don't tell me you have my calendar! A writer like you with a calendar for truckers.'

Fabrizio lied shamelessly. 'I love February.'

She patted her long hair. 'What are you doing here? I didn't think you were the sort of person who came to this sort of party.'

Ciba raised his hands. 'I don't know . . . A hereditary but never before identified form of masochism? An unbearable desire for socialising?'

'Fabrizio, can you smell a sort . . . of yummy smell of sauce and tomato and mozzarella?'

The last arancino that Somaini had eaten had been at her confirmation.

'Hmph . . . No, I can't smell it,' Ciba said, sniffing the air.

Rita Baudo from the Channel 4 news saved him from the awkward situation. She came along with a microphone, and followed by a cameraman.

'So here is the actress Simona Somaini, as always looking gorgeous, with the writer Fabrizio Ciba! Don't tell me I've found a scoop!'

With a Pavlovian reflex, Somaini suctioned up to Ciba's arm. 'What do you mean, Rita? We're just friends!'

'You don't have anything to share with the viewers of *Varietà*?'

Rita Baudo pushed the microphone against Ciba's teeth, and he shoved it away again, annoyed. 'Didn't you hear what Simona said? We're just old friends.'

'Do you mind saying hi to our viewers?'

Fabrizio waved a hand in front of the camera: 'Hi.' And then he walked away with Somaini on his arm.

Baudo turned towards the cameraman with a sly expression on her face. 'I think these two are not telling us the whole truth!'

An inhuman scream came from the infernal circle beyond the barriers. Baudo began to run. Paco Jimenez de la Frontera and Milo Serinov, the centre-forward and the goalkeeper for Roma FC, were getting out of a Hummer.

27

About three hundred metres from the parterre of VIPs, in the courtyard behind the Royal Villa, the Wilde Beasts of Abaddon had been put to work. Zombie was swearing and unloading cases of Fiano d'Avellino from a van. Mantos had ended up in the kitchens working as a skivvy. Murder and Silvietta had been entrusted with polishing six cases of silver cutlery for the Indian-style dinner.

The Vestal rubbed a fork on a cloth, her eyes lowered. 'You did it again.'

Murder snorted. 'Listen, can we let it go just this once . . .?'

'No, we can't let it go just this once. You promised that you'd tell him in the car. Why didn't you do it?'

Murder impatiently threw an unpolished knife in amongst the polished ones. 'I tried to . . . But in the end I couldn't do it . . . After that speech he made, how could I? And hang on, why do I always have to say the difficult stuff?'

Silvietta bounded to her feet. Sometimes she couldn't stand her boyfriend. 'Look, you were the one who said that you'd tell him. That it wasn't a problem.'

Murder opened his arms wide. 'And, in actual fact, where is the problem? As soon as I can, I'll tell him.'

His girlfriend grabbed him by the wrist. 'No, we go and tell him now, straight away! So we can relax. All right?'

Murder got up against his will. 'All right. Sometimes you're so annoying . . . Just think how pissed off he'll be . . .'

The two of them crossed the courtyard, being careful not to be seen by Antonio, who was standing on top of a box, giving orders to everyone. He had turned from a mild-mannered polite person into a kapo.

Murder and Silvietta walked into the kitchens. There were three enormous rooms full of stainless steel appliances, steam, smells and every type of aromas. There had to be at least fifty cooks dressed in white and wearing the chef's hat. And an army of skivvies running around busily. The sound of saucepans and voices was deafening.

They found Saverio sitting on a stool with a small knife in

hand. He was peeling a pile of potatoes that could feed all of Rebibbia prison.

Mantos saw them and softly whispered: 'What are you doing here? Are you out of your minds? If they catch you . . . I told Zombie that we'd meet outside in half an hour for a briefing, then I'll tell you the whole plan. But now get out of here.'

Murder looked at him and, twisting himself in knots, he whispered: 'Hang on . . . We have something important to tell you.'

Mantos got up and took them over to a corner. 'What is it?'

'Well . . .' Murder just couldn't say it.

'Well what? Come on, hurry up!'

A fluted voice with a strong Eastern European accent behind them said: 'Who gave you two permission to enter the temple?'

A sepulchral silence descended on the kitchens. Even the exhaust fans and blenders seemed to have fallen quiet. The swallows outside had been struck dumb.

The Beasts turned around and found themselves facing, enveloped in the steam of broiled meat, a monk. Only his cassock was of black silk, and silver birds of paradise had been woven into the material. He held his fingers crossed beneath the wide sleeves of his outfit and he was barefoot. From beneath the hood you could see a pointy white beard, two square cheekbones, a beak-shaped nose and two grey eyes as cold as a winter day on the Caspian Sea.

The leader of the Wilde Beasts of Abaddon had no doubt that this was Zóltan Patrovic, the unpredictable Bulgarian chef.

Saverio had not seen the great Rasputin, the cursed monk who had condemned the tsar and his family with his tricks and his witchcraft. But he thought that the man standing in front of him had to be his reincarnation.

133

Behind him all of the cooks and the skivvies were absolutely still, their eyes lowered.

'No . . . It's just that . . . You never know . . .'

Saverio's mouth let out words with no construction. He would have owned up, but it was like his tongue had been numbed with an injection of Lidocaine. And he was unable to move his eyes away from the chef's. Two black wells. They were so deep. He felt like he was being drawn in.

Zóltan grabbed his forehead with one hand.

The leader of the Beasts felt a pleasant flow of warmth running through the chef's fingertips into his head, and found himself thinking about the maccheroni omelette that his Aunt Imma used to make him when he spent the summers in Gaeta as a little boy.

He's hypnotising me, he thought for a moment, but straight after that he thought that he had never again eaten such a yummy omelette. It was special because she made it with the puttanesca pasta from the day before. It was thick and tightly packed. Lightly scorched. And it was full of olives and capers. It was a shame Aunt Imma was dead, otherwise he'd have given her a call begging her to make it again. Then he said to himself that, after all, he only needed to beg Zóltan's forgiveness and then he could run home and make that yummy omelette himself. *Have we got eggs in the fridge?*

'I apologise. You are perfectly right. We are wrong and mortified. But in this instant I need to find out whether Serena has bought eggs,' Mantos said seriously.

'On your knees,' Patrovic ordered in a flat tone of voice.

The three of them, as if they were on remote control, knelt down.

'Heads to the floor.'

The monk climbed up on their backs.

It's weird, he doesn't weigh anything, Saverio thought. *Maybe he's levitating.*

The chef stood on them silently for a couple of minutes.

Saverio couldn't see him, seeing as his face was stuck to the floor, but he imagined that the chef was staring at the cooks. Then Zóltan said: 'Good. I see we've reached an understanding.' And he got down off the Beasts' backs.

All of them nodded and went back to work without making a sound.

He's telepathic, Saverio realised.

Then the monk crossed the kitchens, walking stiffly like a wooden statue, as if he was carrying a skateboard underneath his cassock. The cooks bowed and offered him their dishes. He waved a hand over them like a Reiki practitioner.

Every now and then he murmured: 'Less ginger. More salt. Too much caraway seed. It needs rosemary.'

And then, just as suddenly as he had been there, he suddenly wasn't.

Welcome Buffet

28

Even Fabrizio Ciba and the other guests were forced to undergo a similar process to the one the Beasts had gone through to get into the Villa. The writer walked through the metal detector. When it was Somaini's turn, she was forced to leave her mobile phone behind.

'What is this farce?' the writer asked a hostess.

The girl explained that Chiatti didn't want the party to become a public event. Hence they were not allowed to send photos, videos or much less communicate with the outside world. For this reason, no journalists had been accredited.

'Don't worry, there are the photographers from *Sorrisi e Canzoni*. Chiatti gave them the exclusive,' Somaini confided to him in a soft voice – she was an expert in these sorts of things.

The two of them left the checkpoint and found themselves facing a small, missile-shaped train, set upon a monorail. On the top was written: 'VILLA ADA ENTERPRISE'.

They sat in two black leather armchairs. The loudspeakers of their carriage emitted the voice of Louis Armstrong singing 'What A Wonderful World'. Paco Jimenez de la Frontera got into their carriage as well, with his long bleached hair and his chiselled jaw that drove women wild. For the occasion the football player was wearing a sparkly tuxedo and a white silk t-shirt. His woman, the statuesque model from Montopoli di Sabina, Taja Testari, was covered from head to toe in a black organza dress that hid her naked body.

Fabrizio, after the Channel 5 grand gala, had bedded her,

but he'd been so drunk that the only thing he remembered was that while they were fucking she had bopped him on the nose, and he had not understood whether it was an erotic game or retribution because he had ripped her dress.

He was joined by his teammate Milo Serinov, who had hooked up with an ex-showgirl, and was leaving a trail of nauseating aftershave.

Simona Somaini was still squealing as she snuggled up to Fabrizio Ciba's arm again, glueing her tits to him. The writer suspected that she was doing all of this because the rights to *The Lion's Den* had been sold to Paramount, and who knows what she hoped for. She didn't know that he had no control whatsoever over the film. The Americans hadn't even wanted to meet him. They had told his agent that they didn't consider it necessary. They had given him a shitload of money on the condition that he didn't make a nuisance of himself.

The flatscreen TV on the back of the armchair in front of them came to life and the chubby face of Salvatore Chiatti appeared.

'Oh God, he looks just like Minos!' said Simona, covering her mouth with her hand, surprised.

Fabrizio was amazed. He hadn't imagined that the actress was an expert in Greek mythology. 'Minos?'

'Yes, my hairdresser Diego Malara's pug dog. They're identical.'

She wasn't wrong. The Campanian real-estate agent looked incredibly like that little molosser. The exophthalmic eyes, the small turned-up nose, the round skull set atop his wide shoulders. On the sides, above his tiny ears, grew a strip of silver hair, but otherwise he was completely bald.

'Good morning, my name's Salvatore Chiatti. I hope that this party will exceed anything you could ever imagine. I and my assistants have made every effort so that this may be the case. Now, please, close your eyes. I'm not joking, close them, seriously.'

The passengers looked at each other and then, feeling a little embarrassed, obeyed.

Chiatti's voice was becoming more and more honeyed.

'Imagine you are a child again. You are all alone in a little wooden hut, your nana has gone into town. Suddenly the sky starts to grumble. You open the windows and what do you see? At the bottom of the plains a tornado is coming towards you. Terrified, you begin to close the shutters, to lock the door, but the whirlwind is upon the little house in a second and it drags the whole hut, with you inside it, up into the sky. The house is spinning, spinning, spinning . . . And the tornado carries you up high, higher, higher still, beyond the rainbow.' In the background an instrumental version of 'Somewhere Over the Rainbow' started to play. 'And in the end it gently places you in a new, never-before-explored world. In a world where wild and unspoilt nature lives in harmony with mankind. Now you can open your eyes. Welcome to heaven on earth. Welcome to Villa Ada. Hold on tight. One, two, three, we're off!'

'Oh my God.' Simona Somaini squeezed Fabrizio Ciba's hand as the train departed, thrusting them against the back of the chairs. They crossed a few dozen metres of forest at high speed and then the rail, like a roller coaster, pointed upwards, carrying them above the tops of the pine trees. As they went by, flocks of coloured parrots, ash-coloured cranes and huge vultures with mangy necks flew into the air. Then slowly the train descended again and they found themselves in a green field. They went by herds of gnus, zebra, buffalo and giraffes, which seemed unperturbed by the train. They continued along a small highland where a colony of lions slumbered in the sun next to a pack of African wild dogs, and from there down a slope on which shrubs grew.

The passengers screamed in excitement, pointing out the animals. Fabrizio thought he saw monkeys in amongst the vegetation. The train took a wide curve, which slowly carried them back up to thirty metres above the ground. From there, they had a complete view of the park. It was an immense green carpet, with the buildings of the Salario suburb and the Viaduct of the Olimpica only just visible.

In a breathtaking descent, the train slid over a big lake where three house boats were moored. The missile then wedged itself underwater in a jubilation of splashing and screams from the passengers.

Simona was excited. 'I didn't even have this much fun when I went to the Pirate Waterfall at Gardaland.'

The train then turned and headed back towards the turreted building with an Italian-style garden and hedges in geometric designs. There the train slowed suddenly and came to a halt. The doors opened with a puff. Hostesses were standing on the platform, waiting to welcome them with binoculars and leaflets with photos of the animals on the reserve.

'Where are the drinks? I need a bourbon,' Ciba said, stopping himself from expressing all of the profound contempt he felt for Chiatti and that zoo-safari show. Not to mention that little story he had told heavily plagiarised *The Wizard of Oz*. He would let that disdain grow, he would refine it, render it sublime, and then he would detonate it as forcefully as a nuclear bomb in a mega-article in *Repubblica*.

That thought made him feel better. He was still the *enfant terrible*, a writer as acute and cutting as flying shrapnel who would tear that pathetic circus to pieces.

29

At the same time, behind a tool shed, the Wilde Beasts of Abaddon were holding their briefing.

Mantos was seated on a lawnmower.

'Right, disciples, listen carefully.'

He pulled out an old copy of the Rome Streetways. He wet his index finger and began flicking through it.

'This is Villa Ada.' He laid it out on the bonnet and everyone squeezed around. 'We are here, at the Royal Villa. And from what I read on the programme, the three different hunts will start here in about an hour. They will follow three different routes and then each group will end up in a campsite, where they'll have dinner. After they've eaten, all the guests will regroup and there should be the concert with Larita.' He snapped his fingers and grit his teeth. 'What a pity that by then Larita will have been sacrificed. Because we'll kidnap her during the hunt.'

Silvietta raised her hand. 'Can I say something?'

Mantos hated being interrupted while he was explaining a plan of attack. 'Go ahead.'

'I reckon Larita won't take part in the safari. I know her. She's against hunting. She even participated in a campaign.'

Fuck, he hadn't thought of that possibility. Mantos acted as if nothing had happened.

'Good work, Silvietta, this is a hypothesis we need to take into consideration. But we can't be certain. We'll find out. And to do so, we have to be as close to the guests and to Larita as possible. We have to dress up like waiters.'

'Listen, Mantos, there's one thing I don't quite get,' Zombie intervened. 'Who says we'll be able to get her alone during the hunt? There'll be loads of people about.'

This time the leader wasn't caught unprepared. 'Good lad!

You are a good lad! And you know why, Zombie? Because you,' he pointed at him, 'you will be the one who will stop us from getting caught.'

'Me? How?'

'You're an electrician, right?'

Zombie scratched the nape of his neck. 'Well, yeah.'

'Right. At twilight, you'll go to the electricity station, the one we saw on our way in. You'll sneak in and you'll turn the park's electricity off. At that point, without any lighting, taking action will be child's play. Under the cover of shadows, we'll kidnap the bitch. And we'll use this to do it.'

He pulled a small phial containing a transparent liquid out of his backpack.

'This is a really powerful veterinary anaesthetic, Sedaron. They use it for horses. It only take two drops, and you're out of it. This, I found in the workshops.' He showed them a stiff plastic pipe. Then he ripped a page from the street map and rolled it into a cone. He took a pin out of his jacket and stuck it into the tip of the cornet. 'Ladies and gents, here you have a blowpipe. The native Amazonians use this deadly weapon for hunting. At school, I was an ace with the blowpipe. They used to call me El Indio. I'll knock Larita unconscious and then . . .' He showed them the high ground of Forte Antenne on the map. 'We'll carry her here . . . where there are the ruins of an ancient Roman temple. And that's where the sacrifice to Satan will take place.' He looked at them one by one. 'Right. I think I've made it all clear. Are there any questions?'

Zombie raised his hand. 'How am I supposed to cut the wires? With my teeth?'

'Don't worry, there's an answer to that, too. In one of the boxes of cutlery I saw a huge pair of silver poultry shears. You'll use those. Any other questions?'

Murder shyly raised his index finger.

'What's up?'

The adept took a deep breath before speaking. 'You see . . . I was wondering whether you had, by any chance, reconsidered the mass suicide.'

'In what way?'

'I mean . . . Is it really necessary?'

Mantos squeezed his hands into a fist to stop himself from getting angry.

'So you mean it's still not clear? Do you want to spend the rest of your life rotting in jail? I don't. This way, we screw them. They'll never be able to arrest us. We have to sacrifice ourselves to become immortal. Do you or don't you want to become legends?'

'You're right . . .' Murder admitted.

The others silently nodded.

'Excellent. So now we can proceed to phase one of our plan: Silvietta and Murder go pick up some waiter outfits. Zombie, you go look for the poultry shears. I'll . . .'

'Hey! You four. What are you doing?' One of Antonio's men had come up behind him. 'I need a hand. You.' He pointed at Mantos. 'You have to take a case of Merlot di Aprilia to the Villa, quick-smart.'

Mantos whispered to his adepts: 'I'll see you here again in quarter of an hour.'

30

After a thousand doubts about what would be the most effective way to make his entrance, Fabrizio Ciba decided to enter together with Simona Somaini.

A circular piazza stretched out across the centre of the Italian-style garden, with a big hexagonal stone fountain in the middle. Rose petals floated on the surface of the water. Off to the sides Sicilian carts had been set up and filled with everything on God's earth. Ice sculptures depicting angels and fauna melted under the tepid sunshine of a spring day in Rome. Tables had been arranged in a corner. Trained peacocks, pheasants and turkeys wandered amidst the guests. A group of musicians on stilts played baroque arias.

Many of the guests had already arrived. People from show-business, politicians, and the whole Roma football team, whom Chiatti supported passionately.

Fabrizio, arm in arm with Simona, made his way through the crowd. He could feel people watching and envying him. He decided to use again the same attitude as he had during the presentation at Villa Malaparte. Confused and bored, forced for inexplicable reasons to mingle with these people who were so different from him. He saw the hard liquor cart.

'Do you want anything, Simona?'

The actress looked at the bottles of alcohol in horror. 'A big glass of natural mineral water.'

Fabrizio drank a couple of whiskies, one after the other. The alcohol relaxed him. He lit up a cigarette and studied the invited guests as if they were fish in an aquarium. Everyone was watching each other, recognising each other, criticising each other, saying hello to each other with a slight nod of the head, smiling at each other pleased to know that they were all part of a community of God Almighties. Fabrizio couldn't work out, though, if the fact that there was an audience to applaud them unsettled them or made them happy.

Then he realised that off to the side, sitting at a coffee table all alone, was an old man.

No! I don't believe it! He's here, too . . .

Umberto Cruciani, the great writer of *Western Wall* and *Bread and Nails*, the masterpieces of Italian literature written in the seventies.

'Is that . . .?' He was about to ask Simona if she recognised him, too, but then he reconsidered.

What was Cruciani doing there? He had been living in seclusion on a farm in the Oltrepò Pavese for the last twenty years.

The master was staring off in the distance towards the hills, his gaze perplexed beneath his bushy eyebrows. He looked like he wasn't even present, as if a bubble of solitude separated him from the rest of the guests.

'What do you reckon to this party? He's gone all-out. Chiatti is already the winner.'

Fabrizio turned around.

Bocchi was squeezing a huge glass of mojito into his hand. He was already sweaty, purple in the face, and his eyes were feverish.

'Yeah, nice.' The writer kept it short.

'In the end, everyone's here. Do you know how many people said they wouldn't come, not even if they paid them, that it was too kitsch? Not a single one is missing.'

Fabrizio pointed out the old writer to him. 'Even Umberto Cruciani.'

'Who the fuck is he?'

'What do you mean, "Who the fuck is he?"? He is a master. He's up there with Moravia, Calvino, Taburni. Do you realise that forty years after publication his books are still on the bestseller list? I wish *Lion's Den* sold half as much as *Bread and Nails*. I could take it easy, I could even give up writing . . .'

'Has he given up writing?'

'He hasn't published anything since seventy-six. But my agent told me that he's been working on a novel for twenty years that he wants to publish posthumously.'

'He won't have to wait too long.'

'Cruciani belongs to a generation of artists that no longer exists. Hard-working people, bound to their native land, to the farm life, to the rhythm of fields. See how concentrated he is . . . It almost looks like he's trying to find the end of his book.'

The surgeon took a suck on the straw. 'He's taking a shit.'

'What?'

'He's not thinking. He's shitting. You see that Vuitton bag at his feet? It's a fecal collection sack.'

Fabrizio was crushed. 'Poor thing. He's a bit weird, too. He hasn't let anyone see a single comma from his new novel. Not even his editors.'

Bocchi put his hand over his mouth to cover a burp. 'After he dies it will be revealed that he'd written fuck-all, I bet anything you want.'

'He's written . . . he's written . . . Leave him be. Everything he writes, he downloads onto a USB key and then deletes it everywhere else. He's paranoid, he's scared he'll lose it. You see that big gold medal he's wearing round his neck? It's a forty-gig USB stick from Bulgari, he never lets it out of his sight.'

In the meantime, Simona had got herself a plate with one solitary little mozzarella ball.

'You'll never believe how much yummy stuff there is to eat. There's a cart where they're frying artichokes, mozzarelline and pumpkin flowers. Mamma mia, I love fried food. I'd eat it all. It's a pity I can't . . .'

Bocchi picked an ice cube out of his cocktail and rubbed it over his neck as if it was mid-August. 'Why?'

'You're asking me why! I've put on three hundred grams. Can't you see that I'm obese?' The actress showed her perfectly flat and fat-free stomach to the surgeon. 'Can you book me in for lipo?'

'Where's the problem, Simo? The only fat cells you've got left in your body are up there.' He pointed at her skull. And then said seriously: 'I can book you in for some brain liposuction.'

The actress laughed halfheartedly. 'You're always such an idiot.'

The surgeon stood and stretched. 'Whatever. I'm off to take a look around. See you later.'

Fabrizio wrapped his arm around Simona's tiny waist. 'Shall we take a look around, too? What do you say?'

She put her head on his shoulder. 'All right.'

They moved along, following the tide of guests. Fabrizio could smell a delicious perfume coming from the actress's hair and the alcohol made his thoughts feel lighter and his mood lift. People kept stopping them to say hi and pay them compliments. Nobody could deny that they made a splendid couple.

Maybe they're right, I could make Simona my girlfriend.

To be honest, the actress from Subiaco had plenty of strings to her bow. To begin with, she was a total idiot, and Fabrizio loved idiotic women: they drank from his personality like a Friesian at a fountain. The trick was not to listen to them when they started talking about the meaning of life. One of the main flaws of idiotic women is an innate tendency for abstraction, for discussing feelings, personality, life, horoscopes. And in general, they all totally lack practical purpose and irony. Hence they don't criticise everything you do. The day to day, they are manageable. What's more, Mariano Santilli, a film producer who had gone out with Somaini for a year, had told him that in the domestic environment Somaini blended in completely with the furniture. She didn't create any trouble whatsoever. She went into stand-by as soon as she crossed the threshold. All it took was to hand her a remote control and a treadmill, and she would run for hours. She didn't eat, she worked like an animal, and when she wasn't working she was at the gym. And she was the sexiest woman in Italy. Her calendar was hung everywhere. Millions of men wanked themselves to death thinking about her, and they would be envious as hyenas at the idea that he was the lucky one who got to fuck her.

And that's a great feeling.

After all, Arthur Miller had been married to Marilyn Monroe.

'Listen, Simona. What about if we became an item? I reckon we would be *the* couple.'

'You think?' The actress seemed flattered and at the same time disorientated. 'Really? You're so sweet. But I don't know we'd get along . . . We're opposing star signs . . . And then you're a genius, you write books, and I'm a country girl, I don't have anything to say. What would you do with a girl like me?'

'Let me tell you a secret, Simona. Even those writers who seem detached are really nothing more than modern-day story-tellers. They're people who tell stories so that they don't have to work.' Fabrizio pulled her close to him. 'Have you ever been to Majorca?'

Then, out of the corner of his eye, he saw Matteo Saporelli make his entrance.

'They . . .'

The rest of Somaini's words were lost, as if a turbine was blowing wind into his ears. He pulled backwards and touched his forehead.

'I think I've got a temperature,' he stuttered to Simona. 'Excuse me . . . Excuse me just a moment.'

Fabrizio stumbled towards the drinks cart.

I completely fucked up when I decided to come to this fucking party.

In order to comprehend Ciba's reaction, it is important to understand who and especially how old Matteo Saporelli was. Mat, as his friends called him, was twenty-two years old. Half Fabrizio's age. He was the real, true young talent of Italian literature. He had come out of nowhere with his novel *The Misfortunes of a Man with Good Taste,* the story of a chef who one day awakens to discover that he has lost his sense of flavour, but keeps on cooking by tricking everyone. The book had climbed to the top of the bestseller lists with the same impact that the Space Shuttle enters the ionosphere, and there it had stayed. In one year alone, the young man had managed to win the grand slam: Strega, Campiello and Viareggio prizes.

Fabrizio couldn't open a newspaper, or change channels, without Saporelli's obnoxious little nipper face popping up. Wherever there was a question to be answered, an opinion to be given, he was there. The problem of castrating cats in Trastevere? The third lane on the Salerno to Reggio Calabria toll road? The use of cortisone in the treatment of anal fissures? He had the answer ready. But the thing that really made Ciba suffer was that the women drooled over him. They said he looked like a young Rupert Everett. To top it off, Saporelli was published by Fabrizio's own publishing house, Martinelli. And in the last few years he had kicked Ciba's arse, as far as sales were concerned.

He had been told that Saporelli's copy editor (who also happened to be Fabrizio's copy editor) had given him a blow job in the toilets of the Ninfeo of Villa Giulia to celebrate his winning the Strega Prize.

What a slut. She's never given me one. Not even when I won the Prix Médicis in France. Which is a thousand times better.

He stared him down. With his pressed jeans, his moccasins, the white shirt, a sweater knotted over his shoulders and his hands in his pockets, he wanted to look like a typical good boy, modest and undemanding. Someone who hadn't gotten a big head.

What a hypocrite! That devious creature made him sick to his stomach.

But you won't get the better of me. I look forward to seeing you with your next novel.

Fabrizio was so concentrated on being disgusted that it took him a while to realise that Saporelli was talking to Federico Gianni. The managing director of Martinelli gave the young writer a slap on the back and they started pissing themselves laughing.

They're as thick as thieves.

He was reminded of the words that Gianni, that fake, had said at the Indian's presentation. He saw that the two men had been joined by that old gasbag Tremagli and his wife, a troll with tits. Naturally, the literary critic had climbed over himself to praise Saporelli's novel. 'Italian literature takes flight again on the wings of Saporelli', he had had the courage to write.

Fabrizio necked another glass of scotch.

The moment had come to face Gianni. He began to warm up, thinking of the great Muhammad Ali. He took two steps, but then stopped suddenly. What the hell was he doing?

Rule number one: never let them see your envy.

It was much more effective to hit the road, taking the hottest woman at the party with him. He sidled alongside to Simona Somaini, who was at the centre of attention for a group of actors from the series *Crimes in Wheelchairs*.

'Sorry, everyone. I need to steal her for a second,' he said, smiling with gritted teeth. Then he took the actress by the wrist and, purple-faced, he whispered to her: 'I have to talk to you. It's important.'

She seemed a little annoyed. 'What is it, Fabrizio?'

'Listen to me. Let's get out of here. There's a plane leaving for the Baleari soon . . .'

'The Baleari?'

'Oh, right. Well . . . They're Spanish islands in the sea. On Majorca, one of the Balearic Islands, I have a house hidden in the mountains. A love nest. Let's go straight away. If we move quickly, we'll be able to make the flight.'

The actress was looking at him, perplexed. 'But we're at a party now. Why do we have to leave? It's fantastic. Everyone's here.'

He took her by the arm and bent down as if he was going to tell her a big secret.

'That's exactly why, Simona! We can't be where everyone is. We are special. We are *the couple*. We can't be confused with the others. People will notice us a thousand times more if we leave.'

Simona wasn't really convinced. 'You reckon?'

'Listen to me. It's not that hard to underst . . .'

But the words died on the tip of his tongue. Simona Somaini was undergoing a somatic transformation. Her hair was puffing up, becoming shinier and lighter, like in a TV ad for hair conditioner. Her tits were climbing up her chest as if annoyed by the useless dress covering her body. She was staring straight in front of her like she was watching the Messiah walking on the water of the fountain. Then she laid her eyes once again on Fabrizio and sniffed. She was moved to tears.

'I don't believe it! That's . . . That's Matteo Saporelli . . . Oh my God . . . Tell me you know him, please . . . Of course you know him, you're both writers. I love him, and I have to speak to him right now. Morin is making a film from his novel.'

Fabrizio took two steps backwards, horrified, as if he was facing someone possessed by the Devil. If he'd had some holy water in hand, he would have thrown it at her. 'You are a monster! I don't ever want to see you again.' With large steps, he crossed the courtyard and the Italian-style garden, and practically ran to the station.

The train wasn't there.

He went up to a hostess. 'Where is it? When will it arrive?' The hostess looked at her watch. 'In about a quarter of an hour.'

'That long? Isn't there any other way to get out of here?'

'On foot. But I wouldn't recommend it, it's full of wild animals.'

A waiter ran up to him. Before he spoke, he caught his breath. 'Mr Ciba! Mr Ciba! I'm sorry, Dr Chiatti would like to speak with you. Could you follow me, please?'

31

Zombie took a look around and moved over towards some wooden cases that held the silverware for the camps. He began reading the labels on the covers. *Fork . . . Fork . . . Knife . . . Knife . . . Spoon.*

'These are all cutlery.'

He went to another pile of containers. He opened a lid and

wrapped in a blue velvet cloth he found the silver poultry shears. They were so big, they looked like ostrich shears. He picked them up and went back to the shed happy.

Murder and Silvietta were behind the camp toilet, getting into their waiter uniforms.

'Guys, I found . . .' he said, and then fell silent.

The two of them, while they got dressed, were having an argument. Actually, it seemed they were really fighting. They were so caught up that they didn't even notice him. Zombie moved closer slowly, without giving himself away, and he hid behind the Land-Rover to hear better.

'You suck! You didn't tell him, again,' Silvietta was saying.

'I know . . . But I told him a little bit. It's just that I got stuck. This is not an easy situation, you know,' Murder huffed.

'Sure, that's why you were supposed to tell him this morning in Oriolo. Then you said you'd tell him in the car . . . And now what are we supposed to do?'

Murder stiffened, visibly annoyed. 'Excuse me, but why don't you tell him? I don't get why I have to be the one to tell him.'

'Are you mental? You were the one who told me that it was best if you spoke to him. That you've known Saverio for ages and you know how to handle him.'

He sweetened his voice. 'It's just not easy, honey bun. It's delicate stuff, you know that even better than I do.'

The Beast heard Silvietta snort. 'How hard can it be? You go and you say to him: "Listen, we're sorry, but Silvietta and I have decided to get married, so we can't commit suicide." Full stop. Does it sound hard to you?'

The poultry shears fell out of Zombie's hand.

In the former residence of the Royal Family, Mantos, with a case of wine in his arms, walked through the service entrance and found himself in the living room. His mouth dropped. No comparison with that crap from the Furniture Store of the Thyrolean Masters of the Axe. The mix between antique and modern was of very fine taste. This was what he was talking about when, during the brainstorming sessions with old Mastrodomenico, he tried to soften his roughness and bring him closer to the world of interior decoration. He walked through a vestibule and found himself in a studio full of super-tall bookcases.

All of the volumes had been covered in packing paper and the titles written in beautiful handwriting. The effect was that of a light-brown room. In the middle of the room was a single block of solid wood, so big that it had to be from a baobab or a redwood. Atop, a black telephone.

He looked at it.

Don't do it.

He put down the case and picked up the receiver.

I'm about to fuck-up big-time.

It didn't matter. Before throwing himself into this suicide mission, he had to hear his wife's voice one more time.

Holding his breath, he dialled Serena's mobile number.

'Honey . . . It's me . . .'

The answer was: 'Where the fuck are you?'

'Darling, wait . . . Let me explain . . .'

'What have you got to explain? That you're a poor old fuckwit?' Serena attacked him.

Saverio sat down on the armchair. He leaned his elbows on the table.

She had forgotten everything. As if the events of the night before had never happened. She had gone back to being Cruel Serena.

Who knows what I was expecting? That she would change?

No one changes. And Serena was exactly the way she was when she was born. The mirage that over time she would soften had trapped him in a marriage with a witch. This perverse mechanism had kept them tied together. And she had taken advantage of it, making him feel like a gutless halfwit.

With a lump in his throat, he held the receiver away from his ear; but even so, he could still hear her barking.

'Have you lost your fucking mind? I've been calling your mobile for hours. Papa is going mad. He wants to sack you. Today is the first day of Kids' Bedroom Week. There are two thousand kids here, screaming their heads off. And where are you? With those four imbeciles. As God is my witness, I'll make you pay dearly for this . . .'

Saverio was looking out the window. A robin redbreast was cleaning its feathers as it sat on a cherry tree. The image went out of focus, hidden by his tears.

To gain that woman's respect, he'd have to rape her every night. Kick her like a dog. But that was not his idea of love.

At least now I know I've made the right choice.

A strange feeling of calm took hold of Saverio. He felt peaceful. He had no more doubts.

He put the receiver near his mouth. 'Serena, listen to me carefully. I have always loved you. I have tried to make you happy, but you are a bad person, and you make everything around you turn bad.'

Serena's voice was husky, as if possessed. 'How dare you! Where the hell are you? I'm gonna come and get you and punch your face in. Saverio, I swear on my father's head, I'll do it.'

The leader of the Wilde Beasts of Abaddon filled his ribcage with air, and in a clear voice said: 'My name is not Saverio, it's Mantos.' And then he hung up.

'What the hell are you doing here? Who told you to get the poultry shears?'

Zombie didn't have time to turn around and understand, before he was grabbed by the ear and dragged into the middle of the courtyard. He began to scream in an attempt to free himself of that vice-like grip. Out of the corner of his eye, he could see Antonio crushing his auricle.

The veins on the head waiter's neck were puffed and his eyes bloodshot as he spluttered and screamed at Murder and Silvietta: 'Hey! Hey! You two! Why are you dressed like waiters?'

Zombie managed to free himself and rubbed his burning ear.

'You must be out of your minds. Did you by chance think you were at the town festival for the common whitefish at Capodimonte? I'll set you straight.' Antonio shoved Murder. 'Tell me why you're dressed as waiters.'

'We thought we could make ourselves useful. There's not much to do here . . .' Murder suggested.

Antonio got to within an inch of his nose. His breath smelt of menthol.

'"Useful"? Do you think this is a game? And what game would that be? Statues? Tig? You have just come along and decided you wanted to be waiters? You muck around and I lose my job. Have you not understood where we are? In there, are waiters from Harry's Bar, from Hotel de Russie, people who studied hospitality. I turned down people from the Caffè Greco.' Antonio was blue in the face. He had to stop for a second to regain his breath. 'Now, you'll do the right thing. Take off those clothes and get out of here. I won't pay you a lira and that dickhead Saverio will get out of here along with you! Never trust your relatives. Speaking of Saverio, where is that . . .?'

155

Antonio slapped his neck like he'd been bitten by a horsefly. He ripped something off of his neck just above the collar and opened his hand.

In his palm he found a paper cone with a pin at the tip.

'But what . . .?' was all he managed to say, then his eyeballs rolled back in his head, showing the white sclera, and his mouth was paralysed in a sneer. He took one step backwards and, stiff as a statue, fell to the ground.

The Beasts looked at him in astonishment, then Mantos and his blowpipe appeared from a bush.

'He was being a pain in the arse, eh? You can't imagine how much of pain he was at school . . .'

Murder gave his boss a high five. 'You knocked him out. That Sedaron stuff is the bomb.'

'I told you. Well done, Zombie, you found the poultry shears.'

'And him?' Silvietta bent down over Antonio's body. 'What will we do with him?'

'We'll tie and gag him. And then we'll hide him somewhere.'

32

As he followed the waiter towards the Royal Villa, Fabrizio cursed to himself. He didn't have time to waste. He had a plane to catch, and the idea that he had to speak to Sasà Chiatti bothered him. It was ridiculous. He'd been in the presence of Sarwar Sawhney, a Noble Prize winner, without feeling any sort of particular emotions, and now that he was about to meet an insignificant fellow like Chiatti his heart was racing? The truth was that rich and powerful men made him feel insecure.

He walked into the Villa and was surprised. He had expected

anything except that the residence would be furnished in minimalist style. The big living area was a simple cement floor. In a fireplace made of uncut stone burned a big block of wood. Nearby, four armchairs in seventies style and a ten-metre-long solid-steel table with an antique lampshade hanging overhead. Two thin Giacometti statues. In another corner, as if they had been forgotten, were four Fontana eggs, and on the whitewashed walls some Cretti by Burri.

'This way . . .' The waiter pointed towards a long corridor. He led him into a kitchen covered in Morrocan majolicas. A Bang & Olufsen stereo was playing the romantic notes of Michael Nyman's *The Piano*.

A big stocky woman, with a mahogany-coloured helmet of hair, was juggling saucepans over the stove. In the centre of the room, sitting around a rough wooden table, were Salvatore Chiatti, an albino sylph, a decrepit old man wearing a moth-eaten old colonial outfit, a monk and Larita the singer.

They were eating what appeared to be *rigatoni all'amatriciana*, with heaps of pecorino cheese grated over the top.

Fabrizio had the presence of mind to say: 'Hello, everyone.'

Chiatti was wearing a beige velvet jacket with patches on the elbows, a checked flannel shirt and a red handkerchief tied around that limited the length of neck that nature had granted him. He wiped his mouth and threw his arms open as if he had known Fabrizio for a hundred years.

'Here he is, that wonderful writer! What a pleasure to have you here. Please join us. We're eating something simple. I hope you didn't eat anything from the buffet? We'll leave that junk for the VIP guests, right, Mum?'

He turned towards the barge-arse at the stove. The woman, feeling awkward, cleaned her hands on her apron and nodded hello.

157

'We're simple people. And we eat pasta. Take a seat. What are you waiting for?'

Fabrizio's first impression of Chiatti was that he was affable, with a big jovial smile; but he was also aware that he was giving orders, and he didn't like being disobeyed.

The writer pulled up a chair from next to the wall and sat in a corner between the old man and the monk, who made room for him.

'Mum, fill a plate as God commands for Mr Ciba. He looks a little ruffled to me.'

A second later Fabrizio found a gigantic serving of smoking rigatoni in front of him.

Chiatti grabbed a flask of wine and poured Ciba a glass.

'Let's get the introductions out of the way. He . . .' He pointed at the shrivelled old guy. ' . . . is the great white hunter, Corman Sullivan. Did you know that this man met the writer . . . what's his name?'

'Hemingway . . .' said Sullivan, and began coughing and shaking all over. Clouds of dust rose up from his clothes. When he recovered, he squeezed Fabrizio's hand weakly. He had long fingers, covered in depigmented spots.

The white hunter reminded Ciba of someone. Of course! He was the spitting image of Ötzi, the Similaun Man, the hunter found frozen in a glacier of the Alps.

Chiatti pointed at the sylph. 'This is my girlfriend, Ecaterina.' The girl tilted her head, in greeting. She looked like the Snow Queen in a Scandinavian saga. She was so white she looked as if she'd been dead for three days. Through her skin you could see the blood running dark in her veins. Her hair, fiery red, was a mane around her flat face. She didn't have eyebrows and her throat was as thin as a greyhound's. She must have weighed about twenty kilos.

When Fabrizio heard her name, he remembered. She was the famous albino model Ecaterina Danielsson. She was on the covers of fashion magazines the world over. She was undoubtedly the most morphologically different human being compared to Chiatti that nature had ever created.

'And this here . . .' He pointed at the monk. 'You should recognise him. It's Zóltan Patrovic!'

Of course Fabrizio recognised him. Who didn't know the unpredictable Bulgarian chef, owner of the restaurant Le Regioni? But he'd never seen him up close.

Who did he remind him of? Yes, Mefisto, Tex Willer's sworn enemy.

Fabrizio had to lower his gaze. The chef's eyes seemed to sink inside him and sneak into his thoughts.

'And last but not least, our Larita, who will do us the great honour of singing for us this evening.'

Finally Ciba found himself looking at a human being.

She's pretty, he said to himself as he shook her hand.

Chiatti pointed at Ciba: 'And do you all know who he is?'

Fabrizio was about to say that he was nobody, when Larita smiled, showing her slightly separated incisors, and said: 'He's the greatest. He wrote *The Lion's Den*. I loved it. But my favourite is *Nestor's Dream*. I've read it three times. And each time I cried like a little girl.'

A dart had hit a bullseye in the middle of Fabrizio's chest. His legs, for an instant, gave way, and he almost collapsed on the Similaun man's shoulder.

Finally, someone who understood him. That was his best work. He'd squeezed himself like a lemon to finish it. Every single word, every comma, had been painstakingly extracted from him. Whenever he thought of *Nestor's Dream*, an image came to mind. It was as if an aeroplane had exploded in flight

159

and the remains of the aircraft had been spread across a radius of thousands of kilometres over a flat and sterile desert. It was up to him to find the pieces and put the aircraft's fuselage back together. The complete opposite of *The Lion's Den*, which had come out painlessly, as if it had written itself. He was convinced that *Nestor's Dream* was his most mature and complete work. And yet its reception by his readers had been, to put it mildly, lukewarm, and the critics had torn him to shreds. So when he heard the singer say those things, he couldn't help but feel a deep sense of gratitude.

'That's very kind of you. I'm pleased to hear that. Thanks,' he said to her, feeling almost embarrassed.

If you walked past Larita in the street, you would hardly notice her, but if you looked at her carefully you would see that she was very pretty. Each part of her body was well proportioned. Her neck, her shoulders neither too wide nor too narrow, her thin wrists, her slim, elegant hands. Her black bob hid her forehead. Her small nose and that mouth – just a tad too wide for her oval-shaped face – expressed a shy, sincere likeability. But what stood out were her big, hazelnut-colored eyes, with gold flecks that in the moment seemed a little lost.

How weird that, between parties, presentations, concerts and salons, Ciba had met just about everyone, and yet not once had he come across this singer. He had read somewhere that she kept to herself and minded her own business. She didn't enjoy the spotlight.

A bit like me.

Fabrizio had also appreciated the story of her religious conversion. He, too, had felt a strong calling back to his faith. Larita was a thousand times better than that hopeless gang of Italian singers. She stayed at home in a house in the Tuscan–Emilian Appenine mountains and created . . .

Just like I should do.

The same old vision materialised in his mind. The two of them together in a wooden hut. She would play and he would write. Minding their own business. Perhaps a child. Definitely a dog.

Larita flicked her fringe. 'There's no reason to thank me. If something is beautiful, it's beautiful, full stop.'

I'm an idiot. I was about to leave and the love of my life is here.

Chiatti applauded, amused. 'Well. See what a beautiful fan I found for you? Now, to thank me you'll do me a favour. Have you got a poem?'

Fabrizio frowned. 'What do you mean?'

'A poem, to read before my speech. I'd like to be introduced by one of your poems.'

Larita came to his aid. 'He doesn't write poetry, as far as I know.'

Fabrizio smiled at her, then turned to Chiatti seriously: 'Exactly. I have never written a poem in my whole life.'

'Couldn't you write just one? Even a short one?' The entrepreneur looked at his Rolex. 'Can't you jot one down in twenty minutes? It'd only have to be a couple of lines.'

'A little poem about hunters would be wonderful. I recall Karen Blixen . . .' Corman Sullivan stepped in, but was unable to continue as he was overcome with a coughing fit.

'No. I'm sorry. I don't write poems.'

Chiatti flared his nostrils and made a fist, but his voice remained polite. 'All right, I have an idea. You could read someone else's poem. I should have a copy of Pablo Neruda's poetry here somewhere. Would that work for you?'

'Why should I read a poem by another author? There are hundreds of actors out there who would slaughter each other for a chance to do it. Get one of them to read it.' Fabrizio was beginning to get just a bit pissed off.

Zóltan Patrovic suddenly tapped his glass with a knife.

Fabrizio turned around and was captured by his magnetic gaze. What a singular sensation: it seemed as if the chef's eyes had expanded and were now covering his whole face. Beneath the black hood it was like two enormous ocular globes were staring at him. Fabrizio tried to look away, but was unable to. So he tried to close his eyes and break the spell, but failed again.

Zóltan placed his hand on the writer's forehead.

Instantly, as if someone had pushed it forcefully into his memory, Fabrizio was reminded of a forgotten episode from his childhood. His parents, in summer, were leaving on a sailing boat, and they left him with cousin Anna in a mountain cottage at Bad Sankt Leonhard, in Carinthia, with a family of Austrian farmers. It was a beautiful area, with pine-covered mountains and green fields where piebald cows grazed happily. He wore the typical leather shorts, with braces, and ankle boots with red laces. One day, while he and Anna were hunting for mushrooms in the forest, they had got lost. They were unable to remember where to go. They had kept walking around and around, hand in hand, their fear growing as the night stretched out its tentacles between the identical-looking trees. Luckily, at some point, they had found themselves standing in front of a little chalet hidden amidst the pine trees. Smoke was coming from the chimney and the windows were lit. They knocked and a woman with a blonde chignon sat them down at a table, along with her three children, and gave them Knödel, big balls of bread and meat floating in broth, to eat. Mamma mia, they were so soft and delicious!

Fabrizio realised that he desired nothing more in life than a couple of Knödel in broth. After all, it didn't cost him anything to say yes to Chiatti, and later he could always find an Austrian restaurant.

'Okay, I'll read it. No problem. I beg your pardon, but do you know whether there is an Austrian restaurant near here somewhere?'

33

Antonio's head bounced on each step and the muffled sound echoed against the vaulted ceiling of the staircase that disappeared into the bowels of the earth. Murder and Zombie dragged the head waiter by his ankles.

The leader of the Beasts, at the head of the gang, shone an electric torch on the walls of the tunnel carved in the tuff rock. Greenish mould and spider webs were all they saw. The air was humid and smelled of wet dirt.

Mantos didn't have the vaguest idea where the stairway led. He had opened an old door and slipped in before anyone could see them.

Silvietta stopped to look at Antonio. 'Guys, won't all those bangs to the head hurt him?'

Saverio turned to her. 'He's hard-headed. We're almost there.'

Murder was tired. 'Thank goodness! We've been going down for ages. It's like a mine.'

In the end they came to a cave. Zombie turned on two torches screwed to the walls, and a part of the room brightened.

It wasn't a cave, but a long room with a low ceiling and rows of rotten barrels and piles of dusty bottles. On each side of the room a rusty grating closed off a narrow tunnel that led who knows where.

'This place is perfect for a Satanic ritual.' Murder lifted a bottle and dusted off the label: 'Amarone 1943.'

'They must be the royal cellars,' Silvietta suggested.

'You don't perform Satanic rituals in a cellar. At most, in a deconsecrated church or in the open air. In any case, by the light of the moon.' Mantos pointed at a corner underneath the torches: 'Come on, let's dump my cousin and get out of here. We don't have time to waste.'

Zombie, off to one side, was studying a grate. Silvietta went up to him. 'That's weird! Four identical tunnels.' She stuck her hand through the bars. 'I can feel warm air. I wonder where it comes from?'

Zombie shrugged. 'Who cares?'

'You reckon it's safe to leave him here? He won't wake up again, will he?'

'I don't know . . . And I don't really care that much either.' Zombie walked away stiffly.

Silvietta looked after him, feeling perplexed. 'What's your problem? Are you pissed off?'

Zombie started walking up the stairs without answering.

Mantos followed him. 'Let's move.'

The Beasts had climbed one hundred steps when they heard a muffled noise coming from below. Murder stopped. 'What was that?'

'Antonio must have woken up,' said Silvietta.

Mantos shook his head. 'Not likely. He'll sleep a couple of hours, at least. Sedaron is strong stuff.'

And they kept climbing.

If, instead, they had gone back down, they would have found Antonio Zauli's body missing.

Speech by Salvatore Chiatti to the Guests

34

Fabrizio Ciba, the book of poems by Neruda in his pocket, was walking in circles behind a bandwagon that had been transformed into a stage for the occasion. They had put a microphone on him and explained that in a few minutes he would go up and read the poem. He couldn't work out why he'd accepted. He turned down everyone. Even the most aggressive press officers. Even political leaders. Even the advertising executives that promised him a pile of cash.

What the fuck had come over him? It was like someone had forced him to accept. And what's more, Pablo Neruda made him sick.

'Are you ready?'

Fabrizio turned around.

Larita was walking up to him, holding a cup of coffee in her hand. She had a smile that made you want to hug her.

'No. Not at all,' he admitted, feeling distressed.

She began scraping at the sugar stuck to the bottom of the cup and, without looking at him, confessed: 'Once I came to Rome to hear you read excerpts from *The Lion's Den* at the Basilica di Massenzio.'

Fabrizio didn't expect that. 'Why didn't you come to say hi?'

'We'd never met. I'm shy, and there was a huge queue of people wanting your autograph.'

'Well, that was a bad decision. This is serious.'

Larita laughed, moving closer. 'Do you want to know

something? I don't like these sorts of parties. I would never have come, if Chiatti hadn't offered me so much money. You know,' the singer continued, 'with the money I want to lay the foundations for a sanctuary for cetaceans near Maccarese.'

Fabrizio was caught off-guard and took a weak stab. 'It would have been a bad decision not to come, because we never would have met.'

She began playing with the coffee cup. 'That's true.'

'Listen, have you ever been to Majorca?'

Larita was shocked. 'I can't believe you're asking me that. Do you know Escorca, on the north of the island?'

'It's near my house.'

'I'll be spending six months there to record my new album.'

Fabrizio put his hand over his mouth, feeling excited. 'I've got a country house in Capdepera . . . !'

Bad luck would have it that, at that moment, the guy who had microphoned him appeared. 'Doctor Ciba, you need to go on stage. It's your turn.'

'One second,' Fabrizio said, gesturing to him to stay back. Then he laid a hand on Larita's arm. 'Listen, promise me something.'

'What?'

He looked her straight in the eyes. 'At these parties everyone plays a part, people only just brush against each other. That hasn't happened to us. You said before that you liked *Nestor's Dream*. Now you tell me you're going to Majorca, where I will go to write and find some peace. You have to promise me that we'll see each other again.'

'I'm sorry, Doctor Ciba, you really need to get up there.'

Fabrizio stared daggers at the guy and then turned to Larita: 'Can you promise me that?'

Larita nodded. 'Okay. I promise.'

'Wait for me here . . . I'll go, look like a dickhead, then come back.'

Fabrizio, elated, went up the stairs that led to the bandwagon, without turning to look at her. He found himself on a small stage, opposite the courtyard with the Italian-style garden packed full of guests.

Ciba waved to the crowd, ran his fingers through his hair, smiled slightly, pulled out the book of poems and was just about to read when he saw Larita making her way through the crowd and moving closer to the stage. His mouth suddenly went dry. He felt as if he'd gone back to the days of high-school recitals. He put the book back and said bashfully: 'I had planned on reading you a poem by the great Pablo Neruda, but I've decided to recite one of my own.' Pause. 'I dedicate it to the princess who doesn't break promises.' And he began reciting:

My belly will be the coffer
where I will hide you from the world.
I will fill my veins
with your beauty.
I will make my breast the cage
for your sorrows.
I shall love you as the clownfish loves the sea anemone.
I shall sing your name here, now, at once.
And I shall spruik your sweetness amidst the deaf
and I shall paint your beauty amidst the blind.

There was a moment of silence, and then people starting clapping uproariously. He heard a few shouting, 'Bravo, Ciba!', 'You really are a poet!', 'You're better than Ungaretti!'

Larita clapped her hands and smiled at him.

Fabrizio lowered his head, gestured to them to stop, as a shy modest person would do, while the real-estate magnate got up on stage and lifted his arms, spurring on the public. The audience was beginning to lose the skin on their hands. The only thing missing was a Mexican wave.

'Thanks, Fabri. I couldn't have asked for a better introduction.' Chiatti embraced him like they were old friends and pushed him off the stage.

The writer stepped down with his heart beating loudly and the certainty of having done everything wrong.

I overdid it with the poem. Larita will think it was a piece of shit. I love you like the clownfish loves the anemone. Blind people . . . deaf people . . . Oh Lord!

And then, if he was completely honest, that poem wasn't even original. He had re-elaborated in his way, terribly, a poem by the Lebanese poet Kahlil Gibran, which he had learned off by heart when he was sixteen years old, during ski week, to win over a waitress from Bormio.

I've ruined everything.

He had seen her applauding, but, as everyone knows, why begrudge anyone a little clap?

And tomorrow that arsehole Tremagli will write an article in Il Messaggero *saying that I plagiarised Gibran. They'll compare my poem and the real one.*

He had to drink something to try to calm down before Larita returned. He went to the hard liquor cart and had them pour him a double Jim Beam.

Sasà Chiatti, on stage, was boasting about the capital he had spent to fix up the Villa. The crowd applauded him regularly every two minutes.

'Fabrizio . . . Fabrizio . . .'

He turned around, convinced it was Larita, and instead he found Cristina Lotto.

*   *   *

Cristina Lotto was thirty-six years old and the wife of Ettore Gelati, owner of a mineral water consortium and a number of pharmaceutical companies spread across the globe. They had two teenage children, Samuel and Ifigenia, who attended a boarding school in Switzerland.

Cristina hosted a do-it-yourself programme on a satellite channel. She taught viewers how to put together original centre-pieces with driftwood, and how to crochet colourful toilet-seat covers.

She was a bony blonde with long, toned legs, a tight bum and a pair of small balloon-shaped tits covered in freckles. She had the face of girl from a good family, educated at a school run by nuns. High, freckled cheekbones and blue eyes framed by straight golden hair. A thin-lipped mouth and a pointy chin.

Cristina was, undoubtedly, a beautiful woman, with an athletic body. She always wore skirts, angora cardigans and pearl necklaces, and had a whiny voice that didn't convey any sort of sensuality. She was as sexy as a lettuce leaf without any dressing. That had not stopped Ciba from shagging her a few times a month for the last two years. His motives? They were obscure to him, too. It definitely had something to do with the fact that she was the wife of a man who thought he was the boss of the world. The childish idea that, while the businessman was working as hard as a copper pot to become the richest man in Italy, Fabrizio was fucking his wife excited and amused him at the same time. He loved it when Cristina, after inter-course, laid her head on his chest and told him about how much of a puffed-up balloon Mr Gelati was, with his passion for hang-gliding and his claims to nobility. Or when Cristina went on about, with a certain amount of irony, the frustrations of living in the shadow of an insensitive and self-important man. Fabrizio got her to expound all the shabby details, which

169

then transformed this owner of the universe into a poor and miserable man.

There was another element not to be underestimated either. Fabrizio lived in his house in Via Mecenate, which was falling into disrepair, and fed himself exclusively in restaurants. The Gelati family, meanwhile, owned a five-hundred-square-metre penthouse over Piazza Navona, with a white marble bathroom that resembled the Ara Pacis and a fridge as big as a treasure chest full of fresh oysters, Serrano ham and specialities from around the world. Cristina was always on her own, and when Fabrizio felt like relaxing he'd go over to her house. He dipped into the heated pool, watched football matches in the cinema room, and got her to make him nifty little meals.

'Cristina?' Ciba asked in surprise. She never spoke to him in public. She made sure she avoided him, terrified at the thought of someone seeing them together. The boss of the world's wrath, if he ever found out about their relationship, could be as violent and destructive as that of a Babylonian god.

Cristina, for the occasion, was wearing a black tube dress with a low-cut back that came down to her buttocks, and a hat with a veil. She was distraught.

'Fabrizio! I have to speak to you . . .'

The writer felt a wave of nausea hit him. 'What's happened?'

'Something terrible . . .'

35

A pianist played the melody from the film *Out of Africa*. Sasà Chiatti, centre-stage, asked the public for a moment of silence. 'Please, give a warm welcome to Corman Sullivan . . .'

Two black models came onto the stage, arm in arm with the old hunter.

Silvietta put down the tray with the salmon tarts and began clapping along with the rest of the guests.

Maybe it's the Dalai Lama.

The Beasts' Vestal was excited. She would never have imagined in her whole life that she would take part in such an exclusive party. She was convinced that not even in Hollywood did they throw parties like this one. Wherever you laid your eyes, a VIP came into view. Not that she loved VIPs that much, but when you saw them up close they did make a bit of an impression on you. And then she'd just heard Fabrizio Ciba reading such a sweet love poem that she had been moved to tears . . . He had to be a really special person. So shy and introverted. Maybe she could ask him for his autograph. One of his poems would have been perfect on their wedding invitations. She could try to ask him. He looked like someone whose head hadn't swelled too much, despite his success.

Silvietta said to herself that this party could help her to find some original ideas for her wedding reception. Those ice sculptures, for example, couldn't be that hard to make. And the peacocks and turkeys moving around amongst the guests was a nice idea. And the carts with the food on them. But the thing that drove her crazy the most was the old Apecar that gave out ice creams and ices.

We'll never have enough to pay for all these things.

Murder asked for a bank loan to pay for the wedding. Twenty thousand euro, which barely covered the cost of hiring the Vecchio Cantinone at Vetralla, and pay for the catering service and the flowers for the church.

It will be simple but it'll be pretty.

She could see Zombie walking like a ghost amongst the

guests, with a plate of sandwich triangles in hand. He wasn't even trying to be a waiter.

It's a pity he'll be dead when we get married.

The fact that he wouldn't be at their wedding made her too sad. He was her best friend, her muffin, and she had hoped he would be her best man. She looked at him carefully. He looked like shit. As if he'd been run over by a tram. Maybe he didn't want to commit suicide either. If that was the case, she had to talk to him.

She dumped the tray of tarts and ran over to Zombie, who had sat down at a table and was drinking Prosecco.

'Muffin, what's the matter?'

He glanced at her absentmindedly.

Silvietta knelt down in front of him and took his hand. 'Hey, what's up? You're acting weird.'

He shook himself free: 'I heard you.'

Her stomach lurched and she stuttered: 'What? What are you talking about?'

'I heard you. You two are getting married. You didn't even tell me.'

'I wanted to tell you, but I . . .' Silvietta couldn't say any more..

'Well? How long have you been working on the preparations? What were you waiting for? Have you put us on the guest list? Cross us off, anyway, because we won't be coming.'

'Listen, why don't we all just pack it in?'

Zombie picked up another wine goblet. 'Pack it in? Are you out of your mind? Maybe you two think this is a game, that we came to this party to play at being Satanists. But you're wrong. Here, we are going all the way. I will never abandon Mantos. He gave meaning to our lives, he showed us how hypocritical this fucked-up society is. He showed us the Way

172

to Evil. He taught us to channel our hate. Mantos has left his wife, kids and furniture shop, and decided to sacrifice himself to turn us into Italy's number one sect. And you betray him like that?' He stood up and finished the Prosecco in one mouthful. 'Do whatever the fuck you want, but just remember that my last thought upon dying will be aimed at you two. The two biggest villains I've ever met in my whole life.'

And he walked away.

Silvietta collapsed and burst into tears.

36

'What's the matter, what happened?' Fabrizio Ciba was following Cristina Lotto through the crowd, and in the meantime was searching for Larita. But it was hard to find her with all the bedlam.

'Don't talk to me. Just follow me. My husband might see us,' the woman said, talking with her head lowered. 'Let's go inside.'

They nipped behind the buffet carts and walked into the Villa.

Cristina kept looking around. The guests had invaded the living room, too. 'Where would a bathroom be?'

For a second the writer thought that this was a ruse, so they could have a quickie in the loo. But she was too shaken. Also Cristina, even though she was an old nymphomaniac, had always been very careful to plan their trysts. It was for that very reason that Fabrizio had kept meeting her. She would never kick up a stink, she cared deeply about her family, and risked much more than he did if they were ever discovered.

'Listen, can't we discuss this tomorrow? I'm a little busy just now.'

'No.' Cristina opened a door. 'Here it is.'

The bathroom was a big room of seventy square metres. It was covered in staves of oak and wooden beams, worse than a chalet in Cortina. Even in here were crowds of guests who laughed and chatted, with their purple faces and ties. Women fixed their make-up in front of the mirrors. A queue to get into the toilets, where there was definitely something being sniffed, snaked between the columns. There was a feeling of excitement that was totally out of the ordinary for a typical Roman party.

Two fellows in tuxedos were chatting at the tops of their voices.

'I bought a trullo in Piedmont.'

'I didn't realise they had trullos in Piedmont.'

'Yes. They're original. They take them to pieces brick by brick in Puglia and put them back together again near Alessandria. There's a proper residential village of trullos.'

'Do they cost much?'

'Let me see . . . No. Not much at all.'

Cristina put her mouth to Fabrizio's ear. 'Here's no good. Follow me.'

They found a small room, with simple furnishings. It might have been the bedroom of a housemaid. Cristina locked the door and sat down on the bed.

Fabrizio lit a cigarette. 'Will you please tell me what happened?'

She took off her hat. 'Samuel caught us.'

'Who the fuck is Samuel?'

'My son. He caught us.'

Fabrizio didn't understand. 'What do you mean?'

'He caught us . . .' Cristina took a deep breath like she was having trouble breathing. 'While we were making love in the kitchen.'

'Fuck!' Fabrizio sat down on the bed, too.

And if the kid told Gelati about it? He bet his life that that piece of shit would cover everything up before he let word get out that he'd been cheated on. In one way, it would be better that way. The relationship had to end. He wouldn't even need to invent a fake story to break it off. And anyway, now his mind was working like a guided missile that has a single target it must hit: Larita, and their moving to Majorca.

Fabrizio put his hands in his hair, trying to look dismayed. 'Bloody hell . . . I'm really sorry . . . Poor thing, he must be in shock.'

Cristina smiled with tight lips. 'In shock? Him? He wants a pile of cash otherwise our fucking ends up on the Internet.'

Maybe Fabrizio hadn't heard her correctly. 'What did you say?'

'He taped us with his mobile phone.'

'But hang on . . . What the fuck's his name . . .? Wasn't your son off at boarding school in Switzerland?'

'Normally he is. Except that weekend he was in Rome. He had told me that he would stay at his friend's house by the sea. He must have come home early and . . .'

'Have you seen the video?'

'He emailed it to me.'

'How much can you see?'

'You and me. You can see everything. It looks like a porno. The end is terrible, you're fucking me from behind while I'm creaming the *pennette ai quattro formaggi*.'

'He taped that, too?'

'Yes.'

Fabrizio realised that his armpits were cold and wet, and there was suddenly no air in the room. He opened the window and began breathing in, in an attempt to calm down. 'How fucking embarrassing.' They better not panic. 'Come on, he's a good lad, he'd never do anything like that.'

'Oh, he'll do it.' Cristina had no doubts.

'I reckon he's just angry because you neglect him. It's the typical sort of thing teenagers do to get their mother's attention.'

Cristina shook her head.

'How much does he want?'

'A hundred thousand euro.'

Ciba opened his eyes wide. 'Sorry, I didn't hear you properly. Did you say a hundred thousand euro? Is he completely insane?'

'He wants fifty from me and fifty from you. We have to transfer it into his Swiss bank account. He gave me the IBAN.'

'From me? Why from me?'

'"That'll teach him to fuck my mother," he said. And he added that he's given you a friendly discount. If he sold it to a newspaper, he'd make a lot more. You are the first literary star to be caught in a porno. Samuel insists that you could easily compete with Paris Hilton and Pamela Anderson.'

'So he's really a son of a bitch?'

Cristina shrugged. 'Exactly.'

'Can't we negotiate? Get him to lower his price? Fifty between the two of us. What do you think?'

'No chance. He's very stubborn, just like his father. You know, when he grows up Samuel wants to be a movie director . . . He's even put opening credits with our names in the video and the soundtrack from *Gladiator*.'

Fabrizio began walking around the room. 'This is incredible. Your son is a real arsehole. How do we know that he won't keep a copy and continue to blackmail us?'

176

'No! He'd never do that. He's a good boy. He's honest, I trust his word.'

'Honest? He's a shark dressed as a little boy . . . If this leaks to the net, we'd look like total idiots. I would be ruined for ever. What if we had him beaten up by someone?'

'I thought of that. My mechanic's brother-in-law would knock him around for a few quid. I'm convinced he'd become even more evil though. Don't tell me it's a question of money. That's not like you. It's in such bad taste.'

Ciba hated looking like a penny-pincher. 'No, no. It's just that throwing away money like that . . . Tell me one thing, how do I come across?'

Cristina looked at him without understanding. 'What do you mean?'

'I mean . . . um . . .' He couldn't find the words to express himself. 'Do I look good? Can you see my belly? Did I put on a good show?'

'Not bad . . .'

'Thank goodness for small mercies.' Fabrizio grabbed the door handle. 'Send me the account number for the money transfer, and let's hope for the best. What else can I say?'

'What about us?'

'What about us? I'd say that's enough.'

He walked out and shut the door behind him.

37

Mantos, holding a tray with glasses of Champagne, moved like the perfect waiter amongst the guests, in search of Larita. It was like being at the Telegatti Awards. Half of all the celebrities on TV, half of the A-list were there. But most importantly, there was such a high pussy density that it was almost too much to bear.

Ever since he was little, Mantos had never liked sugar. Ice creams, semifreddos, coffee-soaked ice creams weren't for him. He liked savoury food, even for breakfast. Among pizzette, bread rolls and toasted sandwiches, his favourite was the tramezzino sandwich. He liked all flavours, but first place was between chicken tramezzino or prawn-and-rocket salad. At the Bar Internazionale of Fiano Romano they did have many different flavours, but they were often dry. And what's more, they made the serious mistake of heating them up in the electric oven and not on the griddle. Everybody told him that the tramezzini in Rome were a completely different story. They melted in your mouth, and they were always fresh. They kept them hidden under wet cloths, which kept them at the right level of humidity. Saverio imagined that the capital city had houses shaped like triangles, and that the streets were lined with tramezzini exhibitors.

For his birthday he had asked his father to take him to Rome to eat these wonderful delicacies. And for once his father had done what he wanted. In fact, he had gone too far. Following the advice of Uncle Aldo, who worked for the Ministry of Public Education, he had taken him to the House of the Tramezzino in Viale Trastevere, on the corner of Piazza Mastai.

When young Saverio Moneta had walked into that culinary temple, tears had come to his eyes. Before him appeared walls of tramezzini protected in crystal cabinets. They went from simple prosciutto and mozzarella to one with sausage, mayonnaise and Belgian endive. Ocean perch, rocket salad and stracchino. Finely sliced roast lamb, cocktail sauce and scallops. In one, two or three layers. Right up to the Club Sandwich

Ambassador Grand Royal. A twelve-decker beast stuffed full with sixty-five different ingredients.

'You've got three thousand lira to spend. Don't waste them. Pick well,' his father had told him.

The boy ran in a crazed state from one end of the room to the other, without being able to make up his mind. His hands began to sweat and his stomach seized. In the end he had walked out with the banknotes still intact.

Just like now, in the midst of all those headspinning flashes of bare thigh, those lips as swollen as stewed squid, those breasts as rounded as a Brunelleschi dome, Mantos backed up, feeling nauseous, and then noticed a brunette wandering aimlessly amidst all those superheroes.

Larita . . .

She looked like a university student, with her tartan skirt, black jacket and white blouse.

Mantos began manoeuvring closer to her while Sasà Chiatti kept talking on stage. 'We have gone over the top to entertain you . . . There are three different types of hunt. Fox hunt, tiger and lion. The fox hunt is only for those of you who know how to ride a horse properly. It will be carried out according to the old rules of the Duke of Beaufort. A pack of thirty beagles is ready and waiting in the kennels. For this hunt, the uniform is compulsory: red or black jacket, in tweed or in pied-de-poule, white tie, white gloves, light-coloured trousers and, naturally, boots and cap.'

A buzz rose from the audience. The guests looked at each other, shaking their heads. 'What are we supposed to do?' 'Impossible.' 'We don't have those sorts of clothes.'

The host reassured them. 'Don't worry, guys! It's all under control, don't get worked up. The designer Ralph Lauren has generously given us the clothing for the hunts. Behind the Villa

179

there is a campsite where you kind ladies and gents will find everything you need to get ready. The red tents are for those participating in the fox hunt, orange is for the tiger hunt and beige is for the lion hunt. Afterwards, if you wish, you may take the outfits home with you.'

'Chiatti, you're a real gentleman!' someone shouted. 'Ralph, you're the best!' added another.

Mantos had made it to within a few metres of the singer. Larita was standing with her arms crossed, watching the stage, a little bored. She was small, but well proportioned. And she looked out of place.

A beanpole with a black beard and sunglasses, a well-worn leather jacket, snakeskin cowboy boots, threadbare jeans and a flanelette checked shirt had latched onto her and kept laughing and elbowing her, as if they were lifelong friends. She didn't seem to be enjoying herself as much as he was, though.

Mantos was convinced that the cowboy was someone famous. In there, you were either a VIP or a waiter. He had the air of a rock musician.

The leader of the Wilde Beasts of Abaddon's musical tastes ranged between different genres: from Carmina Burana by Orff to Wagner, from Popol Vuh to Dead Can Dance, and last but not least Billy Joel. He couldn't stand Italian music.

When the cowboy took his hat off to wave it at Chiatti, Mantos saw the peace-flag bandana he was wearing underneath.

It was the symbol of Cachemire, the singer of the heavy metal group from Ancona, Animal Death. They were Murder and Zombie's idols.

Cachemire gestured towards Mantos. 'Hey! Waiter, come here.'

Mantos was forced to face him. 'Me?'

'Yeah, you. Come here.'

The leader of the Beasts moved closer, with his head lowered. He offered him the tray with the last glass of Champagne.

'Have you got a beer?'

'No, I'm sorry.'

'Could you run and get me one? Actually, while you're at it, bring me a whole case.'

Mantos nodded.

Larita patted Cachemire. 'I'm going to take a look around. See you later.'

The Beasts' leader was shocked to hear Larita's voice. It was husky and deep. Tattooed on the nape of her neck, beneath her short hair, she had two little angel wings.

And that is where the Durendal will fall.

'All right,' said the cowboy. 'What hunt are you going to go on? I'm not sure.'

'I'm not going. I hate that sort of thing.' Larita moved off, and Saverio followed her at a few metres' distance, swearing silently to himself.

The bitch didn't take part in hunts. He really didn't need this right now. Bad luck was really dogging him.

Larita, suddenly, turned around and walked up to him: 'Excuse me, have you seen Ciba . . .? Fabrizio Ciba?'

Who the fuck is Ciba?

Mantos's tongue was paralysed, and the only thing he managed to do was shrug.

Larita seemed shocked by his ignorance. 'The writer! Don't you know him? The guy who read his poem on the stage before.'

'No, I'm sorry.'

'Don't worry about it. Thanks, anyway.' Larita slipped away into the crowd.

181

Silvietta was right. That slut was an animal rights activist. And now how would they kidnap her?

Mantos necked the last glass of Champagne.

38

Fabrizio Ciba was also necking a double whisky, sitting at a coffee table by himself. He couldn't even contemplate the risk of the porno film getting onto the net.

'Bro!'

Paolo Bocchi advanced towards the table with another mojito in hand. By the way he was swaying, he had to be drunk already. His eyes bloodshot, he was sweating like he'd just finished a game of basketball. Under the sleeves of his jacket two dark rings had formed. He had loosened his tie and unbuttoned his shirt, so you could see the tip of his woollen vest. His fly was down.

The surgeon grabbed Fabrizio by the neck. 'What are you doing here, all by your little lonesome?'

The writer didn't even have the strength to react. 'Nothing.'

'They told me you read a great poem. Pity I was in the loo. I didn't hear it.'

Ciba flopped down onto the table.

'You're looking crushed. What happened?' Bocchio asked.

'I looked like the world's biggest idiot.'

Bocchi sat down on the chair next to his and lit up a cigarette, taking big deep inhales.

The two of them sat there in silence for a bit. Then the surgeon lifted his head towards the sky and puffed out a large cloud of smoke. 'You're so boring, Fabrizio. You still go on about this crap?'

'What crap?'

'That crap about looking like an idiot. How long have we known each other?'

'Too long.'

Bocchi wasn't offended. 'You haven't changed one iota since high school. Always obsessed with looking like an idiot. As if someone were always there to judge you. Do I have to spell it out to you? You are a writer, and you should work out certain things by yourself.'

Fabrizio turned to face his high-school pal. 'What? What are you talking about?'

Bocchi yawned. Then took his hand. 'Right, you haven't got it. The time of looking like an idiot is over, it's dead and buried, kaput. It went out along with the old millennium. Looking like an idiot is no longer an issue, it's disappeared along with the fireflies. Nobody looks like an idiot any more, except for you inside your own head. Can't you see them?' He gestured towards the mass of people applauding Chiatti. 'We roll in shit as happy as pigs in mud. Look at me, for example.' He stood up, swaying. He opened his arms wide as if to show himself to everyone, but his head started spinning and he had to sit down again. 'I did my postgrad in Lyon with Professor Roland Chateau-Beaubois, I am chair at the University of Urbino. I'm head physician. Look at me. According to the old parameters, I would be the epitome of a creature to be avoided at all costs, a poseur rolling in cash, a drug addict, a despicable figure who gets rich taking advantage of the weaknesses of a handful of aging tarts. And yet that's not the case. I am loved and respected. I even get invited to the celebration of the republic at the Presidential Palace, and to every fucking TV medical programme. On a personal note, wasn't that TV programme you did a bit crap?'

Ciba tried to defend himself. 'Well, actually . . .'

'Get over it, it was crap.'

Fabrizio nodded slightly.

'And that whole debacle with that chick, the daughter . . . I can't remember. Anyway, it made you look like a fuckwit.'

Ciba made a pained expression. 'All right, that's enough.'

'And what happened to you? Nothing at all. How many more copies did you sell, with all this theoretically looking stupid? A heap. And everyone says that you're a genius. So, see that? You have to admit that I'm right. What you call looking like an idiot are splashes of mediatic splendour that give shine to your personality and make you more human, more likeable. If ethical and aesthetic principles no longer exist, looking like an idiot disappears as a consequence.' Bocchi stretched out to Ciba and hugged him affectionately. 'And do you know who's the only person in the world who never looked like an idiot in his whole life? Not even once?'

The writer shook his head.

'Jesus Christ. In thirty-three years, not even once. And that tops it all off. Now, though, you do me a favour. Take this little lolly.' Bocchi pulled a purple, oval-shaped pill out of his pocket.

Fabrizio looked at it suspiciously. 'What is it?'

Bocchi opened his eyes wide, his ocular globes popping from their sockets like the eyes of a cane toad, and like a purveyor of old and rare spices, he explained: 'Phenol Hydrochloride Benjorex. This is not any old hallucinogenic. You won't find it on the streets.' He patted himself on the chest. 'It's special. Only Uncle Paolo has this sort of product. You've heard of magic mushrooms, peyote, Ecstasy, MDMA? They are practically the equivalent of Dulcolax in comparison with this little pill. It's a medicine that has been filed by Human Rights Watch as a chemical weapon. It has been used by experimental neuropsychiatrists in Russian jails to make the Chechen terrorists regress to their childhood, and by the Russian Space Research Institute in their research into the psychotropic effects of the absence of gravity. Now let's take one, and you'll see how this circus suddenly turns into the world of Oz, and you and I will have so much fun.'

He chucked the pill into Ciba's jacket pocket, making him jump up, horrified, and take three steps back.

'Bocchi, you really are sick. You are not only a drug addict, you're a psycopath. You want to kill me, be honest. You hate me. Chechens . . . absence of gravity . . . the end of looking like an idiot . . . Let me ask you a favour. I beg you. Leave me alone. You and I have never had anything in common. Not even at high school. We've never been friends, brothers, fuck-all. We have nothing to share, so please do me the favour of leaving me alone, and if you see me on the street, change streets.'

Bocchi smiled at him. 'OK.' He pulled out another pill, popped it his mouth and finished off his mojito.

39

Sasà Chiatti had proceeded with the explanation of the tiger hunt. 'As the Victorian tradition teaches us, the tiger hunt is done with elephants. I have found four wonderful specimens from a circus in Kraków, and I had four wicker baskets handmade in Torre Annunziata mounted on top, which can carry up to four hunters. Each beast will be led by an Indian mahout, who knows his animal like his own skin. The tiger's name is Kira, it's five years old. I bought it after a long negotiation

185

with the zoo in Bratislava. She is a splendid albino female, like my darling girlfriend, who took even longer negotiations to convince her to stay with me. This hunt will last approximately three hours, and at the end there will be a dinner on a fleet of house boats. A self-service feast of Indian cuisine has been laid out there.'

Ten metres or so away, behind the kitchen sheds, the Wilde Beasts of Abaddon had gathered for their unscheduled meeting.

'We're up shit creek!' Mantos commented first.

'What's the matter?' muttered Murder, his mouth full of sea-sturgeon bruschetta.

'Larita's not taking part in the hunt.'

'I told you! She's an animal rights activist,' said Silvietta, smugly.

Mantos was starting to get pissed off, but he tried to keep his cool. 'Congratulations! You knew it! And now what? And now we have to put plan B into action.'

Zombie, who was sulking at the side, jumped to his feet. His eyes were puffy and he was practically shaking.

'That's enough! I can't take it any more,' he exploded. 'Now you start with your plan B? As if there'd ever been a plan A? This, dear Mantos, is the clear demonstration of the fact that you will never be a Kurtz Minetti or a Charles Manson. You . . . you improvise. This is not a Satanic sect, this is a sect of losers. These two here . . .' He pointed to Murder and Silvietta. 'Forget about it. The truth is that none of you are professionals. This whole shit story should have ended that night in the pizzeria. It was a big mistake joining you guys. Even you've disappointed me, Mantos. You got us here and showed us the map of Villa Ada. Are you for real? The Durendal . . . We'll kidnap her in the woods . . . We'll commit suicide . . . We'll become Italy's number one Satanic sect. But you're shooting with a blowpipe! You know what I say? Go fuck yourselves!' And he walked off towards the street.

Saverio looked, shocked, at his two adepts: 'Is he out of his mind? What's happened?'

'I know what's happened,' said Silvietta and ran after Zombie.

Murder, still holding on to the bruschetta, looked towards his leader. 'What's happening?'

'What do I know? She's your girlfriend. Get her.'

Murder snorted and ran off after her.

The leader of the Beasts flopped down in a chair, covering his face with his hands.

He couldn't blame Zombie. There was no plan B. And plan A leaked water all over the place.

Why didn't I accept Kurtz Minetti's offer? I'll never have what it takes to be a real leader. And now what do I do?

He had burned his bridges with everyone, and he couldn't turn back. And when Antonio regained consciousness, he would fuck him over, too.

The only thing left to do was a kamikaze mission. Run quickly towards Larita, and while he quickly recited the Tables of Evil, stick the Durendal in her heart.

'Silvietta! Silvietta, honey, stop. I've got a stitch,' Murder gasped, holding his hand pressed against his stomach while he ran after his girlfriend through the forest. 'Where are you going? There are ferocious beasts in here . . . It's dangerous.'

The Vestal took a couple more steps and then, like she'd run out of battery, she stopped and fell to the ground beneath a huge fig tree with its heavy branches hanging low.

Murder went over to her, stretched out his hand without touching her, as if afraid. 'What's up, sweetie? What's happened?'

She spoke with her face covered by her arms. 'Zombie heard us.'

'What?'

Silvietta lifted her head. Her cheeks were lined with tears. 'The wedding. He heard everything. He's really angry.'

'What did he say to you?'

'He said that we're both traitors. Both wankers. That we're abandoning them. And he's right.'

Murder squeezed his hands into a fist, and stood up. 'Right, but let's not exaggerate . . . All right, we haven't behaved perfectly, but wankers and traitors is too much.'

She grabbed onto his leg and looked up at him, her face half lit up by a ray of sunshine filtering through the leaves. 'Listen to me, I've given it some thought. We can't abandon them. I just can't do it, and it's not fair. We made the Satanic pact. In the Sutri forest we swore to fight together, united, against the Forces of Good. Remember?'

Murder, unwillingly, nodded.

'So we have to commit suicide.'

He looked her in the eye. 'You reckon?'

'Come here.'

He bent down. Silvietta, with her index finger, fixed a lock of hair that had fallen onto his forehead. 'Yes, I reckon we have to.'

Murder began to rock his head backwards and forwards, and snort. 'What a fucking pain! And now what do we do?' He tried to get up, but she held him down. 'I've already paid the deposit at the Vecchio Cantinone, not to mention the booking fee for the trip to Prague. If I'd known, I wouldn't have taken out the loan. And my parents are getting everything ready.'

Silvietta smiled. Her eyes were tearing, but in peace. 'Murder, who cares . . .? We're going to die, anyway.'

'Of course . . . But you know how I am. I hate leaving bills unsettled.'

'Who cares about the wedding? We love each other, and we'll die together. Next to each other. We'll be joined in eternity. Like Romeo and Juliet.'

Murder hugged her close against his thick chest until he almost suffocated her, and then placed her head on his shoulder. 'But I'm afraid . . . I don't want to . . .'

Silvietta brushed her lips against his throat. 'Don't worry, honey. I'll be there with you. We'll hold hands. You'll see, it will be beautiful.'

The shrill call of an unknown bird sang out.

Silvietta raised her head. 'Did you hear that? It sounded like a parrot.'

'You reckon it was a parrot?'

She whispered in his ear. 'I love you.'

Murder kissed her.

Organisation of the Hunting Groups

Wardrobe and Allocation of the Weapons

40

After Chiatti's speech all the guests moved off in hordes from the buffet to prepare for the hunt. There was a sense of excitement and alcohol in the air. The drinks in their stomachs and the drugs in their brains had made them jovial and put them in a good mood. Just as the real-estate agent had promised, they found the tents to get changed in. Off to one side was the armoury. Dozens of shotguns were lined up in racks. The hostesses noted down on pieces of paper the names of the participants on each different safari and made them sign a release form. If anyone got hurt, shot themselves, it wasn't Sasà Chiatti's concern.

Fabrizio Ciba roamed around the camp, thinking about what Bocchi had told him. That wanker wasn't all wrong. The porno film might very well give him a load of publicity, and perhaps the sales of his novels would take off again. Not to mention that he might well become a sex symbol. Nobody would say no to that.

At that very moment the managing director of Martinelli, together with Matteo Saporelli and the literary critic Tremagli, came out of a tent dressed in colonial outfits. Short trousers, khaki-coloured shirt and a pith helmet made of cork. They were holding large rifles in their hands, looking at them as if they had been made by aliens.

The lion hunt is out of the question.

Simona Somaini popped out of the fox-hunt tent wearing a pair of pants that hugged her legs and her ass like a second skin, while the little red jacket left just enough open to show off her pushed-up tits. She was followed by a huge beast of a man with a goatee and a ponytail, dressed in army gear, a rifle under his arm.

Fabrizio had seen the beast of a man somewhere before. He must be a sports star.

The writer took two steps forward and found Larita standing in front of him. He felt like hugging her, but he held back.

The singer seemed happy to have found him again, too. 'I was looking for you everywhere. Where did you go?'

Ciba did what came to him naturally. He lied. 'I was looking for you. So, what shall we do? Don't tell me you want to take part in this clown show?'

'Me? Are you mad? I'm an animal rights defender.'

'Good on you!' Ciba was relieved. 'So let's get out of here, then.'

She looked at him in surprise. 'I can't leave, I have to sing . . . I came here for that purpose.'

Fabrizio tried to hide his disappointment. 'You're right. I wasn't thinking, but . . .' He was unable to finish the sentence because a white Lipizzan stopped before him, lifting itself up on its hind legs. Sasà Chiatti, sitting astride the steed, was pulling the reins and trying to keep the animal still while it reared left and right.

'What are you two doing here? Why haven't you changed? I've got an elephant about to leave only half full.'

Larita waved her hand in sign of a no. 'I'm against hunting. I will never shoot a tiger.'

The real-estate agent leaned down on the shiny neck of the horse so that the other guests wouldn't hear him. 'Who's shooting who? It's fun and games. The tiger has cancer of the colon. It has one month to live, if it's lucky. You'll only be doing her a favour. It's a field trip. When will you ever have the chance to do this sort of thing again? Come on . . .' He then turned backwards and let out a sheep-farmer whistle.

A trumpeting sound echoed across the Italian-style garden. Parrots and crows rose in flight from the branches of the holly oak trees. An elephant emerged from the bushes, shooting rays of blinding light around him. They had painted it orange and light blue and draped it in cloth with hundreds of little round mirrors sewn into it. The long trunk broke off tree branches and carried them to its mouth. They had tied a woven wicker basket on its back. There was an elderly gentleman inside wearing glasses, a green Loden cape and a funny felt hat. He was holding a rifle in his hands. Next to him was a teenager with his eyes half covered by a dark fringe. The two of them held tightly on to the edge of the basket, which pitched with each step the animal took. Sitting on its neck was a small Filipino wearing a white thong and a turban, guiding the animal, whipping it along with a rod.

'Here is your elephant.' Chiatti raised a hand and the Filipino brought the pachyderm to a halt. Then he spoke to the man in the basket. 'Doctor Cinelli, would you be so kind as to throw down the ladder. There are two more passengers.'

The old man was pointing the rifle towards the trees, on the look-out for the tiger.

'Granddad! Granddad! Did you hear him? The gentleman asked if you could throw the ladder down. Yeah, whatever, that'll be the day!' The boy bent over, picked up the canvas ladder and lowered it: 'Please forgive me, he's a little bit deaf.'

Larita looked at Fabrizio, torn. 'What shall we do?'

Ciba shrugged. 'You decide.'

192

Larita, in a whisper, embarrassed, said: 'I don't think we can get out of it. It would be rude for us to stay here. But we won't shoot, though.'

'Don't look at me.'

41

Murder sat down next to his leader, who was sitting with his head bent on his knees, and put his arm around Mantos's shoulders. 'Not everything is lost, Master.'

'Don't worry, Mantos, we'll manage,' Silvietta said.

Saverio was touched. He looked up at them. 'I've disappointed you. I'm so sorry. I haven't got charisma.'

Silvietta took his hand. 'No, Mantos, you've got great charisma, and you have never disappointed us. You gave meaning to our lives. And we will never betray you, we will always be by your side.'

Murder knelt down and asked. 'Who is our Charismatic Father?'

Mantos shook his head, embarrassed. 'Guys . . . Stop it.'

Murder stood up. 'Who wrote the Tablets of Evil?'

'You did!' Silvietta pointed at her leader.

'Who taught us the Liturgy of Darkness?'

Mantos took a deep breath and said: 'I did.'

Zombie was running between the tents.

It was chaos. People grinding their teeth, trying to put riding boots on. An old lady, short of breath, had rolled herself up in a purple sari like a trout in clingfilm. The vice president of the Lazio region, wearing colonial boots three sizes too small, was walking like a robot, carrying a huge

193

rifle. The comedian Sartoretti, the unquestioned star performer of Friday night television on Italia 1, was struggling to zip up plus-fours and shouting at the hostess, 'This is a forty-six. I wear a fifty-two.'

The Beast jumped over Paolo Bocchi, who was lying on the ground, pale and sweaty, looking at the sky as if he was speaking to his maker, and repeated like a mantra: 'Please . . . please . . . please . . .'

Zombie kept running breathlessly until he got to the Italian-style garden.

Silvietta and Murder, sitting at a coffee table, were eating a piece of ricotta-and-spinach pie.

The Satanist stopped and doubled over from the effort. 'What are you two still doing here?'

Silvietta stood up. 'We're not getting married any more. We're going to take the mission all the way.'

Murder stood up, too. 'Forgive us. We've understood our error.'

Zombie was out of breath. 'I don't . . . want to . . . talk to you. Where is Mantos?'

'He's gone to fill up his plate from the buffet.'

Silvietta took him by the arm. 'Did you get it? We're not going to abandon you. We're going to commit suicide, too.'

'Yeah, whatever . . . I don't believe it.'

Silvietta put a hand on her chest. 'I swear. You were right, we were behaving like arseholes. But you forced me to reason.'

At that moment Mantos appeared with a big plate full of crayfish ravioli. 'Zombie! You're back.'

The adept wanted to speak, but he was still out of breath. 'Larita . . . arita . . .'

'What?' the leader of the Beasts asked. 'Larita what?'

'She's left . . . for the tiger . . . hunt!'

Departure for the Safari

42

Between one thing and another, the hunts left two hours behind schedule.

The sun was setting behind the forests of Forte Antenne, talking with it all the colours, but thanks to the skills of the Korean director of photography, Kim Doo Soo, the woods and the fields of the park had been transformed into an enchanted forest. Green moss-covered rocks and tree trunks dotted with mushrooms and silver lichen were bathed in an unnatural light that flooded from several ten-thousand-watt projectors camouflaged by the vegetation. A dense low fog, created by the smoke machines, covered the undergrowth and the plains where herds of gnus, ibex and elks grazed. Thousands of sparkling LEDs scattered across the fields went on and off like swarms of fireflies. Twelve huge fans hidden in the highlands created a light breeze that rippled over the grassy plains where a family of Marsican Brown bears and an old blind rhinoceros were resting between the swings and the ivy-covered slides.

The dogs and horse riders from the fox hunt had already disappeared behind the hills to the east.

The African beaters, followed by the hunters on foot, were sifting through the plains in search of the lion.

The elephants were leaving the Villa. In single file the pachyderms wove their trunks with their tails and, slow but unstoppable, they headed straight towards the swamps in the northwest, where they said that Kira, the albino tiger, was hidden.

Sasà Chiatti, on the terrace of the Royal Villa, observed the parties with his binoculars as they advanced into his immense property.

Everything there was his. From the century-old pine trees to the invasive ivy, down to the last ant.

They had insulted him, mocked him, they had called him a crazy megalomaniac, a poseur, a thief, but he hadn't listened to any of them. And in the end, he had won. They had all come to court to pay him homage.

Ecaterina Danielsson joined him on the terrace. She had changed and was wearing a brown leather corset that squeezed her tiny waist. Her shoulders were wrapped in a silver fox-fur stole. Her legs were bound in boots. She was carrying two crystal glasses.

The model offered one glass to Chiatti. 'Wine?'

Sasà closed his eyes and breathed in deeply. The fine perfume, pleasant, ethereal was perfect. He wet his lips. Dry, warm and lightly tannin-flavoured. He smiled in satisfaction. It was exactly like him, the Aprilia Merlot. He necked it.

Ecaterina wrapped her arms around his waist from behind. 'How do you feel?'

He finished the glass and threw it over his shoulder. 'Like the eighth King of Rome.'

43

Mantos, Murder, Zombie and Silvietta, all dressed as waiters, were marching on sandy, soggy ground dotted with puddles and marshy areas. It was crawling with mosquitoes, midges, worms, flies, dragonflies and a heap of disgusting little animals hidden amidst the reeds, sedges and lotuses.

Mantos turned around in confusion. 'I don't remember this swamp . . . What about you guys?'

'No, me neither,' said Murder, looking down at his muddy shoes.

'I came here a couple of times when I was a kid. My dad used to bring me on Sundays after he'd taken me to hear the Pope. I remember the rides, but not the swamp.'

'Are we going the right way?' Silvietta asked. In reality, she didn't really care. She had to make peace with Zombie. He was at the end of the line and was walking with his head hung low.

'I think so. I saw them heading north.' Mantos overtook Murder to head-up the line. He had tied the Durendal to his backpack. 'What sort of trees are those? They're so weird.'

Trees with contorted trunks sank hundreds of long dark fingers into the sand. A colony of guenon monkeys observed them from the tree tops.

Murder chased off a silver-coloured fly. 'Ummm . . . They're probably olive trees.'

'What are you talking about? They're mangroves. Haven't you ever seen them in documentaries?' Silvietta sighed.

Mantos was starting to run out of breath. 'Hang on . . . Do mangroves grow in continental climates?'

Murder burst out laughing. 'If you don't know what you're talking about, don't talk. This is not a continental climate, it's temperate.'

Mantos pointed at him, using his hand like a paddle. 'Listen to him. The professor is here. You just confused mangroves for olive trees.'

'Would you two stop fighting? Let's hurry up, the mosquitoes are eating me alive,' said Silvietta, hanging back so she could get to Zombie. She began walking next to him. 'Muffin, I know you're really, really angry, but you can't keep sulking right up to when we commit suicide. These are our last hours together, and we're doing the most important thing of our lives. We have to band together and love each other. I am asking you for forgiveness, but you have to give me a smile. Am I or am I not your best friend?'

He grumbled something that might have been a yes or a no.

'Come on, please. You know how much I love you.'

He ripped a reed out of the mud. 'You hurt me.'

'I've asked you to forgive me.'

'Why didn't you tell me you decided to get married?'

'Because I'm an idiot. I wanted to tell you, but I was ashamed. If there wasn't this mission, I would have asked you to be my best man.'

'And I wouldn't have accepted.'

She laughed. 'I know . . . Please, don't say anything to Mantos about us wanting to get married, he'd be so disappointed.'

'All right.'

'Now, will you give me a smile? Just one, little little one?'

For a second Zombie turned his head towards Silvietta, and a smile as quick as the flap of wings flashed across his face before being immediately covered over by his hair.

Hunt

44

As a young man, Fabrizio Ciba had been a fairly good yachtsman. He had crossed the Adriatic Sea on a catamaran, and he had taken a two-masted ship to Ponza. During these crossings he had faced Burian winds and storms and never, not even once, had he suffered from sea-sickness. Now, sitting inside that fucking basket on an elephant's back, he was feeling madly nauseous. He was holding on to the edge of the sedan chair and he could feel the spider-crabcakes and the rigatoni floating around in the Jim Beam.

What a pain. Now that he could finally spend some time with Larita, he was feeling like shit.

The singer looked him over. 'You look a bit pale. Are you feeling all right?'

The writer swallowed an acid burp. 'No, it's nothing, just a bit of a headac . . .' He was unable to finish the sentence because the barrel of Dr Cinelli's rifle hit him on the nape of the neck.

Ciba turned towards the old man. 'That's enough! That's the third time you've hit me in the head with it. Be careful.'

The old man, in his perfect deafness, didn't pay him any attention and kept waving the weapon to the left and right, pointing it into the bushes.

We fucked up big-time when we decided to listen to Chiatti.

Not only were there four of them shoved inside that one square metre of swinging basket with an old fuckwit, but their elephant was at the head of the convoy, which meant they had to watch out for low-lying branches, too. But there was an even more subtle torment that distressed the writer. He had the feeling that he had lost a bit of shine and wasn't as charming as he usually was. Perhaps Larita had made that promise to see him again out of politeness, just as she had accepted to take part in the hunt out of politeness to Chiatti. Unbelievably, he felt like the clumsy teenager he was at high school. Back then he wasn't the confident and brazen Ciba of today, the old smooth sailor, the hitman, but was instead an awkward adolescent with a tuft of messy hair and glasses, hiding inside huge stretched jumpers and grubby trousers. Every time he tried to pick up a girl, it turned into a tragedy. He would put together really complicated plans in order to meet her in the most natural way possible. He hated showing how he felt, appearing weak, so he always wanted them to make the first move. He would lie in wait in front of the entrance to his prey's house, and pretend he was just passing by coincidentally. He would ignore her on purpose or be unpleasant to her, hoping to get her attention. He would think up brilliant Woody Allen-style dialogues in which he would look like an adorable loser.

Now, with Larita, he felt clumsy and as awkward as he had in his younger years.

'Duck!' the singer shouted.

Ciba lowered his head, only barely avoiding a trunk that cut the path in two. Cinelli copped it straight in the face, losing his glasses and spinning a full circle before sticking the tip of the rifle under Fabrizio's armpit.

'Ouch! Bloody . . . I've had enough of this bloody thing!' The writer ripped the gun out of his hands. 'It's even loaded. If he accidentally fires a shot, he'll kill me!'

The boy took his grandfather's defence. 'Who do you think

you are? What a nerve! Do you normally pick on elderly gentlemen?'

Larita offered the grandson a handkerchief. The boy started patting the scratches on the old man's face. He stoically didn't make a sound.

Someone from behind shouted: 'Hey! Get a move on! It's like being in a funeral march.'

Ciba turned towards the elephant that was following them. The basket on its back was carrying Paco Jimenez de la Frontera and Milo Serinov, and their dates.

Fabrizio gestured to them to keep calm. 'Is it our fault? The Indian's the one who's driving.'

'He's no Indian, he's Filipino. And anyway, tell him to get a move on,' said Mariapia Morozzi, the ex-television presenter and girlfriend of the Russian goalkeeper.

Larita turned around. 'Can't you see it's an elephant? If you wanted to go faster, you should have gone on the fox hunt.'

'¡Yo te quiero, señorita! ¡Por la virgen de Guadalupe! Move that big ass!' shouted the Argentinian soccer player. He had the fixed gaze and the stretched smile of someone who was addicted to cocaine.

Ciba stepped in to defend the girl's honour: 'Hey, bello! Calm down. Don't be rude!'

'Desculpe, it's a game . . .' Paco Jimenez giggled nervously and kissed his girlfriend, Taja Testari.

A voice from the third elephant shouted out: 'Excuse me? Does anyone have any Travelgum?' It was Fabiano Pisu, the famous television actor. As green as a string bean, his eyes were wide open. He was with his boyfriend, the Maghrebi designer Khaled Hassan, the head of drama at RAI Television Ugo Maria Rispoli, and the film agent Elena Paleologo Rossi Strozzi. 'Anyone? Anyone got any Travelgum?'

201

'No. I've got a Mars,' said Milo.

In the basket of the fourth pachyderm there was supposed to be Cachemire and his Animal Death, the heavy metal group from Ancona, the revelation of the festival of Castrocaro. But the basket looked empty. A lone army boot stuck out. The four of them were below deck, soaked in alcohol and a mix of mind-altering drugs.

I hate all of you, Fabrizio Ciba thought to himself.

He felt vulnerable and confused, like a non-European Union citizen at the residents' permit office of the police department. He was in a cage, on the back of that elephant. His secret was to keep close to life, in order to observe the horror of humanity with sarcasm, but never get inside it. Right now he was smack-bang in the middle of that circus, and he didn't feel any different from those clowns. He was even looking like an idiot to Larita. It was best if he just kept quiet and behaved as a writer reflecting on life.

He began to study the Filipino pensively, as the man continuously flicked the beast's neck. The track was getting narrower and darker, and there was no sign of the tiger. The last rays of sunshine were cutting through the undergrowth and strange calls could be heard in the air – it was impossible to tell whether they were birds or monkeys.

A weak moan rose up from the third elephant. Pisu's face had taken on the colour of Terra Di Siena. 'Come on, I beg you, give me . . . a Travelgum . . . a travel plaster . . . a banana . . . I'm dying.'

'Again!' the Russian's girlfriend answered impatiently. 'You hard of hearing? We haven't got one.'

'You think it's funny, but I . . .' The poor guy didn't get to finish his sentence because a river of yellow vomit spurted out of his mouth and spilled down the neck of the elephant driver.

The Filipino turned around. 'Fuck you!' he said, and shook the clam-and-baby-calamari-ring salad off his turban. 'Gross!' And with a flick of his wrist, he whipped the soap star in the face.

'Ahhhhhh!' screamed Fabiano as he wobbled out of the basket and flopped down into an enormous puddle at the elephant's feet.

'Hombre at sea!' shouted Paco Jimenez de la Frontera.

Except for Khaled Hassan, who was waving wildly at his fallen companion, nobody really cared what happened to poor Pisu. The elephants, in their ancient wisdom, kept up their slow onward march, abandoning the actor from *Marquess of Cassino* to the mercy of the wild beasts in the park.

45

The leader of the Wilde Beasts of Abaddon was full of energy. He was heading straight towards death, and the Beasts were with him again. He turned to tell them to start singing a conciliatory song to Satan and saw Murder and Silvietta walking along calmly, hand in hand, as if they were off on a picnic.

Murder really is lucky, Mantos said to himself.

Saverio Moneta, in forty years, had never been loved like that. Before Serena, the leader of the Beasts had only had a couple of affairs during the dark years of accountancy. Nothing special, they lasted a couple of weeks, because if you went out with a girl then in the eyes of your classmates you were less of a loser. More than going together, they were associations of mutual aid.

He had noticed Serena Mastrodomenico as soon as he had been hired at the furniture shop. She was so tanned and slim, she reminded him of Laura Gemser, the actress from *Emanuelle Nera*. An onanistic topos of his years of puberty.

He was crazy about Serena, but he saw no way of making her his. He was the last of the accountants and she was the owner's daughter. She paraded like a goddess in a miniskirt through the corridors of the shop and Saverio dreamed of just being able to talk to her, to invite her out to dinner on the Bracciano lake. She didn't even condescend to look at him, though. Even if she walked by him every day, she had never even noticed him. And that was the way it should be. Why should an elegant, worldly woman be interested in a no-hoper like him? A guy who didn't even have a car. A guy whose eyesight had faded reading huge volumes on the mysteries of the Templars and the Bermuda Triangle.

One evening Saverio was in the office, checking over the six-monthly budget again. His colleagues had gone home and he was alone in the furniture shop. He had bought a slice of mushroom-and-prawn pizza, and every now and then he took a bite, making sure he didn't stain the books. He had his headphones on and was listening to 'The Ride of the Valkyries' at full volume.

Suddenly he'd raised his eyes. On the other side of the corridor, the door to Egisto Mastrodomenico's office was open, and the light was on.

It couldn't be the old man. He had left for the Country Style Furniture Fair in Vercelli.

A thief had slipped in and he hadn't noticed? He was just about to call security, when Serena came out of the room carrying loads of shopping bags in her hand. Saverio Moneta's heart had exploded. Shaking all over, he had taken the head-phones off and shyly raised one hand to say hi, but she hadn't even responded. But then she came back in and had tipped her head to study him better. 'All on your lonesome?'

'Ummm . . . yeah . . .' he had managed to say, trying to sit upright in his chair.

She had walked into the accounting office and glanced around as if to check that there really wasn't anybody else there. Saverio had never seen her looking so good. She must have just come from the hairdresser and she was wearing a little pink leotard as tight as the skin on a snake, the zip well splayed over the top of her neckline, and white leather boots that came up to her knees. From her ears hung two gold rings as big as CDs.

'Are you bored?'

'No', Saverio had answered instinctively. But then he'd thought that no right-minded person enjoyed checking the six-monthly budget, and he corrected himself: 'A little . . . But I'll be finished soon.'

She had touched up her hair and had asked him: 'Do you want me to give you head?'

Saverio thought he'd heard her ask if he wanted her to give him head. But he must have misunderstood. She must have asked him if he wanted some tea.

'The drinks dispenser is broken . . . They should fix it by the end of the week.'

'I asked you whether you wanted me to give you head.'

Saverio couldn't believe his ears. Maybe the mushrooms on the pizza were hallucinogenic.

He kept staring at her with his mouth wide open, like an idiot.

'So?' She was chewing gum and had repeated the question just as if she had asked him whether he wanted tea.

'What?'

'Do want it or not?' Serena was getting sick of waiting.

'What?' Saverio's mind had stalled.

'Don't you know what it is? Head is a sexual practice whereby I take your dick in my mouth and I suck it.'

Why was she doing this to him? What had he done to hurt her?

It was obvious. It was a trap so that she could accuse of him of sexual harassment, just like in American films.

'All right, I get it.' Serena walked around the desk, knelt down, pulled her hair up, took the chewing gum out of her mouth and passed it to him. 'Hold this, please.'

Saverio had squeezed the gum between his fingertips while the daughter of his boss, with the cold-blooded ability of a nurse taking the clothes off an injured man, undid his belt and unbuttoned the fly of his trousers.

'You might like it.' She lowered his jocks and looked at his cock without making any comments. Then with her right hand she'd grabbed it, weighed it and squeezed like you do with a cow's teat. With her left, she cupped his scrotum and began to roll his testicles in the palm of her hand like they were two Chinese anti-stress balls.

Saverio, his legs wide, squeezed the armrests of his chair with an expression of terror painted on his face. It was astonishing what this woman was able to do with his reproductive organ.

But the show wasn't over. Serena opened her mouth wide, and with her little pointy tongue she had wet her lips and then swallowed the whole thing, right down to his balls. Saverio was terrified that he wouldn't enjoy it in the least, but then all it took was for him to realise that Serena Mastrodomenico was holding in her mouth the entirety of his cock to bring him to an explosive and embarrassing orgasm.

She had wiped the back of her hand across her mouth, looked him in the eye and asked him in a satisfied voice: 'Listen, tomorrow, would you take me to Ikea?'

He had answered with a single, simple: 'Yes.'

That had been the first yes. The first of an infinite string.

Saverio Moneta, from that day on, from obscure accountant had been transformed into a sherpa during Serena's raids of the shopping centres, the driver of her SUV, her bellboy, her pony express, her plumber, her satellite-dish repairman, husband and father of her children.

Ah, that was the first and last blow job he ever got in ten years of living with Serena.

Mantos studied Murder and Silvietta.

He was tall and big, and she was so petite. She kept pretending to kick him to get him moving along. He was laughing and standing still on purpose.

Saverio looked back through his memory to a stroll with Serena. Never happened. Maybe in Ikea. Him pushing the trolley, her walking ahead and talking on the phone.

Those two instead, looking at them, you could see that they were accomplices. From the moment they met on the train and talked about their passion for heavy metal and Lazio football club, they had not separated since. If one of them read a book, the other had to read it, too. That way of touching each other, of softly caressing each other that they had. They knew that they could count on each other.

As if they had just taken a blindfold off his eyes, he saw the horror. He had convinced a couple of kids who loved each other to kill themselves because of a problem he had.

You don't believe in love, they do. You hate, they don't.

A claw thrust into his throat and sliced down to his heart. He slowed the pace. He took the backpack off his shoulders. It felt like it had been filled with stone.

'Did you see them?' Zombie was walking next to him.

Mantos was unable to say a single word. A lump had formed in his throat. He looked forlornly at his adept.

'Let them go. They're different from us. They live in the light, we live in the shadows.'

Mantos swallowed, but the lump didn't disappear. He was short of breath. The claw was cutting his lungs to shreds.

'You still have time. Let them go.'

Saverio gabbed a hold of Zombie's arm as if he had trouble standing. He squeezed his teary eyes and looked at him. 'Thank you.'

He called to them with the little breath he had left. 'You two, come here.'

Murder and Silvietta moved closer to him. 'What's the matter? Are you sick?'

Saverio put his hands in his pockets, he tried to think of a reasonable excuse, but he was too worked up. He managed to say: 'Go home. Go on.'

Murder stuck out his neck, like he'd misunderstood. 'What?'

'Go off home. No mucking about.'

'Why?'

Bad. You are the son of Satan.

'You do not deserve to be Wilde Beasts of Abaddon.'

Murder had gone pale. 'What did we do wrong?'

The leader of the Beasts squeezed his fists in his pockets. 'You are disgusting. You love each other. You care for each other. It is hate that must nurture you, and instead you are full of love. You make me sick.'

Silvietta shook her head and looked at Zombie. 'You told him about the wedding . . . But why? I asked you not to say anything to him.'

Mantos looked at Zombie without understanding. What was she talking about? He was about to ask him, but the adept rushed to say: 'Yes, I told him that you wanted to get married. I couldn't hide it from him.'

Oh God, they wanted to get married. Why didn't they say anything to me?

Murder looked at him with guilty eyes. 'I tried to tell you . . .'

They didn't have the guts.

'But . . . we changed our minds, I swear. We don't want to get married any more. It was a load of crap. We want to stay with you guys, until the end.'

Mantos wanted to hug them. 'You have broken a Satanic promise. As such, I, the leader of the Wilde Beasts of Abaddon, expel you from the sect.' He said it with all the evil he had in his body, but in doing so he also ripped off a strip of his heart.

'You can't do that. It's not fair.' Silvietta burst into sobs and tried to take his hand.

Mantos took three steps backwards and the girl fell to her knees. 'I decide what is fair. I order you to leave.' He turned to Zombie. 'Come on, let's go.'

Murder hugged Silvietta. 'Don't cry, my heart.'

What was left of the Wilde Beasts of Abaddon walked off towards the forest without turning back.

46

'Not even on the Nevsky Prospekt at eight o'clock in the evening do people drive so slowly,' said Milo Serinov to Paco Jimenez.

'You are right, hombre. Ahora, I show you.' The centre-forward leaned out of the basket, towards the driver. 'Hey . . . niño . . .'

The Filipino turned around and looked up at him. 'Yeah?'

'¡*Descánsate*!' The centre-forward shoved the poor man, who lost his balance, disappearing without a peep into a blackberry bush. With his proverbial agility, Paco jumped on the elephant's neck and began to thrash the shit out of the pachyderm's head. The beast rolled its eye as big as a frying pan and stared the football player over, but he didn't quit. So it raised its trunk, uttering a powerful trumpet, and began to gallop.

Paco, Milo and their girlfriends squealed excitedly.

Ciba saw the elephant coming towards them from the rear like a locomotive without brakes, and then the two animals began to shoulder each other. The baskets wobbled frightfully.

'Where the fuck are you going?' screamed the writer, who almost fell off the edge.

'Move over, slowcoaches!' Milo Serinov was really enjoying himself. 'Let us through,' screeched Taja Testari, but the branch of a hundred-year-old oak hit her on the nasal septum and a spurt of blood reddened Mariapia Morozzi's dress.

'Owwwww! That hurt!' screamed the model, flopping inside the basket.

'One down!' screeched Ciba, who had lost his intellectual aplomb and was getting excited.

Even Paco seemed revved up. Nothing could stop him. '¡Ándale! ¡Ándale con juicio!' And he was about to overtake them when, a dozen metres in front, as fast as a high-speed train, they were cut off by the fox, which, who knows how, had managed to do that to its hunters.

When it passed by, they all screamed: 'The fox! The fox!'

'This is the tiger hunt. What is the fox doing here?' asked Larita.

Old Cinelli came out of his coma and, with a flash of his hand, grabbed the rifle from the bottom of the basket, screaming 'The fox! The fox!' And he began shooting wildly into the forest.

Bullets whistled all over the place.

The singer curled up with her hands over her ears while Ciba grabbed the barrel of the rifle, trying to rip it from the old nutjob, who kept on pulling the trigger. A bullet hit the metal buckle of the basket on the last elephant in line. The belt unlatched and the heavy metal group from Ancona were flipped out. The musicians landed in a field of nettles.

Finally Cinelli's rifle ran out of ammunition. The old man looked around. 'Did I hit it, eh? Did I hit it?'

The elephant race swept away everything. Branches, toppled trees, bushes.

A spine-tingling scream rose from the forest on their left. Astride a stallion, Paolo Bocchi was galloping along, twirling a sabre like a Hussar at the Battle of Marengo. He trotted past the elephants and overtook them, shouting: 'Savoy or death!' He was wearing only riding breeches. His bare chest was whipped by branches and thorns. As the steed went by, the two elephants became even angrier and increased the pace. The surgeon, as quick as the wind, jumped over a hedge and disappeared into the woods. A moment later a pack of howling dogs scurried beneath the pachyderms' legs, following Bocchi and the fox. The elephant driven by Paco Jimenez braked suddenly in terror. Rome's centre-forward and the basket took off like bullets and disappeared into the vegetation.

The sound of an English horn rose up from the shadows of the woods. The stamping noise of hooves grew near. Running in the wrong direction, thirty-eight riders materialised, wearing red jackets and thirsty for fox blood. They noticed the elephants blocking their way only when it was too late. In the ranks of the horse riders many fell, others were dragged with their foot caught in the stirrups for kilometres. Few emerged uninjured.

The elephant carrying the film agent Elena Paleologo Rossi Strozzi, the Maghrebi fashion designer and the head of drama at RAI Television overturned like an A112 Abarth on the bend on Monte Mario.

Fabrizio Ciba, still aboard his elephant, realised that their Filipino guide had disappeared. He tried to stop the animal by hitting it with the butt of the rifle, but the beast simply dodged to the side and headed towards the thick forest. Old Cinelli spun around, flew backwards, bounced off one of the elephant's buttocks and ended up hanging from its tail. The grandson tried for an, at once, heroic and desperate gesture. He got out of the basket and, holding on to the edge with one hand, tried to grab his grandfather with the other. The old man took his grandson's hand. 'Pull, pull!'

The two then tumbled to the ground amidst a lot of butcher's broom bushes.

Ciba and Larita were now alone on the back of a crazed beast.

47

Relief and suffering melted together inside Mantos's tormented soul as he made his way through the reeds growing along the edge of the swamp. Zombie was following him in silence.

Since they had abandoned Murder and Silvietta, neither of them had spoken.

The leader of the Beasts kept seeing them there, hugging each other, watching them as they walked away.

He was reminded of Kurtz Minetti's prophetic words. 'The Wilde Beasts of Abaddon are an INSIGNIFICANT blip. You're over.' He hadn't been wrong; the situation was desperate. Two fundamental members of the team had left and the plan to kill Larita was leaking water. And there was one more thing that didn't make sense to him. Why did Zombie want to commit suicide? Why hadn't he left with his friends? Weren't the three of them always together? He had slithered up to him like a snake and whispered to him to dump the other two.

Don't tell me that loveable Zombie, all hush-hush, has joined the ranks of Kurtz Minetti?

The priest from the Children of the Apocalypse could have corrupted him and charged him to boycott the assassination of Larita, to make Mantos look like an idiot in the Satanic community, and avenge himself for Saverio saying no. Even that scene he made at the Villa earlier was weird.

Mantos stopped, pretending to catch his breath. 'Everything okay?'

Zombie, worn out from the effort, placed his hands on his hips and nodded. His face was a darker olive colour than usual.

The leader of the Beasts looked him straight in the eye. 'Listen, shall we give it up?' It was a trick question to try and understand whether the adept was a dirty traitor. 'Maybe we should pack it in, too . . . This is such a cock-up. The two of us can't do it on our own. And then, what if at the end we don't have the courage to commit suicide? We risk just getting thrown in prison. If we go home now, we're saved.'

Zombie started walking again, with his head lowered. 'I'm not giving up. If you want to, go ahead.'

'But why? I don't understand why you suddenly care so much about this thing. Usually nothing suits you. Tell me why you want to kill yourself now, at all costs?'

'I don't feel like talking about it.'

Mantos grabbed him by the arm and stared at him threateningly. 'No, you tell me about it right now.'

'Let me go.' The adept tried to shake himself free of Mantos's grasp.

'Tell me. I am your leader. I order you to.'

Zombie swallowed and then spoke in a far-off voice. 'A

couple of nights ago I woke suddenly, as if someone had shaken my arm. I thought it was my father telling me that mum wasn't well. But everyone was asleep. As usual I had fallen asleep with the television on. There was a thing in black and white about theatre. Old stuff. The sort of stuff they show on RAI Tre at four in the morning. I picked up the remote and was about to turn it off when the actor, an old man with pointy eyes and a fringe, said something. I'd never heard anything like it before in my life, and since that night everything changed, nothing meant anything to me any more.'

Mantos was unprepared. 'And what did he say?'

Zombie looked as if he wasn't sure whether he should answer or not, but then: 'Do you want to hear it?'

'Yes. Of course.'

'I learned it by heart. I bought the book. But I've never recited it for anyone.'

'Go on, let me hear it.'

'All right.' Zombie put his legs apart, as if waves of pain were breaking over his body. He closed his eyes, opened them again, looked towards the sky and began reciting in a croaky, shaky voice. 'I have of late – but wherefore I know not – lost all my mirth, forgone all custom of exercises; and indeed it goes so heavily with my disposition that this goodly frame, the earth, seems to me a sterile promontory, this most excellent canopy, the air, look you, this brave o'erhanging firmament, this majestical roof fretted with golden fire, why, it appears no other thing to me than a foul and pestilent congregation of vapours. What a piece of work is a man! how noble in reason! How infinite in faculties, in form and moving how express and admirable, in action how like an angel, in apprehension how like a god! The beauty of the world, the paragon of animals! And yet, to me, what is this quintessence of dust? Man delights not me – no, nor woman neither.'

214

Mantos was silent and then asked him: 'Who wrote it?'

Zombie sniffed. 'William Shakespeare. It's Hamlet. I'm worse off than him. And the way I'm feeling, I could even do something good . . . I thought about it . . . But it's a thousand times harder than doing something evil. And frankly, I don't give a fuck about helping, I don't know . . . African babies. They annoy the shit out of me, just like the rest of humanity, and so I prefer to end it and to be remembered as the psychopathic bastard who killed Larita. And don't forget that you were the first to say that. It's all very simple and . . .' He took a deep breath. 'Sad. Anyway, if you want to give up, don't worry, I'll kill the singer. But, please, hurry, the mosquitoes are bleeding me dry.'

Mantos was ashamed to have thought that Zombie could be a traitor. Of course, he was in a really bad way. He must have stopped taking the anti-depressants.

'Zombie, listen to me closely. There are no longer ranks between the two of us. There is no more leader and adept. We're the same. The Beasts are you and me. A duo. Like Simon and Garfunkel, you know.'

Zombie's eyes teared-up. 'You and me. The same and together. Until the end.'

'The same and together. Until the end,' Mantos repeated.

Zombie looked at the sky. 'It's night time. I'm going to sabotage the electrical plant.'

'All right. I'll kidnap Larita and I'll catch you at the temple on Forte Antenne. Tonight the moon is right for ending it.'

48

With a deafening roar, an enormous age-old pine tree fell onto the woods. Beneath the weight of the tree, holm oaks, oak tree and laurel bushes were crushed, and from the earth a cloud of dust and leaves rose up. And, like in a primeval nightmare, the huge elephant emerged. Beneath the beast's stampeding feet the earth trembled. Nothing could stop it. Its brain had shrunk down to a simple and primitive impulse: run. Its famous long-term memory had been re-set, and in the evolutionary chain it had sunk down into the abysses where the sardines flee from tuna fish.

It no longer remembered its infancy spent in a wandering cage. It no longer remembered exercising in the circus ring. It no longer remembered bowing, spraying water at the clowns. It didn't even remember the lashes and the potatoes. It remembered nothing at all, for terror had overcome it. What was this dark, inhospitable place? What were those stakes sticking out of the ground? Those smells? It just had to get away, and thorny bushes, fallen trunks, shrubs, weeds, nothing could stop its running. Every now and then it bent back its long trunk and, giving a heart-rending trumpet, it would rip a tree trunk out of the ground and throw it far away. The colourful quarter-sheet that covered it had been ripped to shreds and blood was dripping from a long gash on its side onto its hind legs. A branch had lodged itself like a harpoon in its right shoulder. It kept hitting its head. One eye was black and the other wide open, with the pupil rolling wildly, as it broke its way through the wall of vegetation.

The half-ruined basket was still tied to its back but it was hanging lopsidedly off to one side. Inside, Fabrizio and Larita were hanging on to the belts of the harness and screaming in terror, just as scared as the elephant.

The beast dodged an oak tree and almost tripped over a tree root as thick as an anaconda, but it regained its balance and began galloping again, diving into a thorn bush. It jumped a ditch, took a step, then another, and suddenly the ground was missing underneath its feet. The crazy eye stopped rolling, it opened its mouth wide in surprise and, waving its feet and trunk, it fell silently down a vegetation-covered slope. It flew about twenty metres towards the bottom of the ravine, hit its head on a stone pinnacle, bounced, rolled over and was jammed between two trees that stuck out like a fork above the chasm.

The animal, its spine snapped, belly up, squirmed and released terrible screeches of pain, which became weaker and weaker.

Fabrizio was thrown from the basket and found himself flopping downwards in the dark, ricocheting off branches, hanging vines and chains of ivy until he crashed into the twisted roots of an oak tree hanging from the rock face.

A moment later Larita fell on top of him and slid towards the precipice.

The writer grabbed her by the collar of her jacket a second before she fell to the ground. Her weight pulled him down and a stab of pain in his tricep ripped the air from his lungs.

Larita, hanging mid-air, was struggling and looking below her, screaming: 'Help! Help!'

'Keep still! Keep still!' Ciba begged. 'If you move, I can't keep holding you.'

'Help me! Please, help me. Don't let me go.'

Ciba closed his eyes, trying to catch his breath. His biceps were trembling from the tension. 'I can't hold on. Grab on to something.'

Larita stretched out a hand towards a bundle of ivy that snaked up between the rocks. 'I can't reach it! I can't fucking reach it!'

'You have to try, I can't take it any more . . .' Ciba's face had turned purple and his heart was booming in his ear drums.

He shouldn't look down; it was a free fall of at least thirty metres.

I am not a man. I am a mooring line. I don't feel pain, I have no brain, he began repeating to himself. But the muscles in his arms were trembling. He could feel, with horror, his fingers losing their grip on the material of the jacket. Out of desperation he bit into the root and screamed: 'I won't drop you. I won't drop you.'

And instead he dropped her.

His face pressed against the hanging vine, he didn't move, almost paralysed. Too shaken to be able to think, to cry, to look down.

Then a feeble voice: 'Fabrizio. I'm down here.'

The writer peeped over the edge and, in the light of the moon, he saw Larita below him, a few metres below, hanging on to the ivy that grew against the rock face.

Neither of them spoke as they gulped air. When Fabrizio had the breath to speak, he asked her: 'Are you all right?'

Larita was wrapped around the plant. 'Yes. I did it . . . I did it.'

'Don't look down, Larita.' Ciba lay back against the root, rubbing his aching right arm.

A tiny stone bounced off his forehead. Then another. Then it began to rain gravel, dirt and dried branches. Ciba looked up above him. The ball-shaped moon was in the centre of the sky. He bent his head and in the middle of the glowing satellite the black outline of the elephant was painted, like a shadow puppet, lying on the oak tree.

It was right above him.

As he put his hand over his eyes to protect them from the falling earth, he heard the sound of wood snapping. The tree was swinging from side to side.

'Oh Madonna!' he murmured.

'What's happening?' asked Larita.

'The elephant! It's about to . . .'

The tree trunk gave way with a deafening crack. The pachyderm let out a last desperate scream and plummeted, along with the oak tree and a fountain of stones.

Ciba, instinctively, wrapped his arms around his head. He closed his eyes. His guts rose into his throat.

No, he was flying in the blackness. The darkness surrounded him like a merciful mother, stopping him from seeing the ground below him coming closer. How many times had he asked himself whether people committing suicide had the time to understand their ending before crashing to the ground? Or if their brain, pitifully, in the face of such a terrible death had a blackout of the senses.

Now he knew. The brain worked perfectly, and screamed: 'You're going to die!'

49

The moon dyed the grass silver. But Edo Sambreddero aka Zombie walked across the savanna, his head lowered, without even condescending to notice it. In one hand he was holding the poultry shears.

A light breeze, cool enough to make him shiver, slipped under his coat. The Satanist rubbed his arms to try and free himself of that chill that wouldn't leave him.

A herd of gazelles passed in front of him, followed by a mob of kangaroos. Not even that sight caught his attention.

What was it that Hamlet said? 'This goodly frame, the earth, seems to me a sterile promontory, this most excellent canopy, the air, look you, this brave o'erhanging firmament, this majestical roof fretted with golden fire, why, it appears no other thing to me than a foul and pestilent congregation of vapours.'

Yeah, the earth really was a disgusting place.

Only in a disgusting place like this can Silvietta marry someone like Murder.

When he surprised the two love birds talking about their wedding, at first he'd thought it was joke. *It can't be true,* he kept saying to himself while the two of them discussed the church, the reception and all that other crap. Then he had seen Silvietta moved to tears, and he'd understood that it was true, and something had shrivelled inside of him for ever.

When he was a boy his granddad used to take him to the vegetable patch, a small piece of land beneath the viaduct of Oriolo, and he would give him a little bottle of poison for getting rid of the weeds. 'You only need a drop,' his granddad would warn him, and Edo would use the dropper so that just one drop, as black as petrol, would fall on the top of the plant. And in less than half an hour, it would lose its colours and shrink until it was nothing but a dried up twig.

The same thing has happened to me. Silvietta had dried up his heart for ever.

How many times had she complained about Murder to him, how coarse and distracted he was, how he always forgot their monthiversary?

'I can't talk to him like I talk to you. You're different. You get me . . .'

How many nights had they spent talking on the phone and watching *Amici* on the telly, hating these talentless monsters who fought all the time, or talking about music, about Motorhead and the historical importance of *Denim and Leather* by Saxon? How many Saturday afternoons had they spent walking up and down Via del Corso, forgetting time as it passed, forgetting the sales in the shops, the people around them, the bus that took them home?

Of course, they weren't a couple. She was Murder's girlfriend. But what did that chubby guy with dandruff have that he didn't?

All right, he suffered from congenital oesophagitis. But he'd read on the Internet that a definitive cure existed using stem cells. It was illegal in Italy, but as soon as his mother died he would have inherited the gold coins of Pope Luciani, and he would have enough money to be cured in America.

Once, Murder had gone to visit his aunt in Follonica, and the two of them had gone out to dinner at the Pizzeria Jerry 2. It had been a special evening, there had been a unique sense of intimacy. She had told him about her fears as a small girl, about her dream to become a death metal queen.

Afterwards he'd taken her home and said goodbye, giving her the usual respectful kiss on the cheek, but with her lips she had brushed against the corner of his mouth. It had been just a moment, and yet the skin, where Silvietta had placed her kiss, had become sensitive like when you burn yourself on a scorching hot fork.

For months he had thought of that kiss. If he, stupidly, hadn't moved his head, they probably would have kissed on the lips.

He placed his finger on the burnt corner. He felt a shiver and gritted his teeth to stop himself crying. He thought back to the night of the sacrifice in the woods of Sutri. The others had simply fucked her and come on her like a pack of horny dogs. He hadn't. It had been different for him. He had put love into it, and when he finally came he had lain on her small white breasts with tears in his eyes, and the desire to pick her up and carry her away.

221

And after they had buried her alive, without letting the others see him he had moved the dirt in such a way that Silvietta could climb out of the grave. When he'd seen her, three days later, sitting on a bench outside the cinema, he'd understood that this incredible girl was the love of his life.

And now he'd discovered that she was marrying Murder. *Muffin.*

There wasn't much else to say, except that there was no sense in living any more.

50

Not even this time did good fortune abandon Fabrizio Ciba. He landed on the flabby stomach of the elephant, which was lying on its side in a rivulet that flowed between stones and ferns. Larita, tangled in a ball of ivy, fell down next to him one second later. The two of them lay there, without moving, grazed, aching and lost for words, incredulous at the idea that they were still alive.

Then Fabrizio pulled himself up, helped Larita to get down off the elephant, and looked around. They were at the bottom of a narrow ravine covered in vegetation. A gravel path stretched right through the middle, dotted with street lamps that created little shiny domes. Everything else – beside them, above them – was wrapped in darkness.

He couldn't bear to think about what had just happened to them. If an elephant hadn't been there to cushion their fall, they would be dead as dodoes right now.

Who organises a safari in Villa Ada? Only a crazy megalomaniac like Chiatti can come up with such a stupid idea.

But it wasn't Chiatti's fault if he'd almost lost his skin.

It's mine. It's my fault for coming to this party. I shouldn't have come. What the fuck am I doing here? How the fuck did I let them convince me to get on that animal? With all those monsters? I am a writer, for fuck's sake . . . I have to write my novel. My novel . . .

He touched his arm. He had difficulty bending it.

If I've dislocated my shoulder, I'll never be able to write again.

It was too much for Fabrizio Ciba. A rage as bitter as vinegar started to bubble in his stomach and rise towards his oesophagus. The more he thought about what had happened to him, the angrier he got. He was so full of rage that he risked exploding like a football. He began to sway his head up and down like a pigeon pecking at grain, and then, gritting his teeth, he started muttering to himself and gesturing with his hands. 'Fuck off! I'm going to fuck them all over. One by one. I'll line them up and I'll fuck them one by one.' His nostrils flared in fury. 'To begin with, I'll fuck over that joker Chiatti . . . I'll write the article and I'll ruin him. That big ball of shit has ended his days of recieving kindness. Who does he think he's dealing with?'

He turned suddenly towards Larita in search of support. 'Can you explain what the fuck those fox hunters were doing . . .?' But he fell quiet, seeing her stock-still, paralysed next to the dead animal.

He felt like he was watching the last scene from *King Kong*. When the girl stays by the side of the big ape fallen from the skyscraper.

Larita really was tiny next to the elephant. In death, the pachyderm looked even bigger than when it was alive. Its trunk stretched out like a snake amongst the stones of the creek. Its feet drew up against its stomach; a broken tusk. The open eye reflected the light of the street lamp. Blood trickled from its mouth and dissolved in the water.

Larita suddenly, as if freed from a magic spell, opened her mouth, trying to breath in deeply, but something stopped her. So she slowly reached her hand and placed it on the elephant's wrinkly forehead. Then, as if the strings that kept her standing had been cut, she slumped down and curled against its rump and began to cry, shaken by sobs.

Fabrizio put a hand over his mouth. How could he have forgotten about Larita? She was the only precious thing amongst all this crap. She was the angel who would save him. She and him were different. She and him had nothing to do with that party. And he had to take care of this beautiful creature and carry her to safety.

He ran to her and hugged her tight, feeling her small body jolted by sobs. She was so small. So helpless.

Larita, her eyes soaked in tears, her face on fire, swallowing air, tried to talk to him: 'Po . . . po . . . poor thing . . .'

Who's she talking about?

'It's not . . . it's not fair . . . He had done no . . . thing wrong.' And she was gripped by sobs again.

About the elephant, you idiot.

He hugged her head and laid it on his shoulder. 'Don't cry. Please . . . Don't cry,' he whispered in her ear as he stroked her hair. But she wouldn't stop. As soon as the rhythm slowed, she'd start over again.

Fabrizio tried to say something. A gabble of senseless sentences. 'No . . . It didn't suffer much . . . It broke its back, it didn't feel anything . . . It has been freed . . . A life spent in chains.'

Nothing, she kept on crying, like she was battery-powered. In despair, unable to find a way to calm her, he grabbed her by the back of the neck, brushed her hair from off her face and, with a naturalness that he had never felt before in his life, he parted his lips and kissed her.

51

Zombie made it to the electrical plant; he was tired, but still determined.

Halogen spotlights created a bubble of light around the building, which shone in the dark like an underwater sea station. The plant was surrounded by three-metre-high metal fencing. To get inside, you had to pass through a gate with a yellow sign. It had a skull painted on it and warned: 'HIGH VOLTAGE. DANGER. KEEP OUT.' In the yard around the little brick building two rows of big metal transformers were lined up and hummed like bee hives. Heaps of wires were wrapped around some ceramic electrodes and then stuck into the ground.

Zombie, in his brief career as an apprentice electrician, had at most dealt with the electrical plant of Villa Giorgini in Capranica, a nine-kilowatt, three-phase system for domestic use, with a safety switch and electricity meter.

Now he was faced with a real, proper miniature power station. He remembered having read something about them in the correspondence course he'd done with Scuola Radio Elettra. There were thermal power stations, hydropower and nuclear power stations. It couldn't be hydropower because there weren't any rivers or dams around. He ruled out nuclear power. So it was probably thermal and, anyway, who gives a fuck, all he had to do was sabotage it.

Luckily there weren't any guards at the power station. The gate was secured with a padlock and chain.

Zombie placed the silver poultry shears on one of the links and squeezed. The steel wouldn't give. He ground his teeth and squeezed harder. His faced turned purple from the effort. Slowly the ring began to bend. He increased the pressure and in one blow the chain and the poultry shears broke apart. He was left holding the two handles of the tool. He threw them away and walked inside.

The little metal door was obviously locked. He kicked at it with the sole of his shoe and it flew open onto a small room full of electronic panels. Ammeters, switches, cursors, lit-up LEDs, levers. Zombie studied the instrumentation, looking perplexed. It was like being in the cockpit of an airplane. He tried to press some buttons, lower a couple of levers, but nothing significant happened. Fiddling with stuff he might succeed in turning it off, but it could always be turned back on again. He needed to destroy it and leave the park in the dark.

Inside a glass cabinet he saw an axe with a red handle. He broke the glass and grabbed a hold of the tool. He noticed that in the middle of all of that equipment a big metal plaque was bolted to a wall. Three cables, as thick as mooring lines for a ferry, wound inside a huge steel switch. In the middle was a lever and a lock to stop anyone from lifting the switch. That was the heart of the power station.

He had to cut one of those cables and . . .

What sort of voltage would it have?

He had no idea. But it was enough to toast him.

He would die, and so he would complete his mission. Even if, to be honest, he didn't give a fuck about the mission, the Devil, Mantos, that Satanist crap.

He felt as sad as a dead duck, but he had the strange sensation that an audience was observing him as he completed his final gestures. He was the cursed hero of his own, tragic, film.

There was a note pad on the bench. He ripped off a page and, without thinking too much about it, he wrote down a couple of lines. He folded it and wrote on the front: 'For Silvietta'.

52

Mantos, naked, was standing on a rock, studying the moon and its craters. The wind caressed his skin.

Arms stretched out. Legs slightly bent. The Durendal in his hands, pointed in front of him. He inhaled and exhaled, freeing himself of useless thoughts. Serena melted away, the old arsehole melted away, Silvietta and Murder melted away, and Mantos concentrated on the miracle of coordination his body held. With every movement he became more aware of the energy running through the fibres of his muscles, of the deadly power held within the Durendal.

He felt the pain of separating himself from his earthly life rising up. He greeted it and bid it welcome. He lowered the Durendal, brought the hilt up against his stomach and raised his left leg. He isolated every tendon, every muscle, enjoying the feelings it gave him. The cold grabbed him by the scrotum.

Mantos was finally at ease. He was able to hear everything. The swishing of the wind in the trees, the guttural grunting of the warthogs in the swamp, the cries from the bat colony from Siam hanging on the pine branches, the traffic on the Olimpica, the tellies in lounge rooms, the sick world.

Then something made him startle. His windpipe closed and a shiver went up his spine. The feeling that someone, hidden in the darkness, was spying on him.

It wasn't an animal. But it wasn't human either. What was it?

He stretched out the sword and began turning around. He couldn't see anyone. The leader of the Wilde Beasts of Abaddon jumped down from the rock and, keeping the weapon ready, took the torch from his backpack and turned it on. The ray of light shone on the laurel bushes, on the blackberry bushes, on the tree trunks, on a rusty bin.

Nobody was there. Maybe his senses had made a mistake. Yet the feeling that someone was observing him remained. Eyes full of hate.

Mantos quickly slipped on his trousers, shoes and the black tunic. He then pulled on the backpack and ran off.

53

Zombie brushed the corner of his mouth with his middle finger – there, where Silvietta had kissed him. He stuck the letter in the panel, spat in his hands, grabbed the axe and, with his legs parted, positioned himself in front of the cable.

The moment had come to show everyone the courage he had kept hidden inside.

'Man delights not me: no, nor woman neither.'

He lifted the handle and, with all the strength and desperation he had in his thin body, he cut the cable.

Twenty thousand volts of electricity were rushing through that copper wire, about ten times as much as is used for the electric chair. The flow of electrons travelled down the blade and the handle of the axe, which, even though it was made of wood, was burnt to ashes in a second.

The hands and the arms of the adept followed the same destiny. The rest of his body caught fire in a spectacular blaze.

The human torch began to knock around and bounce against

the walls of the small room. Then he stopped, threw his arms wide like a fallen angel that wants to fly, and slumped to the ground, burning away until what remained of Edo Sambreddero, aka Zombie, was nothing more than a charred log.

The turbines of the power station stopped. The buzzing was silenced. The lights of the park and the villa went off. Even the computers that controlled the waterfalls, the flow of water into the lakes, the sheds for the animals and everything else, were turned off.

A generator went into action. It turned on the emergency lighting in the house and activated the pneumatic pumps of the solid-steel gate at the entrances, which closed, leaving Villa Ada in the dark and cut off from the rest of the city.

Arrival at the Bivouac and Dinner

54

Fabrizio Ciba and Larita were kissing next to the elephant's corpse when the streetlights on the path went out. The writer opened his eyes and found himself immersed in complete darkness. 'The lights! The lights have gone out!'

'Oh my God.' Larita hugged Fabrizio in fear. 'Now what? What do we do?'

The writer took a while to understand the nature of the problem. The passionate kiss had stunned him. The rage had dissipated and a strange feeling of well-being made him feel weak all over. Now that, finally, he had found love, everything else seemed irrelevant. His sole desire was to wash her, care for her, tend her wounds and make love to her. The elephant ride through the woods, the fall, the certainty of death and the surprise at being alive, that mix of fear, anger and death, had turned him on big-time.

'And now what do we do?' She squeezed up to him.

Fabrizio felt Larita's heart beating strongly behind her tits. 'I don't know . . . But hey . . . Can't we just stay here? What do we care?' He had forgotten that ancient pleasure of feeling the consistency of a pair of silicone-free tits.

'Are you crazy?'

'Why? We wait for dawn. We could hide in the thickets and behave like primitives without rules . . .' If that hadn't been real life, but one of his own novels, the main character would have taken Larita now and, without too much chit-chat, he would have undressed her and then he would have had her on the elephant's carcass, with the blood, the sperm and the tears running together as in an ancestral orgy. Yes, in his new novel he'd include a nice little sex scene like this. In Sardegna, somewhere near Oristano.

Larita interrupted his thoughts. 'The park is full of man-eating animals. The tiger . . . the lions . . .'

He had completely forgotten about the wild beasts. He squeezed her hand. 'Yes, you're right, we've got to get moving. But I can't see a thing. Let's hope they repair the problem quickly.'

'We have to keep to the path.'

'Which way is the house? To the right or to the left?'

'To the left, I think. I hope . . .'

'All right. We'll walk along the path. It's just a few metres away.'

Fabrizio was suddenly decisive. Despite his fear of ferocious beasts, having this woman beside him in need of protection made him feel strong and fearless. He got to his feet and helped Larita to pull herself up. 'Hold on to my belt and stay behind me.' He put out his arms like a sleepwalker and, wobbling over the rocks, he took a few uncertain steps in the dark. 'This way we'll hurt ourselves, though. We're better off on all-fours.'

And so they crawled until the two of them felt the gravel beneath their hands.

There, in the centre of the ravine, where there were no trees, the sky reflected the lights of the city and they were able to make out a fence that surrounded the trench in the middle of the road.

'Here we are!' Fabrizio stood up. 'Let's hold on to the fence and walk along here. But first I need something, otherwise I can't go on any further.'

'What?'

231

'Another kiss.'

He opened his mouth and felt her tongue slide over his, lapping at his palate and tonsils. He hugged her tight, he pulled her up against him, but he held back from making her feel his erection.

Yes, we really are a beautiful couple.

I'm going to marry this girl . . .

I'm so lucky to have met her. And it's all thanks to that clown Salvatore Chiatti and his rubbish party.

All right, Sasà, I'll let you off. I won't write an article against you.

55

'Yes! Zombie, you're the best!' the leader of the Wilde Beasts of Abaddon had screamed, pushing his fists into the air when darkness had shrouded the Villa.

It was about time something went in his favour. Now all he had to do was grab the singer.

Mantos shone the torch around, to try and understand where he was. The road he was walking continued on into a sort of ravine that split the wood in two. He pulled the small map of Villa Ada out of his backpack and studied it carefully.

'Perfect!' He was in the right direction, he had to go down the canyon and would come straight to the lake where they had organised the bivouac for the participants in the tiger hunt. That's where he would find the singer, along with the other guests, all of them afraid. In the confusion and under the cover of the darkness, it'd be a piece of cake to drug her and kidnap her.

Elated, he began to run, the Durendal in his left hand, the torch in his right, and adrenalin flooding his arteries. What a

232

weird phenomenon: now that he was about to die, he felt more alive than he had felt in his whole life, capable of doing anything. Satan was finally on his side. He was a free swinger, an anarchical spirit, a bloodhound of chaos. Someone like him was not afraid of death, and gave his best when chaos reigned.

You'll finally see who you're up against, my dear Mr Kurtz Minetti.

Just as he was jumping over a puddle, a flash of light behind him lit up the road. The leader of the Beasts turned off his torch, threw himself to the side, hiding behind an oak tree.

A car was coming. He could see the headlights coming closer, but he couldn't hear any noise. It had to be one of those electric buggies that they used to move around the Villa.

He stood still and waited for it to go by. There was only the driver inside the small convertible.

And if I hijacked the car? I could use it to load up Larita and take her to the sacrificial spot.

Without stopping to think, he took off, head down, following the small car.

56

Fabrizio Ciba, feeling happy, was thinking that in a couple of days' time he would be with his beautiful girlfriend in Majorca, at Capdepera, in his house. But then he remembered how humid it was, the dead spiders in the bath tub, the central heating with air locks. And the table with the novel on it, waiting for him. He had to reconstruct the entire storyline, cut out some charac . . .

The writer's brain stalled for a second and reset, wiping out that last thought.

What was the name of that five-star hotel with the spa . . .?

They should go on a proper holiday, go to a far-off place where they could unwind and live out their love affair. He laid an arm across Larita's shoulders, as if they were old companions. 'Listen, what do you say to a nice little holiday to recover? How about the Maldives? You know those bungalows by the sea, the sultry nights beneath the dome of stars, the beds with mosquito nets . . .'

'Of course. I'd like that.' Larita was silent for a moment. 'Listen, Fabrizio . . .'

'Yes?'

It took her a few too many seconds to ask him the question. 'Do you have a girlfriend?'

'Me? Don't be silly!' Ciba answered quickly.

'Does the idea make you sick?'

'No, not at all. It's just that I'm a writer . . . Well, you're a musician, maybe you can understand me. I'm a little afraid of my feelings. If they're too strong, I worry they'll dry me up. It's an irrational fear, I know, but I have the feeling that when I let love into my life, I don't have enough to give to the characters in my books.' He was revealing something that he had never told anyone before. 'That doesn't mean that I'm not ready to give it a go. What about you?' He would have liked to look at her, but the darkness only let him intuit her silhouette.

'I ended a relationship with a guy who didn't love himself at all. In other words, an arsehole. And I risked my life following him. Don Toniolo's rehab centre, and my faith, saved me.'

While Larita spoke, Fabrizio recalled having read somewhere that she had been in a relationship with a drug addict singer, and that they both nearly died of overdoses.

'And then since I got back to a normal lifestyle, I haven't

234

had the guts to get into other relationships. I am afraid I'll meet another arsehole. Even if being on my own, sometimes, is sad.'

Fabrizio pulled her towards him and wrapped his arm around her waist. 'The two of us could really be happy together. I can feel it.'

Larita laughed. 'Who knows why, but I was convinced you had a girlfriend. After the lunch back in the Villa, I tried to call my agent to find out, but he had his mobile off. Do you believe in destiny?'

'I believe in the facts. And the facts say that we are both survivors. And they say that we have to give it a chance.' He hugged her hard, as if she might run away, and kissed her. What a pity they were in the dark, he would have liked to look in her eyes.

She suddenly pulled away. 'And if we went to Nairobi instead?'

'You want to go to Kenya? I went there once. Malindi. The sea isn't bad, but nothing compared to the Maldives.'

They began walking again.

'No . . . No . . . What are you thinking? To the slums of Nairobi, to vaccinate children. I do it every year. It's really important. If you came, too, a famous writer, you would be giving them a gift. You would help the missionaries to throw light on this terrible situation.'

Fabrizio rolled his eyes up at the sky. Bloody fucking hell, he wanted to spend a quiet week relaxing and she, in answer, offered him a humanitarian nightmare.

'Well, yeah . . . Sure . . . We could . . . But . . .' he stuttered.

'But what?'

Fabrizio was unable to be insincere. 'Well, I was thinking of a holiday. Five-star. Breakfast in bed. That sort of thing.'

She caressed his neck. 'You'll see . . . It'll be a thousand times better . . . I'm sure the experience will help you to write, too. You can't imagine how many ideas come to mind standing amidst all that pain.'

The writer didn't speak. If he wanted to have a serious relationship with a woman, he had to learn to take into consideration her wishes, and to trust her. And Larita was special. She had a strength greater than he would ever have imagined; she was a typhoon that swept away everything that stood in front of her, and at the same time she was vulnerable and innocent in a way that made you reconsider who you were.

'Yes,' said Fabrizio. 'All right, I'll come. I'll bring my computer so in the evenings, after the vaccines, I'll write.'

Larita squeezed his hand hard and, in a voice charged with emotion, said: 'Come on, let's get out of this place. The real world is expecting us.'

57

Luckily, that little contraption was slow.

Mantos, out of breath, grabbed on to the back hatch and, with a clumsy leap, climbed on board. The driver didn't notice a thing.

There were huge saucepans on a tray on the back, which smelled strongly of curry.

Now he had to knock out the driver. He pulled on his hood, shrank back like a cat and, roaring like Sandokan, he jumped on the man, who, upon hearing that bestial scream and believing it was the tiger, instinctively slammed on the brakes.

The leader of the Wilde Beasts of Abaddon, sword in hand, continued to fly, gliding over the hood of the car and landing bear-rug style in the middle of the street. The Durendal flew from his hand. The bumper bar stopped twenty centimetres from his feet.

Mbuma Bowanda, originally from Burkina Faso, where he'd been a shepherd for years, had seen a strange creature zoom over his head, overtake him and disappear in front of the car.

In his small village near Ouagadougou, the capital of Burkina Faso, there was an ancient belief that, on nights of the full moon, winged demons formed from the mud of the rivers, as black as tar, and stole sheep and cows. They called them Bonindà. He didn't believe in such folkloristic fables, and yet this creature was exactly like the monsters his grandmother told him about when she used to put him to bed as a child.

He got up off the seat, trembling. The demon was still lying in front of the car. It looked dead.

Now I'll just drive over him . . .

But he didn't do it. To begin with, he wasn't sure that demons could be killed like that, and anyway the wheels were too small to drive over the top of it.

He'd put the car into reverse when the black demon raised himself from the earth, his head low, placed his hands on the bonnet and let out a terrifying scream.

Mbuma had been told that people pissed themselves in fear, but he'd always believed they were exaggerating. He was forced to reconsider. He'd just pissed his pants.

He jumped out of the car and, in long strides, ran straight towards the Villa.

Despite his hands and knees being grazed by the gravel, the leader of the Wilde Beasts of Abaddon almost had an orgasm, seeing that poor guy run away in terror.

The Sandokan scream really was scary. He had discovered he had a natural talent for screaming. If he'd known earlier, he would have screamed at Serena to scare her to death when he'd walked into their bedroom naked and armed with a sword.

He limped over to get the Durendal, which had been thrown in the field next to the car. He was about to take off when he realised that someone was shouting at him to stop. He couldn't see them, but they couldn't be far away.

Frightened, eh?

Mantos laughed out loud, and decided to go pick up Zombie. It would be much easier for them to kidnap Larita together, and it would save Zombie walking all the way to Forte Antenne.

Return to Villa Reale

58

When Fabrizio Ciba and Larita had seen the headlights appear, they started screaming and waving their arms about. But the car stopped a couple of hundred metres away and after a few minutes it turned around and drove off.

The writer shook his head. 'How about that!'

Larita was ahead of him. 'Come on, it doesn't matter, we're almost there. I think I can see some lights.'

Fabrizio realised that at the bottom of the valley the shadows diluted into a reddish haze. 'It's true! The camp isn't far off. Let's go.'

They started walking again with more vigour, the gravel crunching beneath their feet. The glare at the bottom of the canyon was strong enough to tinge the road red. A scarlet cloud was rising from the lake, hanging above the trees.

'What on earth are they doing?' Larita wondered aloud.

'They must have lit some fires to grill the meat.' Fabrizio sped up the pace. 'I'm starting to get hungry.'

'I'm a vegetarian. But maybe tonight a little steak . . .'

After another fifty metres a suffocating smell of burnt wood began to scratch their throats. In the middle of the cloud of smoke they could now see long tongues of fire reflected in the black waters of the lake.

Larita held her hand over her mouth. 'Isn't that a little too much smoke for a barbecue?'

Finally the canyon opened out onto a wide plain, with the artificial lake. Right at the centre of the basin a house boat was wrapped in flames. The stern had already disappeared into the water and the bow was lifting upwards, like a funeral pyre.

Larita grabbed Fabrizio's hand. 'What's happening?'

'I don't know. It must be some sort of show. Chiatti would kill his mum to surprise his guests.'

They walked a little further on. Larita pointed at a buggy overturned against a pine tree. Steel saucepans had spilled their contents on the ground and basmati rice was spread everywhere. They looked at each other wordlessly, then Fabrizio took her hand.

'Stay close to me.'

They walked around the edge of the lake to get to the other pontoons that were moored opposite a pier protected by a long gazebo. In the water, where the glare of the pyre could be seen, they could hear strange movements and splashes and the slapping of fins. As if some huge fish were fighting over food.

Moving closer, they found overturned mushroom heaters and buffet tables. Broken bottles. Charcoal paper lanterns. And in the middle of that disaster a herd of warthogs and vultures scratched about in what was left of the Indian-style dinner. It looked as if a horde of barbarians had just passed through.

A sensible voice in Fabrizio's mind suggested that it would be best for them to get away from there as quickly as possible.

Perhaps a pride of lions has attacked the bivouac.

And yet it didn't appear like something done by animals, but by human beings. The tents had all been ripped and rolled into balls.

Larita was looking around forlornly. 'Where is everyone?'

Even the waiters, the cooks, the staff, had disappeared.

The girl headed towards the jetty. Fabrizio unwillingly followed her.

In the moored boats the situation was no different. The

240

buffet had been plundered. The remains of the Indian-style dinner spread amidst the flowers, the statues of the Hindustani gods smashed, an abandoned stage with a smashed sitar on it. Perched on one table a big black crow pecked at pieces of tandoori chicken.

Fabrizio stood next to Larita. 'I would get out of here as fast as possible. I don't like the look of this at all.'

Larita lifted a silver shoe off the ground. 'I don't understand.'

'It doesn't matter . . . Let's get out of here.'

A female voice from behind interrupted them. 'My husband . . .'

A woman was standing in the doorway with a catatonic expression on her face. Her arms hung by her side and she was struggling to stand. The sari she was wearing was ripped and hung between her legs like she'd covered herself with a rag. One of her bra straps was broken and her chest was marked with long red scratches. She was missing a shoe. Her blonde hair, which she must have normally held back in a chignon, was now a tangle blended with blood. A dried rivulet of blood dribbled next to her ear.

At first Fabrizio didn't recognise her; but, looking closer, he remembered. She was Mara Baglione Montuori, the wife of the Milanese art dealer who specialised in contemporary art. He knew her because she was the director of a fashion magazine and once, a long time ago, she had interviewed him. Now she was the ghost of that elegant snob that he had met at Rosati in Piazza del Popolo. She had the same distant and traumatised expression as a woman who had just been raped. As if something, someone, had electrocuted her brain.

Fabrizio went to her and immediately noticed she stank. She smelled of sour sweat.

'Mara, what happened to you? Where are the others?' Fabrizio realised that his guts had shrivelled up.

The woman avoided his gaze, but looked around slowly. 'Where is he?'

Mara Baglione Montuori took off the other shoe and held it in her hand like she wanted to hug it to her. 'My husband . . .'

The singer began to walk around the boat, in search of the husband.

In the meantime Fabrizio took Mara by the wrists, trying to intercept her gaze. 'Listen to me . . . Do you remember me? My name's Fabrizio Ciba, we've met before.'

The woman stared at his face and smiled, as if a funny thought had crossed her mind. 'Tuesday we have to go to Portofino, it's Agnese's wedding.'

Fabrizio had never had much patience with traumatised or sick people, let alone now, in that situation. 'I understand that you are in shock, and I'm very sorry . . . But now you have to explain to me what the hell happened here!'

But she was somewhere else. Probably in Portofino. 'My husband hates Agnese's fiancé. I don't understand why. He's a good lad. He'll go places . . . At his age Piero hadn't done as . . .'

He shook her. 'Where is your husband now? Was he with you?'

She was annoyed, as if Fabrizio was harassing her, and she turned around. There was a silver tray on the ground and she saw herself reflected in it.

'Oh God, I look terrible. My make-up . . . My hair . . . I can't go out like this.' She picked up a fork off the table. 'When my sister and I were little, we used these to comb our dolls' hair.' And she began to comb it through her blood-coated hair.

242

Ciba threw his head back in frustration. 'No. She's lost it.'

'Oh God, gross . . . Come here! Quickly.' Larita was next to the window and was watching something with her hand over her mouth.

Ciba had always loved the satellite TV channel Animal Planet, with its documentaries on nature. Often, while he was writing, he happened to leave the TV turned on to that channel. When there were scenes of a predator, and it jumped on its prey, discharging all of the energy in its muscles with the strength and brutality of hunger, Fabrizio got up and, as if he were under a spell, went and sat on the sofa to watch more closely. He liked the wide-open eye of the gnu, the hit of the lion's paw, the cloud of dust where feline and herbivore met, and the head of the victim that rose up one last time.

He recognised the ferociousness of nature in these clashes. The same thing that governed the affairs of men.

But now that he was seeing live, a few metres away from him, a similar scene, he didn't find it as exciting. He moved his gaze towards the bubbling water so that he could only see it out of the corner of his eye. But the trick didn't work. He couldn't stop looking. Once he'd begun, it was difficult to stop.

The remains of Piero Baglione Montuori were floating in the water and being fought over by three enormous crocodiles. Strings of teeth tore at mouthfuls of adipose tissue from the trunk of the famous Milanese art dealer, famous for having discovered Andrew Dog, the Jamaican sculptor. The reptiles, when they were unable to rip off the flesh, began to spin in a jubilation of bloody splashes. The poor man's head banged against the wall of the raft with the dampened sound of a coconut.

59

The leader of the Wilde Beasts of Abaddon skidded to a halt outside the power station.

He hadn't come across Zombie on the road. Instead, he had bumped into guests running loose. When they had seen him go by, they had waved their arms, yelling at him to stop. What's more, one of them had stood in the middle of the road. Mantos hadn't even slowed down, despite the fuck-yous they had thrown at him. Everything had gone exactly as he had foreseen. As soon as darkness fell, the insipid creatures of the light had panicked and the Villa had turned into a horror theme park. He, being a creature of the shadows, had been rendered more determined and ferocious by the darkness. Durendal in hand, he got out of the little car, turned on the torch and looked around.

Where the hell had Zombie gone?

He probably decided to cut across the fields and the woods, unphased by the wild animals.

He was a Beast of Abaddon, and he was not afraid of anything or anyone.

Before leaving Mantos gave a quick look inside the power station, just to be sure.

As he moved closer to the building, he began to notice a strange odour.

It smells like roast meat.

The gate was wide open. The chain with the padlock and the broken poultry shears were on the ground.

Mantos smiled and pointed the light towards the cabin. The wall around the doorframes and the wood of the doors themselves were all blackened, as if a fire had exploded inside. That crazy Zombie must have set fire to everything.

The leader of the Beasts lowered his torch: 'Excellent work, my brave one.' The ray of light cut across the pavement and lit up some black stuff in the middle of the room. Mantos took two steps forward to understand better what it was.

A piece of burnt tyre? No . . . a shoe.

He took another step forward. It looked just like a shoe. A shoe burnt to a crisp. He could still see the melted studs on the sole.

Mantos swallowed again and again. He held his breath and took another step forward, without the courage to point the torch elsewhere. Then he pointed it upwards.

He saw, attached to the shoe, a leg and the charred remains of a human body. The clothes must have burst into flames and the black, dried-up skin was glued to the bones like tar. Only the rib cage stuck out of the shapeless mass that was the trunk. The arms were raised and the fingers twisted as if they'd been bent by the heat. The fire had literally eaten his head. What remained was a blackened sphere without any features except for a cloister of long white teeth.

Not even his mother would have recognised him in this condition. Mantos, however, knew it was him. The shape of the forehead, the height, the shoes, the teeth.

Oh . . . Jesus. Zombie had burned like a matchstick.

The Durendal fell to the ground. His stomach flip-flopped. He covered his mouth with one hand and had to make an effort not to vomit. His legs gave way so he curled up near the door, unable to believe what he was seeing.

He must have caught fire trying to cut off the electricity.

Saverio stretched out his hand. 'Zombie, look at you . . . Look . . . my friend.' And he would have liked to scream, spit out all his wrath, but he just threw open his mouth and squeezed his head between his hands.

Why? Why this way? It wasn't supposed to be this way. They were supposed to commit suicide together, united, after sacrificing the singer to Satan. That was the pact.

Why did you break the pact?

Pain washed over Mantos like a wave, it drowned him with the force of an oceanic roller. And he was blinded by the ruthless light of the truth.

It's my fault he's dead. What have I done?

If it hadn't been for you . . . It almost looked as if that charcoal mannequin would get up off the ground and point its gnarled fingers at him. *If it hadn't been for you* . . . *I'd be in Oriolo Romano now. With my mother. With Murder and Silvietta. With my whole life before me. Who do you think you are to make me die like this?*

Mantos, curled up near the door, looked at himself. He looked at the black tunic he had sewn with the old cast-off curtains from the Flamingo cinema. He looked at the Durendal bought on eBay. And he realised how pathetic he was.

'What am I doing?' he whispered, hoping that the charcoal mannequin would give him an answer.

A bubble of pain exploded in his trachea. He began batting his eyes as the tears blocked his vision. The dream in which Saverio Moneta, clerk at the Furniture Store of the Thyrolean Masters of the Axe, became mean and merciless like Charles Manson had collapsed on top of him. Satan, the Great Mantos, the Wilde Beasts of Abaddon, sacrificing Larita . . . it was all a load of crap invented by a pathetic little man who had succeeded in killing a young man who suffered from serious depression.

On all-fours, sobbing like a child, he moved towards the remains of his adept. 'Forgive me, Edo . . .' He grabbed the wrist, which crumbled in his hand. 'What should I do? Tell me what I should do.'

But nobody could tell him. He was alone. Alone and hopeless like there was nobody else in the world. Zombie was no longer. Serena and the old bastard wanted to see him dead. Murder and Silvietta were lost to him.

He sat up, sniffing and wiping the snot off his face.

He had to gather the remains and bury them. Or throw them into the waters of Bracciano.

He dried his eyes. 'I won't leave you here . . . Don't worry. I'll take you home. To Oriolo. That's enough of this crap.'

He stood and looked round with the torch. He needed to find a big box. One of those big blue Ikea bags would be perfect.

He noticed a piece of paper folded into four and stuck to one of the panels. He moved closer and saw that it had 'For Silvietta' written on it. He was about to read it when he heard a male voice shout behind him: 'Hey, guys! Can you smell that? The barbecue! It's the barbecue! Woo-hoo. We made it. This party was a total rip-off. Chiatti is a skinflint, he didn't even pay his electricity bill.'

Midnight Matriciana

60

Fabrizio led Larita off to one side and quietly said to her: 'Now you and I, as pretty as the light of day, will leave this place. And quickly. I've got a bad feeling.'

'What about that poor woman?' The singer pointed at Mara Baglione Montuori, who was still untangling her hair with the fork. 'What can we do?'

'We can't take her with us, she'd slow us down. As soon as we run into someone, we'll tell them to come and get her.'

Larita wasn't convinced. 'I don't know . . . I don't think it's right to just leave her here.'

'It's right. Listen to me.' Fabrizio took her hand and dragged her onto the pier. 'I think I remember that one of the entrances to the Villa was near the lake.' He pulled a long piece of bamboo topped with a kerosene lamp out of the ground. 'Let's go.'

They started walking up the long avenue skirted by plane trees, leaving the lake behind them.

A slew of questions were buzzing around in the writer's head. He kept seeing the crocodiles as they ripped pieces of flesh off the art dealer's torn body.

Larita was walking along next to him, with her head lowered, and without speaking.

He was about to tell her to pick up the pace when he sensed, or he thought he sensed, movements in the dark. He signalled to Larita to stop and listen. Nothing. Only the sound of the cars on the Salaria could be heard off in the distance.

I must be wrong.

He looked at Larita. Her eyes were teared-over and she was trembling.

Fabrizio realised that his heart was beating at a thousand miles an hour. He took her hand. 'We're almost there, I think.'

They started walking again.

'What's that over there?' Larita screeched, jumping backwards.

Fabrizio stood still. 'Where?'

'In that tree.'

Fabrizio, his legs as wobbly as tentacles, lifted the lamp towards the spot that Larita had pointed out. He couldn't see anything. He took a step forward, shaking the lamp around. Tree branches stretched out towards the little road. There was nothing there. *What the fuck . . .?* He was shitting himself. Panic grabbed him by the throat . . . *What was that?*

A black silhouette was hanging from a branch.

A monkey?

It couldn't be a monkey. It was too big.

A gorilla?

Too fat. For a second he thought it was a sculpture, a mannequin hanging there.

He stepped away and the feeble light from the lamp lit up the rest of the tree's foilage. There were two others hanging there . . .

Men . . .

Fat men swinging.

He turned around and screamed at Larita: 'Run! Quick!'

He heard a dampened sound behind him, and a wheeze. One of those monsters must have jumped down.

He began running as fast as he could. The lantern extinguished in his hand and the only light left was the far-off glow from the bivouac.

He was galloping desperately, like he had never done before, with the gravel squeaking against the soles of his shoes and the air whirling down his windpipe.

He hoped Larita was keeping up.

And if she's fallen behind?

Turn around! Stop! Call her name! his head yelled at him.

He wanted to do it, but all he could do was run and pray that she was doing the same.

After a couple of dozen metres, he heard her scream.

They've got her! Fucking bloody hell, they've got her!

As he ran, he turned his head. Everything was sunk in darkness, and in the blackness he heard her moans and the guttural sounds of the monsters. 'Fabrizio! Help me! Fabrizio!'

He stopped, bent over in two out of breath, and sighed. 'I'm too old for this shit.' Then, with unexpected courage, he screamed: 'Leave her alone, you bastards!' And he ran back, his fists closed, his eyes closed, twirling his arms, hoping to scare them off, to chase them away, to annihilate them.

But he tripped, fell to the ground and slammed his jaw into the gravel. Despite the pain he got up again, blood between his teeth . . . And just as he was getting up, a fist, a stick, something heavy, slammed down with unheard-of violence on his right shoulder and he found himself back on the ground. Screaming, he tried again, obstinately, to get up, but another fist sank into his stomach.

Fabrizio Ciba sagged like a torn football, and thousands of little orange lights exploded before his eyes. He pushed out all the air in his body, and while he was there dying he felt enormous hands grab hold of him and lift him with the same ease that a human being lifts a bag full of groceries.

He held his breath as he lay placed over the shoulder of the being that was walking. He unclenched his eyes. The pink sky was above him – he could reach out and touch it – and he heard the wheezing of his crushed lungs, which, like empty plastic bags, sucked in air.

And while he was saying to himself that he would find a way to not die, he realised that the darkness was something more than the simple absence of light. It was the substance that he would drown in.

A blow to the back of his neck tore away that last thought.

61

'What are you eating? Give us a bit. Don't be a greedy guts.'

Saverio Moneta saw three guys poking their heads in through the door. The tall one with the big fringe and the frameless glasses was definitely someone he'd seen on TV. He must be a presenter. The other, dumpy and with a forehead two fingers high, had to be a politician. And the third, hmph . . . He didn't know who he was.

With their hunting uniforms designed by Ralph Lauren, their hair full of gel and bottles of champagne in hand, they thought they were God Almighty, but they were just three drunken pieces of shit.

Saverio was an expert on pieces of shit. He had had experience with them early on in life, during his school years. They usually travelled in groups to back each other up. And if they homed in on you, if they worked out that you wanted to be left alone, they would circle you like hungry hyenas.

If things went your way, they would wait for you outside school and, at the first chance, they would pick a fight, beat you and leave it at that. Other times they used to pretend they were your friends. They were funny and polite, and they made you think that you could be one of them – and that's when, like an idiot, you let your defences down and they broke your heart by making fun of you. Then they threw you away like a broken toy. On Sundays, though, they would go to church with their families and would share in the communion. After finishing high school, under the patronage of the family's wealth, they would go overseas to study. They would then clean up, and when they came back to Oriolo they were lawyers, accountants, dentists. They looked like good people, but deep down they were pieces of shit. They often found their way into politics, and they talked about God, family values and country. These were the new cavaliers of the Catholic culture.

Saverio stuffed Zombie's note deep down in his trouser pocket. He squinted and his lips pulled into a sardonic sneer. 'Do you want to see what I'm eating?'

The guy with the goatee gloated. 'You and me, we understand each other, brother. Show me the treasures you're hiding.'

And the politician added: 'Share it with your friends.'

Saverio turned around with wild eyes. He picked up Zombie's body off the ground. He was shocked at how little it weighed. 'What do you prefer, a drumstick or an arm?' And he showed them the charcoaled remains.

At first the three of them didn't understand what sort of stuff it was. The guy with the goatee took a step forwards and then one backwards in a sort of clumsy tarantella.

'Oh god . . .'

'What the fuck is it?' The politician grabbed the presenter's arm.

'It looks like a roasted dead body. That's disgusting,' said the third man, letting go of the Champagne bottle, which smashed into a thousand shards.

Saverio placed Zombie on the ground, then grabbed the

Durendal with two hands and lifted it above his shoulder. 'So, what shall I cut you? An arm? A leg?'

The three losers ran off, pushing at each other to get out of the gate first. The politician let out a desperate scream and sunk up to his chest in the ground, which opened like a mouth to swallow him. The poor guy began to wave his arms around but something, from below, was pulling at him. He tried to hold out, but a moment later he disappeared into the black hole.

The other two stayed where they were, standing on the edge with vacant expressions on their faces, not knowing what to do. Then the presenter found his courage and leaned out over the hole for a second; but a second was enough for a huge arm to grab him by the beard. The man, headfirst, was dragged down into the hole and he, too, was sucked into the bowels of the earth.

The third guy was about to run off when a hand popped out of the hole and grabbed him by the ankle to pull him in. The man fell to the ground and began kicking to free himself of the vice-like grip. With his other foot, he struck the big hand wrapped around his leg. But it did nothing. Those fingers as big as cigars, with their black fingernails, were numb to the pain. He tried to put up a fight, digging his hands into the ground and begging: 'Help me! Please! Help me!' He managed to grab on to one of the gateposts. But then another hand took hold of his free leg, and there was nothing he could do as he too disappeared into the hole.

Saverio Moneta, standing in the cabin doorway petrified, had seen the whole scene. It had taken less than three minutes.

Fuck . . . Fuck . . . Fuck . . . It was the only word that his brain was able to conceive while he watched as slowly, with little effort, two arms as big as legs of ham came out of the hole, followed by a small, bald head set into two rounded shoulders, and then the rest of the enormous human being wrapped in tyres of fat. It looked like it was wearing a green Sergio Tacchini tracksuit.

It must weigh at least two hundred kilos.

Saverio had read a number of treaties on the use of mêlée weapons in feudal Japan, and he knew that there was a mortal blow that the sixteenth-century master Hiroyuki Utatane had called 'The Wind in the Lotus'. It required considerable balance, but if done correctly it made you capable of cutting the head of the adversary clean off.

He screamed, raised one foot, jumped in the air and at the same time did a one-hundred-and-eighty-degree pirouette, holding the Durendal straight out in front of him.

The sword cut through the air while the creature, with the speed and grace of an overweight ballerina, took a step backwards, stretched out a hand and grabbed the blade.

Saverio, thanks to the recoil, flew back and ended up against the wall of the building. He was still holding the hilt in his hands. But the rest of the sword was held tight in the fist of the creature, who now threw it to the ground like a piece of rubbish.

The same old shit from eBay . . .

Saverio threw away what was left of the sacrificial sword.

I don't think I'll have the chance to give those arseholes from The Art of War of Caserta negative feedback.

The big beast stood less than a metre away. Its huge tonnage hung over Saverio.

The leader of the Wilde Beasts of Abaddon raised his head to look at him. An emaciated ray of moonlight shone in the little red, expressionless eyes of the monster, which shook its head and smiled, showing a row of crooked, decayed teeth.

Saverio felt himself being grabbed by the arms and lifted up high. He closed his eyes, trying to suck all the pain into his lungs.

He could smell the rotting breath of the monster. He would have enjoyed spitting in its face, but his mouth was dry.

It doesn't matter. He was ready to die. He wouldn't pray, he wouldn't beg. He would die like Mantos, the Etruscan god of death.

The monster threw him against a tree, and the last thing that Saverio saw before slamming against the trunk was the moon, round and immense, which had managed to find passage through the milky white veils of clouds.

It was so close.

PART THREE

Katakumba

Baron Pierre de Coubertin, born in Paris in 1863, is remembered for having coined the odious phrase: 'It's not winning that's important, but how you play the game.' (The important thing in life is not the triumph, but the struggle; the essential thing is not to have conquered, but to have fought well – which, by the way, is not his, but a Pennsylvanian bishop's). Other than that, de Coubertin is known for having reformed the French schooling system and for having resuscitated the ancient Greek Olympic Games in the modern world. A great supporter of the role of sport and physical activity in forming the personality of young people, the Baron was charged by the French Government with founding an international sporting association. After consulting fourteen nations, he set up the International Olympic Committee, which, in 1896, organised the first modern Olympic Games in Athens. It was an enormous success, repeated four years later in Paris. The third Olympic Games was held in 1904 in St Louis, in the United States. For the fourth edition, the Baron hoped to bring the Olypmic Games to Rome, in the hope of recreating the legendary rivalry between Rome and Athens, the two powers of the ancient world. But at that time Italy had economic problems (no change there), and declined the offer.

On the 16th of June 1955, the dream of Baron de Coubertin finally became reality: the city of Rome, after having won an exciting head-to-head with Lausanne, won the right to host the Games of the Seventeenth Olympiad planned for 1960.

The Italian Government invested approximately one hundred billion lira to prove to the world that Italy was part of the exclusive club of rich countries.

The Eternal City turned into a construction site in preparation for the event. New roads were laid and, between Villa Glori and the banks of the Tiber, a huge Olympic village for hosting the athletes was built, comprising many modern buildings immersed in greenery just a few kilometres from the historical town centre. Two brand-new stadiums were erected, and the Olympic stadium was rebuilt to hold up to sixty-five thousand spectators. And then new swimming pools, velodromes, hockey fields. And for the first time in the history of the Olympics, images of the races would be broadcast across Europe by the RAI.

Rome stood out all over the world for the beauty of its playing fields: the Terme di Caracalla hosted the gymnastics events, the Basilica di Massenzio held the wrestling, while the marathon took off from the Capitoline, followed the Appia Antica, and ended under the Arco di Costantino. And it was during the marathon that something extraordinary happened. Abebe Bikila, a small athlete of the Imperial Ethiopian Guard, won the race running barefoot. He crossed the finish line with the new world record.

With an astonishing medal count of thirty-six, Italy came third on the medal board, behind the Soviets and the Americans.

All of this is common knowledge. What few people know, however, is what happened to a small group of Soviet athletes during the closing night of the Games.

The USSR had only started participating at the Olympic Games in Helsinki, in 1952. Before then, the leaders of the Communist Party said the Games were 'a means for distracting the workers from the class struggle' and providing participants with 'training for new Imperialistic wars'. In reality, the mistrustful behaviour of the Kremlin veiled the Soviets' intention to show themselves in the Olympic limelight only when the USSR had the possibility of playing a starring role. So from 1952 onwards, the two global superpowers, frozen in the cold war, found, in the Olympic Games, the perfect battlefield for showing all of their strength. On one side the Soviet Union, with an ironfist paramilitary organisation consistently improved through scientific studies, causing suspicion and insinuations about the use of medicines to improve their athletes' performances. On the other side, the United States, star of every edition of the Games from 1896 onwards, supported by the possibility of choosing the best from thousands of college and university athletes.

Humiliated during the Olympics in Helsinki, and winners by a long shot in Melbourne, the Soviet Union came to Rome with the intention of proving the superiority of the Communist regime.

The Soviet representatives were separated from all the others and occupied private apartment buildings. The athletes were not allowed to have any contact with people from other nations, who were the epitome of the corrupt capitalism of the Western world. They were under the constant control of Party employees.

The athletes included Arkadij and Ljudmila Brusilov. He was a javelin thrower, she an artistic gymnast. They had married in 1958 in Kutuko, a town near Moscow. Both of them held a dream in their hearts: to abandon the USSR and go live in the West. They hated the authoritarian Communist regime, and they wanted to give birth to their children in the free world. But that was only a dream, for no one could leave their country. This applied even more so to those athletes considered to be official representatives of Soviet ideology and strength in the wider world.

During the Games, the couple began to plan to escape and hide out in the West. The day after she won the silver medal, Ljudmila let this slip to Irina Kalina, a pole vaulter who shared lodgings with her. Irina begged them to take her with them. They explained to her that it was dangerous, and that that choice would haunt her for the rest of her life. The KGB would never leave them alone. They would have to hide out in a secret location and live underground.

'It doesn't matter . . . I'm prepared to do anything,' said Irina, whose grandfather had ended up in a gulag in Siberia.

Slowly the secret did the rounds of the athletes. And in the end, there were twenty-two of them, men and women, planning their escape.

Given the results of the races, it was evident that the Soviets were to conquer the palmarès. And after the Games closed, they would surely toast to their having beaten, for the second time and in such a humiliating way, the American imperialists.

And so it was. The managers organised a dinner for the whole delegation, with Russian salad, boiled carp, baked potatoes and stuffed baked onions, all washed down with litres of vodka. By nine in the evening, the organisers, trainers, athletes and employees of the Party were drunk. Some sang, some recited old poems, some played ballads on the piano. The atmosphere was that of apparent joy, but actually hid a terrible feeling of nostalgia.

The twenty-two dissidents had filled their bottles of vodka with water. At a nod from Arkadij, the whole group met in the pavilion garden. The two guards had fallen asleep on a bench. It was easy to climb the fence and run off under cover of the Roman night.

They ran quickly along the banks of the Tiber until they reached the Acqua Acetosa sports ground, from there they climbed up towards Parioli without stopping. They then found themselves in front of a big hill covered in woods. They didn't know it, but that was Forte Antenne, the outermost point of a huge park called Villa Ada.

They ran into it, and nothing more was ever heard of them.
Naturally the Soviet authorities denied the whole thing. They

couldn't admit to the world that some of their most glorious athletes had escaped, repudiating Communism and their own country. They unleashed the secret services on a hunt to find them and make them pay. For years the agents searched for them all over the world. Nothing. It was like looking for a hole in water. They appeared to have melted away, as if a Western country had helped them to disappear without a trace.

As we've already mentioned, the subsoil of Villa Ada is criss-crossed with the ancient Catacomb of Priscilla: more than fourteen kilometres of tunnels and cubicles dug into the tuff rock, divided into three floors packed full of ancient remains of Christians. The underground necropolis's name comes from a Roman woman Priscilla, born in the second half of the second century AD. It appears that the woman donated the land to the Christians, who dug their cemetery there.

That's where Arkadij and the company of dissidents hid. After having scoured the necropolis from top to bottom, they set up their living quarters on the deepest level, more than fifty metres below the earth's surface. That area, cool in summer and warm in winter, had been explored, mapped out and then closed to the public and forgotten. The tourists only visited a part of the first floor, in the area in front of the Convent of the Benedictine Nuns.

The Russians, during night time when the park was closed, would climb up the tunnels and go outside in search of food. Their nutrition was principally based on what the Romans abandoned during the daytime: leftover panini, fried food, potato chips and Cipster, snacks and the dregs left in Coke cans. Their economy was substantially based on rubbish collection. Similar, in a way, to the gatherers of the Paleolithic era. They wore tracksuits, sweatshirts and caps that people absentmindedly left behind on the lawns or lost at the fitness tracks. Ethnologists might compare the relationship established between the Soviet athletes and the Romans to the symbiosis that exists between hippopotamus and herons. These splendid birds live off the back of the huge mammals, feeding themselves on the parasites on the skin. In the same way the Romans always found the Villa clean and tidy, and the Russians found food and clothes.

Inside the tunnels of the catacomb the small community began to breed and it slowly grew. Obviously, considering the fact that the population was small, crossbreeding between blood relatives happened regularly, generating an uncontrolled and accelerated genetic drift. Even the hypogeous lifestyle, in the darkness of the tunnels, and a diet rich in carbohydrates and fats contributed to transforming them morphologically. New generations were obese, with serious dental problems, and very pale skin. On the other hand, they were able to see in the dark and, being direct descendents of athletes, they were extremely agile and strong.

It sounds unbelievable, but in almost fifty years nobody noticed their presence. Except for the bin men and maintenance workers of Villa Ada, who told of the legend of the Mole Men. It was said that at night they came out of the air holes of the catacomb and cleaned up all the rubbish in the park, freeing them of the bulk of the work. There were others who swore to have seen them jumping from one tree to another, performing amazing acrobatics. But it sounded like just another urban myth.

The sale of the park to Chiatti broke the delicate balance between the park and its underground guests.

From one day to the next, the Russians no longer found the bins overflowing with leftover food. And slowly the park had been repopulated with wild beasts. As they were not hunters but gatherers, and had developed a metabolism that required constant intakes of glucose and cholesterol, the dwellers of the catacomb began to suffer and feel sick, feeding as they must on mice, insects and other small animals.

Breaking the ancient and hard-and-fast rule that they had imposed on themselves when they'd entered into the catacomb, which forbade them from going into the open during the day, the old king Arkadij sent a small squad of explorers armed with sunglasses and led by his son Ossacatogna to find out what the hell was happening inside the park.

When the explorers returned, they reported that the park had been closed and had become a sort of private zoo for the amusement of a very powerful man, who was organising a big party.

The council of Old Athletes was immediately convened, governed also by the king, who was now totally blind and ravaged by psoriasis. He knew what was happening: exactly what he had always feared during fifty years of underground living. The Soviet Empire had finally triumphed, its armies had invaded Italy, and now Communism reigned the whole planet undisputed.

That park had most certainly become the residence of a bureaucrat, a Party bigwig, and the party was a celebration for the Soviet victory.

'What do we have to do, father?' Ossacatogna asked.

The king took a couple of minutes to think before answering. 'During the night of the celebration, we will show ourselves. We'll attack the Soviets, and we will take what we need to survive.'

Concert by Larita in Villa Ada

62

Sasà Chiatti, in a satin robe, striped boxer shorts and infrared glasses, was standing at the centre of the terrace of the Royal Villa. With his right arm he was holding on tight to a gold-plated TAR-21 assault rifle with a Swarovski crystal-studded butt, and in his left an M79 grenade-launcher with an alabaster butt and a silver-plated barrel. In between his teeth he held a Cobina Behike cigar, rolled by the able hands of the Cuban torcedora Norma Fernández.

He walked over to the big staircase that led down to the garden, and opened his arms wide in greeting. 'Welcome to the party.'

He never thought that they would have the guts to show up on the day of his incoronation. He had been naïve not to consider it. It was obvious. Like that, in front of everyone, his downfall would have been complete and conclusive. A warning to all those who tried to think and act for themselves.

He walked down a couple of steps, fired at the hard liquor table and sent it into thousands of pieces. 'Here I am. Come on, show me what you've got' he screamed in the green night of his goggles.

He felt like laughing. They were coming to punish him because he had dared to rise up, because he had shown everyone that even a poor boy, son of a humble mechanic from Mondragone, had become, thanks to his entrepreneurial skills, one of the richest men in Europe. Because he had given work to the unemployed and hope to a heap of desperate losers.

Because he had revved the engine of the economy of this fucked-up country.

That sainted woman his mother, she hadn't studied but she was smart, had warned him. 'Savlato, sooner or later they'll find a way to fuck you over. They will band together and drown you in shit.'

For years Sasà Chiatti had slept in fear, awaiting that moment. He had hired troupes of lawyers, accountants, economists. He had had a wall built around the Villa to defend himself, he had had an underground bunker excavated to hide out in, recruited Israeli bodyguards and armour-plated his automobiles.

It hadn't changed a fucking thing. They'd got to him, anyway. They had sabotaged his power station, they had ruined his party, and now they wanted to finish him off.

Through the night-vision goggles he saw a couple of them, nice big ones, running around the buffet leftovers with bags full of food. 'You losers. Do you want to hear something interesting? I'm glad that we can finally end this stand-off.' He loaded the grenade-launcher. 'And do you want to hear another interesting thing? The party, the guests, the VIPs can all go and get fucked, kill them all. And I don't even give a shit about this crap old Villa. Destroy it. You want war? You've got war.' And he blew up the big water fountain. Marble shrapnel, water and water lilies were sent flying over tens of metres.

He walked down another three steps. 'Do you want to know who the fuck I am? Do you want to know how the fuck a lowlife from Mondragone can afford to buy Villa Ada? Let me tell you now. I'm going to show you all who Sasà Chiatti is when you piss him off.' He began to sweep through the buffet tables with the machine gun. The plates of truffle tartines, trays of chicken nuggets and carafes full of Bellini disintegrated under the gunfire. The tables fell to the ground riddled with gunshots.

It was a beautiful feeling. The machine gun had warmed up and was burning his hand. As he was pulling another magazine out of the pocket of his robe and replacing the empty one, he thought back to the book he had read about Greek heroes.

There was one guy he admired in particular, Agamemnon. In the film *Troy*, he was played by a really good actor whose name he couldn't remember. The Greek hero had beaten the Trojans and he'd taken Chryseis, a nice piece of skirt, as a war prize. One of the gods, an important one, one of Zeus's helpers, had offered him a shitload of cash in exchange for the girl, but Agamemnon hadn't accepted. Agamemnon wasn't scared of the gods. And the gods had taken their revenge, and unleashed a terrible pestilence on his camp.

'This is your vendetta . . .' He looked up towards the greenish sky. 'Except that the Greek gods were great and powerful. The Italian ones are miserable. You've sent these fat gits to kill me.' He took aim at a sort of molosser that was dragging a big bag full of drinks away, and he sent it crashing to the ground.

He came to the bottom of the staircase. 'Should that be democracy's goal? An opportunity for everyone?' Chiatti, with a flick of his arm, reloaded the grenade-launcher. 'Cop this opportunity to get the fuck out of here.' And he blew up a fatso carrying an entire roast pig on his shoulders.

'You greasy lowlifes . . . Viva Italia!' He spat the cigar from his mouth and began running and wildly shooting, cutting down these obese killers. '*Fratelli d'Italia, l'Italia s'è desta . . .*' he sang, while the cartridge cases from the TAR-21 were splattering all over the place. '*Dell'elmo di Scipio si è cinta la testa . . .*' He hit one, its skull opening like a ripe watermelon.

'Idiots, you haven't even got any weapons! Who the fuck do you think you are to come in here like that? You're not immortal. Tell the people who sent you that it takes more than that to kill off Sasà Chiatti.' He stopped to catch his breath, then he burst into laughter. 'I think you won't be able to tell them a bloody thing, you'll all be blown to smithereens.' He stuck in another grenade and slammed the Algida ice cream Apecar. It caused an explosion that, for a second, lit up the Italian-style garden, the boxwood maze, the information gazebo and the hunting tents as if it were daytime. The front tyre of the three-wheeler Apecar popped out of the fireball, overtook the tables with the aperitifs, the remains of the fountain and the hydrangea flowerbed, and hit the real-estate magnate on the forehead.

Sasà Chiatti and his ninety kilos wobbled, and seemed to withstand the impact; but then, like a skyscraper whose foundations have been undermined, he fell back. While the world around him was being overturned, he pulled the trigger of the machine gun with his index finger and shot off the tip of his blue velvet slippers with his initials embroidered in gold thread. Inside were four toes and a fair bit of his foot.

He ended up on the ground, hitting his head on the corner of a glass table on the way down. A long triangular sliver stuck into his neck just above the nape, cut through the periosteum, the dura mater, the arachnoid, the pia mater and through the soft tissue of the brain like a sharp blade through a Danone vanilla pudding.

'Ahhhh . . . Ahhhh . . . Owwwww . . . You've got me,' he managed to mumble, before vomiting the semi-digested remains of the matriciana rigatoni and the meatballs with pine nuts and sultanas all over himself.

With the crooked night-vision goggles, he studied what was left of the tip of his left leg. The stump, a mass of raw flesh and bits of bone, was leaking a dark-green liquid like a thread-less tap. The real-estate magnate stretched out one hand, grabbed a table cloth from an overturned coffee table and wrapped the injury as best he could. Then he grabbed a bottle of Amaro Averna liqueur and necked a quarter of it.

'You arseholes. You think you've hurt me? You're wrong. Come on, surprise me, show me what you can do. Here I am.'

He gestured with his fingers for them to bring it on. He grabbed the machine gun and kept shooting around until there was nothing left to shoot. He was quiet for a moment, and then he noticed that his neck and shoulders were soaked in blood. He touched the back of his neck. Felt a piece of glass sticking out of his hair. He grabbed it with his thumb and index finger and tried to extract it, but it slipped his grasp. Gulping for air, he tried again, and as soon as he moved it a pink flash blinded his left eye.

He decided to leave it there and collapsed against the rest of the ice sculpture of an angel. Then, with the little strength that he had left, he necked the rest of the liqueur, tasting the bittersweet flavour of the Averna mixed with the salty flavour of his blood. 'You haven't fucking hurt me . . . You haven't . . . A conspiracy of dickheads.' The head of the angel and the melted stubs of the wings were dripping a frozen rain that dribbled down his smooth skull and into the infrared goggles, down his chubby cheeks and onto the swollen stomach, the robe, and finally watered down the puddle of blood he was sinking in.

Death was cold. An ice octopus had wrapped its frozen tentacles around his spinal column.

He thought of his mother again. He would have liked to have told her that her little chiappariello loved her, and that he'd been a good boy. But he had no air left in his lungs. Luckily, he'd hidden her away in the bunker.

Fucking hell . . . , he said, ironing out a smile. It was nice to go like this. Like a hero. Like a Greek hero in a battle. Like the great Agamemnon, the king of the Greeks.

He was sleepy and felt exhausted. How strange, his foot didn't hurt any more. His head wasn't throbbing any more either, it was lighter. He felt like he'd risen out of his body and was watching himself.

Right there, collapsed beneath a melting angel.

His head fell onto his chest. The bottle slipped between his legs. He looked at his hands. He opened them and closed them.

My hands. These are my hands.

In the end, they had won.

They who?

Salvatore Chiatti fell asleep with a question to carry into the hereafter.

63

Fabrizio Ciba regained consciousness like he was coming out of a bottomless well. With his eyes closed, he stayed curled up in a foetal position, swallowing and spitting air. He remembered the darkness and the bunch of fat bastards hanging from the trees.

They've kidnapped me.

He kept still, without opening his eyes, until his heart began to slow down. He was aching from his toes to the tips of his hair. As soon as he moved, an unbearable pain streamed along his shoulders . . .

That's where it hit me.

(*Don't think about it.*)

. . . and through his neck muscles, radiating out like an electric shock behind the ears and up to his temples. His tongue was so swollen that it struggled to stay inside his mouth.

They fell from the trees.
(*Don't think about it.*)

Right, he shouldn't think about it. He just had to stay still and wait for the pain to pass.

I have to think about something pretty.

All right, he was in Nairobi, lying on a bed. The linen curtains were moved by a warm wind. Beside him was Larita, naked, vaccinating Kenyan kids.

Where's Larita?
(*Don't think about it.*)

Soon he would get up and he'd take a Nimesulide pill and squeeze himself a nice fresh grapefruit juice.

It's not working.

He was lying on ground that was too hard and cold to allow him to fantastise.

He placed a hand on the ground. The floor was wet, and felt like it was made of pressed dirt.

Don't open your eyes.

He'd have to open them sooner or later, and find out where the monster had taken him. At the moment it was better to wait. He felt too shit and he didn't want other ugly surprises. He preferred to stay there, behave, and imagine Africa.

But there was a strange smell of damp that made him feel nauseous. It reminded him of the odour in the cellar dug out of the tuff rock in his uncle's house in Pitigliano. And it was cold, just like there.

I'm underground. There were at least five of them in that tree. They've kidnapped me. It was a ploy just to kidnap me.

A group of obese terrorists had swung down from the trees and kidnapped him.

Slowly at first, then more and more quickly, his brain began to elaborate this mad idea, to knead it and let it rise like a piece of dough for making pizza. And he would bet his bottom dollar that the kidnapping had been coordinated by that son of a bitch Sasà Chiatti, a real mafioso who colluded with the powerful. The party, the safaris, were all a smoke screen to hide a global plan to get rid of a troublesome intellectual who pointed his finger at the moral downfall of society.

It's obvious, they want to make me pay for it.

Throughout his whole career he had exposed himself, uncaring of the consequences, against the hidden powers. He considered it to be the civil duty of a writer. He had written a fiery article against the Finnish woodcutting lobbies that scythed down thousand-year-old forests. Those big beasts that had kidnapped him could very well be an extremist phalanx of Finns.

Another time he had openly declared in the *Corriere della Sera* that Chinese cuisine was crap. And everyone knows that the Chinese are a mafia, and they don't let anyone who has the courage to attack them publicly go unpunished.

Of course, those colossuses were a little too beefy to be Chinese . . .

What about if they'd united with Finnish woodcutters?

Salman Rushdie and the Islamic fatwa came to mind.

And now they'll execute me.

Well, if that's how it went, at least it would be a death that guaranteed him being remembered as a martyr for the truth.

Like Giordano Bruno.

He was so caught up with unwinding himself from the tangle in his mind that the writer didn't realise he wasn't alone until he heard a voice.

'Ciba? Can you hear me? Are you still alive?'

It was a low voice, almost a whisper. It came from behind

him. A voice that had an annoying inability to pronounce its r's properly. A voice that annoyed the shit out of him.

Fabrizio opened his eyes and swore.

It was that shithead Matteo Saporelli.

64

The day he had been called to organise the catering for the party, the unpredictable Bulgarian chef Zóltan Patrovic had set his eyes on an oil painting by Giorgio Morandi in Chiatti's studio that represented a pair of flagons on a table.

That work by the Bolognaise painter would add prestige to the Emilia-Romagna room in his restaurant Le Regioni.

His place, situated in Via Casilina on the corner of Via Torre Gaia, had been at the top of the European restaurant guides for years. It was designed by the Japanese architect Hiro Itoki, in 1990, like a miniature Italy. Looking at it from up above, the long building had the same shape and proportions as the Italian peninsula, including the major islands. It was split into twenty rooms, which corresponded in shape and culinary specialities to the regions of Italy. The tables took the names of the capital cities.

Morandi's painting would have been perfect hanging above the cellar-fridge where he kept the Lambrusco.

The Bulgarian had decided that, after the party, he would get Salvatore Chiatti to give it to him as a gift. And if, as he imagined, the real-estate mogul resisted, he would convince him to donate it to him by pushing a little confusion into Chiatti's mind.

Now that the party had fallen to pieces, the guests were lost in the park and he had seen the lifeless body of the entrepreneur lying in a pool of blood, there was no reason for him not to pay himself for the work he'd done by taking the piece of art.

In the darkness, a candle in hand, he set off as silently as a black cat up the big staircase that led to the first floor of the Villa, which had been abandoned by the waiting staff and the other employees.

The steps were littered with pieces of furniture, clothes, dishes, broken statues.

The fatsos had sent the residence to rack and ruin. The chef didn't care who they were and what they wanted. He respected them. They had appreciated his cooking. He had seen them fling themselves at the buffet with a primeval enthusiasm and violence. He had recognised the ancestral ecstasy of hunger in their eyes.

For quite some time he had been returning home from his restaurant tired and frustrated. He couldn't bear the way people used their fork to investigate what was on the plate, how they interrupted their chitchat with mouthfuls, how they organised work lunches containing useless antipasti. To retain his sanity, he was forced to watch documentaries about hunger in the Third World.

Yes, the unpredictable Bulgarian chef loved hunger and hated appetite. Appetite was the expression of a replete and satisfied world, on the verge of surrender. A people that tastes instead of eating, that nibbles instead of feeding themselves, that's already dead but doesn't know it. Hunger is a synonym for life. Without hunger the human being is only the pretence of himself, therefore becomes bored and begins to philosophise. And Zóltan Patrovic hated philosophy. Especially when applied to cuisine. He regretted the passing of war, hunger, poverty. Soon he would up sticks and move to Ethiopia.

The unpredictable Bulgarian chef was on the top floor. The

air was heavy with smoke, and wherever he pointed the dancing flame of the candle he could see destruction. He could hear murmurs and flashes of flames coming from the bedroom.

He didn't care what was going on in there, he had to go to the studio, but curiosity got the better of him. He put out the candle and moved closer to the door. A huge wall tapestry and the brocade curtains were on fire, and the flames lit up the room. On the four-poster bed lay Ecaterina Danielsson, completely naked. Her hair, like a red cloud, framed her angular face. Around the woman a dozen men were on their knees murmuring a strange chant and they stretched out their hands and brushed her tiny white breasts and plum-coloured nipples, the flat stomach with a goblet-shaped belly button, her pubis covered by a strip of carrot-coloured fur, and her long legs.

The model, her back arched like a cat, moved her head lazily, her eyes half-closed in an expression of ecstasy, her large, moist mouth wide open. She was gasping, placing her hands on the heads of the men bowed down around the bed like slaves worshipping a pagan goddess.

Zóltan moved along. He lit the candle again, followed the corridor and went into Chiatti's study. He lifted up the flame. His painting was still there. Nobody had touched it.

Something that resembled a smile appeared on the chef's face for an instant. 'I don't want it, but I have to have it.' He took a step towards the painting, but then he heard sounds coming from the dark corner of the room. He flattened himself behind a bookcase.

More than sounds, they were disgusting cries.

Zóltan moved the candle slightly and saw, between two bookcases, in a corner, a man on his knees. He was all skin and bones. His little bald head, bent towards the floor, was hidden behind thin shoulder blades and Zóltan could see his backbone, with the vertebrae protruding like a mountain range. His skin, as fine as tissue paper, was covered by a network of wrinkles and hung floppily from his arms, which were as frail as twigs. He was ripping something and stuffing it in his mouth, producing guttural sounds and gurgles.

Curious, the chef took a step forward. The parquet creaked underfoot.

The man on the ground turned around suddenly and ground the few rotten teeth he still had in his mouth. The small eyes shone like a lemur's. His shrivelled face was smeared with a dark, oily liquid. He pulled away, growling, his back against the wall. Between his legs he had the leftovers of a big tray of aubergine parmesan.

The chef smiled. 'It's delicious, isn't it? I made it. It uses strained tomato sauce. And the aubergines have been fried in a light oil.' He moved closer to the painting.

The old man craned his neck, without losing sight of the chef.

'Take your time eating. I'll just take this and leave,' the chef said in a low, reassuring tone of voice. But the old man grabbed the tray from the floor and, hissing like a cat, he threw himself at Zóltan. The chef stretched out his right hand and squeezed the spherical cap of the skull.

Aleksej Jusupov, famous marathon runner, stood still instantly. His eyes went blank and his arms fell to his sides. From the tray that he was holding on to in his hand, the rest of the parmesan dribbled to the ground.

How strange. Suddenly he was no longer afraid of that black man, and in fact he realised that he loved him. He reminded him of the old monk from his village. And the hand on his forehead radiated a wholesome warmth all down his arthritic skeleton. It seemed to be absorbing a healing energy that surrounded his bones and softened joints stiffened over time with the dampness of life underground. He felt strong and fit, like when he was a young boy.

He hadn't thought back to that time in his life for years.

He used to run kilometres and kilometres along the frozen banks of Lake Baikal without ever getting tired. And his father, tempered in his overcoat, would check his times. To celebrate, if he had beaten his own record, they would go fishing on the long pier from where you could see the Barguzin Mountains covered in snow. In winter it was even more beautiful, and they would open a hole in the ice and drop their bait in. And if they were lucky, they would pull up one of those big brown carps. Vigorous animals, who fought proudly before giving in.

That fatty meat was so tasty, boiled together with potatoes, black cabbage and horseradish. He didn't know what he would have given to experience again the sensation of those fillets melting in his mouth and the horseradish tickling his nose.

Aleksej found himself back in the fishing hut lit by just a kerosene lantern and the glare from the wood-fired oven. Papa gave him a glass of vodka to drink, told him it was fuel for his runner's body, and then they got into bed together, beneath layers of rough blankets smelling of camphor. One next to the other. And then Papa would hug him tight and whisper in his ear, with his breath stinking of alcohol, that he was a good boy, that he ran like the wind and that he didn't need to be afraid . . . That it was a secret just between the two of them. That it wouldn't hurt, in fact . . .

No. I don't want to. Please . . . Papa, don't do that to me.

Something snapped in Aleksej Jusupov's mind.

The wholesome warmth disappeared from his limbs and

terror doused him like a cold shower. He squeezed his tear-filled eyes, and standing before him he saw his father dressed as a monk.

'Пошёл вон! Я тебя ненавижу'[1], said Aleksej and, channelling all the strength he had in him, he thumped the perpetrator of those days with the solid, reinforced-steel tray.

The unpredictable Bulgarian chef, incredulous, fell to the floor and the Russian athlete finished him off by walloping him with the tray again.

---

[1] 'Go away! I hate you'

Fireworks display by Xi-Jiao Ming and the Magic Flying Chinese Orchestra

65

The ex-leader of the Wilde Beasts of Abaddon woke up in the pitch black, being tossed about like a sack of potatoes.

It took him a while to realise that he was over the shoulder of the monster that had slung him up against a tree. He kicked his legs, trying to free himself, but an arm squeezed him so hard that he understood it was best he behave, if he didn't want to suffocate. The fatso was marching along at a fast pace without tiring, and he seemed to see perfectly in the darkness, turning right and left as if he had been born in that labyrinth. Every now and then a sliver of moonshine managed to slip through the cracks above the vaulted ceiling, and from the shadows little skeletons lying in niches along the long underground tunnel appeared.

I'm in the catacomb.

The ex-leader of the Beasts was familiar with the Catacomb of Priscilla. At middle school he had gone there on a trip. Back then, he was in love with Raffaella De Angelis. She was as skinny as a sardine, with long brown hair and a pair of silver braces stuck to her teeth. He liked her because her father had a dark blue Lancia Delta with light blue Alcantara seats.

In an attempt to be funny, while they were walking through the catacomb, Saverio had snuck up behind Raffaella and pinched her calf muscle, whispering: 'The Etruscan kills again.' And she'd let out a scream and flapped her arms in terror. Saverio had been hit in the hose and fainted.

He remembered, like it was yesterday, waking up in the Cubicle of the Velata. All of his classmates had gathered around him, Mrs Fortini was shaking her head, the old nun from the convent was making the sign of the cross, and Raffaella was telling him he was an idiot. Despite the pain, he had realised that for the first time in his life he was the centre of attention. And he had understood that you needed to do something extraordinary (but not necessarily intelligent) to get noticed.

Raffaella's father had driven him home in his Lancia Delta, which had that lovely new-car smell.

He wondered where that cute girl had ended up?

If he hadn't played that stupid joke on her, if he'd been nice to her, if he'd been more confident, if . . . Maybe . . .

'IF' and 'MAYBE' were the two words that they could carve on his tombstone.

Saverio Moneta threw back his head and let himself relax on the shoulder of his kidnapper.

66

Fabrizio Ciba studied the vault of a cave lit up by the red flashes from a fire. The ceiling had a crude geometrical shape. A crypt carved into the rock. A torch hung from the wall, its thick black smoke floating upwards and channelled through holes that worked like flues. Carved into the walls were dozens of little niches, in which piles of bones accumulated.

Matteo Saporelli kept annoying the shit out of him.

'So . . . How are you? Are you able to stand?'

Fabrizio continued his inspection, ignoring Matteo.

Gathered against the walls, all of them curled up on the ground, he could see the silhouettes of a heap of people. Looking more closely, he realised that they were all guests from the party, waiters and a couple of security guards. He recognised a few actors, Sartoretti the comedian, an undersecretary from the Ministry for Cultural Heritage, a showgirl. And, strangely enough, no one was talking, as if they had been forbidden to do so.

Matteo Saporelli instead continued to torment him in a quiet voice.

'So? What do you say?'

Worn out from the constant questioning, Fabrizio turned around and saw the young writer. He was in a bad way. With a black eye and that cut on his forehead, he looked like the poor man's version of Rupert Everett knocked about by someone bigger and nastier.

Fabrizio Ciba rubbed his aching neck. 'What happened to you?'

'Some fuckers kidnapped me.'

'You, too?'

Saporelli patted his swollen eye. 'They beat me when I tried to escape.'

'Same here. I hurt all over.'

Saporelli lowered his head, as if he had to admit to a terrible sin. 'Listen . . . I didn't mean to . . . I'm so sorry . . .'

'For what?'

'For this whole mess. You've all been involved because of me.'

Fabrizio turned so he could look at him better. 'What do you mean? I don't understand.'

'Exactly one year ago I wrote a snappy little essay on corruption in Albania for a small publisher from Foggia. And now the Albanian mafia wants to make me pay.' Saporelli brushed his injury with the tips of his fingers. 'Anyway, I'm prepared to die. I will beg them to save you, though. It's not fair for them to take it out on you. You've got nothing to do with this.'

'I'm sorry to have to tell you this, but I believe you're making a mistake.' Fabrizio patted himself on the chest. 'It's all my fault. It's a subversive group of Finnish woodcutters who have kidnapped us. I exposed them for the havoc they were reaping in the thousand-year-old forests in Northern Europe.'

Saporelli burst into laughter. 'Oh, come on . . . I heard them talking before, they're speaking Albanian.'

Fabrizio looked at him with a perplexed expression on his face. 'Of course, because you speak Albanian now?'

'No, I don't speak it. But it sounds just like Albanian. They use those consonants typical of the Balkan languages.' He kept on tapping his bruise in an obsessive manner. 'Listen, tell me the truth: how do I look? My face is disfigured, isn't it?'

Fabrizio looked at him for a second. He didn't look too bad, but he nodded slowly.

'But will I go back to normal?'

Ciba gave him the bad news. 'I don't think so. It's a bad blow . . . Let's hope your eyesight isn't affected'

Saporelli collapsed. 'My head is throbbing. You don't have a Saridon? Ibuprofen?'

He was about to say no, then he remembered the magic pill that Bocchi had given him. 'You're the same old lucky guy you ever were. I've got this pill. You'll feel so much better afterwards.'

The young writer examined it with his healthy eye. 'What sort of stuff is it?'

'Don't you worry. Swallow it.'

The Strega winner, after a moment of hesitation, swallowed.

At that moment, from the depths of the dark tunnel they

heard the slow sounds of percussion instruments. It sounded like a heart beating.

'Oh God, they're coming. We're all going to die!' shouted Alighiero Pollini, the undersecretary for Cultural Heritage, and he hugged Magic Daniel, the famous illusionist from Channel 26. The showgirl began to whimper, but nobody made any effort to comfort her. The beating was getting louder and echoed around the crypt.

Fabrizio, overcome with fear to the point where even his fillings ached, said: 'Saporelli, I . . . I . . . I admire you.'

'And I consider you to be my literary father. A model I try to imitate,' the young man answered in a moment of sincerity.

The two of them hugged and stared at the entrance to the tunnel. It was so black that the darkness seemed tangibile. As if millions of litres of ink were on the verge of overflowing inside the crypt.

The tribal rhythm, hidden by the shadows, seemed to be made up of percussion instruments and drums, but also hands clapping.

Slowly, as if freed from the darkness that imprisoned them, some figures appeared.

Everyone stopping whining and complaining, and kept silent to watch the procession.

They were enormous. As white as chalk, with small heads set into rounded shoulders. Rolls of fat hid their waistline; their arms looked like legs of ham. Some of them were holding bongos under their armpits and the others beat their chest, creating the ancestral rhythm. There were women, too, shorter and with tits like flat, wide mozzarellas. And children – barge-arses, too – who held their mothers' hands in fear.

Slowly the shy, clumsy gang came forward. They were wearing bits and pieces of tracksuits, stretched sweatshirts, the remains of a gardener's uniform. On their feet they had trainers that were out of shape and sewn back together with pieces of string and metal wire. Around their chubby biceps, dog collars. Some of them were wearing broken headphones with charms hanging from them: bottle tops and dog tags, with names and telephone numbers. Others had bicycle tyres around their chests.

Their skin had no pigmentation and their small eyes, red and beady, seemed annoyed by the light. Their colourless hair had been braided with the strips of red-and-white plastic tape used to cordon off workmen on building sites.

Suddenly, all together, they stopped beating and stood silently in front of the guests. Then they divided into two wings to let someone through.

A group of old people so spindly they looked like they'd walked out of a concentration camp, moved between the fat people. They were extremely white, but not albinos. Some of them had dark hair.

The fatsos got down on their knees. Then a man and a woman were placed in the middle of the room, on white plastic chairs.

The old man was wearing an ornamental headdress that looked vaguely like the ones the American Indians used, made up of Bic pens, little bottles of Campari Soda and coloured plastic spoons. Huge Vogue sunglasses covered nearly his whole face. On his chest he was wearing an armour made of colourful plastic frisbees.

The woman was wearing a blue sandbucket on her head, and big cords of hair plaited together with inner tubes and pigeon feathers framed her face. She was wrapped in a disgustingly dirty North Face down jacket, with two skinny legs with varicose veins sticking out the bottom.

The king and the queen, Fabrizio said to himself.

67

Those two are the king and queen, Saverio said to himself, on the other side of the crypt.

The fatso had put him down among all the other guests. They were silent and shook their heads in unison, like dolls on a car dashboard. Larita was in a corner, curled up on the ground, and she didn't look too good. She kept wiping her face and neck obsessively, as if they were covered in insects.

Saverio felt strangely peaceful. A terrible sense of tiredness had fallen upon him. Having to pick up Zombie's charcoaled cadaver had made him insensitive. Like a Buddha, he sat still, his face relaxed, beside the faces of fear, twisted with tears, of the other guests.

Perhaps this is the spirit of the samurai that Mishima talks about.

There was a substantial difference between him and those people. Unlike them, he didn't care about life any more. And in a certain sense he felt closer to these monsters who had appeared like a nightmare from the earth's entrails. Except that they had succeeded in doing what he and the Beasts had not managed to do: bring terror to the party.

A fatso holding a bicycle wheel as a shield thumped a stick on the ground and spoke in a foreign tongue: 'Тише!'[2]

The old king, sitting on his plastic throne, observed the prisoners and then, with a sliver of voice, he murmured: 'Вы советские?'[3]

Saverio would have liked to be one of them, he would

---

[2] 'Hush!'
[3] 'Are you Soviet?'

have undergone any sort of initiation necessary, he would let them hang him up with hooks in his skin to prove he was a valid element, a fighter. A member of the people of the darkness.

The guests looked at each other, hoping that someone understood that weird language.

A guy with a fringe, a black eye and a gash on his forehead stood and asked for silence. 'Friends, relax, they're Albanians. They're here for me. I will set you all free. Does anyone here know Albanian and can translate for me?'

Nobody answered. Then Milo Serinov, Roma's goalkeeper, said: 'Я русский.'[4]

The old man gestured at him to stand up.

The football player obeyed and the two began chatting amidst the general surprise. Then finally Serinov turned towards the kidnapped guests. 'They're Russians.'

'What do you want from us?', 'What have we done to them?', 'Why won't they let us go?', 'Have you told them who we are?' They were all asking questions, all wanting answers.

Serinov, in his shaky Italian, explained that they were dissident Russian athletes who escaped during the Rome Olympics and have been living in the catacomb for fear of being killed by the Soviet regime.

'And what do they want from us?'

The football player smiled in amusement. 'They thought . . . Well . . . they thought we were Communists.'

Uproarious, spontaneous laughter rose up from the guests. 'Ha ha ha . . . Us? Haven't they seen what we look like? We hate Communists,' said Riccardo Forte, an emerging businessman in the aluminium laminate field. 'Have you explained

---

[4] 'I'm Russian . . .'

to them that Communism is dead and buried? That Communists are rarer than . . .' He couldn't think of a paradigm.

'Than Paninari,' added Federica Santucci, the DJ from Radio 109.

'Of course, I told them. And I told them that the Soviet regime no longer exists, and that Russians are much richer than Italians. I told them that I, too, am Russian, and that I am a football player, and that I do whatever I like, seeing as I make a shitload of money.'

Suddenly there was a light, fizzy feeling in the air around the guests. They were all happy and they patted each other on the back in solidarity.

The old king spoke to the football player again, who translated: 'The old man here has said that they will set us free if we promise not to tell anyone of their existence. They aren't ready to leave the catacomb.'

'No problem. Who would we tell?' said one guy.

'What's the problem? I've already forgotten it,' said another.

A girl with long red hair was looking around. 'How weird! I can't see them any more.'

Michele Morin, the director of the TV series *Dottoressa Cri*, stood up.

'Guys . . . Please! I'm serious! Your attention, please. Let's cross our hearts and hope to die. So they'll relax. They deserve it.'

'They could let us take a couple of photos, though. They look like something out of a fairy tale. I work for *Vanity Fair*'.

'Anyway, I've had a great time. I can't wait to tell Filippo about it. . . '

They all stood up and were wandering around the crypt, studying this underground population with interest. Finally, they were starting to have fun. Much better than Chiatti's organised hunts. This was the real surprise.

'Darling fatsos.'

'Look at the children. So cute.'

68

During the period when Rome local councils managed the park, the old sluice gate that regulated the flow of water into Villa Ada's big artificial basin had created a lot of problems for the maintenance workers. In the last ten years it had broken at least six times, and each time it had been repaired. Time passed, the huge rusty valve began to leak again, and the lake dried up, leaving behind a carpet of dark, vile slush.

When Villa Ada had been bought by Sasà Chiatti, the water works had been replaced with a new, more sophisticated system. The ingenious young Texan engineer Nick Roach, who had become famous for overseeing the building of the Stanley Dam in Albuquerque and the Aqua Park in Taos, had been flown in directly from Austin to design the complex hydraulic network that would fuel rivers and creeks, two artificial lakes, the animal troughs, the fountains and the skimmer pool.

The technician had spread sensors throughout the basins in Villa Ada. These would continuously send information on the water levels, temperature, carbonate hardness and pH to the computers in the control room. A programme designed by Roach with the help of the Douphine Inc. software company managed, via the pump system, the flow into all of the basins, recreating the natural conditions of Lake Victoria, the Orinoco Basin and the Mekong Delta.

While he was there conducting the construction of the water

works, the engineer had come across the old sluice gate in the big south lake. The valve was a piece of industrial archeology: huge, covered in lichen and with a cast-iron wheel. The factory trademark was moulded on the top: 'Fonderie Trebbiani. Pescara. 1846.' Roach had stood there studying it, dumbfounded, and then knelt down on the ground and begun to sob.

His mother's name was Jennifer Trebbiani and she was originally from Abruzzo.

In the last days of her life, when the cancer had invaded her intestine, the woman had muttered to her son that her great-grandfather had left Pescara for the Americas, leaving the family-run iron foundry in his brother's hands.

Hence, strictly speaking, that valve had been produced in the iron foundry of his ancestors.

In a moment of nostalgia, Nick Roach had decided to leave the sluice gate where it was within the new water works. He knew that it wasn't the right thing to do from a technical point of view and that probably, should there ever be a blackout, it would expose the valve to pressure above its capacity. But he did it anyway, in honour of his mother and his ancestors from Pescara.

When, on the night of the party, the electricity had failed, all of the computers that regulated the water flow, and the pumps that kept the level of the basin constant, had shut down and the lake had begun to fill with water, subjecting the pipe-works and the water sluices to exceptional pressure levels.

At 4:27 a.m. all of the joins in the pipes were spraying water like sprinklers, but the old valve seemed to be holding up. Then there was a sinister sound, a metallic screech, and the cast-iron wheel popped up in the air like a Champagne cork. The pipe exploded and two million litres of water contained in the basin were sucked down into the outlet pipe at the centre of the lake, creating in just a few minutes a maelstrom that sucked down crocodiles, turtles, sturgeon, water lilies and lotuses.

That great body of water opened up an abyss in the ground and smashed through a tuff-rock tunnel in the catacomb that passed right under the lake and began to fill with water just as if it were a huge pipeline. It took less than three minutes to flood the first floor of the ancient Christian cemetery, and dragging with it everything it found in its path – bones, stones, spiders and mice – it threw itself spitting and gurgling down the steep staircases dug tirelessly with the Christians' rudimentary chisels, and onto the floor below. There the water, hindered by the narrow diameter of the staircases, seemed to lose power. But then a huge slab of tuff rock crumbled like a sandcastle beneath a wave and the water forged a new course that allowed it to express its unstoppable rage and to drown everything in its path. The ancient affrescoes representing two doves in love, which had been there for two thousand years, were ripped off the walls of the tomb of a rich fabric merchant.

And then the fearful torrent, humming like a reactor, continued in the dark towards the great crypt where the guests and the Russian athletes were gathered.

New and Revival Dances by
DJ Sandro

69

The guests were chatting, expressing opinions, crowding around the Russians like they were at the opening of an art exhibition. Federico Gianni, the Managing Director of Martinelli, covered in shreds of the lion hunt uniform, was talking to Ciba. 'Listen, this is an unbelievable story . . . Soviet athletes who have been living in Rome's subsoil for fifty years. This would make an incredible novel. Up there with *The Name of the Rose*, if you know what I mean.'

Fabrizio didn't want to give too much away. That man was a great big fake. 'You reckon? I don't think it's that special. These sort of things happen reasonably often.'

'Are you kidding? This could turn into a great novel. This story, with the right sort of marketing campaign in the shops, would walk off the shelves.'

The writer rubbed his chin. 'I don't know . . : I'm not convinced.'

'You have to be the one to write it. Without a doubt.'

Fabrizio couldn't help himself. 'Why don't you get Saporelli to write it?'

'Saporelli's too young. This would take a much more experienced pen, someone of your calibre. Someone who changed modern Italian literature.'

Those compliments were starting to soften the armour of the author of *The Lion's Den*.

To be honest, the arsehole wasn't wrong: that story was

much better than the great Sardinian saga, but he couldn't drop his pants straight away.

'I'll have to think about it . . .'

Gianni wasn't prepared to weaken his hold. His eyes were sparkling. 'You are the only one who could write this sort of book. We could even include a DVD.'

The idea was beginning to inspire Fabrizio. 'A DVD? You reckon? Would that work?'

'You bet. Tons of extra content. Like the history of the catacomb . . . and loads of other stuff. It's up to you. I give you carte blanche.' Gianni put an arm around his shoulder. 'Listen, Fabrizio. We haven't spoken much lately. That's part of the deal of keeping this whole kit and caboodle running. Why don't we get together for a work lunch in the next few days? You deserve more.' He paused for effect. 'In all senses.'

A terrible burden disappeared, his tense diaphragm suddenly relaxed and Fabrizio realised that since the presentation for the Indian he had been living in a state of continual physical unease. He smiled. 'All right, Federico. Let's talk tomorrow and we'll organise a date.'

'Great, Fabri.'

How long had it been since he'd called him Fabri? Hearing him say it again was honey to his ears.

'Listen, I saw you with that singer . . . What's her name?'

Fuck me. Larita! He had forgotten all about her.

Gianni's eyes softened at the thought of the girl. 'Nice bit of skirt. Have you nailed her yet?'

While Fabrizio was looking around to see where Larita had ended up, a loud rumble resounded inside the ancient necropolis.

At first the writer thought it was an explosion above ground, but then he realised that the rumbling kept on going. In fact, it was getting louder, and the earth was shaking beneath their feet.

'What's happening now? I can't take any more . . .' Magic Daniel snorted, feeling fed up.

'Must be fireworks,' his boyfriend, the stage actor Roberto De Veridis, answered, excited. 'Come on, let's hurry . . . We missed out on the Midnight matriciana and I don't want to miss out on the croissants for no reason. . .'

No, these aren't fireworks, Fabrizio said to himself. It sounded more like an earthquake.

His infallible instinct which normally informed him whether it was worth his while to go to a certain party or not, that let him perceive whether or not to do an interview and suggested to him the right moment to appear and disappear from the limelight, this time informed him that he should immediately abandon that place.

'Excuse me just a moment . . .' he said to Gianni.

He started looking for Larita, but he couldn't find her anywhere. He did find Matteo Saporelli, who stripped in a corner and was covering his body with dirt while he hummed 'Livin' la Vida Loca'.

He went over to his colleague. 'Saporelli. Let's go. Quickly. Let's get out of here'. He stretched out his hand.

The young writer looked up at him through goggle eyes with pupils the size of pinpricks and started rubbing dirt under his armpits.

'No thanks, sweetcakes . . .' he said. 'I think this is a magical place. And I'm convinced that we should all try to love each other more. That's the problem today. We've forgotten that this planet is our home and will have to house our offspring for thousands and thousands of years to come. What do we want to leave them with? A handful of flies?'

Ciba looked at him, feeling shattered. The pill had already gone to his head. 'You're right. Why don't we go outside so you can explain it to me better?'

Saporelli was touched. He hugged him. 'You're the best, Ciba. I would come with you, but I can't. I will erect a temple in this place to the future memory, so when the aliens come they will find the ancient remains of this sick civilisation. And remember that this land belongs to nobody. Nobody can dare to say that this is mine, this is yours . . . The land belongs to mankind, and that's it.'

'All right, Saporelli. Good luck.' Ciba made his way through the crowd. Everyone had stopped chit-chatting and was silently listening to the sound as it became more and more deafening.

Where the fuck has Larita disappeared to? Maybe they didn't bring her here.

A puff of hot, damp air, like you feel when an underground train passes by, ruffled his hair. Fabrizio turned around and a black, winged cloud was expelled from the tunnel and splattered around the subterranean cavern.

He didn't have time to understand what it was before a bat as big as a glove landed on his face. He felt the animal's filthy hair rubbing against his lips. Screaming in disgust, he slapped it away and crouched down, covering his head with his arms.

The guests began to squeal as if suddenly possessed by the tarantella, jumping up and down to avoid the rats that shot between their legs, flapping their arms to keep the bats away.

Why are the mice fleeing? Because they're abandoning the sinking ship.

Fabrizio realised that the Russians were moving away quickly through a tunnel opposite to where the rumbling was coming from. The men had gathered the children into their arms, and even the king and queen had been thrown over the shoulders of two fatsos. He had to follow them.

As he elbowed his way through the people, he saw Larita. She was on the ground and hundreds of rodents were crawling over her. The ground was shaking more and more violently. Tibias, skulls, rib bones were falling from the crypts.

Fabrizio stopped. 'Lar . . .' An old senator from the Central Democratic Union party ran into Fabrizio, screaming 'It's the end!', while a woman holding a femur in her hand, trying to slap the bats away, hit the writer on the bridge of his nose. Ciba covered his face. 'Ahhh . . . Fucking stupid bitch!' He turned towards the singer. She was still there, on the ground. Defenceless. She looked like she'd fainted.

The cave was shaken with swarms of vibrations and it was difficult to keep standing.

It's going to fall to pieces.

He couldn't die. Not like this.

He looked at Larita. He looked at the tunnel.

He chose the tunnel.

70

Even though bats were sacred animals for students of Satanism, they grossed Saverio Moneta out. Luckily the hood of the habit protected him. Stones and dirt were falling from the ceiling of the catacomb and everything trembled. The guests seemed to have gone crazy, flapping around amidst mice and bats. Nobody dared to venture into the dark tunnels, though. The only thing they managed to do was scream like gangs of monkeys locked in a cage.

In the meantime, the Russians had sneaked out without making a sound.

He had to follow them and find a way out. But it was impossible to make headway in that madhouse. He moved towards the wall, creeping along the rock face.

'Master! What joy!' A young man, naked and covered in dirt, had jumped towards him and grabbed him by his robe. 'Master, you're here! What a relief. I am erecting a temple in remembrance.'

'What?' Saverio didn't understand. The young man had got down on his knees in front of him. The screams of the people, the vibrations of the cemetery and the far off rumblings were deafening. 'What did you say?' He bent down to hear better.

'It's time. The horror is here.'

A huge fragment of the vault collapsed in the middle of the crowd. A cloud of dirt covered everything. The guests were running into each other like shadows in the dust.

The ex-leader of the Beasts looked the fellow in the eye and realised that he was off his nut. 'Excuse me, I have to go.'

The man hung from him.

'The horror! The horror! The earth belongs to no one.'

Mantos tried to free himself from the grip. 'Leave me. Let me go, please.'

'You should understand, and you don't understand. Brother killing brother. This is our world.'

The rubble had buried a woman. Her legs poked out from beneath the stones. On her skinny calf muscle, disappearing into the debris, was a long tattoo of an ivy branch.

Saverio, in desperation, dragged the madman along with him. 'You must show me the road, and instead you want to abandon us,' he went on.

Mantos kicked at him and finally managed to shake him off. 'What do you want from me?'

The nutter, kneeling in the dirt, stared him in the eyes.

'You know what you have to do.'

Mantos stepped back, terrified. For a second he had thought it was Zombie.

'Who the fuck are you?' the ex-leader of the Beasts stuttered, and began running towards the tunnel, pushing through with his head down.

He then saw Larita in a corner.

Saverio screeched to a halt.

The girl was curled up on the ground and people were running all over her.

You must finish off your task! You must sacrifice her. At least my death will have been worth something, he thought he heard Zombie telling him.

He screamed and, fighting against the tide of the guests, making way by punching and elbowing, he got to the singer.

The young woman's mouth was wide open, her cheeks were aflame, and she was trying to swallow air like she was having an asthma attack.

Saverio shielded her with his body. He would get her out of that hole and take her up to Forte Antenne. There, he would sacrifice her in Zombie's honour.

Larita was sobbing. 'I had a panic attack. I couldn't breathe. Everyone was walking on me.'

'I'm here now.' Mantos hugged her in his arms.

The girl slowly began to breathe again. She dried her eyes and looked at him for the first time. She looked at his black robe. 'Who are you?'

He stayed silent, without knowing how to answer. He would have liked to tell her the truth. Whisper it in her ear. *I am your killer.* But he said: 'You don't know me.'

'You're so kind.'

'Listen, we can't stay here. Can you walk?'

'I think so.'

'Well, come on, let's give it a go.' He lifted her by the hip and stood her up.

She took his hand. 'Thank you.'

He looked into her hazelnut eyes.

And who knows, perhaps Saverio Moneta aka Mantos would have told her that she shouldn't thank him. Perhaps for the first time in his life he would have had the balls to say . . . What had the nude guy called it?

The horror! Yes, the horror of a life lived wrongly.

Who knows what he would have said to her if a wave of dark, foamy water hadn't swept them away.

71

Fabrizio Ciba was moving through a tunnel, using a cigarette lighter to light the way. He couldn't see shit, and every ten steps he tripped over a pile of dirt or a hole.

He was sorry to have abandoned Larita. But if he'd brought her with him, he'd never have made it.

Only the strong survive. If they don't weigh themselves down with lead.

The noise behind him had become deafening.

He turned around quickly, and by the light of the little flame he saw a wall of water coming towards him, black and furious.

'Fucking hell . . .' he managed to say before the water flipped him over and carried him off like dead wood.

72

Piero Ristori was seventy-seven years old and lived in Via di Trasone, a few metres from Villa Ada. He had been retired for ten years. And since he'd stopped working, he'd had trouble sleeping. He woke at two a.m. and lay in bed awake, waiting for the light of day. Nailed to the bed next to the sleeping body of his wife, he would remember. The ticking of the alarm clock beat out the rhythm of the silence while, like boiling gnocchi, images from his childhood in Trentino floated to the surface of his mind. He remembered his teenage years, the boarding school, the holidays in Liguria. With longing, he saw his wife as a young lady, in her swimming costume, so beautiful she took his breath away, lying on a raft at Cesenatico. The first time they had made love without even being married. And Rome. Writing for the newspaper. Thousands of articles written in a rush. The sound of typewriters. Ashtrays full of cigarette ends. Lunch at the La Gazzella osteria with his colleagues. And in particular, he remembered all his trips. The Summer Olympics in Helsinki. The World Athletics Championships in Oslo. The World Swimming Championships in the United States. A Portuguese woman with a fringe and freckles whose name he couldn't remember.

In the dark of his bedroom, a heartbreaking yearning gripped Piero Ristori and tore the breath from his chest. Of his whole life, only useless, disconnected memories were left. Sensations, smells and the desire to turn back time.

What a fantastic life he'd had. At least until he'd retired.

From that moment onwards, it had been clear to him. He was an old man, and that was purgatory on earth. At times he regretted not being addled enough (like the majority of his friends) to not realise. He was painfully aware that his personality had changed. He got annoyed by any old crap, he hated young people, confusion, and anyone who would still be alive when he had become wormfood. He had collected all the cons of old age and not one single pro.

The only moment of the day that he loved was when the light began to filter in through the blinds and the birds began to sing. He got out of bed with a feeling of freedom and left that burial ground where his wife lay unconscious, got dressed and took Max, their little Jack Russell, to do his business. The city was quiet and peaceful. He would buy milk and fresh bread at the market, and then get the newspapers. He would sit on a bench of the Nemorense Park (he used to go to Villa Ada before, he was incredulous at the idea that the council had sold it) and leaf through the papers, leaving Max free to run around a bit.

That day he had got to the newsstand on via Salaria ten minutes behind his usual schedule. He had taken a sleeping pill the night before, so that he wouldn't have to listen to Salvatore Chiatti's hellish party. The whole suburb had been blocked so that that mafioso could do as he pleased.

Piero Ristori bought *Il Messaggero*, *La Gazzetta dello Sport* and *La Settimana Enigmistica* from Eugenio, the newsagent, who was still finishing opening the packs of newspapers that had just been dropped off.

'Good morning, dottore. Did you hear the clashes between the police and the protestors yesterday?'

Max loved, for some obscure reason, to do his business in front of the newsstand. Piero Ristori pulled the leash, but the dog had already begun. 'I heard them. I did indeed hear them. They have to die.'

Eugenio stretched his aching back. 'I heard that Paco

Jimenez de la Frontera, Milo Serinov and the whole Magica were there.'

The old man pulled a little plastic bag out of his jacket pocket to pick up Max's turd. 'Who cares? You know, sport doesn't interest me any more.'

Eugenio was about to answer, and ask him why he bought *La Gazzetta dello Sport* every day then, but he didn't feel like getting into an argument with that cranky old man. Such a shame. He had been a great sports journalist, a likeable person, but since he had retired he'd shrivelled up and hated the world.

When I retire, I'll be a better person, the newsagent said to himself. *I'll finally be able to go to Lake Bolsena to fish. I've just got to grit my teeth for another twenty-two years.*

Piero Ristori took a look at the front page of the *Gazzetta*. The news was about the transfer of a French footballer costing millions of euro. 'See? It's only a question of money now. Sport, the real stuff . . .'

He would have liked to end the sentence by saying what he repeated to his wife every day. Sport, the real stuff, the stuff the old Olympic Games were made of, is dead.

But a sudden roar silenced him. He turned towards the Salaria, but he saw nothing. The sound continued, though.

He wiped a hand across his forehead . . . It sounded familiar. The roar you could hear walking along the dam wall of Ridracoli, in Emilia-Romagna, where they used to go for their summer holidays with the kids. It was an unmistakable sound, similar to the noise of a jet turbine.

The old journalist, with the dog shit in one hand and the newspapers under the other arm, squinted behind his glasses and kept looking around. Via Salaria was empty, and eveything seemed normal.

Even Eugenio was looking around in confusion, scowling.

Max was going crazy, pulling at his lead and whimpering like he'd seen a cat.

'Settle down . . . Jesus . . .'

For the second time, the noise shut him up. This time it sounded more like a high-pitched whistle.

Eugenio looked upwards. Piero Ristori moved his gaze upwards and saw in the cloudless sky a black object spinning higher than the buildings, above the street. He had enough time to understand that it was a manhole cover before the bronze disc fell back down again, straight as a rail, and wedged itself in the roof of a Passat Variant. The windows exploded, the wheels folded outwards and the alarm rang crazily.

Out of the corner of his eye, the old journalist noticed that from the footpath opposite him a column of white foam was lifting up, like the neck of a cobra. The stream of water went over the top of the fence of Villa Ada.

Then it appeared that the manhole spat out something black.

'What the hell . . .?!' Eugenio said.

Ten metres above their heads a human being was flapping his arms and kicking his legs in the air. He fell out of the sky like someone who has dived off a cliff, and plummeted to the ground.

Piero Ristori closed his eyes. A second later, when he opened them again, he saw that the man was standing on the white line in the middle of Via Salaria. His legs were shaking a little from the impact but, miraculously, he was unharmed.

As the water flooded the pavement, the journalist took two steps towards him.

It was a skinny old man covered in a tattered black tracksuit. His long white beard and hair were soaked and stuck to his body. He didn't move, as if his feet were glued to the tarmac.

The journalist took three more steps and overtook the cars parked alongside the kerb.

No, it can't be . . .

Despite the fact that half a century had gone by, despite the arteriosclerosis that was hardening his arteries, despite the long beard that covered half of the man's face, Piero Ristori's old temporal lobes, as soon as they saw those eyes as cold as the Siberian plains, and that big nose, remembered.

He was taken back in time, to the summer of 1960. Rome. The Olympic Games.

That there was Sergej Pelevin, the great pole vaulter who had won gold. He had disappeared during the Games, along with a group of other Russian athletes, and nobody had ever known where they had ended up. Piero Ristori had interviewed him for the *Corriere della Sera* newspaper after the medal ceremony.

But what was he doing half a century later in the middle of Via Salaria?

The journalist, his hands shaking, dragging the dog behind him, moved closer to the athlete, who was still as stiff as a statue.

'Sergej . . . Sergej . . .' he stuttered. 'What happened to you? Where have you been? Why did you run away?'

The athlete turned around, and at first he didn't even seem to see the journalist.

Then he closed and opened his watery eyes, as if the sun on the horizon bothered him. He showed his toothless gums and said 'Свободу я выбра . . .'[5]

He wasn't able to finish his sentence because a Smart Fortwo, coming from the Via Olimpica at over one hundred and twenty kilometres per hour, ran straight in to him.

---

[5] 'I chose freedom . . .'

73

Saverio Moneta had managed to never let go of her, to keep hold of her hand even as they were being slammed around and turned over by the current that dragged them through the black tunnels of the underground necropolis. They had swallowed litres of water, and they hadn't taken a breath in what seemed like forever, and then, without knowing how, they had risen up inside a pocket of air that was trapped beneath the vault of one of the tunnels.

Saverio had the tip of his nose up against the ceiling. With his mouth open, he breathed and coughed. Larita, who was next to him, couldn't stop coughing either.

'Can you make it?' the singer gasped.

Saverio attempted to improve his hold with his hands and feet against the funeral niches. The current was so strong, if he let down his guard for a second it would drag him away. 'Yes. I've got it.'

Larita used one hand to grab on to a jutted rock. 'You all right?'

'All right.' And to be more convincing, he repeated himself. 'All right.'

It wasn't true. He must have broken his right leg. While they were being dragged by the current, he had slammed violently up against a wall.

He released his grasp with this right hand and touched where he was feeling pain. He felt . . .

Oh God . . .

. . . a long, pointy shard sticking out of his leg.

A piece of wood, something, has been driven into my thigh . . .

en he understood and almost let go of his grip.

was his broken femur that was sticking out of his leg like knife. His head started to spin. His ears were burning hot. His oesophagus squeezed tighter and stomach acid rose up and touched his palate.

I'm about to faint.

He couldn't. If he fainted, the current would suck him in. He stayed still, squashed up against the rock, waiting for his head to stop spinning.

'What should we do?' Larita's voice echoed from far away.

Saverio vomited and closed his eyes.

'Should we stay here? Wait until they come and save us?'

He made a huge effort to answer her. 'I don't know.'

I'm losing blood.

The water stopped him from being able to see the wound. A small mercy.

'Neither do I,' Larita said after a little while. 'We can't wait here, though.'

Please, help me, I'm dying, was the only thing he would have liked to say to her. But he couldn't. He had to be a man.

How ridiculous . . . Less than forty-eight hours earlier, he had been the sad employee of a furniture shop, a failure oppressed by his own family. And now he was next to the most popular singer in Italy, in a flooded catacomb, bleeding to death.

A weird twist of fate was offering him an opportunity. That woman there, who knew nothing about him, or about his inbred bad luck, would see him and judge him for who he was in this moment.

At least, for once, someone would see him as a hero. A fearless man. A samurai.

What was it that Yamamoto Tsunemoto said in *Hagakure*? 'The Way of the Samurai is found in death.'

He felt his willpower strengthen like a hard blood clot in his aching guts.

Show her who Saverio Moneta is.

He opened his eyes again. It was dark, but he could see the bones of the dead floating around them. There had to be light coming in from somewhere.

Larita was struggling to hold on. 'I think the water's rising.'

Saverio tried to concentrate and not think about the pain. 'Listen to me . . . The air will run out soon. And who knows how long it will take for the rescue teams to get here. We've got to make it on our own.'

'How?' Larita asked.

'I think I can see a glimmer of light coming from over there. Can you see it, too?'

'Yes . . . only just.'

'All right. Let's go over there.'

'But if I let go, I'll get dragged under.'

'I'll take care of you.' Mantos moved towards the voice of the singer, digging his fingers into the crumbly tuff rock. 'Wait . . . Hang on to my shoulders.'

The pain was blinding him. To stop himself from screaming, he grabbed a tibia that was floating by and gripped it between his teeth. Then he moved right up to the young woman, who grabbed on to his shoulder and wrapped her thighs around his chest.

74

Matteo Saporelli was a fish.

In fact, he was a yellowfin tuna fish. No, actually, he was a dolphin. A splendid male dolphin swimming through the mysterious remains of Atlantis. His arms held close to his body, he moved his head up and down in time with his legs, which flapped in unison.

I am a marine mammal.

He was exploring the remains of a great civilisation sunk into the depths of the ocean. Now he found himself in the long corridors that led to the royal chambers. With his sharp eyes he could see gold, precious stones, antique jewels encrusted with seaweed and coral. He could see crabs and lobsters walking over mountains of gold coins.

He felt at ease. It had been a long counter-evolution, which had lasted millions of years and had led the mammals back into the sea, but it had really been worth it.

Water life is so much better.

There was just one problem that ruined that magical state of grace.

The air. He needed air too much, considering he was a dolphin. This disappointed him. He remembered that cetaceans could stay under water for a long time, but instead he felt a desperate need for air.

He tried to give a shit. There were too many fantastic things to see down there, he couldn't waste time breathing.

Along with the jewels, and the hot pink octopus, there was also amazing coral that he would have spent hours admiring.

Hey, you know what I'll do? I'll grab a bit of air and then I'll come back down.

He flippered his way to the surface, like the man from Atlantis, and popped his snout out of the water in a small pocket of air beneath a vault in the catacomb.

75

While Saverio Moneta was struggling along towards the glimmer, with Larita grasping on to his neck, the head of a man popped out of the water less than a metre away.

The leader of the Wilde Beasts of Abaddon, after a second of amazement, spat out the tibia and screamed: 'Help!'

Larita began to squeal, too: 'Help! Help!'

The man puffed and unpuffed his cheeks, looked at them for a second, let out a strange guttural call, a sort of ultrasound, and then dove back down.

Saverio couldn't believe his eyes. 'Did you see him, too?'

'Yes.'

'He's a nutter. You don't know what he said to me before. Who the fuck is that guy?'

Larita took a moment to answer. 'It looked like Matteo Saporelli to me.'

'And who's he?'

'He's a writer. He won the Strega award.' Her voice went up an octave. 'Look! Look over there!'

A beam of light fell down from a hole in the vault of the catacomb and died in the slimy waters.

Saverio, fighting against the current that tried to pull them in the opposite direction, put in a huge effort and managed to get them under the hole.

It was a long cylinder dug into the earth. The walls were covered with roots and spiders' webs. Up top they could see the branches of a fig tree swaying in the wind, and behind that the pale sky of the Roman dawn.

Larita let go of Saverio and grabbed on to the rock. 'We can make it . . .' She stretched out her hand, but it was too high. She tried to push herself upwards by kicking her feet, but nothing. 'If I had some flippers . . .'

She won't be able to make it, Saverio said to himself as she tried again to push herself up to the edge of the hole. It was about seventy centimetres from the water's surface and there was nothing to grab on to on the tuff rock, as smooth as a slab of marble. She would never make it, kicking with her legs alone.

Larita was out of breath. 'You try. I can't do it.'

Saverio pushed up with his kidneys, but as soon as he moved his leg he let out a scream of agony. A stab of pain as sharp as a scalpel shot through the flesh of the injured limb. He fell back down, without any strength. He drank in a heap of water.

Larita grabbed him by the hood of his robe before the current carried him away. She pulled him to her. 'What's the matter? What happened to you?'

Saverio squeezed his eyes tight and struggled to keep himself afloat. In a soft voice, he murmured: 'I think I have a broken leg. I've lost a lot of blood.'

She hugged him, laid her head against the nape of his neck and began to sob. 'No . . . What do we do now?'

Saverio could feel a lump of tears pushing against his sternum. But he had sworn he'd be a man. He took three deep breaths and said: 'Hang on . . . Don't cry . . . I might just have an idea.'

'What?'

'If I prop myself against that niche, you climb onto my shoulders, and then you grab on to the walls of the hole. From there, the rest is easy.'

'But what about your leg?'

'I'll just use my left leg.'

'You sure?'

'I'm sure.'

Saverio took a hold of the wall. Every movement took a huge amount of effort, and he was slowed down by a tiredness like he had never felt before in his life. Every cell, tendon and neuron in his body had run out of energy. Along with his blood, he was draining out his final reserves of energy.

Come on, I beg you, don't give up, he said to himself, as he felt his eyes fill with tears.

With his good foot, he touched the wall until he found a niche he could push up from. He stretched out his arm and grabbed on to a small outcrop. 'Quickly! Climb up on me.'

Larita climbed up, using him like a ladder. She put her feet on his shoulders and then one on top of his head.

He was forced to push down on his other leg as well, so that he wouldn't lose his hold.

Please . . . please . . . hurry up . . . I can't take it any longer, he screamed into the water.

He suddenly felt the load lighten. He looked up. Larita had made it to the hole and was propping herself up with her legs on the edge. With one hand she held on to a root protruding from the rock face.

'I made it.' Larita was out of breath. 'Now give me your arm and I'll pull you up.'

'You can't . . .'

'What do you mean, I can't?'

'The root won't hold our weight . . . You'll end up back in the water.'

'No. It's strong. Don't worry. Give me your hand.'

'You go. Call the rescuers. I'll wait here. Go on, hurry up. Don't think about me.'

'No. I won't leave you here. If I leave, you won't be able to bear up and you'll be carried away by the current.'

'Please, Larita . . . Just go . . . I'm dying . . . I can't feel my legs any more. There's nothing you can do.'

Larita began to cry, shaken by sobs. 'I don't want to . . . It's not fair . . . I'm not leaving you. You . . . what's your name, I don't even know your name . . .'

Saverio had only his mouth and nose above the surface of the water. 'Mantos. My name is Mantos.'

'Mantos, you saved my life and I can't leave you to die. I beg you, let's at least give it a try.'

'But if we don't succeed, will you promise to leave?'

Larita dried her tears and nodded.

Mantos closed his eyes, and with the little strength he had left he pushed himself upwards and stretched his hand out towards Larita's. He managed just to touch her but then fell back, his arms wide open as if he'd been shot in the chest. His body sank, bobbed to the surface again for just a second, and then the current pulled him under. He didn't fight it. He was carried down to the bottom.

At first his body didn't want to give up, and fought not to be overcome. Then, beaten, it quietened and Saverio could hear only the water ringing in his ears. It was beautiful being able to let himself go like that, let himself be carried downwards in the dark. The water that was killing him was extinguishing the last flames of life.

How liberating, he said to himself, and then he could think no longer.

76

A tiny little spot kept the sun anchored to the horizon, when Fabrizio Ciba opened his eyes again.

He saw a vaulted ceiling of golden leaves, clouds of midges, butterflies. Bird calls echoed all around him. And he could hear the water running and dripping softly, like in a shower. He breathed in the smell of wet earth. On his shoulders, the back of his neck, and on the wet rags he was wearing, he could feel the soft warmth of the sun.

He lay there, without thinking about anything. Then slowly the memories of the night, the catacomb, the wall of water that had buried him, clotted together into one thought. A very positive thought.

I'm alive.

This awareness cradled him, and he began to reflect on the fact that this terrible experience would be left behind. Over time it would lose its dramatic force, and over the next few months he would begin to remember it with a mixture of amusement and regret. And it would mean something.

The human mind works that way.

He was surprised by his own wisdom.

The time had come to figure out where he was. He pulled himself up onto his elbows and saw that he was lying on a bed of mud and sand spread over two small, tree-covered hills. A stream of water flowed through the middle. There were bones everywhere, shoes, a riding hat and a huge crocodile, tummy-up, its abdomen swollen and white. Flies were buzzing around it.

He stood up and stretched, happy to not have any injuries, feeling a little battered but otherwise in good shape. And he realised he was hungry.

That's a good sign. It's a sign of life.

He walked in the direction of the sun. He overtook the woods, yawning, but then had to stop when faced with a breathtaking vision.

A small opening appeared in the vegetation. He could see

the Via Olimpica off in the distance, with the usual morning traffic jams, the deserted rugby fields at Acqua Acetosa, the still, grey bend in the Tiber River. Further down, the viaduct of Corso Francia covered in cars, and the Fleming Hill covered in luxuriant vegetation.

Roma.

His city. The most beautiful and oldest city in the world. He had never loved it as much as he did in that very moment.

He began to conjure up a café, a Roman café, any one would do. With the waiting staff in their jackets and bow ties crowded around the sugar-strewn bench. The custard-filled croissants. The apple tarts. The tramezzini. The sounds of saucers and cups being knocked against the sink. The tinkling sound of teaspoons. The *Corriere dello Sport.*

He almost skipped down the hill. If he didn't remember wrongly, the exit was in that direction. He found a path and began to descend the staircase, two steps at a time, that led across the woods towards the lake.

There was something, a strange object, right in the middle of the path. He slowed down. It looked like it was made of metal and had wheels. He moved a little closer until he realised what it was.

A wheelchair.

It was knocked over onto its side. As well as the chair, there was also a body lying across the steps. Fabrizio, holding his breath, moved closer.

At first he didn't recognise him, but then he saw the bald head, the ears that stuck out. The Vuitton fecal-collection sack.

He put his hands through his hair. *Oh God, it's Umberto Cruciani.*

The old master, on the ground and without his chair. He looked like a soldier crab that had its shell removed.

Fabrizio didn't need to touch him to understand that he was dead. His eyes were wide open beneath his thick eyebrows. His toothless mouth was agape. His hands curled up.

He must have fallen down the stairs.

Fabrizio bent over the cadaver of the great writer and closed his eyes.

Another great had departed the earth. The author of *Western Wall* and *Bread and Nails,* the masterpieces of 1970s Italian literature, had departed, leaving the world a poorer, sadder place.

Fabrizio Ciba was shaken by a sob, by another and by another again. He hadn't cried once during that whole crazy night, but now he burst into tears like a little boy.

He wasn't crying for the suffering, but for the joy.

He dried his tears, caressed the bony face and with a flick of his wrist he ripped the 40Gb USB key from around Cruciani's neck.

He smiled as he sniffed. 'Thank you, Master. You saved me.'

And he kissed him on the lips.

77

Larita had managed to emerge from the well. The roots had helped her to clamber up to the top.

Now she was walking, with her head lowered, across the field where gnus, buffalo and kangaroos calmly grazed.

She couldn't stop thinking about the image of Mantos's hand brushing against hers as he gave her a letter before disappearing into the black waters.

She pulled the saturated piece of paper from her pocket. There was something written in faded but legible handwriting.

'For Silvietta.'

Who was Silvietta? And, above all, who was Mantos?

A hero who had appeared from nowhere and had sacrificed himself to save her.

Maybe Silvietta was his sweetheart.

The singer was about to open the note, when she heard police sirens.

With the piece of paper in her hand, she began to run.

Croissants

78

The fire brigade, after many hours' work, had finally managed to breach the wall surrounding the Villa. It was easier than knocking down the solid steel gates. They had sealed off the zone, which had filled with onlookers, police cars, dozens of ambulances, journalists and photographers. The guests were coming out in dribs and drabs. Many of them were only just able to stand and were greeted by medical teams, who laid them down on stretchers. Corman Sullivan had been wrapped in an inflatable hyperbaric chamber. Antonio, Saverio's cousin, his head bandaged in a huge gauze turban, was sipping hot tea. Paco Jimenez de la Frontera and Milo Serinov were talking on their mobiles. Cristina Lotto was hugging her husband. Magic Daniel was down to his underpants, and was arguing with old Cinelli and a Chinese dressed up as an acrobat.

Larita pushed her way through the people. Her heart was beating loudly and her hands were trembling with excitement.

A young nurse came up to her with a blanket. 'Come with me.'

The singer gestured to her that she was fine. 'One moment, just one moment.'

Where was he? *And if* . . . She didn't even want to finish that thought. Too sad to think.

She couldn't see him anywhere. Then she noticed a knot of journalists pushing to get closer to someone. Fabrizio was there, answering the interviewers' questions. Even though he was enveloped in a grey blanket, he looked in great shape.

A burden was lifted from Larita's heart. She moved closer to get a better look at him.

Oh man, I like him so much.

Luckily, he hadn't seen her. She would surprise him as soon as he'd finished talking to the journalists.

79

'So, tell us . . . What happened?' asked Rita Baudo from *TG4*.

Fabrizio Ciba had decided not to talk to the press, to be cranky and stand-offish as always, but when he had seen the journalists running towards him, forgetting about all the other VIPs, he had given in to the temptation to bask in the attention. And then there was the fact that the hand he had in his pocket was holding a USB key that instilled him with 40Gb of strength and courage. With the other hand he touched the lobe of his ear and put on the expression of a survivor.

'There's not much to say. We ended up at the party of a psychopathic megalomaniac. This is a sad parable of a presumptuous and proud human being who believed that he was Caesar. In a certain sense a tragic hero, a figure from another age . . .' He could have gone on pontificating for the rest of the day, but decided to cut it short. 'I will soon write the chronicle of this night of horror.' When a photographer focused on him, he brushed back the tuft of rebellious hair that fell in front of his teary eyes.

Rita Baudo wasn't satisfied, though. 'But what do you mean? Can't you tell us anything more?'

Fabrizio waved at them with his hand, as if to say that although he was emotionally unsettled, he'd had the decency to speak to the press, but now he needed some privacy. 'Please forgive me, I'm very tired.'

Just then, with the tact of a prop in a rugby match, Simona Somaini burst in amidst the journalists.

The blonde actress was wrapped up in a microscopic Red Cross blanket that strategically revealed her flat tummy, a tiny thong covered in mud, and her amazing tits with nipples as big as thimbles hidden beneath her tattered bra.

'Fabri! There you are! I was afraid . . .' she said, kissing him on the mouth.

Ciba's green eyes flew open, and for a tenth of a second they expressed a doubt, then closed again whilst the two of them remained entwined, amidst an explosion of flashes.

Right then Simona, as if it was a curtain on a stage, let the blanket fall to her feet, showing off her 40-26-36 figure.

When they ran out of oxygen, she laid her head, with its savannah-coloured hair, against his neck and dried her sparkling eyes for the cameras.

'During this terrible night, despite everything, we have found out . . .' She turned to Fabrizio. 'Do you want to tell them?'

Fabrizio raised an eyebrow, looking perplexed. 'What, Simona?'

The actress paused, but then she recovered, bent her head to one side and whispered in embarrassment. 'Go on, let's tell them. For once, let's not hide. We are human beings, after all . . . especially today. After this terrible adventure.'

'Can you be more explicit?' the journalist from *Rendez-vous* asked.

'Well, I don't know whether I can say.'

The correspondent for *Festa Italiana* pushed a microphone in her face. 'Please, Simona, speak up.'

Fabrizio realised that Somaini was a genius. He squeezed the USB key in his pocket, and knew that he loved her. That was the final *coup de theatre*, the just conclusion that would make him the most important man at the party, the most envied of them all. He breathed in deeply and said: 'We've decided to get engaged.'

The journalists, paramedics and the onlookers behind the barriers started clapping enthusiastically.

Simona tickled her nose against his neck like a pussycat. 'I'll be his Marilyn.'

Fabrizio asked for a moment of silence. 'And I wanted to celebrate by giving you an exclusive preview. I have finally finished my new novel.' And he added: 'And I won't be publishing it with Martinelli.'

Somaini hugged him tightly, lifting up her delicious ankle. 'Darling, what wonderful news! I can't wait to read it. I'm sure it's a masterpiece.'

A big Porsche Cayenne now came into sight, honking its horn. The fat head of Paolo Bocchi popped out of the window. His face was still flushed. Sitting in the passenger seat was Matteo Saporelli, snoring away. 'What a fantastic party! The best I've been to in the last few years! Guys, do you want a lift?'

Fabrizio took Simona's hand. 'Yes, to the airport.'

'No worries!' said the plastic surgeon.

'Where are you taking me, darling?' asked Simona, all excited.

'To Majorca.'

80

Larita had watched the scene up until the two of them kissed.

Then she had slipped on a tracksuit, hidden beneath the hood and managed to slip away from the circus before anyone could recognise her.

She had had the same bad luck as ever. That night she had met another arsehole. But luckily he had disappeared from her life before he could do any real damage.

In the palm of her hand she still had the note that Mantos had given her. She opened it carefully, so as not to tear it. Smudged, but still legible, was written:

I FELL IN LOVE
WITHOUT KNOWING WHAT LOVE IS
AND I LOSE MY LIFE
WITHOUT HAVING EVER LIVED IT.
EDO AKA ZOMBIE

The End

PART FOUR

Four Years Later

Villa Ada, following the terrible night of the big party and Sasà Chiatti's death, had returned to local council ownership. And Romans began to hang out there again as if the Chiatti era had never existed.

To be honest, very little was left of all that splendour. A memorial plaque at the entrance from Via Panama with the names of the VIPs who'd died. The train tracks already bound in the branches of the ivy.

A couple of warthogs and a pair of vultures called Gino and Nunzia, both as fat as turkeys from scavenging around the rubbish bins. All the other animals had ended up in bioparks around the peninsula.

Everything else had returned to being the same old Villa Ada. Immense, tangled, dirty, thorny, dusty, a hideout for stray dogs, sewage rats and non-European citizens without residency permits. The hundred-year-old pine trees, sick to their core, continued to fall on passers-by. The fields were once again overrun by thorn bushes. The green smelly lakes nests for tiger mosquitoes, coypus and turtles. Dogs had reappeared without their muzzles, policemen flirted with au pairs, cyclists dressed in reflective clothing, bongo-players, joint-smokers, and old men sitting on park benches.

But on the 29th of April, exactly four years from the night of the party, on a sunny but chilly Roman day, Murder and Silvietta were there.

Lying on a tartan blanket, they were having a picnic with maccheroni omelette, supplí and mushroom pizza.

For the last three years they had decided that that day

325

would be dedicated to the memory of Mantos and Zombie.

Not that they did much to honour their friends, but they were happy like that. They took a day off work (they had opened a family business for treating terracotta tiling in Oriolo), hopped into the Ford Ka and headed to Rome. And if the weather was nice, like today, they had their picnic, read a bit and sometimes even squeezed in a nap in the open air.

That's how they remembered their friends.

This year was special, though. They had brought along Bruce, their two-year-old son, who was now able to walk and, if you didn't keep an eye on him, could take off on those shaky legs and end up who knows where.

Silvietta glanced up from her book. 'Go on, go and get him . . .' she said to her husband.

Murder stood up and yawned. 'You really like that book, don't you?'

'*A Light in the Fog* is fantastic. I can't stop reading. I reckon it's even better than *The Lion's Den*. Ciba has become a much more mature writer. And these stories about the farmers from lower Padania are so touching.'

Murder bit into his pizza. 'How does he know so much about those people? He's always lived in Rome.'

'He's a genius. Talent, pure and simple. I remember when he read that poem at the party. He's such a special person.' Silvietta looked around. 'Go on, get going. Be a daddy. Go and get Bruce.'

Murder stretched his arms above his head. 'All right, my queen, I will return your child to you.' He gave her a kiss and walked off to the rides, where the baby had headed.

Silvietta stared after her husband, for a second, as he wandered away. She really needed to sew the hem of his torn jeans. Then she dived back into the novel. She was fifty pages from the end. But not even three minutes later, she heard Murder calling her.

'Honey . . . Honey . . . Come quickly.'

Silvietta closed the book and left it on the blanket. She found her husband and son next to a German Shepherd puppy. The little boy kept stretching out his hand towards the animal, which was running around him, wagging his tail.

Bruce wasn't afraid. The opposite. He was giggling and trying to catch him.

Silvietta moved closer to her son. 'It's nice, isn't it, honey?'

Murder patted the puppy and it threw itself tummy-up, ready for a proper scratch. 'Maybe we could get one for him. Look how much he's enjoying it.'

'Who'd take it out?'

Murder shrugged. 'Me. No worries.'

'I don't think so.' Silvietta gave her husband an affectionate punch on the shoulder.

Murder picked up Bruce, who immediately started whining. 'Come on, let's go and eat before it all gets cold.'

But when they got back, the picnic had been plundered. Someone had taken the bag with the supplí, and the omelette had disappeared, too.

Murder put his hands on his hips and set his legs apart.

'Sons of bitches! You can't leave anything alone for a minute . . .'

Silvietta grabbed her bag. 'They didn't even touch my money, though.'

Murder pointed at a crushed supplí beneath a laurel bush.

Husband and wife, silently, trying not to make any noise, sneaked over. At first they couldn't see anything, but then they realised that, beneath the branches, crouched down, was a man wearing an old tatty tracksuit and a strange headdress made of pigeon feathers and small bottles of Coke. He was stuffing down their picnic.

'Hey! You! Thief!' Murder yelled at him. 'Give that back!'

The man, caught redhanded, jumped back in fear. For a second he turned around and looked at them, just for a second, then he picked up the omelette from the ground and, limping, disappeared into the vegetation.

The two of them stood there, petrified.

Silvietta put a hand over her mouth. 'Don't tell me that that was . . .'

Murder was staring at the bushes, then he swallowed and looked at his wife.

'No. I won't tell you.'

Acknowledgements

And now we've come to the thank-you page.

First of all, I have to thank Antonio Manzini. Thank you, my friend, without your tightrope-walking fucking around, your inventions, your encouragement, this story would never have existed. Then I thank Lorenza, who sees further than I do, and I thank my wonderful family. A special thanks also goes to Vereno, Marino, Massimo and Sauro for having built me the best hideout in the world, and to Marco, the orchestra conductor of a little act of foolishness. Then come Severino Cesari and Paolo Repetti, Antonio Franchini, Kylee Doust and Francesca Infascelli, for having supported me while I paddled upstream.

And of course, how can I forget Nnn . . . nnn . . . nnn . . . ntwinki and Nicaredda, my silent and caring life companions.

Obviously, this novel is the product of my imagination and of turbulent dreams. If you see any things or facts that remind you of reality, that's your problem. For the history of Villa Ada and the Olympic Games, I plundered Wikipedia and other websites. I would like to say one last thing. Villa Ada is in a state of terrible decay. One of the last green lungs of a metropolis smothered in smog and stunned by noise is about to die. If the public institutions don't intervene soon, by attempting to treat the sick pine trees (treat doesn't mean decapitate), reclaim the lakes and repair the buildings, which are crumbling, we will lose another piece of this old and tired city that is Rome.

See you next time.